Praise for *The Biographer*

'Duigan's novel is a gripping study of the duel between the woman with a secret and the biographer who senses her fear. Beautifully paced, and even more sinister for its decorous setting, *The Biographer* offers the elements of a detective story and a debate on biography's methods and ethics in a sympathetically drawn human situation.'
Brenda Niall, *The Age*

'Her vocabulary is adroitly chosen, her sentences beautifully balanced, her minor characters vividly sketched.'
Judith Armstrong, *Australian Book Review*

'A clear light on the ruthless habits of biography. Marvellous.'
Drusilla Modjeska

'The backgrounds have a physical richness, and the portrayal of artistic life and conflicts is convincingly achieved.'
Christopher Koch

'Duigan is a wonderful writer . . . who intelligently explores notions of love and sacrifice, regret and forgiveness, and the dogged nature of truth . . . she serves up a psychologically compelling and thoroughly delectable read.'
Lucy Clark, *The Sunday Telegraph*

The Biographer
VIRGINIA DUIGAN

VINTAGE BOOKS
Australia

A Vintage book
Published by Random House Australia Pty Ltd
Level 3, 100 Pacific Highway, North Sydney NSW 2060
www.randomhouse.com.au

First published by Vintage in 2008
This Vintage edition published in 2009

Addresses for companies within the Random House Group can be found at
www.randomhouse.com.au/offices

National Library of Australia
Cataloguing-in-Publication Entry

Duigan, Virginia.
The biographer.

ISBN 978 1 74166 715 8 (pbk).

A823.4

Cover images by Getty Images and iStockphoto/Thomas Bradford
Cover design by Nada Backovic
Typeset by Midland Typesetters, Australia
Printed and bound by Griffin Press, South Australia

Random House Australia uses papers that are natural, renewable and recyclable
products and made from wood grown in sustainable forests. The logging and
manufacturing processes are expected to conform to the environmental regulations
of the country of origin.

10 9 8 7 6 5 4 3 2 1

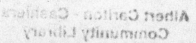

To my brother, John Duigan, and my uncle, John (Tig) Duigan.
And to my sister- and brother-in-law, Helen and Jan Senbergs.

1

Wednesday 5th July
Today I met an extraordinary man. Oddly enough, or perhaps
not, I knew straightaway he was someone out of the ordinary.
Well, you'd have to be blind, deaf and monumentally dumb
not to notice that Mr S. is on the right side of unique.

It was a medium-sized notebook about the width of a woman's clutch bag, with a shiny red cover that hadn't been opened for twenty-five years. The pages were bone dry but otherwise unaffected, the words crowded together and sloping to the right, fast and energetic. Greer looked at the flamboyant script, the extravagant surge of the writing. Myself when young, she thought. Someone I hardly recognise.

Last month had brought a letter from Antony. The envelope, with its address printed in indelible black marker, stood out from the rest of the post, which was mainly bills and art-world bumf. Normally Antony preferred email, and she thought it was significant that this time he had chosen to write. A handwritten letter was challenging, tangible, it lay there in front of you. You could pick it up as often as you liked and re-read it, or tear it up and chuck it away. Or put a match to it, perhaps. Even the act of opening the envelope, which Greer had finally slit with a slender-bladed letter opener, set up an expectation.

The letter lay on her desk all afternoon until she brought herself to open it. After reading it she hadn't crumpled it up, tossed it in the bin or burnt it, but put it down, her heart thumping. Antony had written: 'I wonder if you could look out for any material you might have from the early days. Press cuttings, of course, and reviews. But also photographs, letters, appointment books and general detritus – especially mad ephemera like doodles on the side of laundry lists . . . Dare one hope for a diary or three? But absolutely anything you may have salvaged from the Australian period would be of use.'

The Australian period. Reading the three words made her mouth dry. They lay there on the page in strong, masculine handwriting: three words, clear and unambiguous. Might they have been innocently put down?

She stared at the writing as a graphologist might, as if it could be deciphered, searching for clues, but it told her nothing. After looking at three words for a while, she thought, any three words, they become meaningless and the implications that may or may not swirl around them cease to exist. They are like words in an unfamiliar language, mere arrangements of letters that have lost their power. The power they may have had to make your heart stand still.

In any case, a graphologist would be looking for revelations of character, and not of knowledge.

The letter still lay face up on her desk. What kind of a person wrote in this way, as if people's lives were like segments of an orange, to be pulled apart? Or worse, labelled, dissected and denounced? Greer had mentioned the letter to Rollo. She knew it was unfair to expect Rollo to take those three words at anything other than face value, and he didn't. They sounded perfectly innocuous to him.

'It's a necessity of the biographical process, darling,' he'd said. 'What did you expect? This is what happens from now on. Your lives will be annotated, analysed and arranged in alphabetical order. Reduced to lists in a filing cabinet. They're not your lives any more, you see. You're in the process of being reinvented for public consumption. You belong to posterity now, and Trivial Pursuit. It's tedious, but exciting. Don't look so tragic, wallow in all the fuss. Lie back and enjoy it.'

But you don't understand, Rollo, she thought. You haven't a clue. If you had, you wouldn't joke about it. Even Guy, you see, even Guy might hesitate.

Most of Antony's communications had been with Mischa, but he had addressed this particular letter to her. 'Allowing for my admittedly patchy knowledge of Mischa's habits, I have a suspicion he hasn't bothered to record a great deal. You are probably the archivist of the partnership.'

The archivist. Another word that branded him, in her eyes, as an outsider. An enemy alien.

After four days she had steeled herself to write back. 'If by "archivist" you mean the one who throws things into boxes, then yes, I suppose I qualify. But it's a very grand title for what has been woefully piecemeal and amateurish – Mischa hates keeping anything and I have been neither systematic nor thorough. There are a few boxes of jumbled cuttings, exhibition invitations, reviews – that sort of thing. Completely unsorted. Your job will be cut out to get them into any useful order, I'm afraid . . .'

Before posting the letter she tore it up and emailed her reply instead.

During the four intervening days before Greer answered the letter, the unknown Antony had followed her around. He was there in the bedroom in the morning, a critical voyeur, watching her dress. Instead of reaching for clothes unthinkingly she found herself pausing to make selections and looking at herself in the mirror.

He was a third, faceless presence at dinner. Mischa was oblivious to him, shovelling food with his usual gusto. Greer felt unusually constrained to make conversation. Companionable silence might too easily be misinterpreted, might be put down to imagined tensions and resentments. Might, in the mind of a silent arbiter, be put down to something else altogether.

When she picked up an English glossy magazine she felt him looking over her shoulder. He was inquisitive about what she was reading, curious about every aspect of her. She discarded the magazine and from a pile of books picked up one of J. B. Priestley's more obscure novels, which Rollo had lent her last week. Be flattered by the prospect of his scrutiny, Rollo had advised. Wallow in it. But she did not find it flattering.

One night she even dreamt of Antony, but when she tried to recall his appearance she could remember nothing. There had been an uneasy feeling pervading the dream, though, an aura that still lingered. An aura of threat.

She tried to redefine him as benevolent. A benign authorial presence who was only concerned to put on record the life of a successful painter and give Mischa his due. And in so doing to impose a semblance of order on his, and later on their joint, ragtag past. Wasn't that the main purpose of biography? An attempt to define a life by tracing its chronological evolution?

If you were to put a life, any life, under the microscope you might conceivably work out a formula to separate the random elements from the deliberate choices. There were conundrums here that Greer had thought about a great deal lately. Still, when considered in this way a biography sounded fairly harmless, beneficial even, with the potential to enlarge the range of human understanding.

Until the relative calm of the past decade Mischa's life, and by assumption her own, had been so nomadic and almost wilfully undocumented that the most assiduous biographer would have his work cut out trying to make any sense of it. There wouldn't be much time left for anything on the periphery. It would be a matter of imposing an artificial order on chaos.

It's Mischa's business anyway, she told herself. I am on the periphery.

She tried to put herself in Antony's shoes. A biographer, she supposed, would take the raw materials – birth, character, personality – and superimpose on them the achievements of the will and the accidents of fate. Attempting, in the process, to answer a recurring question that could never be answered with absolute certainty: was this the result of that?

But a life could be affected forever by an accidental meeting, a chance encounter of two people. There was no avoiding that. It was what made the world go round. Two lives could be fundamentally changed, to be specific. And not only two, to be more specific still. There were causal questions Antony would certainly ask, to which the answers were unequivocal.

How far might he wish to go? If it was legitimate for a biographer to ask, to what extent has this person dictated his or her own fate, might he not also ask, to what extent has this person dictated the fates of others?

I was the only one there when he came in. I knew he was coming, Verity had told me to look out for him, she'd said, 'He's noisy, big, you won't mistake him.' Well, that was accurate, I suppose, but what she hadn't told me was how potent, how archetypally male he was. That's typical of Verity, she probably hadn't even noticed. She's kind of impervious to men – I think she must've been desexed. Or else everything's atrophied from lack of use. How awful would that be? Unthinkable.

Anyway, he came staggering in carrying a huge painting, which was covered in a mouldy bit of felt, dumped it down without a word to me & rushed out again, and lurched back in with another. Then he yelled, 'Are you a real person? Are you a fragment of my imagination? Is it too much to ask for help before it pelts with rain?'

'You mean a figment of your imagination,' I said. 'But I'm impressed with your vocabulary, so I'll help.' He had a very thick accent, not sexy like a Frenchman but not unappealing. We lugged pictures in from this ancient ute he'd borrowed that looked as if it had been rotting in a paddock for centuries. He looked a bit like

that himself. Inches of stubble, long hair that looked dirty, frayed t-shirt hanging out under his sweater, filthy canvas shoes tied up with string.

I told him he could do with a wash. 'So, you are being rude to me now, as well as lazy!' I couldn't tell if he was affronted or not. It was true, he stank. I said he could use the shower in Verity's flat, but he wouldn't have it, & insisted on starting to hang the pictures. I tried to tell him V. would have a fit because she always wants things hung her way, but he just ignored me & started banging in nails.

Greer shivered in the pale sunlight, clasping her arms under her breast. Mischa had asked early that morning, and unusually for him almost tentatively, 'What is this albatross on your mind?'

Mindful of Antony's scrutiny, she plucked something out of the air. 'I was thinking, does first imply second?'

'First? First of what? First love?'

'If you say the first something – anything – does it imply the existence of a second?'

'Mrs Smith, you are a mystery to me. You are my first true love. You know that. I have no strength for a second, not at my stage of life.'

She had gone on to say, but he hadn't waited to hear, 'It's not just a position, is it? It's expressing a potential. The potential for a second.' She would discuss it with Rollo sometime. He was always interested in everything – the more fanciful, the more pointless, the better.

She thought, in actual fact, Mischa, what you just said was not strictly true on two counts. I wasn't your first true love at all. Your first and enduring love is something quite different. And neither was I your first carnal love. But – you were mine. Oh yes, you were mine.

She had no doubt in her mind of that. The conjunction of ideas and memories gave her an ache in the heart. As if something lying there, which had not made its presence felt for years, was turning over.

The weak April sunlight lay on the wide windowsills and rebounded off the stone. Greer lifted her hands from the red exercise book and held them in the light. The hands of a middle-aged woman, she thought. No age spots, no wrinkles, but a certain puckering of the skin when the fingers were spread.

She turned them over. The palms were soft, unmarked by calluses or scars. Not the hands of a woman who did hard physical work. What kind of a woman's hands, then, were they? They looked capable enough, the long fingers pleasing in their symmetry, the square palms marked by well-defined grooves, like an etching. They might strike an observer as a confident woman's hands. Were they?

On the fleshy mound below each thumb was a tangled grid of tiny criss-crossed lines. Years ago, a clairvoyant in Sydney had told her that meant passion. She had been unsurprised to hear this. It confirmed something she had recently discovered about herself: she was a passionate woman.

She remembered exactly how old she was when she made this discovery. Almost thirty years of age. Somewhat advanced in years, many might think, to arrive at such a momentous realisation. This part of her must have been there before, must have been there always, but until she was nearly thirty she was unaware of it. It had needed something, an impetus, to rise to the surface. No, that was not right – it had clawed its way out, like a tigress. Tearing, shattering, destroying.

I'd gone back to finish some paperwork from the last exhibition when I suddenly heard a roaring sound. It took me a moment to realise it was him singing. It was the hymn 'Jerusalem', of all things. 'And did those feet, in ancient time, walk upon England's mountains green?' He'd hung a painting and was staring at it, his face was transfixed. Absolutely lit up with joy. And he was bellowing this, but like a rock song, his own rollicking tune, not the usual dirge. He was so loud I could see people passing in the street peering inside & grinning.

I looked at the picture. It was of a piano in a paddock. Standing on the keys, feet apart, was a little barefoot Aboriginal girl dressed in oversized dungarees, staring the onlooker down with a truculent expression. She and the piano were painted very beautifully and meticulously. The paddock was recognisably Australian – brown, parched, with a huge expanse of blue sky & an extraordinary atmosphere of heat & blazing light – all that was painted very freely and expressively. I could see immediately what Verity meant. She'd said, 'Greer, he is, without question, the most profound talent I have ever represented.' I remember that, word for word, because it's unprecedented for Verity to engage in anything approximating a rave. The way she said it actually made my spine tingle.

He stopped, having sung every verse of the entire poem, and stood there with his eyes shut and a beatific expression on his face. I said to him, 'That's really, stunningly good.' He said, his eyes still closed, 'My painting or my singing?' 'Your painting, of course.' He opened his eyes, seemed to see me properly for the first time, enfolded me in his arms and kissed me on the lips. Kissed me passionately.

She covered the page with her hands. The nails were painted in a transparent gloss, the whites as bright and the half moons as boldly defined as they had been all her life. Her toenails were painted red. Once she had never bothered, but now it was a habit. A habit of twenty-five years. The colour was identical to the scarlet cover of the exercise book, but that was a coincidence. The colour of passion, she thought. I might never have discovered that I was a passionate woman.

This thought was so provocative, such a series of life-changing events evolved from it, that her mind reeled. Were there other innate qualities lying below the surface, hidden and unsuspected, awaiting only an unknown agent – an experience, a word, a special person – to bring them to life? How many people lived out their lives in ignorance of another self, a shadowy form that they carried within them but knew nothing about? This might, she thought, be the real meaning of the fairy story 'The Sleeping Beauty'. The princess who lay asleep for years, until awakened by a kiss.

What had happened to Verity after Greer left the gallery? How old would she be today? The twenty-nine-year-old Greer had considered Verity an ancient monument, but she was probably only in her mid fifties at the time. Around Greer's present age, funnily enough. That would make Verity what, about eighty by now? Almost certainly she wouldn't still be running the gallery in South Yarra. Was she, even, still alive?

Had Antony managed to track her down? All Greer's mental pathways converged here in the same blind alley, no matter what strategies she employed to divert them. Verity had played a pivotal role in her life and Mischa's. Quite unwittingly, Greer thought, and decidedly unwillingly, she had been a manifestation of fate.

Wasn't a biographer, in essence, a detective investigating a life? If so, Verity was an essential clue for Antony. A primary source. Clues were the seedbeds of his raw materials, and the quality of his work must depend to a large extent on his forensic skills. It couldn't be that hard to find Verity, could it, even though she had been an unsociable woman? Everyone knew everyone else in the Melbourne art world of the 1970s. It would be all too easy to locate an elderly former dealer.

But there was an outside chance, there was slightly more than an even-money possibility, that she was no longer around. She might have retired to Queensland, to Port Douglas perhaps, or even to an apartment on Manhattan. Verity had once admitted to a weakness for New York City. She might have developed cancer, or Alzheimer's, or some other incurable disease. In Greer's mind was the wish, almost inaudible: let Verity be dead.

Greer hadn't thought of Verity for years. Her young self had viewed the older woman, absorbed with her work and her artists, uninterested in any form of social life, apparently without friends or even family, with a kind of uncompre-hending pity. But she remembered her now as that comparative rarity: a woman who appeared content. An unencumbered woman.

Greer's own relationship with Verity had exerted an influence she was unaware of at the time. For it was a kind of friendship, she could see that now, even if it had not always looked like one. The type of lopsided, inter-generational friendship that is possible between mentor and pupil. I learnt a lot from Verity, Greer thought. I learnt how to approach paintings, to read them. She taught me the language of art, or more precisely some of its many languages.

Who had replaced Greer in the gallery? Her departure would have left a gap. No, she corrected that. Her departure would have left a void.

Greer had worked there for nearly five years on her return from London. She'd taken an art history major at university, but Verity made it crystal clear she regarded her new employee as a greenhorn. She was a dogsbody to begin with, Verity's lowly assistant, but gradually took on wider duties and more responsibilities until, almost imperceptibly in the fourth year, she had been aware of herself evolving into a kind of equal – Verity's trusted right-hand woman.

It occurred to her now, belatedly: Verity was grooming me to take over from her. Not in the immediate future, perhaps not even for some years, but eventually. Verity was like that. A meticulous forward planner. She liked everything to be mapped out, all contingencies anticipated and taken care of. Forewarned is forearmed. This, thrown more than once at her young protégée, was one of a set of key maxims on which she structured her life.

Verity cared for no one except her artists, in Greer's opinion. But she was fond of me, Greer conceded now. I knew that very well, even though she never said it. And I walked out on her without a word.

It was always going to be difficult for Verity to find someone to take my place. Few young people would have the tolerance to put up with her brusqueness, her autocratic ways. Her bloody-mindedness, let's face it, and inflexibility.

I made allowances because I recognised her wellspring. Art was the core of her life. And she believed it was mine. That was the thread that linked us, two such disparate personalities – opposites even – drawn together by a mutual obsession. That was the mistake Verity made.

But I believed art was my life, too, for almost the entire time I worked for Verity. Until the cataclysm happened. Strange, to remember it like that. But that is how it was. I can see it now, from this distance, in the generous spring warmth of this classical landscape that is not foreign to me, but is somewhere, unmistakeably somewhere other than the land of my youth.

He released me – it was that way round, I found myself kind of immobilised with surprise – and started humming, & turned back to what he was doing, hanging another smaller picture, a detailed drawing of a street corner piled with rubbish & an old dero sitting on a moth-eaten Queen Anne (?) sofa. The street was in St Kilda, I recognised a shopfront.

'Is that where you live?' I asked. He had a nail hanging off his lip, like a cigarette, but he clenched it in his teeth and immediately said, 'Yes, and it is not a self-portrait, in case you are about to ask me.' He turned his back and got on with it, and I went back in the office. My mouth was still tingling. When V. came back she didn't have a tantrum, as I was expecting, but was quite mild. She made a couple of suggestions to move things around, which he rejected out of hand. Instead of pursuing it she just raised her eyebrows, with a tolerant 'have it your own way' smile. Pretty amazing. He was smoking, too.

I made coffee for us but he wouldn't stop, he just went on in his own private ferment of activity. I watched him for a bit. He seemed extraordinarily decisive; he'd take a quick look at the relevant bit of empty wall & bang a painting up. Very precise, no hesitation, no changing his mind. 'Don't you ever make a mistake?' I called at one point. He seemed to find this amusing. 'Of course, but only when it is a matter of love or death.'

'You mean life or death.'

'Don't try to tell me what I mean. I mean love. Perhaps you know nothing about this area.'

Soon after 5 he put the last one up. He and Verity stood in front of it (he was admiring it just as much as her, if not more) then, without warning, he grabbed her by the waist & started waltzing her round the room and belting out 'The Blue Danube' — 'da da da da DA, da da, da da . . .' V., breathless, didn't know how to react. Probably the first time anyone had dared to touch her for years, maybe since her mother. Then she started giggling almost girlishly. Bizarre. It didn't suit her. I had to leave at that point, because of the drinks party at C.'s work.

But he'll be back tomorrow, for the opening.

Why am I writing all this??

'G.' Guy was there, drumming on the open door. She shut the exercise book and slipped it inside her desk drawer. 'You were in exactly the same position when I saw you at the window two hours ago. Unmoved and unmoving. Unnervingly sphinx-like. What are you doing?'

'Just the wretched accounts.'

She preceded him down the three stone steps into the kitchen, where a soft beam of sunlight fell on the table, taking in the stove top and the wall behind, hung with pots and pans and gadgets. Fine motes floated and swam in the air, caught in the light and then extinguished. Like the teeming, fleeting life on earth, she thought, and, billions of years into the future, like the destiny of the earth itself.

Greer loved this kitchen. She could never occupy it without remembering that it had been a kitchen for four hundred years. She took the coffee out of the fridge.

'You should keep it in the freezer, you know.'

'Oh, you always say that. I'm not convinced it makes any difference.'

'Better make enough for three. His Unholiness might grace us. He's intolerable when he's got a blockage. The real problem is that he's miffed, of course.'

She unscrewed the biggest of the three pots, filled the

bottom half with cold water and spooned ground coffee into the middle container.

'Miffed about what?'

'You know what. The bloody bio. He wants one.'

'Well, he can have Mischa's, for all I care.'

'Don't say that. Mischa's as chuffed as hell. Isn't he? I've never seen him in such an elevated mood for such an extended period. It's almost as revolting as Rollo's sulks.'

She lit the gas with a match.

'You really wish it wasn't happening, don't you?' Guy was as acute as ever. 'Why? You're not jealous. You haven't a jealous arrow in your quiver.' Behind him, Rollo's bulk filled the doorway, ahead of a plodding black pug. 'Oh Lord, it's him already. Trailing clouds of gloom and doom.'

'Hello, darling.' Rollo heaved a lugubrious sigh and deposited a kiss on Greer's cheek. He planted himself in a chair. The pug jumped on his lap. 'Forgive me crashing your elevenses, but I'm slavering for civilised discourse. I've only had that,' he indicated Guy, 'to talk to for the last forty-eight hours, and the gloss has worn off. The gilt's off the gingerbread.'

Guy snorted. 'It wore off decades ago.'

'I'm exhausted today. I think I'm fading fast.'

'You're eighty, what do you expect?'

'But I'm a loveable octogenarian at the height of my powers. Everyone says so.'

'Oh, just slink off into your fetid hole and paint, you silly old queen.'

Greer only half listened to them, two grown men bickering like children. Mischa refused to humour the daily charade, accusing them of living a clapped-out routine. She maintained that it was purely for show, a modus operandi that amused and sustained them both. Besides, she rather enjoyed the performance. It took her mind off things.

Rollo looked much the same. He always brought to her mind a certain portrait of Henry VIII, the bluff exterior masking a core of steel. She could never decide whether he was good-looking, with his trim moustache and small beard, his military bearing, his pale, shrewd blue eyes and enigmatic visage. It was irrelevant, she always concluded. Rollo Sonabend was himself, that was all there was to it. Guy Crewe, on the other hand, was a blatantly handsome man with a fine leonine head. Her age exactly, a generation younger than Rollo.

They were still at it. 'I don't think I'll ever paint again, darling. The inspiration's gone. It's just not there. Flown out of the window and migrated. It's probably landed on some art student nonentity from 'uddersfield.' Rollo hailed from Yorkshire, although he liked to assert that he was unsullied by his origins.

'Oh, shut up about it. You're the nonentity from 'uddersfield, and you're pea-green with envy, that's all. You want some mewling boy to swan in from overseas and ask you obsequious questions. And formulate drivelling academic theories about the significance of the banana in your work.'

Lately, Rollo's very accomplished still lifes had been featuring domestic objects against elaborate backdrops rather than the flowers and interiors of his earlier career.

'Only a mewling pretty boy with flattering theories of the banana. Longitudinally flattering.'

'You want to be able to drone on about yourself, un-interrupted, for – how long is the Antonioship staying?'

'A week or two, I think,' Greer said. 'Maybe more. Or less.'

'He'll have to be out of the cottage by the end of May. The crumbling ruins are coming, remember.' Guy's parents were strikingly active and showed no signs of flagging. As far as Greer could see they spent their retirement in ceaseless travel round the world, visiting their three sons. Guy never tired of reminding Rollo that they were in fact younger than him, though by a slender margin.

Greer put the coffee pot, cream and English digestive biscuits that Rollo loved onto a tray. Guy took three earthen-ware mugs from the shelf. They went out of the kitchen on to the terrace, with what Rollo called its vertiginous view.

'Thank you, darling.' Rollo took three biscuits. He looked unperturbed. 'Am I jealous?' He ignored Guy's hoot. 'Only up to a point. One has to ask oneself, would one really want someone pissing on one's murky past? The honest answer to that is possibly not, or not in its unadorned entirety.'

'The answer to that is, yes, one would adore every moment of it. One would dig out every pongy scrap of dirty linen and wave it under his nose.'

Rollo turned to Greer. 'But Mischa's expecting a hagiography, surely, not a warty type of bio, isn't he?'

Guy interrupted. 'Warty ones are the only kind there are these days. No sleazy sexual sod left unturned. That's what she's so worried about.'

'Are you worried, dear heart? Not on Mischa's account, surely. No sleazy sexual sods there, he's just a tortured artiste with a one-track mind, like me.'

'What are you talking about, "like me"? Your past is littered with compulsive lechery. Far more than those disingenuous, prim, anal retentive little titbits you chose to disgorge in *The Whitewash*.'

The Whitewash was Guy's name for Rollo's autobiography, published to considerable acclaim ten years earlier. It had been translated into Italian and, to Rollo's rather mystified pleasure, Japanese. He had become, he liked to tell journalists, very big in the Orient ever since.

Rollo chortled at Greer. 'Isn't it sweet? Thirty-three mentions, its own paragraph in the index, and it's still shirty. Anyway, darling, we all know Mischa's as pure as the driven snow. A boring subject for your poor unfortunate biographer.'

'The driven snow he skied across? There's always the Iron Curtain aspect, remember, Roly.'

'Ah yes, the crepuscular Czechobosniak Dark Age no one knows anything about.'

'I can see the chapter heading now: "Svoboda's Secret Shame: the Unexpurgated Expose".'

Rollo gurgled. '"Karlovy *Vari*: the Unvarnished Truth".'

They were rubbing along quite well now, and Greer was the outsider. Guy turned on her, smiling.

'What about your secret years, then? Life before Mischa. You never talk about it.'

She wanted to say, I wrote about it once. To myself. Instead she said, 'I was just a mewling girl. There's nothing much to tell.'

She was on the point of adding something, but she could see they believed her. They were easily satisfied, these two men who knew her so well. Who thought they knew her.

2

Saturday 8th July
The opening went fantastically well (except for one thing).
Nearly two-thirds sold. V. tickled pink, in her phlegmatic way.
Other people wouldn't necessarily have known, but I could tell –
the corners of her mouth that are normally turned down were
horizontal at least. I'm pleased for her, she needs a hit.

He was waiting outside when I got there at 4, looking in
worse shape than yesterday, if possible. I was positive he
hadn't even changed his shirt. I asked him if he'd slept on the
pavement.

'I do have somewhere that is not the pavement to go. Do
you want to come and inspect it? Is that why you are rudely
asking?'

'You seem to have this effect on me. I'm sorry, I'm not
usually like this.'

'What effect are you talking about?'
'Well, asking questions you think are rude.'
'What are you usually like?'
'I'm usually quite polite.'
'You are a very bourgeois little girl then, aren't you, in
your nice white suit?'

That really annoyed me, and I pushed past him & started
turning on all the lights. Verity came in & I buttonholed her,
away from him, & suggested she at least get him to go and

have a shave & a wash. She said it was not her place to tell him what to do, he was a grown man. And she's normally sooo fastidious. Then she added, 'You wouldn't think of telling Francis Bacon to go and have a shave, now, would you?' She laughed, quite light-heartedly.

She's not only putting him in the big league, now she's making jokes as well.

A column of smoke split the horizon in two equal, and equally decorative, halves. The smoke is the colour of pewter, Greer thought, and the sky is lavender. If I were a landscape painter I would be sitting here with an easel on the terrace, or up among the olive trees on the hillside, translating this sublime view. The way the land lies, the changing shape of its moods. It has the open, responsive countenance of a face.

I was never a landscape painter. I was always more drawn to people. People and appearances. The unlimited variety of the human face, with its capacity to hint, to express, to reveal. And equally, of course, to lie. In the same way as the landscape painter observes the bones of the earth's crust, the way the land lies, you might say that I was a student of the lie of the face.

I was a competent portraitist. Possibly more than that; Verity was always encouraging me to do more drawing, to go to art school part-time, to explore and develop my talent. She urged me to push the boundaries. I was about to, of course. That was the plan. And I suppose I did push them, but not in the way she meant. Not remotely in that way.

A corner of the diary page curled slightly. She felt the sun move between clouds on her back. She had brought sunglasses on to the terrace to take advantage of the brightness and warmth, which would not last. And to take advantage of this unaccustomed free time, which she had set up for the duration of the biographer's visit.

From her chair she saw that part of the gutter was coming adrift. It needed fixing. So did the cistern in their bathroom, which was making a constant low-level flushing noise. She noticed a couple of loose bricks in the archway over the kitchen door, where the mortar had crumbled away. There was always something, with an old house.

A silky drift of perfume hung in the air. The old wisteria vine clinging to the east wall of the house and, she thought, practically holding it up, was in full flower. The speckled stones were only intermittently visible behind prodigious spouting fountains that cascaded down the wall like blue waterfalls. Heliotrope-coloured flowers, she maintained, largely because she liked the old English word. Not a bit of it – Cambridge blue crossed with gentian violet according to Guy, a pedantic King's man.

There were a couple of Guy's discarded wine casks directly below the small terrace, planted with spiky rosemary bushes. Next to them were smaller, sawn-off barrels of lavender. The rosemary was coming out early too, dotted with its more reticent blue flowers. Very soon, on the cusp of summer, when it was especially still and there was a particular configuration of sun and wind and light, the air on the kitchen terrace would fizz with a broth of wisteria and rosemary.

In the corner of the terrace she kept pots of jasmine. It had been warmer than usual this year and already they were starting to bud, the stems sporting silvery slivers of magenta. Long sultry evenings were just around the corner. In a week or two – it couldn't be long now – with the lavender out in force and the jasmine in full rampaging flower like the clouds of a child's snowdome, the air would vibrate once more with the scent of seduction.

I'd only just got the cheese & biscuits & wine put out when the GP started arriving. All the usuals, but a few extra VIPs. Verity's obviously been putting the screws on around town. There was a distinct buzz. I was run off my feet putting red stickers on.

The Aboriginal girl went first, then there were a couple of photo finishes that almost turned nasty. Jane C. & Stephen S. both wanted the dero, & the charcoal drawing of the woman in an apron doing the vacuuming had two others after it. I told V. she should've charged more. She said, 'Next time we'll double the prices.'

He was quite low-key, relatively well behaved. Maybe Verity had had a quiet word. She steered him round the bigwigs & the silver-spoon brigade. You could see people thinking, wow, a real live Bohemian artist! The genuine article – grotty & eccentric, none of your modern, suave art-school product. They were lapping it up.

He came over to me at one point, to get his glass filled. He leant over & shouted (it was v. noisy), 'I would like to offer you dinner tonight.'

I must have looked flabbergasted, & he immediately said: 'You are alive, so you probably eat food? It would be a pity to waste that nice white suit. And now I have lots of money.'

I said, 'Thanks, but I'm not wasting the suit so you needn't worry.' I was meeting C. at Mietta's. As I said that I realised it sounded quite ungracious. Then something made me add, 'It's cream, by the way. Not white.'

He made a series of silly faces & yelled, 'Oh, really? You don't say! Is it CREAM? I am SO SORRY for my STUPID mistake!' He was trying (unsuccessfully) to do an exaggerated English accent. I realised he was actually quite drunk.

He went off to eat with Verity afterwards.

Why did I say that? But his invitation was pretty damn ungraciously expressed too. What did he expect?

C. goes to the NZ conference tomorrow, for 3 days.

His overreaction was ridiculous. Childish.

She picked up the diary and went inside, into their bed-room, a cool, sparsely furnished space that squared off one corner of the house. The windows on the two outer walls were flung wide open. If you stood at the door and looked through the gap of the far window, the room seemed to extend into the sky. Zoom further in, as if through the lens of a hand–held camera, and the panoramic vastness of the landscape swung into view.

On the right-hand wall the windows had a different function: to illuminate the domestic arena. Across the drive and a swathe of lawn dotted with daisies and yellow celandines – the piazza area they called the parade ground – sat Rollo and Guy's house. It was clearly visible now, its cloak of Virginia creeper still a wintry tracery of branches, and the vine leaves on the pergolas tightly furled. Soon the creeper and the vines would be out, concealing the house behind an impenetrable green wall of foliage.

Normally she loved this airy bedroom, with its contrasting outlooks. She thought of it as giving a physical voice to the two halves of her existence, the outer and the inner life. Her mind's eye, the imaginative play of the mind, was as crowded and colourful as a kaleidoscope. There were times when she wondered if she was more occupied with the world of the mind than with what people called real life.

But in recent weeks the imminence of the biographer's arrival had achieved a kind of upheaval. It was as if her private horizons were no longer unrestricted. They had contracted into a small claustrophobic space, rather like a safe house. She had begun to think of herself as living under a house arrest of the mind.

Beyond the perimeter of her mental safe house lay a cordoned-off area, a dark no-man's land ringed by shadows. It was an ominous and forbidden place, and yet time and again she would find herself drawn towards it. There was a pattern to this apparently unconscious process. It was always the same. She would find herself out there, stealing towards that dangerous forbidden boundary, creeping up on it. When it dawned on her she recoiled and drew back. Both moves, the cautious advance, the shocked retreat, were like reflex actions, each as involuntary as the other.

The zone that lay beyond the perimeter was not empty.

She knew there were things out there. She sensed, but could not grasp, their amorphous shapes.

Always, the bedroom had a calming effect. The walls revealed the fugitive presence, both physical and ethereal, of previous generations. Unlike the rest of the house, which was mostly plastered and hung with pictures, she and Mischa had left these walls untouched. They were flecked with spectral tints of pigment, these walls that had once been menaced by brambles and worn away by wind and rain. For four desolate decades the house had lain uninhabited, abandoned to the elements, before Mischa and Greer arrived to live in it. Like the other two main houses it had once been divided up and occupied by two or three families.

It was Rollo and Guy more than thirty years earlier who had stumbled across the Castello: a medieval hamlet with chapel and watchtower in a state of extreme dereliction. The cluster of buildings on an isolated hilltop had been abandoned for at least twenty years, since the inhabitants of the day, a small community of sharecroppers, were left destitute by their landlord. He was known in the district as the wicked count. These days some less feckless descendants of the wicked count still lived in the grand villa further up the hill and were cordial friends of Rollo and Guy.

The farmers had all dispersed to cities and villages in search of work. Local lore had it that some of them had gone to Australia and ended up in Melbourne, Greer's home town. An example, she thought, of the random circularity of destiny.

Patches of cracked stucco still lay on the bedroom walls, floating like clouds. To Greer, the grainy surfaces, with their layers upon layers, hinted at other lives. The remnants of paint and wash were small testimonies, modest but eloquent, bequeathed to posterity. She speculated often with Rollo about those who had left them. She liked to think of herself and Mischa as the natural descendants of these unknown forbears.

They may be unknown and mysterious, she thought, but I am not unaware of them. We are their posterity and they are not forgotten. She sensed that in some visceral way this ancient house was aware that it had been rescued from rack and ruin and was grateful. Her predecessors, she was certain, had responded to it just as she did. She felt imagined presences at times. She had never once felt lonely in this room, or this house.

She saw now that the stippled smudges of ochre were fragments of autobiography. A human version of spoor, the track or scent of an animal. What inadvertent traces would she and Mischa leave behind? Even if it were only a subtle shift in atmosphere, they would leave their spoor. Proof that the terracotta roof and these limestone walls had once sheltered this woman and this man, the successors and inheritors of all those who had gone before.

The house is not mute. Our ancestors may be unnamed but they are not entirely anonymous, Greer thought. There are certain facts about them that I know, certain important truths. They too had their human failings. They were capable of particular things, deeds in their lives that they regretted, which caused them shame; deeds to which this house has borne patient witness. It sustained them in times of joy and passion, anguish and loss. Through infidelities, betrayals and remorse. This house sustained them throughout their lives, and after centuries it is still here, an unprejudiced observer, accepting everything, judging nothing. I find this knowledge strangely comforting.

On her left next to the door was a gold-framed drawing in red chalk, the head and bare shoulders of a man. Signed with a flourish, with a pair of ornate initials, two capital Gs interlocked by curlicues, and a date in the bottom right-hand corner. Her own initials, and a date she knew by heart.

She considered the drawing critically, as if she were Antony the invader coming upon it with no preconceived ideas. It showed a man who looked the age she knew he was at the time: nearing the end of his fortieth year. A strong, square face, fleshy and lived-in, shadowed with heavy stubble. Long straggling hair, almost shoulder length, piercing deep-set eyes, and a complicated expression full of challenge and triumph.

It was, she decided, both a good likeness and a success-ful rendering of a sensuous and virile man. But it was neither an objective portrait nor a dispassionate one. It shouted disclosure. In the bold, suggestive strokes of the chalk a perceptive onlooker might recognise the feelings, the full-on complicity of the artist.

On the wall opposite, next to the window, the chalk man was reflected in an old octagonal mirror whose carved wooden frame had been painted, like the bedroom walls, layer upon layer. Greer stood next to the drawing and posi-tioned her face close to his. She examined the two reflected images.

The new portrait was in colour, but looked slightly overexposed. It showed a middle-aged woman, faded blonde hair pinned up untidily, no make-up. Full lips, which matched those of the man next to her. A sensual mouth, unquestionably. Long, narrow nose, pale blue eyes.

She couldn't read the expression in the eyes or the face. It wasn't that it was an enigmatic face, exactly. It was hard to read because it did not give much away. And although it was so familiar, the face, after all, whose every detail she knew, every blemish, there was a sense in which it remained a mystery, even to her. Would it suggest to the onlooker that it was the face of a woman with secrets?

The man and the woman, side by side. How did they go together? Did they fit? The woman looked older than the man, which was not surprising since he was still young and radiated vigour. But he was fixed at a point of historical time, and she, existing in real time, had aged twenty-five years. How would a biographer read them as a couple? He would see that this man was anything but secretive. His emotions were there for the asking, ready to jump out of his skin.

Sunday 9th July
He was in for less than half an hour this morning. Only 5 left unsold by 6 o'clock. He looked in bad shape.
    We ignored each other.

3

From the kitchen terrace, scanning across the valley floor Greer could just make out a moving speck. It was a car, coming from the north. She watched as it crawled along the curving road, sliding in and out of sight as it dipped below the scrub of ilex trees, hawthorn and poplars. Could it be Antony? He'd said late afternoon, well after yardarm time, and it was only just after midday.

Besides, he might not be coming today at all. Greer handled the computer, Mischa being useless with any kind of technology, and she had accidentally erased the email. It might have said tomorrow, or even the day after. Then she saw another car trailing behind, and another. She turned her back on the view. This was absurd. It must be the beginning of the tourist season, if indeed it ever came to an end. She had better things to do than watch the road, than wait for the arrival of an unknown visitor. A person whose impending arrival was unwelcome. Whose arrival, she faced up to it, filled her with dread.

Mischa appeared to have no such qualms. Guy was right: he had been full of ebullience since the emails stepped up and the biographer's arrival became imminent. But there was an edge to this sustained, almost bombastic, good humour. Mischa had used it to deflect all attempts to broach the subject, by Greer or anyone else, almost as if the biography were some whimsical construct, a poem by Edward Lear or an unsuitable joke. In any case, Greer had found the subject well nigh impossible to broach. From its very first mention the biography had assumed the loaded status of a taboo topic between them.

Mischa had not referred to Antony Corbino's introductory letter for some time. And had he in fact been the first to mention it? Greer couldn't even be certain of that, not entirely. Her first inkling that a biography was on the cards may well have been a concerned remark from one of Mischa's dealers. It was so unlike Mischa to agree to such a thing she could only conclude that he must have been diverted, briefly, by some notion of seeing himself silhouetted on a canvas, pictured through the prism of another's eyes. She suspected he would rapidly lose patience with the interviewing process. He had never much liked talking about himself.

It was always likely that Mischa would be the target of a biographer, sooner or later. Greer knew this perfectly well, but until recently the idea had been simply that – a vague possibility that might never eventuate. She felt angry now, and principally with herself. Why had she been so passive? Her attitude had been like that of a passenger on an aircraft, suspended in limbo between two points and unable to influence the outcome.

Not that Mischa was susceptible either to other people's opinions or for the most part to persuasion, whether gentle or robust. She firmly believed that in all his life he had probably never once asked of anyone: what do you think I should do? He always knew what he wanted to do, and whether he should or should not be doing it didn't come into it.

Greer knew that she could, on occasion, and if she put her mind to it, divert him from his chosen course and get him to do what she wanted. She knew she might have had a good chance of success if she had come right out and spoken her mind. If she'd said: this biography is a very bad idea. It would only get in the way of your work. It's not too late to withdraw your permission. Then he might have said: if you really want me to, Mrs Smith, I will. Fuck it, let him waste some other bugger's time. And that might have been the end of it.

But I couldn't say that, she thought. It would be like sabotage. A biography is a natural outcome of a successful career. It's inevitable. If not this one there would be others, and behind Mischa's back and mine, which might very well be worse. Besides, Rollo would think I was mad. And mean-spirited. Rollo would be bemused to know, she felt sure, how much she valued his good opinion.

Greer and Guy were the winemakers, working through changing seasons and in all weathers. They saw themselves as extracting treasure from the stony soil, and saw each other nearly every day; their friendship – jokey, rooted in practicalities – thrived on it. Yet it was with Rollo that she felt she had the more organic relationship. She found it hard to believe she had not known him all her life. Rollo was like a close sibling. In her imagination she positioned him as a much older fraternal twin. Mischa, on the other hand, was nothing like her sibling or her platonic, jokey friend.

She was unprepared for the thought that arrived without warning: these are the only men in my life.

The first letter had arrived nearly three years ago, soon after the appearance of an article on Mischa's recent work in the journal *Artnews*. The writer of the article and the follow-up letter was an up-and-coming young art critic from Los Angeles named Antony Corbino. The article was a well-written, perceptive piece and Mischa approved of it.

Corbino's letter introduced himself, presented his credentials and declared his wish to become Mischa's first biographer. He wanted primarily, he said, to focus on Mischa's career path, his place in the annals of contemporary art, rather than what he called the banal personal detail.

He asked for Mischa's permission to go ahead. Mischa had written straight back, without consulting his dealers in London or New York, and without a word to Greer. He'd only mentioned it to her in passing, days later. He had given the project his blessing and then put it aside.

Antony Corbino had kept in regular contact with Mischa by letter or telephone during the next couple of years, and sometimes via Greer by email. Mischa enjoyed these little communications, which were pithy and rather witty. They were mainly concerned with the location and provenance of particular paintings, and reconstructing Mischa's meandering route over several years from Prague to Melbourne. And then trying to pin down the sequence of Mischa and Greer's wanderings, post-Australia, pre-Italy.

There was ongoing light banter over inconsistencies in printed biographical details. Arty in-jokes abounded. In addition, Antony had set up a website with an email address and posted updates on articles and references to Mischa's work in publications around the world. It had all been straightforward enough and, Greer had to admit, in her role as aide-mémoire and fact-checker, completely unthreatening. Mischa was happy – he felt that he and Tony, as he was already calling him, had a good rapport. He was chuffed, as Guy said, and it seemed almost churlish to cast a pall over his pleasure.

From below the terrace she heard her name called. It was Guy, with the three Welsh wine buyers who had been staying in the guest cottage for the last couple of days. She ran down the kitchen steps to say goodbye. The men were clients of several years' standing, a convivial, blasphemous trio. There had been a dinner, a very rowdy dinner the night before, with Guy and Greer presiding over the table, a virtual couple for the evening.

The men loaded suitcases into their boot. Guy was about to take them up the road to a friend's vineyard for a farewell lunch. They pressed her to change her mind and join them. Leave the artsy critic to fart around. He'd get lost on the way, anyhow. And she already knew what he'd be like: a poncy bugger, like all of his ilk. They kissed her warmly. Singing wine bores like themselves were more amusing in their fashion, weren't they?

Oh, loads more laughs, she smiled. 'And in the normal way I would. But I think I should stick around, just in case he inflicts himself on us . . .' She didn't add, I'd give a great deal, you know, if only this were in the normal way.

She had been part of the business for so long now it was hard to recall the time before it. When she and Mischa first arrived Guy was already in the process of establishing himself as a winemaker. From the start he had put much stock into building personal relationships with his buyers and suppliers. He liked to dispense hospitality, and one night he'd roped in Greer as his date and social hostess. The evening had been a success, and she found it surprisingly congenial. It had quickly settled into a habit during the buying season.

When Guy was laid low with bronchial flu one November, Greer had found a way through an administrative labyrinth of red tape that had entangled him for months. Guy put this triumph down to three factors: her appalling Italian, incomprehensible accent and entirely bogus air of feminine helplessness. She had, he said, achieved a mathematical first by transforming three negatives into a positive. Whatever, it disarmed the men he needed to rubber stamp his future and he began to make use of it on a semi-regular basis.

Then there was the discovery, wholly fortuitous, that she had an exceptional palate. Asked to adjudicate in a tea-making domestic between Rollo and Guy – a row over whether milk should be added before or after – Greer, blindfolded, had correctly identified which cup was which. Her prowess hadn't settled the interminable argument, but it was often reprised as a party trick for visitors.

Looking back it had been a seamless transition, her march towards a hands-on role in the winery. From Guy's virtual wife she had morphed into his decidedly existential wine-making partner, and normally at this time of year she would be based in the office co-ordinating business. Dealing with buyers and the daily round of consignments, ordering bottles and corks, checking the pigments of labels. Endlessly schmoozing, as Guy put it, the bloody bureaucracy.

She could easily wander over to the office and give Giulia a hand. But Giulia, who was relieving her and having boyfriend trouble, would think she was being checked on. There were friends less than twenty minutes away, or at the end of a telephone. And there was always Mischa, who never minded her coming in. He pleased himself, simply went on working away through any kind of disturbance; he was capable of turning his back on anything or anyone. But she didn't feel like talking to Mischa's back, or to a friend.

Rollo would be in his studio again after his half-hour coffee break. Generally he disliked being interrupted, but during his episodes of painter's block he courted distraction. On impulse she threw some things into a basket: salami, pecorino, tomatoes, this morning's loaf. And an opened bottle of workaday wine, their flinty, quaffing white that Guy referred to as the dregs. Rollo was partial to a glass at lunch. She almost ran across the wide expanse of the parade ground to the chapel abutting the house opposite. She knocked on the door.

Rollo was lounging on his squashy sofa with two pugs, listening to Wagner. He held up a cautionary hand as Greer pushed open the heavy wooden door, introducing a shaft of bright light into the murky interior. When Rollo was in full flight the door would be ajar and all lights burning. Now he sat sunk in classic gloom. She waited until the *Siegfried Idyll*, a favourite of theirs, drew to a close.

Rollo's paintings hung everywhere and were stacked up against the walls. He was preparing for a Christmas exhibition in Milan. Two easels carried works in progress, both stalled. She examined the pictures while she listened and waited. They looked the same as they had a week ago. One was a large expanse of untouched canvas surrounding a half-finished, painstakingly detailed washbowl and jug, next to a silver photo frame.

Beyond the easel was a backdrop set up on the old altar, containing the objects in the picture. The photo in the silver frame was of Rollo's mother. Behind it and still to be painted were a woman's Edwardian riding hat and cape draped over a mahogany clothes horse, roughly and whimsically carved in the shape of a stallion with tossing head and tail.

The other canvas was even more sparsely covered and stood in front of a pair of heavily pitted medieval doors from Sicily. Over one door knob hung a man's cravat, on which was pinned an extravagant filigree brooch in the shape of a pear tree, whose fruits were seed pearls and emeralds. Greer knew that the brooch, which had been found the year before in a Viennese street market, would most likely end up in her hands, exquisitely wrapped, as a Christmas or birthday present from Rollo.

Whenever he was away, Rollo made a point of seeking out the local markets – antique, flea, or trash and treasure. He was an obsessive hunter of fabric samples and bric-a-brac, from which he would construct sought-after miniature stage settings, the backdrops for his pictures. There had been several sell-out exhibitions of these charmingly theatrical pieces. Guy maintained Rollo was just a window-dresser at heart.

Even in the incomplete form on display, Rollo's technique was dazzling. It had a trompe l'oeil quality that flirted with the surreal and was much admired. They may try to emulate but they never equal, as he said himself of his many imitators. His blockages often struck in the middle of a prolific period, as now, and their origin mystified everybody except Guy, who claimed that they were an invention when Rollo wanted to be waited on.

'Darling, you're an angel.' Rollo turned the volume down. 'I couldn't stand my own indolent shadow a moment longer. I've always known you were psychic. Is it warm enough to eat outside? Should I bring my fur coat?'

They carried the food to a long table under the pergola at the front. There were pergolas all along the south and west walls of the house, supporting thickets of wild climbing roses and mature grapevines. This one, with its shaggy hammock of a canopy, was in bad shape. The old beams were bent, visibly rotting in places, and about to be replaced.

Guy had cobbled his early attempts at making drinkable fermented grape juice from these very vines, plus the few stragglers remaining in the home paddock, picking up the basic tricks of the trade from local farmers. For his first vintages he had gone to the lengths of crushing the grapes in traditional style, or so he liked to boast, using sticks with branches like horns.

'It still might never come to anything, Roly. The biography. Don't you think?'

Rollo plonked the magnum of olive oil he had fetched from their kitchen on to the table. He poured a lavish amount on to a plate and dunked a wedge of bread. He rolled it around on his tongue. 'This is his best yet. Gooseberry-ish, lovely and peppery, almost a hint of jalapeño, wouldn't you say? But not *too* hot. Just right. He's getting better at it all the time.'

He winked at her. '*And* at the olive oil. But don't ever tell him I said so. He's so big-headed about everything since your grog gong.'

Their most recent release of Brunello had been awarded the coveted five bunches, top score of the Italian Sommelier Association, and *Wine Spectator* had given it a score of 92 out of 100.

Greer didn't respond. Rollo chewed noisily. 'He's quite well regarded, isn't he, your Yank? His first book was all right.' Corbino had sent them a copy, a competent biography of a turn-of-the-twentieth-century Boston artist.

'A bit dull, if anything.'

'Dull is good,' Rollo boomed. 'If you're anxious to avoid salacious,' he peered at her, 'you want dull. Pedestrian, straightforward, boring. Then no one will buy it.'

She looked at him suspiciously. He cut two thick slabs of cheese and passed her one, adding, 'The Boston one's wife died early, didn't she?'

'Yes. Why?'

'There was a bit of a shortage of sex angle. You want the full rich tapestry in a bio. I expect your Mr C. is well pleased that Mischa has such a palatable distaff side. He's been cultivating you, hasn't he?'

'Well, I've had a couple of letters. And emails.'

'There you are. That's what they do. He's thinking to himself, I will get to him through her. She will unlock his cabinet of curiosities. He'll be grovelling charm itself, wait and see.'

'But it's Mischa's biography, isn't it? Not mine.'

'Of course it is. But you're the love interest. It's your bounden duty to supply the sexy bits. Is this pecorino from Mario? It's very good.'

She nodded.

'You're distracted, darling. *Distraite*, I can always tell. Listen, if you haven't got any secrets you can always make them up. I'll help you. We will devise an irresistible scenario. Mischa was a spy for the West – well, that's probably true, isn't it? He used to smuggle out information encoded in his pictures. Then, when he was sprung, he had to get out fast. And that's where you came in. You provided a safe house. But it was daggers drawn at first sight. The attraction crept up unawares and exploded one blazing tropical Aussie night, when hate turned to unbridled passion.'

He looked at her expectantly, his eyes keen. She thought, how wily he is. To please him she said, smiling, 'Very good. But not hot. It was Melbourne. It was pouring with 'uddersfield rain.'

Sun 16th July
Isle of Pines
I thought he wasn't going to come in on Wednesday. Then, at nearly 6, there he was. I was about to lock up. V. had already

gone. There was nobody else there. He looked even more daggy than last time, and kind of volatile, as if he was living on compressed petrol or something. He barrelled round inspecting the red dots. When he got to the big oil of the people lined up and staring he yelled out, 'Hey, what's-your-name!' It was a summons not a question, & it sounded full of pent-up dislike. I kept right on with what I was doing – typing, not looking at him. Then suddenly there he was in the office right beside me, holding out both hands in front of him like a supplicant with the palms up. He said, in a fairly normal voice, 'This is a peace offering.' I saw that his palms were sweating.

'What is?'

He stared at me. I said, 'If it's genuine, you have to be offering something. I might want to make conditions.' There was a long silence between us. For a dreadful moment I thought he was going to go beserk. He was breathing fast, I could hear it. Then, out of the blue, he seized my left hand. 'There is something genuine I am offering. I am offering you a kiss.'

He said it like a question this time and I came right out in goosebumps. It was quite a cold evening. I said, 'All right. I accept.' He put my hand up to his lips. I felt them moving against the tips of my fingers. He kept my hand there, for a full minute it must have been, our eyes fixed on each other, then he said, 'Come with me.'

Again, it was a question. I got up and he led me by the hand over to the same painting, the queue of staring faces. 'Tell me, why don't they like this?' It hadn't sold. I said, 'I suppose it's a bit disturbing. But it's very powerful. Like you. Don't worry, I'm sure it will go. They'll come to like it.' We stood there in front of it, very close together. He was still clasping my hand, pressing it hard against his thigh. Neither of us spoke.

He must have pulled me sideways, because suddenly I was right up against him. Heat from him hit me like an electric current. I think I was rigid with shock. I don't know how long we stayed like that. It was as if neither of us wanted to move, we were sort of mesmerised. Eventually he said, 'Well? Do you want to make a condition?'

'Yes, actually, I do,' I said. It came out hoarse. I cleared my throat. 'I was expecting a proper kiss.'

She snapped the exercise book shut and rammed it in the drawer. It was 3 o'clock. An hour since she had left Rollo. Looking down at her arms in the warmth of her study, she was unsurprised to find the fine light hairs were standing on end. She snatched a key from a hook in the kitchen and with fast steps crossed the courtyard to the third stone house, about 50 yards from her own.

At the top of the steps the front door stood open. Loud music issued from inside – American country music. That meant Agnieszka. She nearly turned back, then went in.

Agnieszka was vacuuming one of the rugs in the sitting room, her back to Greer, who waited until she turned round so as not to give her a fright – Agnieszka was famously highly strung. It was not a long wait. Everything Agnieszka did was done fast and furiously. She reached the edge of her rug, saw Greer, switched off the machine with one hand and the portable CD player with the other, and darted over to enfold her in a beaming hug. They had seen each other the day before but this was a ritual that never varied.

'I like it do the house today, make sure everything is perfect for your man. When he come? Tonight? You tell me when and I finish before he come. He is taking the train from Roma to Grosseto?'

'He's driving from Pisa. But he may not come today, I –'

'He come from Pisa? He must see the leaning tower, he is coming all the way from America. Or Roma, he can see the Colosseum. Why he no want to see these things?'

'He's been here before, Aggie,' Greer said patiently. 'Not here, but to Italy. And he's not coming from America, he's been in London.'

'Oh. *London.*' Agnieszka's voice dropped an octave. She looked disappointed and disparaging. Her year in England as a Polish casual worker was a bad memory.

'I'm not sure exactly when he's coming, anyway. It may not be today at all. I deleted the email.'

'You no write it down, the time? You no remember the day?' Greer was familiar with the tone of voice and the expression on Agnieszka's face. She was aware that this model of domestic efficiency considered Greer a lost cause in that department.

'I give you notebook. There is book with,' Agnieszka gestured wildly, 'things – round things – metals – on the top. You can get in supermarket –'

'A spiral notebook?'

'Yes, you know it? You write it to yourself, each time you want to remember. Then you tear off, and put by the front door. Maybe hang from a string. You like it I get you next week? There is game I play with Silvio,' Agnieszka's fourteen-year-old, Silvio, was regularly hired to solve computer glitches at the Castello, 'very good for the memory. One person say, I go to the supermarket and I buy one apple. Then the next person say, I go to the supermarket and I buy one apple and one dog biscuit for Rocco, then the next person –'

'Yes, I know that game. It's for children.'

'You know? Then you play with your husband. At breakfast. If you do this every day, you soon find you remember everything, and no forget important thing like when guest is arriving!'

Greer regretted coming in. She went up the short staircase into the bedroom on the right. Agnieszka chased after her. 'All the sheets from wine men are changed, and rooms nice and tidy. So your man can choose where he like it. Maybe he like it big room. Or maybe small room with balcony. The other one big but dark, I think, but if he like it no matter, bed is made up. And towels – everything is perfect. You like it I put flowers?'

'I was going to do that, but if you –'

'I do it, no trouble. What you have tonight, for dinner?'

'Oh, I'm not sure, Aggie. If he comes we'll probably take him out.'

'Yes, you go out, you no want it do cooking. You take the bad boys with you?' For obscure reasons of her own, which Greer interpreted as conveying both disapproval and affection, Agnieszka liked to refer to Rollo and Guy as the bad boys. 'I doing nice big fettucine alfred today for my family, like I make for the boys last night. And a big tiramis-you. I tell you what I put, and you do it next week.'

Greer heard this without listening. Having been suspicious of Italian food for most of her life, Agnieszka was a recent convert. This was Guy's doing. She cooked dinner for him and Rollo two or three times a week. Last year, announcing the transformation of their house into a flaczki-free zone, Guy had paid for her to attend a week-long Italian cooking and conversation course in Perugia. This had nearly precipitated a terminal rift with Rollo, as Guy well knew it might. Rollo was an offal man from way back, and flaczki – Agnieszka's hearty tripe stew – was his favourite.

It was Rollo who'd found Agnieszka in the first place, a young Polish bride adrift in the village. 'She was dazed and confused, and we took her in,' was Rollo's somewhat self-serving version.

Agnieszka, waitressing in London's Greek Street, had encountered Angelo Brogi, the most boisterous and disorderly of a local gang over on the razzle in Soho, and an unlikely but sizzling holiday romance had ensued. This probably should have been the end of it, but Agnieszka had become pregnant and her will, which despite her youth had come into being fully formed, ensured that Angelo toed the line.

Now, twenty years and a daughter and son later, the marriage soldiered on through storms and separations that came and went as regularly as wars and famines in the world at large. Angelo was employed periodically at the Castello to do odd jobs requiring muscle but not much else, and was known as Angelo who-is-no-angel-o.

Agnieszka had returned from the week in Perugia with no discernible improvement in her Italian conversation but with a new fixation on the cuisine of her adopted land. Everyone except Guy was astounded at the success of his plan. Now the pieroszkis and the krupniks, the borscht and the bigos were well on the way to becoming a distant memory. Once Agnieszka had discovered the practical advantages of pasta and risotto there was no looking back. In her life it was a small revolution, and like all revolutionaries she was a crusader, wishing to convert everyone in her path.

It's like the arrival of the pill, Greer thought, backing away from the tidal wave of Agnieszka's words and making her excuses. The birth-control pill had unleashed a tsunami of sex. Sex was always there, of course, just as Agnieszka had always known about the existence of pasta, but before the pill's arrival it had taken more of a background role, a controlled position, as if it were on a leash. Let off the leash it immediately leapt to centre stage, impinging on every-thing. Dominating everything.

Or was that merely a consequence of being young, and nothing to do with science or sociology or anything else? Because these days, these less frenetic and desperate days, sex was in the background again; it had retreated to its old historical position. It was still there, oh yes – in her mind's eye she saw Mischa standing in the shower, head thrown back – but it had lost the feverish primacy it had claimed for so long.

The gradual decline of the primacy of sex in their lives must have released tracts of spare time. Rather like an unex-pected bonus awarded for long and dedicated service, she reflected. They had given years of dedicated service to the pursuit of sex. But any time awarded more recently as a bonus seemed to have been filled easily, as time invariably tended to be. Swallowed up by other things, such as work in Mischa's case.

And in her own too. There was no question of that. She imagined a dialogue with the biographer. Without any false modesty I am on the way, she would tell him, to my surprise and probably everyone else's, I am well on the way to becoming rather a talented winemaker. She knew Guy would confirm this. He may even – no, he would very likely – add, perhaps a potentially outstanding one.

But the biographer could decide to tease this out further. He might want to play around with the elastic subject of time. In fact, and she knew this was a given because it was beyond reasonable doubt, Antony Corbino was going to be interested in more than the last decade.

You had, what was it, about fifteen years together before you fetched up here, he might remark. That was a long time to be on the move. How did you fill it? What did you do while Mischa was working? You had years to get to know yourself, right, he might joke, in his American way. But a light remark such as that one might carry a hidden agenda. Behind every throwaway line was the possibility of an ulterior motive. She knew she would be well advised to remember that.

During sex's obsessional heyday, there had been neither pause nor inclination for such new-worldly pursuits as getting to know oneself. She found it was not hard, not at all difficult, even from this distance, to conjure up the atmosphere of that hot-blooded time, to inhabit again that urgent body with its explosive desires, its ardour.

But it was unwise. She knew she was in danger of trespassing again, of breaching those inflexible mental boundaries. Of venturing towards the territory where she could not go. She retreated a little way and breathed deeply, like a woman in labour, concentrating on her surroundings: the beauty of the stone, the diving swallows on the porch, the sound of a distant bell. The cypresses that were like lissom limbs against the filmy April sky.

For a moment she imagined these bright images confronting her alternative landscape, becoming entangled in its darkness, before it overwhelmed them.

4

Greer walked quickly away from the guesthouse towards her own. As she climbed the steps to the kitchen door she again had a glancing view of the distant valley floor with its slow trickle of cars. She paused at the top as she always did and looked out over the face of the landscape, the rolling panorama that she could have drawn on paper blindfolded, whose every swelling and indent she could have reproduced with meticulous exactitude.

Antony Corbino will surely think I am spoilt, she thought. A privileged woman with an enviable life, living closeted away from the outside world. That is, if he is a charitable man. If he is not, and if he's a good detective, will he think all this beauty, all this creativity, are in some respects ill-gotten gains? He won't see into my mind. How could he? And even if he could, what difference would that make? Would it be enough to stop dead in its tracks the suspicion that I must be a monstrous woman?

Before I had time to think what I'd said, he was kissing me – so violently I nearly fell over. He backed me up against the wall, there was this incredible ravenous hunger coming from him, and from me too – oh God yes – we just kept on going, kissing, oblivious to the windows & the lights – it was dark outside, rain pelting on the windows – until suddenly he jerked his head back & it dawned on me where we were. In the GALLERY for God's sake, lit up, in full view of the street & passers-by – heaven knows who might've seen us – and he just looked at me wordlessly without any question and went over & turned off all the lights & bolted the front door. And we fell on the ground right there, on the polished floor, under his pictures.

The sloping writing had grown more and more undisciplined, veering over to the right until it was almost horizontal, careering off the faint blue lines of the exercise book, the words so crowded they were nearly joined together. A line of dots, thick and heavily indented, followed the last sentence. Several of them had speared through the paper. If dots could be expressive, thought Greer, these were.

She leant back in the chair in her study and closed her eyes. She remembered the force of the kisses, the bruises on her mouth. How, for the first time in her life, she had felt sick with desire.

After, I remembered I hadn't locked the connecting door to V.'s flat! She could've come in from the garage, she could've come down!! BLOODY HELL!!! While I was fumbling with it, he said, 'We must go somewhere, very fast. Where can we go to?'

There was some light from the street but my legs were like water & I was shaking so much I couldn't get the key in the lock. He came up behind me & put his hands over mine. 'You live in an apartment? A house?'

'Yes, in Eltham, but it's miles away and . . .' I didn't know how to tell him. 'What about your place?'

'You would hate my place. You have a boyfriend, yes? Is that it?'

'Yes. He's away tonight. But . . .' Even then, I couldn't say it. He could see, though. Some of it. Not all. Not the worst. He said, 'A hotel then. What is the best one in Melbourne? The Hotel Windsor?' I said yes, but it would be horribly expensive, more

maybe than one of his paintings. 'So, no problem, I will just paint
another one!' I tried to insist on paying half, but he wouldn't hear
of it. 'I am rich. Don't forget.'

I told him he'd have to have a shave or they wouldn't let
him past the portals.

'So, you are bossing me about now.'

'I thought that since we've just made love I might take the
liberty.'

'Is that what you thought?' He cupped my face in his hands,
very gently, & closed my eyelids. 'That was not love. When we
make love you will not just think, you will know.' I felt a jolt in
the pit of my stomach.

We went in my car to his place to get something to look like
luggage, & money — he said he had some that Verity had advanced
stashed behind the loo(!). He obviously hasn't got a bank account
yet. We got drenched racing to the car. I let him drive, I felt faint
all the way. I think I was in shock.

He drove like a maniac, but well. The rain was bucketing
down in torrents, flooding the windscreen.

She saw the two of them again, clear in every detail, pressed
hard against each other on the front bench seat of her
Holden station wagon. Hurtling along in a metal capsule
insulated from the outside world. And oblivious to that
world too, self-consciously sharing a Gauloise, like the
leading actors in a noir film. Outside, the rain was sheeting
down, surging in glistening rivers on the road, and inside the
car suffocating clouds of cigarette smoke swirled against
the glass and almost obliterated the windscreen.

Rubbing portholes in the steam that immediately
fogged over again, clutching on to his arm and chest as if she
were drowning. The backs of his hands, knotted and dense
with coarse hairs, paint embedded in the fingernails. One
hand abandoning the gearstick recklessly and enclosing both
of hers, gripping them with a kind of desperation. The
sensation of giddiness, of being drugged on air that fairly
reeked of carnality. Both of them too tense to say a word.

We got to the grungy St Kilda corner I recognised from the picture. He was in and out in less than 5 minutes, but when he came back he'd actually scraped some stubble off his face & tucked his shirt in, but he still wore the holey old jumper & was carrying a dirty holdall thing that he obviously uses for paintbrushes, & he still looked like a scarecrow, not remotely like your average Windsor patron.

We got in somehow. I think the man took pity on us, or else he was terrified – we may possibly have looked deranged. We kissed again in the lift & missed our floor, finally got there & shot down the corridor, pelted into the room & he dived at the bed & pulled me down on top of him.

Another line of dots followed. At the end of the line was a scrawled star. Greer's eyes scrolled down to the bottom of the page. She already knew what she would find there: a corresponding star, and the single word: *Paradise*. The letters were small and emphatically printed.

He was right, Greer thought. I did know. It was a revelation.

She couldn't recall anything about the hotel room or the feel of the bedclothes under her skin. Later she was aware of starched sheets and feather pillows. And then the same pillows scattered on the floor, and tangled sheets and blankets hanging off the bed like sails shredded in a cyclone. The top of his head, clumps of black hair matted with sweat. Her heart juddering, streams of sweat mingling with the slap of skin and rasp of breath. Sounds she had never heard herself make. Tears she found herself shedding – scalding, confusing tears, for reasons she had never known before that moment.

She saw them both in the shower, his head thrown back joyously under cascading water. Soaping him.

He grabbed the soap from me. 'Am I clean enough for your high standards yet?' Then he launched into, 'If I was a rich man' from 'Fiddler on the Roof'. He broke off & said, 'I forgot. You hate my singing.'

'I didn't say that. I said I loved your painting. I didn't say anything about your singing.'

'Why not? And why are you not wearing red toenails? Don't you know that is not allowed?'

We had a wild pillow fight that ended up on the bed. At two in the morning we ordered room service, three courses & champagne. As we sat in the hotel dressing gowns eating oysters, he said, 'Since we have now made love, before you start to boss me about you had better tell me your full name.'

Greer Gordon, she said. G.G. Like a horse. Like the '50s actress Greer Garson. Like the Governor-General. Not at all like the Governor-General or old Greer Garson, he'd retorted, or especially a horse. Like Gigi. And Gigi, eventually, she had become. Instead of Greer Gordon she had become known in the limited circles of the art world as Gigi Svoboda. None of her old friends from the Australian period would know her by that assumed name, that frivolous name. They might know she had done a bunk, but they wouldn't know what had happened to her. Unless the biographer detective had tracked them down and filled them in.

Svoboda is a common name in Czechoslovakia, like Smith. It means freedom. Mischa is his nickname. He told me he had to get out of Prague fast after the Russians invaded in '68. He escaped by skiing across the border into Austria. I just tried to blot things out by bombarding him with questions. I could still eat, but inside I was all clenched up.

Suddenly he gripped my shoulders & said, 'Where is your boyfriend? I have to kill him.'

The feeling I'd been fending off surged & I thought I was going to vomit. I burst out, 'Actually, it's worse than that. I'm married.' Then I realised I really was going to throw up & rushed to the bathroom. I told him that C. was coming back from NZ tomorrow & after that we were going on holiday. Those two dreaded items were all I could manage.

'You don't wear a wedding ring so you can't be married.
It's a mistake. A mirage.'
'I wish I wasn't. It is a mistake. I wish it was a mirage.'

The long, shuddering sigh. The conviction that at the age of
twenty-nine she might have ruined her life.

'Why are you not wearing a ring?'
'I think because I've never felt really married.'
'You see? Your feelings know the truth. You're not really
married. How long are you going away?'
'Three weeks.'
'Three whole weeks? Not three parts of weeks? Where?'
'The Isle of Pines. It's part of New Caledonia. Off the north
coast of Australia.'
'I know where it is. Thousands of miles from me. For 3 weeks.
With your husband.'
'Yes.' I started crying.
'You can't go. I won't allow it.'
'I have to. It's all booked. I have to go.'
We went on & on until we crashed from total exhaustion.
Woke up at 8 when breakfast came in. He said he'd been up for
ages, he'd used up all the hotel writing paper sketching me, there
were sheets all over the floor. Then we had this dreadful row, he
wanted us both to arrive at the gallery together, but he doesn't
know what that would mean . . . I tried to tell him that I
couldn't face it with Verity, but of course he didn't understand
& I couldn't explain . . . He kept saying 'Why does it matter?
Why do you care what she thinks? You're ashamed of me, are
you, is that it?'
It was dreadful. Terrible. Finally we went down in a deathly
silence & he paid the bill & turned his back on me in the street &
strode away from me.

Then, as now, his emotions had a direct conduit to his
actions; the two were inseparable. He is so direct, so single-
minded, whereas my mind is more of a filter, Greer thought.

Or should I say devious? She closed the exercise book. There was a limit to how much of this she could read at one sitting. She forced herself to take a break, to try to think about it in a more objective way.

Here were her first encounters with Mischa. She had never shown him the diary. It occupied a place that was too revealing, too private, even for him. And not only for Mischa. Although she had carried it with her for a quarter of a century and always knew where it was, after making the final entry she had never wanted to look at it again.

Until now. This is how it all began, the diary was saying, this is how it began for me. For us. But there is a filtering system at work here, she thought. This is truly how it was, on one level, on its own terms. On that level it is surprisingly detailed. On its own terms it is a thorough, almost exhaustive account. The writer clearly couldn't budge from her position until she'd got it all down.

Whereas if Mischa had written about the same sequence he would have got it down and over with in a few bald sentences. Where he acts without thinking, I mull over, premeditate. At least, I do now. I tend to think too much about consequences. The biographer might prefer to call it making up for lost time.

Because consequences seem scarcely to have crossed the mind of this young writer. If I had no connection to her, if I stumbled on her diary with no preconceptions, how would I feel? I would probably picture its writer as a randy, reckless young woman. It's quite vividly written, in its juvenile way. Wouldn't the biographer just love to get his fingers on it?

This was a thought to make the flesh creep.

I crashed into work feeling totally wrecked. Told V. I'd stayed at a friend's & the alarm hadn't gone off. I had to plaster make-up on in the loo, my face was rubbed raw from his bristles. V. noticed I was wearing yesterday's things (rather crumpled). She said, 'Forgot to take a change of clothes, did you?' Annoyed rather than knowing, I thought.

C. rang from NZ, wanted to know where I was last night.
Said I'd gone to Lambie's. Had to ring & word her up. Cut her
off before she could lecture me . . . Restless & anxious all
morning. Bought more cigs, smoked the lot in spite of V.'s
disapproval. Kept going hot & cold – an icy feeling of dread, then
a rush of soaking sweat. She must've thought I was having
premature hot flushes. I wish that's what it was.

He didn't come in. V. furious because there was a buyer he
was supposed to meet. Of course he doesn't have a phone. Finally
she wrote down his address & told me to go & drag him out of
bed. I shot off, was in the car & outside his door before I realised
we were rumbled – I hadn't even stopped to take the address from
her hand . . .

She'd found the front door of the huge two-storey terrace
unlocked. Inside was a dingy central passage of scabby, mud-
coloured lino with doors off it on both sides and what
looked like a kitchenette at the end. There was no way of
knowing which was his, so she'd knocked on all the doors.
Only the last one was opened, by a bare-legged emaciated
girl wearing a man's nylon shirt. She was friendly, told Greer
the artist lived in the front room upstairs.

He'd yelled out when she knocked: 'Go away!' When
she turned the handle disobediently and found it open she
couldn't see him at first. The room was the width of the
house with tall, once-elegant Victorian windows and double
doors opening on to a balcony, but the windows were caked
with grime and a whirling fug of tobacco smoke smothered
everything. She was aware of a strong smell of turps, of a
room chaotically crowded with canvases propped three and
four deep against the walls, a trestle table littered with junk.
Of an unmade mattress on the floor with a grimy under-
sheet and grey army surplus blankets screwed up in a heap.

He was standing in the far corner, quite still, his back to
her. She saw his hair tangled with splodges of paint. As she
took a few steps into the room, treading gingerly across bare
gritty floorboards and weaving a path through squashed

paint tubes, jam jars full of brushes, clothes, newspapers, scummy paper plates, she saw that he was at work on a drawing. It looked half-finished, but she could make out a tousled female figure, nude and spread-eagled across a bed.

'Is that by any chance me?' she'd said. It came out more belligerently than she intended.

His hand stopped on the paper. 'Of course it is. Can't you *see*, now? Do you need glasses? Or do I need to get your permission?'

'It would be nice to be asked.'

'That's too bad then, because I never ask.' He hadn't turned round.

'Mischa,' she said, 'I've come to get you.'

'But you are leaving me.'

'Only for three weeks.'

'And then you are coming back?'

'Of course.'

'Back to me?'

He hadn't moved. She felt a sensation of vertigo, as if she were teetering on the rickety verandah rail outside his window.

'Yes.'

'If I come now, Gigi,' he said, 'there is a condition I want to make. Do you agree to it?'

'Well, I don't know what it is yet.'

'We will go in together.' It was a statement, not a question. He still hadn't moved or looked at her.

She took a deep, steadying breath in an effort to find her balance. 'All right. I agree. We will go in together.'

He clasped my hand tightly as we came into the gallery. Verity looked up. She registered, I saw her eyes. Then she whisked him straight back out of the door to the lunch meeting. When she went past my desk she shot me a look.

I had to leave at 4 to pick up C. from the airport. I had to lock up first because they still hadn't come back. I drove to the airport in a manic state, radio at full blast, smoking, very nearly smashed into a turning tram in St Kilda Rd. C. didn't notice a thing, but told me off for smoking.

I'm writing this sitting on the sand on the Isle of Pines. C. has gone out in a boat fishing for a few hours, thank the Lord. It's day 3 of the 'holiday', the first chance I've had to be alone. 18 more to go, an eternity. My life is in the worst sodding mess it's ever been or ever could be in, & I'm sitting in this ravishing tropical paradise with waving palm trees & pristine white sand that's like the softest, silkiest clay.

It's all lost on me. I might as well be locked up in a dungeon, living on bread & water.

The page was creased and smudged. A few grains of sand were stuck in the spine. Small greasy blotches punctuated the writing. Suntan oil.

What would an objective person make of this? To Greer, looking down the long lens of retrospection, the remarkable thing was the selective nature of the writing. What was not on the page was as important as what was included, and in some ways more telling. And quite apart from the back story, what was left out was the other side of her life. The flip side of her interior life, one might call it. The young diarist's omissions were, on any objective reckoning, breathtaking.

An objective reader was, of course, a detached person in full possession of the facts. Until this time only one person came close to fitting this description: the writer herself. But she was personally involved. And now there was a detective abroad, nosing and prying. Who might be hell-bent on putting back in what had been left out.

Unlike the hot-headed young diarist, the biographer had a balanced narrative to construct. He was unlikely to be wilfully or self-servingly selective. His bias should be neutral and dispassionate, which made it diametrically opposed to hers. Was there any reason why Antony Corbino should view Mischa and herself benignly? Any reason why he would give them, and more particularly her, the benefit of the doubt?

Greer thought: I'm the only one who is thinking like this. Mischa is obviously and inexplicably not. He seems oblivious. He seems almost wilfully blind. And yet there must be, and there are, because I know about them, assumptions that were made and people he hurt. Certain things in his past that he can't help but regret. Or rather, she amended, things that he might well feel guilty about, if he ever stopped to think about them. Once something was done it was past, gone, out of his head. If it could not be changed he wasted no time regretting it. She envied that.

A voice in her head added: but nothing he has done, or left undone, is of this order. That's what an objective biographer would surely think, were he to uncover it. It may be Mischa's biography, as Rollo says, but it is my problem.

At last she'd wandered into Mischa's studio and said something. 'He's going to be observing us all the time. And judging. I can't bear the thought of it.'

Mischa was playing a cassette of Charles Trenet, one of a dusty collection that had rattled round in the glove box of the car for ages, before they acquired a new car and a CD stacker. He must have salvaged it and brought it into the studio.

He was intent on mixing three shades of blue with a palette knife. 'What are you talking about?' He didn't look up.

'You know. The biographer. Antony.'

'So? Aggie sees us all the time. Roly, Guy. The dogs see us. Who cares about Mr Antony bloody Corbino? We don't know him and he doesn't know us.'

'But that's the whole point. He'll be spying on us, Mischa.'

'Rubbish. What is there to spy on? Have you been living a secret life from me all these years, Mrs Smith?'

Well, in a sense I have, she thought. Doesn't everyone?

We can't see into each other's heads. Why was it so hard, so impossible to say, of course I don't mean the present. I mean spying on the past. Not yours – ours, Mischa. And mine. Why can't you understand that?

She sat in an armchair and listened to Trenet singing 'La Mer'. She had always found it an emotional song.

'This tape's terrible, Mischa, I don't know how you can bear to listen to it. The words are so distorted.'

He grunted, 'I don't need the words. It's the atmosphere I want.'

She understood what he was saying. She watched him as, slowly and with intense concentration, he drew his brush across the canvas in a long arching line, like a violinist drawing his bow.

She tried to shut out the scratchy words and concentrate instead on the nostalgic line of the music, but it seemed to her suffused with an almost unbearable melancholy. Mischa's brush reached the end of the line and he swept it skywards, flinging out his arms in a triumphant arc. He held the pose, his eyes on her, willing her, but she would not smile.

5

The path from Mischa's studio skirted the laundry at the back of the house. The laundry door stood open, and Greer was pounced on. Several oily stains on the best white tablecloth had been removed successfully, and Agnieszka brimmed with a glee she wished to impart.

There was no view from the laundry's single small, high window. Helping to fold the newly pristine cloth, Greer missed her chance to spot a compact blue Fiat as it traversed the valley in her direction. It was a rental car driven with unusual circumspection by a young man who now and then took his eyes off the road and checked the map on the empty seat next to him. This was no ordinary map, but a coloured photocopy of a print, decorated in antic style with sketches of gross peasants climbing olive trees, toiling in a vineyard and tilting at wild boar.

The original had been made over thirty years earlier by Rollo, soon after he and Guy completed their bold purchase of the hilltop hamlet with its collection of abandoned buildings. Copies of the print were regularly faxed to first-time visitors, and later very often framed to be hung as mementoes in studies and sitting rooms around the world. Rollo and Guy liked to tell their guests they lived in such a backwater that the instructions for locating them had not altered a jot in three decades.

The driver passed an acute-angled turn to the right, on a bend in the road and concealed by two massive cypress trees, immediately realised his mistake and executed a smart U-turn. He re-positioned the map on the steering wheel with one hand and headed inwards along a bumpy road that wound through an unruly scrub of turkey oak and strawberry trees, hawthorn bushes and ilex, the glossy evergreen oak.

Ignoring two rutted laneways off to the right and a narrow intersection, he proceeded steeply upwards until, at precisely 2.3 kilometres from the turn-off, a second pair of sinuous cypresses flanked a well-used gravel track to the left. He was in among the vineyards now, the vines still bare and skeletal, marked by the proprietorial symbol he recognised: the *leccio*, acorn, fruit of the ilex tree. Another kilometre further and, just as the map depicted, a white gate and the sign: *Castello di Monte Leccio.*

The driver unlatched the gate and drove in, pausing again to shut it behind him. The track meandered across the slope of the hill through more vineyards, these ones slightly more advanced and coming into bud, and then an extensive olive grove. There were signs of activity, men with trucks and a bonfire. A short distance ahead, at the crest of the rise, he saw clearly the first of the group of buildings that comprised the hamlet.

He drove through a second gate, propped wide open, and followed the track around to a large gravelled area bordered with showy rows of purple iris. A two-storey stone house faced him, with a low wing extending out to the right. An iron roof was attached to this wall, with three cars parked in its shade. A fourth car and another truck stood in the open. He pulled up next to the truck, switched off the engine and opened the driver's door. But instead of getting out he removed a small dictaphone from the back pocket of his jeans and at once began speaking into it.

'April fourteen. First impressions. I reach the Castello at

5.15 pm. It's a two-hour drive from Pisa, quite hidden away until you get there, invisible from the road except for occasional glimpses of the watchtower from about 5 miles back. (NB Check with Mischa: the cypresses guarding the entrance gate are the ones in the *Guardians* picture in Tate Modern?) I can see the three handsome stone houses and an artistically ruined tower – which must be Mischa's studio – all well separated from each other and grouped around a wide central courtyard. A parking lot at one side and a number of outbuildings, well maintained, including a barn-like structure attached to the right-hand house, which could be the winery.'

He climbed out of the car and continued to speak while walking forwards.

'On my left is a bigger house facing the other two. This would be Rollo Sonabend's. It's square with fine, almost Georgian proportions, tall windows below, shorter ones above, all with dark green shutters, walls artistically clad in a spidery climber – Virginia creeper? – still bare but a few buds. A vine-covered terrace extends the full length of the house and a good 20 feet beyond. There's a long rustic table under the terrace, a bunch of chairs, a small lawn and a luxuriant garden at the side, with pergolas on all sides.'

He came closer.

'It's a longer house than I thought. It has a side building stepped down, joining it to the vestry maybe, and a small attached church which would be Sonabend's studio – yeah, next to a neat little war memorial. The whole set-up is pretty damn gorgeous. House opposite must be Svoboda's, with masses of blue wisteria coming out on the wall facing me, and scarlet geraniums and other plants in pots on the side steps and window boxes. The sun on the mottled stone walls and terracotta roofs, the crumbling tower against the blue sky, a sense of ancient stillness and isolation – your classic artists' retreat. I wouldn't mind living here, it's almost too perfect to be true. Where are they all?'

At that moment his eye was caught by a flurry from his

left. A small, extremely thin woman in jeans and a pink t-shirt had emerged from the big house and was galloping towards him, shouting and energetically flapping her hands. Behind her, two black pugs waddled a few steps, barked and then sat down.

He replaced the dictaphone in his pocket. Had she not, in addition to the shouting and waving, been distinctly smiling, he might have stepped back in alarm. She closed in, and he began to decipher a series of disconnected phrases. 'Are here . . . today, no next week – computer it lost – accident – perfect!'

She almost skidded to a halt in front of him, sentences rushing on unabated. 'You like it see the rooms, and you choose which one you like?'

He began lamely to introduce himself, but she interrupted. 'Yes, yes, I know, I know who, Antony the writer from America, but not from America this time, from London, come to do the job on Mr Mischa. That is good! My name is Agnieszka. You get it luggage and I take you to your house over there where you stay, and then I tell Gigi. You know Gigi?'

'No, I just got here. We didn't meet yet.' He hoisted his canvas holdall and a hard-topped suitcase from the boot and dumped them on the gravel.

'You no meet? Oh. But Mr Mischa you know.' She reached for the computer case, but he slung it over his shoulder.

'Thanks, I'll take it. No, not even Mr Mischa. Although we have talked.'

'Oh, you talk. But you like it know everything about him, very soon, because you write nice big book all about him and everybody read!'

They both laughed. She chatted on, observing him with lively curiosity as they walked the short distance to the guest house. The building alongside the car park butted up against it. She followed his gaze.

'In old day before that was dirty old shed with

machines, now new winery inside. Beautiful, very modern with all steel. Very clean. Tidy, you know, and very nice?' She made emphatic horizontal gestures with her outstretched hands. 'No messy with bits and books in piles, like in all these people houses. Big, *very* big barrels, you don't believe me, filled up with wine that Gigi make with Mr Guy, but waiting, not ready for drink yet. If you like it see, you go through office, underneath your house. Gigi can show it.'

He saw that the ground floor of the house was an office, complete with shelving, files, computer table and a classical beauty with dark waving hair, all clearly visible through the wide-open French doors. The young woman was fetching her coat and bag, saw them and emerged. Agnieszka sketched an openly reluctant and pointedly one-sided introduction.

'Mr Antony just arrive from London.' The dark-haired girl flashed an interested smile. 'I quickly show him house, then he must go straightaway to Mr Mischa.'

The girl put out her hand. 'Hello, I'm Giulia.'

'Hi, Giulia. You work in the winery here?'

Agnieszka interrupted, 'She do Gigi job while Gigi tell you everything you want to know about Mr Mischa.'

The girl added, 'Everything you always wanted to know but were afraid to ask.'

'Hey, how come your English is so good?'

'Oh, I studied in the UK, at Bristol.'

Agnieszka, transparently irritated, had already bounded up the steps to the first floor. She called down in a loud, reproving voice, 'Say goodbye, Giulia, Mr Antony must wash and unpack clothes and meet his people before it dark, he no like it waste time now.'

He winked, and was treated to a merry look. 'I think she wants to protect you. Or keep you for herself.'

'Well, how very flattering. If you're around this week, maybe I could take a look at the winery?'

She was locking the office doors with two keys from a big bunch. 'Sure, I'm here every day because of you. Come in, you know where to find me. Ciao.'

The heavy door to the apartment upstairs had a cumbersome latch but appeared to be unlocked. Agnieszka threw it open and ushered him in. She tugged the door shut behind them and shook her head.

'That Giulia, she very naughty girl, she have two good boys in love with her.' She spoke in a low, confidential tone, although they were demonstrably out of anyone's hearing. 'Each boy think they get married, but she holding them on string. She not marry either of them, I think so, and Gigi think too.'

'What does Mr Mischa think?'

'He?' She gave a dismissive trill of amusement. 'He no think anything! He very famous man. He no very interest in people, interest only in painting.'

'And in Gigi?'

She nodded impatiently. 'He need her very much and he love her, oh yes of course, but he no understand proper talking, or communicate. He no nice young modern man like you.'

Before he could ask what she meant by nice modern man, she was off on another tack, beckoning him through the sitting room.

'You have all these bags, for the clothes?'

'Just one for the clothes. The hard one's got all my research material.'

She gave him a satisfied nod. 'You are very good travelling, only one bag for the clothes, but you stay long time. Easy for the man. He take one pair shoes, do for everything. The woman need different shoes for each thing – jacket, evening, skirt, trouser. Swimming. Jeans. It not so easy travelling for the woman, you don't believe me.'

'Oh, I believe you all right. All those shoes. What a nightmare.'

They laughed again. 'You are lucky boy, wine men all gone and you have nice big house for yourself. This is good big sitting room, fireplace here with wood, very comfortable for listen to music, or read magazine. Bedrooms up there.'

She collected a jug of tulips the colour of fresh cream from the mantelpiece of the living room and moved a yellow pottery vase of irises into the centre. 'You start writing your book in one room and sleeping in the other, and if you have friend come there is still one more left over. I show you.' She darted ahead of him up three stairs.

Antony listened to a running commentary on the pluses and minuses of the three bedrooms. Realising that a prompt but considered response was expected, he selected the one whose two wide-open windows overlooked the valley.

'I'll take the middle-sized room with a view,' he said.

Agnieszka deposited the shiny green jug of tulips on a chest of drawers. She looked pleased.

'This one I like, good big bed, very nice, very good choice. Very warm today, you like it turn off heating?' He was about to answer, but there was no pause. 'I think better wait, it still cold in night and maybe rain again tomorrow. Now, you want it little time for unpack and shower before you like it meet Gigi?' She patted his luggage. 'You put on nice clean shirt after journey, no problem, and I wash tomorrow. Only five minutes for unpack – not many shoes.'

When he came down twenty minutes later he saw a group of men in shirtsleeves emerging from the winery, stretching and moving slowly in the slanting, late afternoon light. Agnieszka was scurrying across the courtyard towards him, carrying a stack of folded white towels.

'You have shave. Look better!' She eyed his sweatshirt in khaki cotton and olive green chinos, and gave him an approving pat on the arm. 'Very nice trouser – no creased from packing.'

'Ah, well, you see, I did a secret touch-up.'

'You do iron yourself?'

He grinned. 'Oh, yeah. I'm a nice modern man, remember? I do the iron real good.'

*

Tony lay on his bed, arms folded behind his head. He was stripped to the waist, the dictaphone balanced on his pectorals.

'Eleven pm. Day One: the names made flesh. Greer slash Gigi first. I am escorted into her presence by Agnieszka, one deeply bizarre and hyper Polish housekeeper. Early to mid forties, does for all of them, which is promising. Over-familiar and decidedly chatty – also promising. Complained about the number of shoes women have to pack – Polish sense of humour? Dished some dirt on Giulia, the Botticelli siren who works in the office on the ground floor of my house, who gave me the eye. Agnieszka seemed to approve of me too. Says Giulia is two-timing a pair of beaux. File them both under: to be cultivated.

'Greer slash Gigi. Not at all what I expected. First thought was: she reminds me a bit of Virginia Woolf. A dishevelled version thereof. That elongated, horsey face and narrow, high-bridged nose. Not unattractive for her age, horsey as in thoroughbred, not cart. Good bones. Blue-grey eyes. Would've been a looker. But unexpectedly refined really. Hard to recon-cile with things. But that's mostly the case when you come face to face with people for the first time in their middle age. They generally don't give their past away. It's not written on the face, contrary to received wisdom.

'And she doesn't give much away at all. Greeted me politely but not warmly. Wasn't keen to be alone with me. She watched me a lot during dinner, when she thought I wasn't looking. Seemed to be studying my face. That follows – she used to do portraits. Wary, is how she was. Guarded. When she did speak to me she avoided making eye contact. Well, is that surprising or not?

'Mischa's her polar opposite. Like he's always described, a big, grizzly bear of a guy, messy, no dress sense, pronounced Czech accent, excitable, up-front emotional. He presents as totally straightforward and spontaneous, unlike her. I'd say she's heavily into self-censorship, won't let anything out without giving it a mental makeover. Whereas he just lets rip, couldn't care less what he says. I get the impression political correctness doesn't get much of a look-in with him, or with Rollo Sonabend either, for that matter.

'Mischa's never still, always fiddling with objects. Within minutes he'd picked the wine cork to bits then set about building little heaps of cork and breadcrumbs. At dinner he was making patterns with the salt, chewing matches, drawing. The moment we sat down they brought out butcher's paper, covered the tablecloth with it for him to doodle. And a box of crayons. They obviously do that for him every time, like he's a kid with hyperactivity syndrome. Or their tame Picasso. They're very proud of him and Rollo, that's obvious.

'Mischa proceeded to draw this incredible intricate maze. Well, it started as a maze; ended up more like a jigsaw puzzle. I took it home. Yet I don't think all this activity is a nervous habit or attention deficit or anything, it's just surplus energy boiling up and spilling over. For sixty-five, that's something. He looks his age, but kind of doesn't act it.'

Greer turned over in bed. Mischa had an arm flung out, wedged under her neck. He was snoring. She tried to re-position herself more comfortably, then gave up and slid down in the bed. His arm followed her, resting heavily against the top of her head, hot and sweaty. He had fallen asleep imme-diately, as he usually did. She had lain awake for some time, eyes open in the darkness.

Before she met Antony she had a clear mental picture of him. It had arrived of its own volition just the other morning, when she heard Mischa loudly singing in the shower. He was belting out his own rock 'n' roll adaptation of Blake's 'Jerusalem', an arrangement he neither varied nor tired of and which never failed to remind her of their first encounter. When he reached the last couplet, 'And was Jerusalem builded here, Among those dark, satanic mills?' Greer had seen Antony Corbino. Two words clinched the vision. Antony's face would be dark and satanic, she was certain of it.

Instead, as she stood on the steps and watched him materialise in Agnieszka's excitable wake, she saw that he was light-haired and boyish, and far too urbane to betray anything much. He had a good-looking face in a conventional, regular-featured way. Open and round, with unblinking blue eyes. Voyeuristic blue eyes?

Strictly speaking he should have a cleft chin, she thought, but even without one he reminds me of those illustrations of fair-haired, clean-cut young men from the *Boys' Own* annuals of my father's childhood. Athletic, smiling chaps who were clones of each other, wearing sleeveless Fair Isle sweaters and holding tennis racquets, well-mannered and eager to please. His manner's faintly old-fashioned too, although he may have adopted that out of a misplaced consideration for our seniority. He's younger than I imagined.

They shook hands. I am very likely shaking the hand of my enemy, Greer thought. His handshake was firm and cool. He was smiling, and she noticed unusually white, even teeth in a smooth, tanned face.

'I hope you were vaguely expecting me,' he said. 'I heard about the computer glitch.' As he said this he inclined his head in Agnieszka's direction. He had a pleasant voice, well modulated. It reminded her of Gene Kelly's. And his clothes lay on his body with the same casual elegance. Last week she and Mischa had watched *Singin' in the Rain* again at one of Rollo and Guy's regular video nights.

'Your email flew off into the ether . . .'

He gave her a wide smile. 'As they do. Hey, what a place you have here. I'd heard about it, of course, but the real thing —' He shook his head.

'Did you have any trouble finding us?' she asked.

'Absolutely none at all. I had that cute little cartoon by Rollo Sonabend. I'm going to have it framed.'

Rollo would enjoy that description of his map. She looked at her watch, then across the courtyard. Sure enough, there he was emerging on cue from the chapel, pugs in tow. At home his habits never varied. Six pm on the dot was knock-off time, the signal for Campari or a gin and tonic (sherry in winter) or champagne if there was any going. With an airy, 'Look, there he is now, in the flesh,' she signalled to him and beckoned.

Rollo's solid flesh could be a bulwark, for the moment, between her and Antony. Mischa could wait. His working hours followed no pattern and were completely unpredictable. If they had nothing arranged, and sometimes even if they did, he frequently worked into and through the night.

'That's *the* Mr Sonabend? Wow.'

She led Antony through the sitting room and down the steep steps to the south terrace. They talked landmarks, while Rollo and the pugs ambled over. Antony had done his homework. He knew the layout already: Mischa's studio in the tower, Rollo's in the chapel, even the old walled cemetery and the path that wound through olive trees and horses on agistment to the swimming pool on the side of the hill.

They could hear Rollo's grumbles before he showed up, mopping his brow. 'It's never like this in April. It's all this global warming and dimming. You'd think they'd cancel each other out, wouldn't you?' He winked at her.

She knew he was well aware that she needed him there and why, and she observed him closely as he was introduced. It was Rollo's impression of Antony that she most wanted to hear. Rollo had been mastering the art, he said, of character assessment (you mean assassination, Guy would say) for close on eight decades, and no one could touch him for accuracy. Greer was inclined to agree, with him and with Guy.

Antony came forward, hand outstretched. 'It's a great honour to meet with you, sir. I'm an admirer of your work from way back.'

Rollo turned to Greer. 'Did you hear that, darling? He's one of my admirers, not that way back is very far back, in his case. But he's very good-looking, which is an excellent thing in a biographer, and he's got off to a good start by sweet-talking me. He knows I can be a big wheel in this bio. An essential primeval source.'

He plumped himself down with a satisfied grunt. Greer knew without looking that his appraising eyes were still actively focused on the visitor. He had a tendency to stare on first meeting, which some people found disconcerting.

'So, this is the unscrupulous young pup who will disclose to the world where the bodies are buried.'

'Absolutely, sir, and I'm hoping that you're the trusty mole who's going to divulge all the locations,' Antony was saying as Greer went inside for drinks.

She reached for things slowly as if on autopilot, reluctant to return: gin and tonic, mineral water, a plate of crostini and a bowl of bright green Sicilian olives. When eventually she came back, put down the tray and retrieved ice and cold glasses from the second fridge on the terrace, Rollo wasn't sir any more, one of the dogs was lying in his lap, the other in Antony's, and Rollo was recounting stories about his life as an art student after World War II.

'I've been regaling him with my Slade period, darling. Like your Australian period, only more sordid and sleazy. I'm hoping he'll do me next, you see, after Signor Svoboda. In fact, it's a condition of my indiscretion. If I'm to be the Deep Throat in this bio, I must be bought off.'

Antony was grinning. 'Deal.' They shook hands on it.

'But how soon can you get this little number out of the way? You've been at it for years, haven't you?' Rollo paused for a beat. 'The book, I mean,' he added roguishly.

'Oh, you mean the *book*. Well, I've done pretty much all the research, the travelling around and hard slog. The solid background work. Now is the fun part, when I get to colour things in, you know, fill in the foreground. All the up-close and personal bits.'

'It's like adding reclining nudes to a landscape, isn't it? Well, you'd better not take for ever. I might not be around. There can't be that much to say about Mischa, surely? He's far too lacking in notoriety. How much longer are we talking?'

'That depends a bit on what comes up. I haven't interviewed any of you Castello people yet.'

'You're talking to us now, already.'

'In private, I mean. People are way more indiscreet in private.'

He's smiling at me again, Greer thought. The face is bland, but those guileless blue eyes are sparkling.

'Oh, *way* more, you're right on the knocker there. I'll give you a completely different story when Gigi's out of earshot.'

'I haven't even got to meet with my subject yet. Your maid was appalled at my tardiness.'

'Oh, he doesn't need to meet with his subject, does he? It would be quite superfluous. We can tell you everything about Mischa. Besides, he's spectacularly inarticulate about his work, isn't he?'

'He is, rather,' Greer said. Rollo's trying to include me, she thought. I ought to say something. She added, 'He's an instinctive painter, not an analytical one.'

'Pretty amazing instincts, huh?'

She nodded. He was still smiling. His teeth were really quite small, but remarkably white and regular. The top and bottom rows were equally visible, like the picture of a gleaming porcelain smile in a toothpaste advertisement.

Rollo said, 'You mustn't give too much credence to what people say in interviews. There would be a gruesome amount of best behaviour going on, I should have thought. Lashings of sanctimonious spin.'

'That can certainly be true, but you make allowances for embellishment, and everything gets massively cross-checked again anyway. On the other hand, I have to say it's more than balanced by the amount of bad behaviour you get thrown at you.'

'Really? You don't say.' Rollo's ears were pricked.

'People out to settle old scores, and so on. The most lavish informants are not exactly devotees of their subject. Mostly failed painters in this case, blaming Mischa for their own less than stellar careers and lack of talent.'

Antony looked at Greer. 'But don't worry on that score,

the grudge groupies are wildly transparent. They're child's play to see through. Most of them haven't even set eyes on Mischa in years.'

'Well, who has, really, apart from us? And even we don't see that much of him, do we?' Rollo laid his hand over Greer's. 'This is probably just another failed painter talking, but our young friend here will have to confront the bitter truth in his bio eventually, won't he? Your soul mate's got a serious dose of the workaholics. Full on, he's not just a recovering one like me. He's never been a social flutterby or a nightclubable chap.'

She made an effort to play along. 'He doesn't feel the need for what most people think of as essential – a busy social life, the kind where you keep up with a wide circle of friends. He's happy with a select few. And with them he can be quite,' she looked at Rollo, 'he can be quite extrovert.'

'Ain't dat de truth.' Rollo chuckled.

'That's why it's so great to get here at last and meet with you guys, the inner circle who really do know him. I've been itching to put faces to the names I've had in front of me for so long.'

'But surely you've already seen photos of us guys? And interviews on the telly? There must be a few home movies gathering dust under people's beds too these days, although we've never gone in for them here. Far too incriminating.'

'There are, but it's not the same. Even when you've seen photos and TV clips. People are usually nothing like you imagined. In the flesh.'

He's looking at me again, Greer thought. He's hardly touched his drink. She refilled Rollo's glass, added the two ice blocks he liked, and said, immediately regretting it, 'Are they better or worse?'

'They're neither. Just different. The same way you get a mental picture of someone from a voice on the telephone, and when you go face to face with them you're gobsmacked.'

'Isn't that spot on? And isn't it extraordinarily odd? They're usually the exact opposite of your mental picture.

Why do you suppose this is?' Rollo leant forward. He could chew over this kind of discussion for hours. When she tuned back in they were roaring with laughter over something, and looking at her expectantly.

'She's in a dream,' Rollo said. 'You'll have to get used to that. Don't take it personally. She's apt to go off at any time, whether you're Nelson Mandela or Cary Grant. Or, I suppose, Brad Pitt.'

'Especially Mr Pitt,' she said.

'I was just telling him, darling, that although we'd never spoken on the phone I had a definite conviction he'd be a receding brunette with horn-rims, like your standard prune-lipped critic. Not a nice blond preppy. How did you visualise him?'

'Oh,' she looked down, 'I don't think I had any mental picture.' She felt Antony's eyes on her again. He knows I'm lying. He may be fair-haired but my conviction was right: he is dark, deep down. He has a dark gaze.

'Mrs Smith! Where are you hiding?' Mischa's shout, although she had heard it a thousand times, made her jump.

She called, 'We're out here.' She turned to Antony and said, looking over his head, 'He always does that. Even though he could have seen us on his way here from the studio, if he looked up, and there's a limited number of places I might be . . .' Why was she explaining this, she wondered. She went to the bar fridge for his beer.

'Antony's here, and Roly,' she added loudly and unnec-essarily, feeling foolish, as Mischa lumbered in on them.

'Have you got a beer for me? Ah, what a good woman.' He gave her a smacking kiss then seized the bottle and pumped Antony's proffered hand. '*Salve*, Tony! This is my authorised biographer, base rabble, and nobody told me he was here!'

Greer thought, he's still sounding awkward.

Another drink later and the four of them had given up on Guy and his wine buyers and gone down to eat in the village. Just a jumped-down tratt, Rollo told Antony, nothing fancy for you. But the biographer couldn't fail to see that the group were regulars there, knew all the other diners, were hailed by Maria Paola the moment they set foot in the door, had their chairs ceremoniously pulled out and, what was more, Rollo's own special chair, upholstered in worn velvet, carried ceremoniously in.

'I am very partial to a well-padded seat,' Rollo said, looking at Antony. 'Especially since me piles.'

'Shut the hell up about seats and piles, Roly. We will have straight-talking because the straight majority rules, that's right, isn't it, Tony? Maria Paola, meet Tony, my authorised biographer from LA. If you treat him well he will give you a rave write-up and you will become rich and famous –'

'And our nice quiet place will be rooned.' Rollo laid a hand on Antony's shoulder. 'She doesn't understand a word of English, you know. Especially Mischa's. We can assassinate critics and shred reputations in here to our hearts' content. It's so very therapeutic and restful.' He looked around approvingly. 'You see? Not a horrible tourist in sight.'

6

21st July
Isle of Ps
*What's really ironic is that people come here for a rest cure, it's
so unbelievably quiet & peaceful. I must be the only guest who's
in a permanent massive turmoil. It's only a week since we came
and it seems like a year. We've settled into a routine – getting
up late, having breakfast on the porch, collecting a packed
lunch and biking off somewhere in our togs. Picnicking at some
idyllic spot with no one else around, going for a swim, then
back for a siesta & read. A sail or another swim, then dinner.
The food (Frog) is divine. You couldn't find a more gorgeous
place for a holiday.*

*Charlie's so happy & I'm trying to act as if I am too, when
inside I'm cold & apprehensive and full of dread. He keeps
urging me to do some drawing, but I've got no motivation at
all. He even offered to sit for me, to mark 'this auspicious
occasion'. I just felt ill. He keeps making advances at night
and I keep making excuses, which he's accepted, so far. He's
always so understanding. I just can't face it.*

What am I going to do?

'What are you up to, Mrs Smith?'
Greer's hand flew to her heart. 'Don't come in like

that, Mischa, you gave me a terrible fright.' His eyes were accusing and blurry from sleep. He was naked.

'Why are you in here? I woke up and you weren't there. I was worried. Come back to bed.'

He advanced. She pushed him away, gently. 'I couldn't sleep, that's all. I came to get a book.'

'Why couldn't you sleep? *I* was asleep.'

He always relates everything back to himself, she thought without rancour. 'I know you were, you were snoring like a steam train. Go back. I won't be long.'

He looked hurt. He always claimed he couldn't sleep without her in the bed. 'You'll catch cold. Bring the book back to bed and I'll warm you up.'

'I'm looking for it. Go away, you'll catch cold too. I'll come back in a minute.'

He padded off, apparently satisfied. She waited, then went through the kitchen door and out on to the side steps. She looked across to her left at the smaller of the two neighbouring houses. Antony's house. Tony's. There were no lights burning. Under the clear moonlight it was the same as it had always been, much as it had looked for centuries, yet she found she could not think of it in the same way as friendly territory. Because of the person within, it had ceased to be neutral. It had taken sides.

Was Tony in bed, fast asleep? Or was he lying there in his upstairs room, blue eyes wide, shutters open to let in the moon, idly regarding the beam of its light on the wall as he mulled things over? He would think, wouldn't he, that the evening had gone well?

It had been a convivial table, jolly, the three-cornered conversation of the men ranging over art, inevitably on to conspiracy theories (Rollo's speciality) and thence progressing naturally to European and American politics. Mischa found politics baffling but he enjoyed discussions about their Machiavellian complexities. His naïve amazement at what he heard tended, as on this occasion, to rouse his informers to competitive heights of hyperbole. He had begun to draw a maze on the paper cloth, using the flattened edge of a black crayon.

Greer hadn't contributed much. The reason for Antony's being there at all didn't come up until late in the piece. Until they started on the Bilbao art gallery. He had written about it.

'Talking of galleries,' he went on casually, 'what do you think of the one in Melbourne?' None of the others had seen it. 'Huge mosaic stone walls: it's like great sheets of crazy paving have been levered off a sidewalk and hoisted a hundred feet in the air. Lots of angled glass that doesn't seem to be held up by anything. Natural light as far as possible, a very Southern Hemisphere openness.'

He gave Mischa and Greer a surprised look. 'You haven't gone back at all? You should definitely do a pilgrimage. It's a changed city, I guess, from a quarter of a century back. Cosmopolitan, lots of buzzy little laneways full of bars and cafés. Very multicultural.'

'It was multicultural then,' Mischa said. He was drumming his fingers on the table. His nails were encrusted with paint in a variety of colours.

'Wouldn't you like to see the place again?' This question was definitely directed at Greer, she wasn't imagining it. She let Mischa reply. She knew what he would say.

'Never go back.' Mischa started to draw a path of arrows through the maze. 'It's not a good idea, under any circumstances. You should live in the present and look forwards, not sideways or back. You can write that down if you like, Tony.'

Rollo perked up. 'There you are. Now you see what a dire subject you've got for a bio. Relentlessly simplistic. What a depressing task lies ahead. However will you cope?'

'Oh, I guess I'll muddle through, by dint of relentless interrogation. It's still going, you know, Mischa, the little Corbett Gallery where you started off. You wouldn't recognise it now though – they expanded into another property at the back. But they showed me how the old place was, the room where you had your first exhibition. They even had photos in an album, of your original pictures on the wall. In colour, so some had faded a bit, of course, but others were pristine. It was pretty exciting to see.'

Greer had taken those photos. She heard herself ask, 'Who runs it now?'

'Good question. The old lady Verity Corbett handed it over to her nephew, Simon Corbett, a couple of years back. They all thought she'd die in the saddle and never relinquish it. Simon runs it now, in theory, with his son, Alex, but she still comes in most days and drives them all nuts.'

Greer felt her heart flutter. She's still alive. I never even knew she had a nephew. But I think I knew Verity would be still alive.

'The amazing thing is, I met Alex, that's her great-nephew, when we were both students in London, at the Courtauld. We were friends before I even knew he had an ancient great-aunty with a seminal connection to Mischa Svoboda.'

He turned at Greer, who was sitting next to him. 'It's what gave me the idea for the book, in fact. You hear about these uncanny strokes of fate sometimes, when biographers get together to chew the fat. Everybody seems to have synchronicity stories like that.'

Rollo said, 'I suppose you desperately need a spy, an initial whistle-blower to spill the beans.'

'Right. You need someone to give you that first crucial breakthrough. It was Alex who handed me the intro to Verity Corbett.' Tony looked at Mischa and Greer. Neither responded. He turned back to the more rewarding Rollo. 'Did he ever tell you about Verity?'

'I doubt it, he never tells anyone about anything. Who was she? Not an old flame, shurely?' His eyes twinkled at Greer.

Mischa interjected, 'That's because Roly talks all the time and no one can get a word in. She was a character. I liked her.'

'She discovered you, didn't she? It's a good story. Quite romantic, you know,' Tony glanced at Rollo, then at Greer, 'in the aesthetic sense of the word. If there is one. Can I tell him?'

Mischa was drawing two little figures in the maze, a male and a female.

'You may as well, Tony,' Rollo said, 'then we can skip that bit in the bio.'

'Mischa was painting Verity's bedroom –'

'Did you know about this, darling?' Rollo gave Greer a quizzical look.

'Ah, but wait for it, Rollo. Mischa was painting houses for a living, OK, and doing his own work at night. He'd only been in Melbourne like a couple of years. Well, besides her pied-à-terre above the gallery, Verity had a run-down old family home out in the suburbs. One day she blew in unexpectedly and found him drawing the cleaning lady in the bedroom instead of painting the walls. The cleaning lady was vacuuming the room – she was of mature years and fully attired, I hasten to say – and Verity, being a gallery owner, could immediately see that the picture –'

'That's enough of that,' Mischa interrupted. Greer saw that the maze had turned into pieces of a jigsaw puzzle now. They had covered his side of the butcher's paper and were creeping towards hers. 'Let him read about it in the book. I don't enjoy being talked about in the past tense when I am right here sitting at the table. I feel like I am at my own wake.'

Maria Paola's daughter arrived just then with strawberries and plates of homemade gelato, profuse with graceful apologies for covering over the artwork. Greer tried to eat the rich scoops of hazelnut and vanilla. Finally Mischa grabbed her plate and devoured the melting leftovers.

She stood on the stone steps in her long-sleeved nightgown. Although the night was unusually still, she was visited by a sense of abundant life surrounding her, going about its secret work in the dark. Plants growing, nocturnal birds, animals and insects on the prowl. The playing-out of countless other stories, tiny dramas of life and death. As crucial to each one as ours are to us, she thought.

Far above, galaxies swarmed like living beings. The almost full moon had the cold intensity of a floodlight, washing the hamlet in a glow that seemed to her unearthly. There had been a sharp shower as they left Maria Paola's, forcing Mischa to sprint around the corner for the car. Now the clouds had dispersed but the ground still glittered. The buildings looked different. They had a crystalline sheen they never possessed in daylight.

She thought, I know these buildings are made of solid stone, yet tonight they're diaphanous, as if Mischa has given each one a slick of varnish. Or Rollo has draped them in a lacy veil. They could be an illustration in a picture book, with the moon suspended over the sleeping houses on chains of silver stars.

And I could be someone else, a character in a child's fairy story, stepping out of my bedroom into an enchanted village. But I'm not, I am here, in another story I cannot get out of. Mine. We are all trapped in our own stories. We can't write ourselves out of them. We can never write ourselves out of our past. What a burden that is.

Opposite, Rollo and Guy's house was in darkness, save for a solitary light from the porch. That meant Guy was still at large. Her eyes moved to the outlines of the other house, the nearer one, a mere fifty paces away. As she watched, a light came on in the room she knew was Tony Corbino's. Through the open windows, the glow of a bedside lamp. He hadn't closed the shutters.

For a moment she was too startled to move. So he was not asleep after all; he was awake, like her. But unlike her he would be calm and unworried, musing. He would not be gazing at the moon, as if its two faces held the answer to her troubles, he would be planning his strategy.

A wide-winged bird, probably the barn owl that lived

in the top of Mischa's tower, swooped towards her, then veered abruptly to the left. It had something in its sights, a fieldmouse perhaps. It looked, briefly and terrifyingly, as if it would fly into Tony's open window, sucked in like a giant moth to the light. At the last moment it braked and plunged vertically, but in the split second before her reflexes flung her backwards, out of sight, she saw the round silhouette of Tony's head.

Behind the concealing shelter of the wall her heart pounded. She hadn't seen his expression or even his profile, he was too far away and the glimpse was too fleeting. Only the smooth circle of his head in the light. Had he seen her? She sank to her knees, winding the thin wool of the night-dress tightly around them. She realised she was shivering. Why did it matter anyway, whether he had seen her or not?

She knew why it mattered. If he knew why she was there outside in the dark, unable to sleep, standing alone in the chilly night air, if he knew that, then he would surely know that she was agitated and cold not so much from the night air as from fear.

Tony Corbino unlatched one of the open windows and pulled it closed. It had an old-fashioned catch. He leant towards the lamp on the bedside table, speaking into his small dictaphone.

'One thing I forgot to say. She got a big shock when I mentioned Verity Corbett. She asked who was running the gallery now, very cool. But when I said the old lady was still around she went a distinctly whiter shade of pale. *He* wasn't worried though. Freely admitted he'd liked Verity, but didn't ask any questions. He lives only in the present, he claimed. Doesn't believe in looking backwards or forwards. He's a simple, uncomplicated guy, if you believe Rollo, who's anything but.

'Maybe Mischa works off his obsessions through his pictures. Or maybe he's evolved the way he is through living with her – the classic reaction. She's either a natural-born cold fish, which doesn't square with her past, or she has to be a bunch of neuroses. The question is, which? And has it impacted on his work?'

The other three had waited inside the restaurant while Mischa went off into the pelting rain. He had roundly dismissed the younger man's offer to fetch the car.

'Don't try and take him on in the macho stakes, Antonio,' Rollo advised, 'you'll get nowhere fast. Mischa's got machismo overload. It's part and parcel of that deeply ingrained Eastern European suffering addiction, don't you think, darling? It must be so nice to be married to. Guy can't bear rain, it ruins his hair, and phrases like "Empty the mousetrap" or "Fetch my stole" are simply not in his repertoire.'

'However, he makes excellent wine and olive oil,' Greer said. 'And cooks and sings and plays the piano. All good things in a husband.' She was feeling slightly better. Probably the sedating effect of Maria Paola's coarse pork sausage with cannellini beans. And liberal quantities of wine.

'But the sentence "I'll run and get the car while you stay warm and dry" has never issued from his lips?'

Tony is remarkably at ease with us, Greer thought. He's probably a bit tight too.

'Has never emerged from that sybaritic orifice and never will.' Rollo adopted a mournful face.

'He sounds like a fine, well-grounded person. Will I get to give him the once-over tomorrow?'

'I don't see why you can't give him the twice-over, he's got nothing better on the go at the moment.' Rollo gave Tony an ironic look. 'And the wine makes itself at this time of year, doesn't it, darling? Tony should be given the run of the place, don't you think? Then he can just front up and give any of us the once-over whenever he feels like it.'

She nodded. Rollo added, 'So, Antonio, what is your plan of campaign for the morrow?'

Tony looked at Greer and smiled. 'Good question. What *is* my game plan?'

They worked something out on the short drive back to the Castello. It would be a loose arrangement. Tony would spend the first few days or so mostly with Mischa, starting chronologically with the early years in Czechoslovakia and his birthplace – the old spa town of Karlovy Vari.

'Karlovy *Vari*, the un*var*nished truth,' Rollo said, turning round to smirk at Greer, who duly laughed. He was ensconced in the front next to Mischa. Greer was aware of Tony's presence beside her, and of the narrow space that separated them.

Tony said pleasantly to her, 'Maybe I should drop by tomorrow and start checking out your archives. When Mischa needs to take a break from my gruelling interrogation?'

'You mean the cardboard boxes? Of course, yes.'

'Mischa has a ludicrously short attention span.' Rollo swivelled round again. 'You'll find the breaks will vastly out-number the gruelling grillings.'

Tony asked her, 'Did you manage to unearth much?'

'A few things, I suppose. All jumbled up, as I said.'

'Letters?' He was clasping his hands together in a prayerful pose. 'Please say you kept some letters.'

'He doesn't write letters, Tony, so why would he get any?'

'Shut the fuck up, Roly, if you don't mind,' Mischa said mildly. He turned the car up the hill. The rain had eased to a drizzle.

'There are letters –'

'Yes!'

'But nearly all from the last ten years, since we came to the Castello. We moved around so much before then. We were constantly shedding things.'

This was a safe enough topic. She felt quite expansive. 'We were like gypsies for years, weren't we?' She looked at the back of Mischa's head, but he seemed intent on driving. 'We wanted to be free to take off and go anywhere, with no encumbrances, nothing to tie us down. Except his equip-ment, which didn't boil down to much more than a handful of favourite brushes in a cigar box.'

And my equipment too. The biscuit tin of pencils, charcoal and chalks, brushes and watercolours. She added rapidly, to suppress this thought, 'That's a lot of years without much documentation, I'm afraid. How awful for you.'

She stopped. They were winding upwards on the unlit dirt road, and it was too dark to make out his face without turning and staring, but something told her he was smiling again.

'Don't worry about it. They're not entirely without documentation, those years. You'd be amazed how much inadvertent flotsam gets left behind. It's the other guys, you see, the motley crew you hang out with on your travels. They hold on to things, remember stuff, keep diaries, even. To be honest, it's a bit of a relief you don't have a whole bunch of material from that time.'

'I'm sure she's got more bunches than she's letting on.' Rollo searched for the outlines of their faces in the rear-view mirror. 'Every little twiglet is grist to his mill, Gigi, remember. Who was that Aussie composer who hung on to every scrap of paper he ever had in his life? You know, the self-flagellating one? Not just the dirty-linen bits, he kept all his dry-cleaning bills, shopping lists – a biographer's wet dream, Tony. Of course, Mischa's never had anything dry-cleaned in his life so Gigi couldn't have kept the chits even if she'd wanted to.'

'It was Percy Grainger,' Greer said.

Tony added, 'And all those chits would be more of a biographer's worst nightmare, I'm here to say.'

'Come on, admit you'd love the flogging.'

'The flogging would be knockout, I give you that.'

'The flogging would be knockout.' Greer heard Rollo's appreciative snicker. 'Well, he won't be tripping over any birch rods at your place, will he, darling? I fear you may be confronting a tragic dearth of debauchery instead.'

Mischa interjected forcefully, 'You can find that at the priest's house, Tony. That's Roly's house, if you didn't know yet.'

Rollo chuckled at this. 'Ah, well, all wives secretly love to dish the dirt on their husbands, don't they? I'll do what I can, but Gigi's probably your best hope.'

They were feeling their way through the second entry gate now. The movement triggered an outside light that thinly illuminated the parking area.

'Well, I'll just have to put the screws on you then, won't I, and hope for the best.' This time she distinctly saw the whites of Tony's smiling teeth.

7

23rd bloody July
What am I going to do? It's impossible, I can't bear C. to
touch me. I can't conceal it either, he can tell. I couldn't help it,
last night when I tried to go through with it I actually recoiled,
gorge rising. He thinks he understands but he knows nothing.
There's not a single thing I can do to change this. I know now
it could never work with C. If it ever did work before, in some
kind of disabled way when I didn't know anything about
anything, it couldn't any more.

   What on earth am I going to do? What am I going to
what what whatwhatwhat is there available for me to do?
What the fuck can I in fact actually do?
   WHAT THE FUCKING HELL CAN I POSSIBLY DO???

The night before, for the first time on the holiday, she
had yielded to Charlie's sensitive overtures. Forced
herself to go through the motions, in a resigned spirit of
experimentation. It had been a disaster.

The diary page was torn and ragged. The letters were
agitated, getting progressively larger, more fevered and out
of control, until the ballpoint pen had ploughed into the
paper and ripped it. The brief entry filled the whole page.

She had let the pen and diary fall on to the sand. It took

no effort to recall the scene. Her hunched figure in the blinding light, sitting with her back to the sea on sand that was as refined and pale as finely milled face powder. A young woman in a straw hat and burnt-orange bikini, slender, with long blonde hair. It could have been any hackneyed photo in a travel magazine, except that the sun-tanned legs were drawn up to the chin, the eyes squeezed shut and the mouth clenched in a grimace.

She had groped for a cigarette and found the packet empty. At precisely that moment a young man, French, had come up and offered her a Camel. He must have been watching her. She'd taken a cigarette automatically and accepted his light, then had trouble getting rid of him. He was personable, polite, insistent. What was the matter, he wanted to know. Why was she so upset? Was it love?

Instantly the tears spilt over. His handkerchief came out. Was it a letter she was writing? he demanded. Had he broken it all off, *le salaud*?

'No, no, not that at all! It's only my diary!' It was as if a tap had been turned on and, just like the tears, a torrent of words had spilt out.

For the rest of the morning, while Greer's husband, oblivious, threw fishing lines over the side of a swish catamaran, the two young people who didn't know each other (and one who would never meet Charlie) had thrashed out a problem he didn't know he had. The foundations of his future and the fates of several others would be sourced as a result of this casual encounter on a beach, and the intense conversation that ensued.

It was a shamelessly frank conversation. In later years, whenever the meeting with the young Frenchman crossed her mind in the seconds before being dismissed, Greer had thought of it as a secular variant of an epiphany. She had told this unknown Frenchman private things that she could not imagine saying to anyone else. The fact that he was a total stranger and foreign to boot had made such candid confessions possible. He was sympathetic, with no axe to grind.

And he was young and attractive. These facts too could not be discounted.

They had been like a pair of spies having a covert rendezvous on an empty beach. Or, more accurately, conspirators. She knew nothing about her fellow conspirator beyond his Christian name, Jean-Claude, and his occupation. But he spoke English fluently, being a graduate student attached to a medical research lab in Canberra. And as they groped towards an outcome she had hardly dared conceive of, he was prepared to envisage the unthinkable. Not only to imagine it, but to say it out loud. Which eased the way for her.

'No, it is easier for me,' he countered, 'because I don't know your husband. He is Mr X. If I know Mr X, maybe I cannot talk like this. But I see you, and I see that you cannot be unhappy for the rest of your life.'

'You don't find the idea terribly shocking?'

'Shocking? Perhaps, but only if you are a bourgeoise.'

That's the second time in two weeks I have been accused of being bourgeois, she thought.

'To be bitter and frigid, and not to have great sex again, ever. Those things are shocking to me,' he added.

Once the unthinkable had been given an imaginative existence, they were able to take it further. By the end of the morning they had worked out a plan. It depended on contingencies that were both considerable and unpredictable. It had no guarantee of success. The very word success was inappropriate.

She said again, 'Wouldn't it be impossibly ruthless? And – unnatural?' She felt her heart race.

'Youth is always ruthless. That is its nature. Love is the most ruthless of all.'

'What about unnatural?'

'What does that mean, natural? It is a meaningless word. The whole of civilisation has been a process of improving on the natural.'

'How do *you* know all this?'

'Everyone knows it in their heart. That's what great art is all about. The great novels, the work of Tolstoy, Flaubert, Zola. Music, paintings. You say Mischa Svoboda is a great artist. Well, he will have no difficulty with it. You just wait and see.'

They had been so engrossed in the conversation on the beach that when she looked at her watch she was amazed to find it was lunchtime. Charlie would be back from his fishing trip, anxiously seeking her out.

The Frenchman got to his feet first, then pulled her up and kept hold of her hands. He said, 'But all of this, it rests on the hypothesis that the great artist Mischa Svoboda you have only known a week is the true love of your life.'

'It's not a hypothesis. It's a certainty.'

The love of my life. The phrase stirred a physical response.

'*Je comprends*. When it happens, you know.'

They stood in silence, hand in hand, facing each other. She remembered how they had suddenly and spontaneously embraced, and the way the embrace had morphed like a computer-generated image into a passionate kiss. How she had let it happen, with her eyes closed, with no resistance. The release of it.

At least I was the first to pull back, she thought now, wryly. At least, I always like to think I was. It hadn't felt reckless, or even disloyal, just natural. Whatever that was. She had disengaged herself. They were both left smiling, rueful, and distinctly breathless.

'So,' he'd said, 'then you will have to go through with this plan. When you get back, you must make a start by coming clean with him.'

'Yes. Oh, God.'

'If it's going to work out between you, it will work. You don't need God.' He grinned. 'Love has a famous habit of finding a way.'

She remembered his parting words. '*Bonne chance*. I wish it was me.'

It was the last day of his vacation and she had seen Jean-Claude only once more, that same evening, at the far end of the resort dining room. Just an impression of his face, angled towards her as she walked in ahead of her husband. She had turned sharply on her heel, gasping involuntarily, as if stung. At dinner outside on the candlelit verandah she kept her eyes fixed on her innocent husband seated opposite, as if she were wearing blinkers.

Even at the time Greer had retained no clear picture of Jean-Claude's face. He remained a blur, like the fleeting glimpse that night in the hotel. Sometimes she found herself wondering if she had imagined the entire incident. Was he some kind of ghostly scapegoat she had conjured up, so she could tell herself: it was his idea, not mine. He planted it in my mind; I would never have contemplated it. Had he been an agent provocateur, prompting a sequence of events that she might not otherwise have had the nerve, the heart, to embark upon?

But her recall of the conversation was total. And she had no memory of ever asking him whether he thought she would find the strength to go through with it when the time came. The possibility that she might find herself unable to go through with it, she suspected, had never even entered her mind.

In Greer's study lined with floor-to-ceiling bookshelves was a fine walnut writing desk with two lockable drawers. For the last ten years she had left the diary lying at the back of the left-hand drawer, unlocked. She turned the key of the drawer now, and put the key in her purse. The diary was an incriminating document, without any doubt. She could burn it. She was surprised to find herself strongly disinclined to do this. Because hidden between these covers is the person I was then. The answers to the questions are right here: the how and the why. This is the evidence, with no excuse and no apology. Just the raw feelings on the page.

There was something abhorrent about the idea of

destroying the evidence, however incriminating it might be. She felt some pride in taking this attitude. Even if it was never used, either for biography or autobiography, it was the personal equivalent of a historical document, a primary source. And a primary source, she felt instinctively, should be sacrosanct.

She had been thinking of the diary as a fragment of autobiography. She revised this idea now. It was a mistake to think of it like that. The diary was too immediate, with its heat-of-the-moment roughness, its shameless partiality.

An autobiography was another thing altogether. It required distance from events. You had to take a step back, make an attempt perhaps to view the past through the eyes of a second self – a more dispassionate and grown-up version. A self that had become, you might even say, a different person.

The obvious analogy, she thought, is right here in front of me: wine. A mature wine contains all the elements it displayed in youth, but they have undergone an alchemy, a sea change. Life has tempered them. Or tampered with them, more to the point. If one could freeze a particular red wine in its rackety youth, then drink it years later alongside a mature glass of the same vintage, to claim they were one and the same wine would be effectively meaningless.

In what sense, then, am I the same person as the writer of this diary? Must I take responsibility for what she did? Or could I legitimately disown her?

Mischa, she knew, had a remarkable, even eerie, ability to disconnect himself from his past. Unlike Rollo, he could never write an autobiography. He might get a kick out of reading a perceptive account of the evolution of his work. But he would read his own biography much as he might read someone else's, as an intriguing story. As a fiction, even.

His identity and his sense of self were rooted in the present tense, as this man, this working artist, anchored today in the here and now. His younger self was another person altogether, one with whom he felt no particular sympathy and in whom he had only minimal interest. Was there any particular reason for this, and was it normal or abnormal? Healthy or unhealthy?

How did writers of autobiographical works deal with questions like these? Like all authors, they would use their major resource, the mind. They would then channel it through the crafty constructions of the pen, or more likely the keyboard. Because an autobiography, essentially, was calculated. It was the considered presentation of a life story.

And a unique marketing opportunity – not always taken up, she had to admit, by persons of integrity – to finesse the truth and present the author in a favourable light. It bestowed on the writer the precious gift of hindsight in the form of distance from events and a free hand to put a particular slant on them.

And leisure, she thought, to tamper with those events. The chance not only to tweak, shape and embellish, but also, on occasion, to censor. Or to excise. It offered the chance to delete unwanted events from the author's life.

She recalled Guy once delinquently dismissing Rollo's lauded memoir as the written equivalent of creative accounting. What an alluring concept this now appeared to be. She envied the ingenious autobiographer, free to rewrite history through the filter of selective memory. Free to flirt with dishonest self-interest. At liberty to leave things out.

Unless, of course, a biographer had already pre-empted that freedom and was planning to put on record a full and frank account. Unless he felt it incumbent on himself to put on public record an uncensored, unabridged and essentially unimproved version of events.

Greer had got up late, unusually for her, and shuffled into the kitchen in dressing gown and sheepskin boots. Mischa had left a fire burning in the grate. She stood with her back to it, reminded of how at school in the frosty Melbourne winters the girls had lifted their skirts and backed up against the radiators, luxuriating in the warmth on their bare legs.

It was cold again today, leaden and overcast, a reminder

that winter was not about to yield possession without a struggle. She felt an unease encircling the house as if some giant creature, an extinct flying reptile, had invaded her territory and was hovering overhead, blanketing everything in shadow. The feeling would persist all day, she knew, until the interloper himself arrived smiling at her door.

Mischa was already in his studio. The kitchen table was strewn with papers, today's *International Herald Tribune* and a pile of letters, which meant that he had been down to the village. She saw the current *Guardian Weekly*, and the remains of his breakfast – coffee, toast crumbs, a jar of peanut butter and the empty shells of two boiled eggs. Mischa was indifferent to any theories of healthy eating and cholesterol, just as he always forgot to put things away or turn off the radio. It was tuned to the BBC World Service.

Also on the table in a glass of water was an indecently huge and showy pink peony from Rollo's garden and a handwritten note in his meticulous calligraphy: 'Please attend confab soonest.' She felt a rush of gratitude that lasted as she showered, dressed and pinned up her hair. The feeling that she was being watched was still there. She was a woman under investigation. She took her time.

She smelt burning logs and fresh coffee well before she reached the front door of the big farmhouse. Some of Rollo's person was visible through the kitchen window, sprawled in an armchair, not reading but gazing out. He saw her coming and clambered to his feet, enveloping her in a hug at the door.

'At last, you lazy slattern. I've done you a fire, very possibly the swan song of the season. Coffee's made, crumpets are poised, and I'm busting for a bitchy debrief.' He appraised her: ankle boots, black wool trousers and grey-green cashmere sweater over a silk shirt. 'You've scrubbed up again, and you're wearing that celadon-coloured number I like. *And* a discreet touch of lippy. I know it's not for me, but you look *molto* svelte and ornamental, darling. You'll impress him no end.'

The fire blazed in the capacious grate at the dining end

of the L-shaped room. At the business end, on Guy's new ultra high-tech stove, the coffee in a sleek Alessi pot was bubbling into the upper chamber. A fresh packet of English crumpets, flown in for Rollo every week by friends in London, sat by the stove.

He placed four crumpets on the grill and led her by the arm to the sofa. One of Rollo and Guy's stylistic quirks was to have comfortable sofas and armchairs around the kitchen table instead of wooden chairs.

'Well? Did you like my pulchritudinous peony? His Majesty thinks it's vulgar. He can be so *prissy*, can't he? All right, so what did we make of our nubile young bio-meister?'

He poured coffee into two old pink and white Spode cups from an incomplete set displayed on the vast dresser. Like other pieces of furniture in the house, the dresser had been rescued years earlier from the refectory of a disused monastery in Urbino before the building was converted into apartments. It occupied the length of the wall and provided a theatrical showcase for Rollo's eclectic and ever-expanding collection of crockery. Jugs, plates, bowls, vases and pots of every derivation – singular finds all – each one there solely because he had stumbled upon it somewhere, usually off the beaten track, and fallen for it.

The sense of threat retreated for the moment. Rollo always made Greer feel wanted – almost, she thought, in the way of a love object. Other friends were as affectionate, but only Rollo habitually convinced her that she was, then and there, the person in the world whose company he most craved. They sat close together, elbows touching on the table.

'I'm not at all sure what I made of him. I found the teeth a bit unsettling.'

'Flawless and dazzling? That's because he's from California. They all have spotless ceramic choppers there.'

'What did *you* think? Choppers apart?'

'Well, he's a gay boy, for starters.'

She was startled. 'Is he?'

'Of course. He'll be off to Rome with Guy at the drop of a *capello*. Hear the prophetic words of the sage.'

She considered this. 'Is he really Guy's type? He's not at all like Mischa.' Guy's unrequited penchant for Mischa and other big bear-like men of his sort was a running joke at the Castello.

'Oh, Guy's type is completely flexible, you know that. It bends with the wind. It's like that man's famous theorem, you know the one – work expands to fill the time available. Guy's type expands to accommodate the goods on offer. Besides, one can pretty well guarantee Guy will be *his* type.'

'That's very true, I suppose.' Guy's raging sex appeal had never gone unnoticed by a visitor of either sex.

'He's a bit of a looker himself, our young Antonio,' Rollo looked prim, 'if you like that sort of winsome blondie thing.'

'Come on, you love that blondie thing. You're as bad as Guy.'

'Not any more, I'm not. Age has wearied me and the years condemned.'

'What utter nonsense. You'd be gadding off to Rome every weekend if you had your wicked way.'

He turned the crumpets. 'Really, you know, I can't remember when we last went to Rome. *A deux*, that is. It must have been before your time.'

When Rollo and Guy first came to live in the Castello they had embarked on the lengthy drive to the capital most weekends. 'No rest and intemperate recreation' was the slogan. These less edgy days, the euphemism 'going to Rome' was usually employed only in relation to Guy's activities, Rollo stressing that he used it purely in an unprejudiced and non-judgemental fashion.

He cut a large slab of butter, bisected it into two perfect triangles and deposited one on Greer's plate.

'It's depressing, isn't it, the decline of the sex urge?' This was a regular conversational gambit of his. Before she could respond, he added, 'Sorry, sorry, I know you don't want to talk sex this morning, only him. Not that the two topics are unrelated, necessarily.'

'Well then?' She turned and gazed at him.

'What do we make of him? What manner of chap, apart from being a fragrant figure of one, is he?' He doled out the crumpets, buttered his lavishly and spread them with Fortnums thick-cut English marmalade. She waited. His habits were as ingrained a part of his personality as his patterns of speech.

'He's bright. Very bright. And adaptable. I admired that, didn't you? The way he tuned in to the wavelength, put his feet up, metaphorically speaking, and enjoyed himself.'

She agreed. Visitors to the Castello often found it a daunting experience. The intimacy of the self-sufficient little community could be hard to penetrate. There were those who found the intimacy suffocating and the self-sufficiency elitist and smug.

She said, 'He struck me as one of the most confident young men I've ever met.'

'Too right. One of those enviable creatures who is entirely at ease in his own skin. The cut of his cloth was nice too. Very trendy clobber. I have to say that I'm not altogether sure that I'd trust him.'

'Whatever do you mean?'

'That's clear enough, isn't it? *Molto* engaging, in fact *moltissimo* charming, but I don't think he's got an off-the-record button on his dashboard. Which, let's face it, is only to be expected in his line of work.'

'Charming or ingratiating? Confident or cocky?'

'Ah. He's a charming devil, so shall we err on the generous side? And probably rather good at his job.'

'Good at getting people to tell him things? A plausible bugger?'

'You said it, not me. Just bear in mind that any passing remarks are likely to be regurgitated, unexpurgated. Don't let anything drop that might come back to haunt you.'

He quartered his second crumpet with a surgeon's

precision. Greer knew that he did this in order to make it last longer.

'I'll implore His Majesty to keep mum, but that's a lost cause, as you know. Once he lays his lascivious eye on young Tonio he'll be falling over himself to curry favour by scandal-mongering. The fact that he may not have much scandal to monger is neither here nor there.'

'Do you think Tony's –' She hesitated for some time, unsure how to phrase it. Rollo waited with no sign of impatience. He very rarely interrupted or finished her sentences, a courtesy that he and Guy had long since dispensed with between themselves.

She passed him her second crumpet and watched him heap on the butter and marmalade. Finally she said, 'In spite of the above, do you think he's fundamentally a kind man?'

'Ooh. What a heavy question. I should think he's as ruthless as all get-out, wouldn't you? I'm not sure that kindness is considered a virtue in the contemporary bio. More of an irrelevance. Or a hindrance.'

'But wouldn't most biographers of living people be well disposed towards their subjects? Why would you take the project on, otherwise?'

'One assumes you'd be interested. Well disposed? That depends. Maybe that has to be earned by the subject. But *self*-interested? Yes and yes again. And there's the rub.' Rollo wiped his mouth with an Irish-linen napkin starched by Agnieszka. 'Because we all know the megabucks are to be made from muckraking. The golden olden days of gentlemanly discretion are long gone. That's one of the facts of modern life, even for someone as hopelessly old hat as Mischa. It's not an optional extra. You take it on board as a freebie when you agree to a bio.'

'I hate that.' She shook her head vehemently. 'I just hate it. The idea that you let someone into your life knowing they're going to be poking around, trying to unearth a . . . something to your detriment. It's horrible, Roly, it's like inviting a spy from MI5 inside, throwing open the cupboards, tossing him the keys to the filing cabinets and then blithely going away on holidays.'

'Darling, the spook's well and truly over the threshold now, so the gnashing of teeth – here we go again – is a touch academic, isn't it?'

'Why did we ever agree to it, Roly?' She was filled with despair at her own comprehensive stupidity.

'Because Mischa's a major cheese,' Rollo repeated patiently, 'and this is what you get when you get to be the consort of a *grand fromage*. People want to come and write you up. You can't reasonably expect to be famous *and* have a private life, it's just not on.'

He looked at her more closely. 'You've been done over before, in heaps of glossies.'

'Maybe, but they were just articles about Mischa's work. Serious stuff. Not – gossip. I've kept out of the way. I've hardly featured in them at all.'

'Well, Mischa's success is less than half of his own making, as any woman worth her salt will confirm, so here's your chance to take centrestage for a change. Strike a blow for the sisterhood. Blow your own bugle. Let's face it, you'd make a much better subject than Mischa.'

When her face remained set he took her hand. 'Look, maybe I've gone and overdone the scaremongering. You know me – it's that dreadful drama-queeny temperament I'm saddled with. Let's forget everything and give young Tony the benefit of the doubt. He's probably just a pompous little prick with massive probity and not a skerrick of salacious intent.'

She managed a small smile. He said in an altered tone, 'Is there something you want to tell me, darling?'

In the moment's silence she heard a rushing wind start up in the three tall pines that shaded the house.

'I wouldn't mind what it is. It wouldn't make any difference. You know that.'

'I know.'

Through the kitchen windows they both saw Agnieszka

rushing in her usual frantic fashion from the car park towards the house. Her long black hair streamed behind her
like the tail of a kite.

'There's nothing.'

But she had wavered, and she knew Rollo had seen it.
She knew she should have confided in him, and Guy too for
that matter, well before this. Their pique, and Rollo's hurt,
would be further factors to contend with.

She thought, I can still get in first. If it ever comes to that.

31st July
I've found a little beach with no one on it. Thank God – I
couldn't face talking to anyone. C.'s stuck to me like a limpet
until today, when I persuaded him to join some of the boys on
an all-day fishing safari.

Only 2 days left. Now it's nearly time to go I don't want
to leave. I want the next 2 days to drift on for ever. I'm scared.
Terrified. Dry-mouthed, sweaty-palmed, gut-churning terror.
I can't believe C. can't tell. It proves he doesn't know me at all.

Am I really going to go through with this? I think I might
be going quietly insane. It's one thing to nut out a desperate plan
with a total stranger, another thing entirely to put it into practice.
Jean-Claude's a foreigner, he's from a different culture. He's not
involved, and he's a male too, so he could look at the situation
from a detached perspective. It was just a fantasy to him – he
doesn't have to go through with it.

What about C.?? And what about M.? Mightn't his feelings
change when he hears about all this? Why aren't I more concerned
about his reaction? Why aren't I tearing my hair out over that?

Why indeed? The writer on the beach had laid aside her
pen at this, but only for a second. It was true, she had enter-
tained scarcely a doubt over Mischa's role in all this. He was
central and problematic, yet he was the least of her worries.
He had made the strength of his feelings plain and known
in no uncertain terms. She found that she believed in them
absolutely.

Well, on that score maybe — conceivably — when I see him again I won't feel anything, it'll have all dissolved away like some bizarre mirage and I won't need to do a thing & can just get on with my former life as if nothing had ever happened. Then I can push the boundaries, as Verity says, enrol in art school part-time and become a successful portraitist.

That's a delusion, I know perfectly well. I've got a terrible conviction that nothing will have changed. Even the idea that it might have is anathema. The thought of never seeing him again makes me feel dead, to all intents & purposes. I couldn't live like that now, not any more. He's made it impossible. There's me before I met Mischa, and there's me after. Two totally different people.

It's weird how everything around me here on this island brings back his presence. The sheer raw energy he exudes. It's explosive. The thought of everything about him — his face, the texture of his skin, his mouth — provokes a reaction in me, instantaneously. An internal shudder of rapture.

Everything I see here is sensuous — the vibrant colours and shapes, the steamy atmosphere, the brilliant flowering shrubs & willowy palm trees, the sand — especially the supple, velvety feel of this amazing sand. It's like rolling in clotted cream, I find it supercharged with eroticism. I think something in me's been switched on & I've evolved. My body's gone through some elemental chemical change & now, if I fantasise about making love with him, virtually anything can turn me on, just by being in my orbit. It's as if I've been smitten with sunstroke — the sun is beating down & I'm burrowing into the sand in a kind of mad, erotic trance. It's as if I've gone demented, crazy with longing for him.

I have to go back to him, whatever it may involve. Yes, yes, yes. Like Molly Bloom, no doubts. I have to do it, whatever it takes.

How could something as familiar as sand be arousing? She was a Melbourne girl; sea and sand were part of her daily environment. Yet she saw herself clearly on that remote beach, shutting her eyes against the groaning drumbeat of the sun and letting the sinuous bleached threads run through her fingers, over and over like an hourglass endlessly revolving.

Saw herself lying face down on the silky powder and working her hips rhythmically and ecstatically into it until she had hollowed out a shallow depression in her own image and lay there spent, spread-eagled in a sticky bath of sweat.

When she came to, sunspots danced in front of her eyes. It took a while, minutes perhaps, before she became aware of the muffled sound of giggles and a tickling sensation on her back. She'd been oblivious to what was a little mound of feathers, leaves and flowers tossed by three brown islander children, crouched a few yards away in undergrowth at the edge of the sand. Had they stolen up in her oblivion and draped them on her writhing back? There was nothing for it but to laugh with them and she did, guffawed helplessly until her eyes streamed and her stomach muscles ached.

I must have been delirious, she thought now. In a hallucinatory state, I needn't mince words, of near-constant arousal. Mostly frustrated, mostly suppressed, and always adroitly concealed from my husband. I suppose they were three weeks of delayed shock, really.

The proverbial clouds hovered on the horizon beyond the blurring of blues that separated sky and sea. And remained there in the forgettable distance, exiled to the outer reaches of my consciousness. In the stakes of love, I can be brutally honest about it now, intimations of some future reckoning had negligible bargaining power.

I had taken a bite of the apple. It was an addictive drug I had tasted, and notions of duty and caution hadn't a hope of competing with that. The scarlet blaze of passion and euphoria versus the dun colours of duty and responsibility – it was that simple. A classic, no-contest situation.

8

Tony Corbino lost no time in making his presence felt. After breakfast with Rollo, Greer drove down to the village for a cappuccino with friends in the bar. Then she forced herself to do a circuit of the co-op and pick up items for Tony's kitchen to supplement the basics that were always left in place in the guest cottage. This task had been neglected in advance of his arrival. It was a case, she knew, of wilful neglect.

They had agreed Tony would cater for himself at breakfast and sometimes lunch too, as was the custom for visitors. Mischa himself rarely stopped for a midday meal. Instead he ate bananas or apples and gnawed chunks of bread and cheese more or less continuously as he worked. Agnieszka reported finding caches of chocolate in dark corners.

Greer saw Tony emerging from the studio as she got out of the car and unloaded the boot. The sight was unwelcome. Their paths were on a collision course and they intersected on the parade ground. He looked cheery and chipper. Today he wore a leather bomber jacket over an oatmeal polo-necked sweater, with a denim version of a briefcase slung over his shoulder on a strap. The denim was rope-trimmed, like espadrilles, she noticed.

'A few iron rations for you,' she said, avoiding his gaze by looking up at the sky. It was heavily overcast and the wind was frigid. She was wearing a belted raincoat of cherry red, hooded against the wind.

'Hey, you didn't need to shop for me, but major thanks anyhow.' He took the basket from her. 'What a cool outfit. You look like Little Red Riding Hood.'

His tone was playful. For a second she toyed with saying, do I now? And who does that make you?

'What time do you generally knock off for lunch?' he went on. 'Should I drop by afterwards for a bit of a chat? Start the ball rolling?'

'You can start the ball rolling whenever you like. I'm on holidays this week.'

I should offer to share my lunch with him, she thought, but I won't. Come and get it over with, was the unspoken subtext. She had a feeling he was wise to that.

'Well, I'll go stash those goodies in my fridge, fix a bite to eat and see you in a bit.' He turned away, then looked back. 'How about we make it in around an hour? I need to get some urgent housekeeping done. If I don't cross-reference every single interview tape as I go along there's a scarily high risk of systems failure.'

'Fine by me, I'm not going anywhere.'

In the house she pulled the boxes out from under the bookshelves in her study and assembled them in the neutral space of the sitting room floor. Only two were proper archival containers with fitted lids. The others were cardboard grocery boxes. She was amused to see that one had contained Kellogg's cornflakes. That had probably come from Rollo.

Before Tony's arrival she had given the boxes a cursory going-over. She was confident there was nothing to be afraid of in them. Nothing incriminatory. Nothing much, indeed, to do with her.

The doors to the office were firmly bolted against the weather, but Giulia's shapely back was visible. She was talking animatedly on the phone. Tony observed her before heading up the stairs to his front door. He went to the fridge, poured a glass of mineral water and made a submarine sandwich with cheese and ham. He bit into it and sat back with a notebook in a winged armchair upholstered in a faded cotton weave of pastel flowers, conical shells and leaves.

The cottage had been done up and furnished for guests by Rollo as a top priority, long before the arrival of Greer and Mischa. Its village name was Casa Nova, contracted to Casanova to no one's surprise by the first sparky guests back in the 1970s. Greer and Mischa had camped here themselves for a year while their future home, Casa Vecchia – the old house – was rendered liveable again and the watchtower reclaimed from the vipers and shoulder-high brambles that had colonised it.

Rollo and Guy had naturally picked the plum for themselves: Casa Canonica, the priest's digs – always the biggest and best in any village. And indeed a stooped old monsignor had finally moved out only weeks before Rollo and Guy moved in, the sole remnant of a little community that had numbered fifty-eight in its heyday. The priest's house had also functioned during his tenure as the village bar, boasting the only working TV in the area. A dressmaker once lived in the basement. Now it was Guy's wine cellar, with a perfect year-round temperature.

The guest cottage was full of Rollo's decorative fingerprints: a bedhead delicately painted with fruit baskets, a Jacobean high-backed sofa, rugs, cushions and bedspreads in splashy, variegated fabrics picked up from markets around the world. Rollo liked to claim that he was Matisse's soul mate, colour-wise if not in all other-wises. On the mantelpiece facing Tony was a collection of old pottery fragments and bottles of milky glass that had been found during the restoration period.

Tony wrote, 'Tape one: Mischa's studio', and the date. A second cassette recorder was already sitting on the side table. He spoke into it, fluently and without a pause. 'Mischa's studio is in what they call the watchtower. You reach it through a small grassed courtyard with a covered well. The tower itself was built,' he consulted the notebook, 'in 1170 as a lookout post for the Sienese republic. The studio occupies what were once living quarters.

'The first floor's like an airplane hangar divided by an archway, with a bathroom tucked away in one corner. He does the big pictures and murals here, but it's mainly used as a workroom and for storing paintings and materials. There's some of the largest painting racks I've ever seen. And stacks of firewood. A basic structural renovation's been done, it's plumbed and wired, the ceiling's been fixed and concrete posts put in for support.

'The walls are rough and unplastered, at least five feet deep. And the floor's original, still paved with flagstones, heavily worn and uneven. Beautiful. Plenty of natural light streams in from two vast windows that have been cut through the south wall to look over the valley. That must've cost a bundle in itself.

'You climb eighteen steps and shove open a mother of a great door to get into the main studio. This was once four rooms – some jagged slabs of the dividing walls are still in place, buttressed by steel struts. There's coir matting on the floor, and he's added radiators and rows of lights with conical shades suspended from ropes – each one on a pulley and individually adjustable. He has a bar fridge and a primeval stone butcher's sink sitting next door to a state-of-the-art coffee machine. He's very proud of that – made me a neat espresso.

'Huge arched windows look over the internal courtyard and the tower. Opposite, that's to the south, you get stunning panoramic views over the countryside and distant mountains to the sea, forty miles away. There's no way in the world an invading army could've snuck up here without being spotted, but now that Mischa's commandeered the tower they could surround the place and he wouldn't even notice.

'It's a view to die for, but when he's working he insists he doesn't even see it. I believe him because his powers of concentration are awesome. There's no clock in the studio, and he wasn't wearing a watch. When I remarked on that he looked at me like I was some kind of a retard and retorted that he doesn't need to know the time, and if he does his belly will tell him.

'There's a humungous fireplace which he still uses. You could roast an ox in there – it must have been butt-numbingly cold in the old days. Today all the lights were on and he had a fire blazing away and roaring up the chimney. It threw out such a blistering heat you couldn't get near it, and it did a pretty amazing job of warming that cavernous space.'

He broke off and drank some water.

'It's impossible to describe the studio in words. It's kind of like a visual cacophony. We'll need full-colour photo spreads to do it justice. Alongside all the usual junk, the literally hundreds of squashed tubes of oils and acrylics, tins and jars of brushes and so on, it's crammed with personal stuff from their travels. Probably stuff she won't have in the house. A wild boar's head with a paintbrush in its mouth, paper kites in the shape of weird hybrid birds suspended from the ceiling, a row of spears and tribal figures with bulbous tits and/or dicks. Whatever's at hand – the edge of a table, bar stool, school desk, even an old wooden bed – he's liable to use it as a palette. They're everywhere, encrusted with historic pyramids of paint.

'He assembles his stretchers from cedar and even occasionally still makes his own easels, like he always did, even though they all say he's no handyman. I told him Rollo says only amateurs make their own easels. He just laughed and said, yeah, that was right, that's all he was. There's a stack of tools on one wall: hammers, set squares, drills and saws. Rolls of the Belgian linen he favours, and heavy French paper that he cuts with a metal ruler and Stanley knife.

'He loves to draw on thick, lush paper, he told me. The

way he confided this, it was almost like he was an informer divulging a secret about himself. If he thinks that was revealing information, I guess it was.'

Tony stopped speaking and took another large bite of the chewy bread. He ran his index finger along an elaborate panel on the narrow side table to the left of his armchair. It was incised with an intricate design, a vine trailing bunches of grapes and pears, pine cones and acorns. Animals and birds were shown running along the stem and gobbling up the fruits. They had beady eyes and voracious gaping beaks.

He started again, more slowly this time. 'I didn't expect to find the studio such a profoundly –' He broke off once more, gazing at the etched creatures frozen in their telltale moment. He got to his feet, picked up the dictaphone and paced around the room with it.

'The studio is a total shambolic mess, sure, but it's a hugely atmospheric space and what I didn't plan on finding is this: it's kind of an emotional place to be in. Why's that? I think maybe it has something to do with the ancient history of the place, its original purpose, which was a vigilant purpose to warn and protect its people. Then you juxtapose that with this anomalous present usage that the original inhabitants could never in their wildest dreams have imagined, but which has something satisfying and right about it too.

'I guess, and this is the nub, it's because the place is being used with passion. It's not just another crumbling heritage ruin, it's lived in and used. More than that – it's potently alive, crammed with the raw materials and oily, pungent smells of an artist's trade. There are a few gestures here and there to civilian life, like worn leather armchairs and the corduroy sofa with a threadbare patch where he puts his feet up sometimes, but basically what it says is this: I don't arse around here, guys. This is the place where I do what I love.'

Tony left the machine recording and switched the first one on. His own voice issued forth on the tape.

'Mischa, I'd somehow assumed you were always going to be a painter, but your friend Evzen said that way back you wanted to be an astronaut.'

'Rubbish.' Mischa's dismissive voice sounded far off, as if he had turned away.

'Evzen Kolar. You were pals through primary school.'

'I don't remember him.'

'Well, he remembers you. Said when you were both six he wanted to make movies and you were going to be a spaceman.'

'That's right. I am a spaceman, not an astronaut. And what did he do?'

'Evzen? He produces movies now. How do you mean, you're a spaceman?'

'I fill spaces.'

Tony stopped the tape and spoke into the second machine that was recording this. 'He points to the eight by six he's working on. It's going to be another picture about loss or displacement, but it's blank except for a road snaking from lower right to centre left. As I watch he makes fast emphatic charcoal marks on the virgin canvas. Just a few strokes, but enough to create people, their backs to the viewer, vanishing into a distant black hole. And he turns to me triumphantly.'

He switched on the other tape.

Mischa's voice rang out: 'There, you get it now, Tony? I dictate what occupies the space. Sometimes I'm a benevolent dictator, sometimes not. Whichever way it goes.'

'And how do you choose which way it goes? According to what?'

'According to the feel of it.'

'The feel of it? How you're feeling about yourself? Or about the subject?'

'The feel of the picture.'

There was a short pause.

'So, you do think about the picture when you're painting.'

'No. I don't do that.'

'You don't think about what you're painting? What you're communicating? The structure and meaning of it?'

'I paint the painting, but not with any of that in mind. I just let it do its job. It's a mistake to search for meanings, Tony. You shouldn't look at pictures that way.'

'But there's something guiding you as you paint, right? Your hand is responding to something, impulses, in your mind.'

'No. I don't think through my mind. I think through the brush.'

Tony switched off the first recorder.

'With that he turned his back on me and ripped into his work. The old trick where you zip your lip and wait for the subject to fill the silence or drop his guard doesn't wash with Mischa. I left him to it for a bit while I poked around. At one end of a rack of pictures against the wall I found a couple of very small, very detailed studies from the "Old Cypress" series. I lifted them out. They were from the latter experimental period when he was exploring the interior of the trees, where the small tight cones transmogrify into dark, semi-abstract forms suggestive, like McCaughey has written, of fecundity and amniotic fluids.'

Tony activated the other tape. 'What was it with the cypress trees, Mischa? When you first arrived at the Castello you were obsessed with them for quite a while, weren't you? You've never really let them go.'

'Like Van Gogh. They spoke to him too. I have good company there.'

'They speak to you?'

A laugh. 'They are always communicating.'

Laughing with him. 'How do they communicate? What do they tell you?'

'Nothing.'

'How do you mean, nothing?'

'I mean they say nothing.'

'You mean, nothing verbally?'

'That's right. They make a poem or a song. They have a tune, but without words and music. All things do it, Tony, not just nature. Pylons are the same.'

'Electricity pylons? Are you saying that you pick up on things, atmospheres, feelings, which kind of emanate from them?'

'You are saying that.'

Tony stopped the tape. 'He'd been using both hands to make big expressive circles, sort of humorously pushing the air around his face. Then he just laughed at me again and shrugged. And then – here's a funny thing – he went over to a high shelf on the wall and reached up for a little glass jar. He took it down and rubbed it, kind of tenderly and abstractedly like it was a magic genie lamp, against his pants. Then he put it away again and produced a bar of chocolate from behind it, threw me a few squares, and went back to the canvas.

'Something told me not to make any comment, but I took a close look at the jar later, when he had his back turned. It was just an old jam jar with some white sand in it and what looked like old faded flower petals.

'I'm picking up on a short attention span here. He'll toy with me, kid along indulgently, and then he loses interest – bang – just like that. He never loses the thread of what he's working at though, there's a powerful force-field of concentration there. You can almost feel it – but then that's his reality, I suspect. I get the impression that life as others live it is perilously close to an irritation, almost an irrelevance, distracting him from his real thing, which is work.'

He made a pencilled note: was it always the case? And how does she cope with that?

'Why does he call you Mrs Smith?' Tony was on his knees between the boxes and the fire, which was throwing out sparks. He'd peeled off his sweater. The knobs of his spine stood out against his straw-coloured shirt. Greer had a mental image of a row of pith helmets on a sandbank.

'That's just a joke. Because of Svoboda being such a common Czech name, like Smith or Brown.'

'But you never bothered to get formally married, right?'

'No. We never bothered.'

'Was that because you didn't want the formality?'

'It was because we didn't need it.'

'You did take his name though?'

From her armchair behind him she thought, he's not looking at me at all. He's trying not to appear to be interrogating me, while he pretends to study the material. Probably thinks I'll be more at ease that way. Less on my guard.

'I never took his name, not legally. It just somehow happened that people assumed I was called Gigi Svoboda. After a while it seemed hardly worth the trouble of correcting them.'

He said, 'It was more convenient, huh?'

She chose not to answer that.

He was persisting with this. 'People didn't call you by that name in Melbourne. It's like they lost track of you altogether after you went away.' She caught a breath of hesitation, before the almost absent-minded punchline: 'They didn't even know you *were* Gigi, half the time.'

And I'm sure you took pleasure in wising them up. I bet you didn't have to tell Verity though. She would have known.

'Look at this, will you?' He sounded excited, sifting through the earliest papers from the bottom of the first box. He held out two yellowed sheets stapled together. 'The list of paintings and drawings from the first show at the Corbett Gallery. And the reviews. Take a look at those prices. Three hundred dollars. Five hundred dollars. The most expensive is nine-fifty. Oh boy, all you art collectors, eat your hearts out. Typed on one of those early electronic machines and roneoed off, by the look of it.'

'Yes. I typed it.' And Verity invested in a word processor soon afterwards and enrolled me in a three-day training course on my return from holidays, which I never went to.

'Typed by you. Well, there you go. And the old lady, Verity Corbett, told me she had the temerity to buy one of those alarming new computers the week after that sell-out show. She said she felt like she was a hominid standing upright for the first time. Nothing wrong with that mind or memory. I'd like to be that sharp at eighty.'

'Rollo's that sharp at eighty.'

Instead of taking this up, he said, 'So how come you got to be Gigi?'

'Oh, that was Mischa, of course. He has nicknames for everyone.'

'Greer Gordon. Was it your initials? G.G.?'

He was sharp, too, at thirty.

'And what do you prefer to be called, Gigi or Greer?'

'I don't really care. Everyone calls me Gigi here.'

'But they're such different names. Opposites. Greer is like, elegant and poised, a tad enigmatic maybe, and Gigi's kinda ditzy, isn't it?'

'Well, maybe I'm a ditzy kinda dame.'

He looked up at her then, with an easy grin. 'Is that right?'

When she proffered only a tight smile in response, he said, 'I think I'd be more comfortable with Greer. That's if it's all the same to you, of course.'

'Whatever makes you more comfortable is fine with me.'

'Verity said you were the very model of a resourceful, insightful personal assistant. And super-bright. But her warm and fuzzy feelings for you flew out the window when you shot through, I have to say. She was mad at you, she told me, livid. And ropeable. I never heard that word before. I like it.'

I should have told her in advance. Even at the time I knew perfectly well that I should have confided in her, but I couldn't bring myself. It was a very unwise thing to do, to make an enemy of someone like Verity. Both unwise and unnecessary.

'She said Mischa rang her from a public callbox the

morning after you left, but you didn't give her any notice. You just didn't show up.' There was an implied question here, an upward inflection.

'Yes, that's right. I didn't.'

Was he going to ask why?

'You were anxious to get out of there, I guess.' It was a plain statement of understanding, giving no indication of what shoals might lie beneath. She nodded.

He added, 'She blames you more than him, I'm afraid.'

'He could have lit bonfires in the gallery and trashed it like a rock star and she wouldn't have blamed him. She was fifty-five or so, but I think he swept her off her feet, in a way.'

Again she saw Mischa whirling Verity in her severe navy suit around the floor of the gallery to his exuberantly improvised 'Blue Danube' waltz, until she was out of breath and giggling like a schoolgirl.

'How would you describe his relationship with her?'

'He flirted shamelessly. And the amazing thing was she responded. He brought out something unexpected in her, something rather awkward and – arch. Well, it was amazing to me at the time. It was quite sweet, when I think about it now.'

'Sweet?'

'Well, touching. I suppose I'd always thought of her as dessicated and virginal. Not lesbian but definitely sexless.'

Somewhere in the conversation he had switched on his tape. Should she be going on like this? Would he quote her, for Verity to read? Perhaps it was a sound tactic to divert him with a few indiscretions that were comparatively immaterial.

Tony rocked back on his heels. 'People have said that at the same time she treated him like a favourite son.'

'She certainly indulged him.'

'How did she do that?'

'She was a bit of an autocrat, Verity. Headmistressy towards all her other artists. Mischa got away with things they were never allowed to do, like hanging his pictures wherever he chose, eating and smoking in the gallery. Putting his arm round her – no one else would have dared do that. She was always strictly untouchable.'

'Were you at all jealous of their relationship?'

'Jealous?' He had swivelled round to look at her. She stared at him. 'Not in the least. I was amused, if anything.'

'It never occurred to you to wonder if there'd been anything between them?'

She felt her face going hot with annoyance. 'That's absurd. You've met Verity.'

'OK, but you know how it is when you meet somebody new and they're eighty years old? It's kind of hard to envision how they might have been.'

'Well, I knew Verity how she was.'

'And how was that?'

'She was, very categorically, chaste.'

He grinned.

She was incredulous. 'Did someone really cast aspersions about Verity and Mischa?'

'You know what folks are like with those wretched aspersions. They'll cast them about anyone, given half a chance.'

Or given half an invitation.

'People also say that she treated you like a favoured daughter.'

Who were all these people? 'I think she was fond of me, yes.'

'She feels you stole something from her, the greatest artistic discovery of her career. Perhaps the only one. She still thinks Mischa would have stayed in Melbourne if you hadn't run away with him.'

'And did you interrogate Verity on the subject of her possible dalliance with Mischa?' The idea was so preposterous that she found herself on the verge of laughing.

'I kinda danced around it. It's a tough call to raise that type of subject with a touchy old lady her age, as I expect you can appreciate.'

'Oh, I can see it might well be delicate for you. Just as well it's not so touchy to raise with me, eh?'

'You're a lot younger than she is, Greer.' He threw her an almost skittish glance. She thought, and you're younger than me by not much more than Mischa was younger than Verity, Tony.

'What about Mischa? Did you raise this intriguing subject with him?'

'Well, yeah, I had a shot at it, and he just laughed at me.'

'There you are then.'

'I just thought, you know, it might have been one of the reasons why you left Melbourne. To get him away from her.'

The casual, quick-fire audacity of this took her breath away. He had his head down, his hands carefully sifting through folded papers, reviews and invitations, and creased newspaper photographs.

Did he seriously expect her to address the line of inquiry that followed on from the dismissal of that leading question?

In the pause that followed, various responses went through her mind. It had been a light, almost throwaway remark. There was nothing to differentiate it in tone from what had gone before. Did he even know what he was saying?

In the end she merely dryly stated, 'That never entered my mind,' leaving the coda 'as I'm sure you well know' unspoken, yet quite as surely understood by both.

A few minutes later, Guy looked in on his return from lunching with more wine buyers.

'I've had far too much to drink, G., you were well advised not to come,' he declaimed as he strode through the kitchen. 'Have you got the dreaded biographer here?'

At the sight of Guy, Tony sprang to his feet. Greer introduced them. They shook hands.

'Rollo's told me all about you. He ordered me to summon you to our place for dinner tomorrow. He specifically said not to invite *you*,' he looked at Greer, 'so we can gossip about you and Mischa with maximum impunity.

Aggie's doing her lamb with artichokes, it's very good. Has he run into Aggie yet?' He turned to Tony. 'You'd know if you had.'

'Would that be Agnieszka, the diminutive Polish dynamo? Absolutely, we had a memorable encounter yesterday and she escorted me over here. Thanks. I'd love to join you and the lamb.'

He dropped on to the floor and sat cross-legged, his back against the sofa. Again, Greer noticed the easy way he fell into conversation with a new acquaintance. She also observed, with a mental nod to Rollo's acumen, that his manner had become just a little heightened.

'You'd better *dress*, I'm afraid,' Guy said, selecting Mischa's rocking chair to sit in and positioning it directly opposite Tony. 'His Lordship will insist on parading you before some toffy friends. I don't mean tie, just no frayed denim. He's got a queenie thing about jeans, probably because his bum's too big to wear them himself.'

He rocked backwards. 'Now, I'm not going to disrupt your session, I'm going straight home for a little siesta any minute now. By the way, G., I saw my two hoopoes on the lawn again this morning, I really think they may be here to stay.'

To Tony, again, 'Are you up to speed on hoopoes?'

'Not to speed. They're birds, aren't they?'

'Adorable birds. Handsome, with an *erectile* crest of pink feathers and black and white splashes, is how the book describes them. There's going to be a plague of cuckoos this year, I've never heard as many this early. We're quite good at wildlife here, Tony. Buzzards, porcupines, wild boar, Giulia . . .'

'Ah, I had an encounter with Giulia too. A brief encounter – Agnieszka was somewhat over-protective of my virtue. But she offered to show me around the winery tomorrow.'

Guy's eye met Greer's.

'You'd better watch your back with her, or perhaps more to the point your front. She eats men, our Giulia.'

Greer demurred. 'She's a perfectly normal twenty-four-year-old.'

'She's lethal, but Gigi's feminine solidarity won't allow her to admit it. Just don't let her lure you behind the wine barrels, Tony. Especially the thirty hectolitre brutes.'

'If it comes to that, there's a bunch of barrels lying on the ground outside my house. Would they be Giulia's rejects?'

'Those are our *botti*.' Guy grinned at Greer. 'Svelte Slovenian oak casks bound for the knackery, waiting to be picked up. They've reached the end of their working lives. Their tannins are exhausted and they're being put out to grass.'

He yawned and stretched with the slow, sensuous deliberation that informed all his movements. 'This is what we find so satisfyingly allegorical and anthropomorphic about wine. It follows the same life cycle we're all prisoners of, only it's bottled. Callowness of youth, through to prime of life and eventual senility.'

Greer added, 'Of course, one should always exercise responsible altruism and drink the bottle before senility kicks in.'

'Which in wine circles is known as compassionate euthanasia.'

The crackling fire underpinned their joviality. The soughing of the wind in the cypresses and the soft cooing of doves, a change of pace, rose above it. Guy cocked an ear.

'Has Gigi told you about her babies?'

Tony did not answer immediately. His eyes flicked towards Greer. She was looking out of the window towards the sounds of the birds, which always reminded her of creamy pearls on a silk cushion in one of Rollo's paintings.

'Uh, no. She hasn't.'

'She bought ten pairs of caged doves a year ago at the local market. Tell him.'

'They had been born in their cages. I released a pair at a time. They all flew away and established their own territories. Some went back to the village. One pair stayed here to nest in the cypress. They chose the nearest one to the house, the one that's bending in the wind.'

Tony smiled. 'That's so neat. And it reminds me of a thing,' he extended his legs, engaging Guy, 'there was an incredible moon last night. I was leaning out, just drinking it all in – you don't need to be told how beautiful it is here – when *wham!* this great big bird nearly slammed into my face. I thought it was coming for me through the window. I got the shock of my life.'

His gaze, wide-eyed with the memory, wheeled and came to rest on Greer. She got out of her chair and threw another log on the fire.

Guy said, 'Most probably our barn owl. Did it have a white face and feathered legs?'

'I didn't see what it had. It was like this monstrous winged creature from a manga comic.'

'There are owls in the tower. They have an impressive wingspan and a remarkable repertoire of sounds. Screeches, whistles, and an extraordinary grunting noise, a cross between an orgasmic groan and a snore.'

'Thanks for the warning. I think I got such a fright because it had been so quiet and still out there. And the shimmering light from that full moon after the rain was just dreamy.'

He switched back to Greer. 'Too bad you didn't see it.'

This time their eyes met, briefly. She was reminded of a child's card game, long forgotten, in the course of which players stealthily revealed their hand. On impulse she said, 'Do you play poker, Tony? We should have a game.'

She was pleased to register his momentary flicker of surprise.

2nd August
I of Ps
Sneaking a moment – C. doing laps in pool. Happy in his ignorance. Is this the last time he will be really happy? No, he is the kind of person who will bounce back. I was always the wrong

one for him, he just couldn't see it. He will find someone else who will love him properly, I'm sure of it.

We go back tomorrow. Back to face the Music with a capital M. What an inadequate, woeful phrase – sword of Damocles is more apt. Whatever that was. I feel as if it's dangling above my head. I feel sick all the time. I'm thinking about Mum's reaction. If she thought I was impulsive & headstrong before, now she'll think I'm positively criminally reckless. She'll probably disown me. I'll be cast aside like some nineteenth-century trollope who transgressed society's mores.

And what about Josie? What if she will have nothing to do with this? Is it too much to ask? It is a very big thing to ask, of any sister. But my instinct makes me hopeful. There's her situation, and her nature is so radically different from mine, people have always said that. I've seized life with both hands & jumped in, whereas she's always somehow been on the sidelines, observing. Waiting for this? Is it possible? Since it all fell through with ratty Richard it's not as if she's got anything much else going on in her life . . .

That sounds terrible. Callous and calculating. Has love got me by the throat and shaken every shred of decency out of me? Is this even the real me talking?? Perhaps I've turned into a changeling now, substituted for my old self by Cupid's fairies.

That reference, Greer supposed, had been prompted by the opera, a recent visit she and Charlie had made, at her instigation, to Britten's *Midsummer Night's Dream*.

She sat with her elbows on the desk, chin in her hands.

What does it ever mean, 'Who is the real me?' Was it the rash young woman I was then, contemplating the transgression of society's mores? There was another self lingeringly present, one whose desultory, whispered words – words like betrayal, words like duty and responsibility – were suppressed and ignored. Was she the real me? Or have those two evolved into a descendant who is another person altogether?

When Greer looked back on the former self who was the writer of this diary it was as if she had arrived from nowhere, a visitor from outer space. At the time it had felt like being reborn inside her own skin. Mischa is right in a sense, she thought. In the way he refuses to engage with his past, as if his early lives belonged to a series of prototypes of himself. I had to rethink my identity after I met him. My sense of self imploded. I felt it had been wrenched from my control.

It was like living through an earthquake. Such a powerful one that twenty-five years afterwards I am still living through the impact. What I should have remembered, of course, was that all earthquakes are followed by after-shocks, which do not necessarily come immediately. These, though, have been delayed for two and a half decades, and I did not anticipate their arrival. I have immersed myself in an alternative reality all these years, in an altered landscape. I am, in the deepest sense, unprepared for these aftershocks and what they may herald.

After Tony left the house carrying, with her permission, a box of papers with him, she retreated to the safety of her study, unlocked the left-hand drawer of her writing desk and sat in her chair. A silver clock on her desk, which she had polished herself that morning, told her she had been sitting stiffly in the same position for forty minutes. She felt an emotional and physical exhaustion.

She rotated her neck and shoulders. What was it that she was really afraid of? Public exposure and judgement of that ruthless youthful self? Or was it something other than that?

The Art Deco clock in the shape of an aeroplane with two propellers was one of her first presents from Mischa. He had bought it soon after their first New Year's Eve together. It was a potent image of escape, of their mutual flight to freedom. At the time she had seen it as marking their liber-ation from a more recent past. The clock aeroplane in sterling silver symbolised their emergence not so much from their separate years in Melbourne or Prague as from the five months they had spent closeted together in Sydney.

There was an empty space at the bottom of the page where the previous diary entry had skidded to an abrupt halt. On impulse she unscrewed a fountain pen and wrote some new words there, but slowly, without pausing, and deliberately, in the way of an automaton:

15th April 2006
It is not public exposure I am afraid of. It is the realisation that I have lived as if I hadn't done the thing.

The pen came to a stop, the nib remaining on the paper. Then she added one brief question:

What does it mean, that I am afraid of this?

She thought, but did not write: I am afraid for what it means.

9

Greer showed Tony around the house. He had already admired the virtuoso painted frieze of hill towns and distant watchtowers, stone houses and panoramas of corn-fields, vineyards, olive trees and cypresses that wound in an undulating ribbon around the sitting room, and had identi-fied it – no prizes there – as Mischa's.

'They're all views of and from the Castello,' she told him. 'Mischa did it out of pique one day, right at the beginning when the furniture was still being moved in here and his studio wasn't ready for him. They were still securing the upper floor with steel struts, and he got very stroppy because they wouldn't let him work in there. He just stood on a chair which he moved along as he went, and painted directly on to the wall, without any prior drawing and without hesitation.'

She brought out an album and showed him photos of Mischa at work on the unfinished frieze, up on the chair, back to the camera and wielding his brush like a truncheon. 'He only did it to annoy me, but of course it's wonderful and I love it.'

Tony was being very agreeable today. In her study he whistled at the wall-to-wall, floor-to-ceiling bookshelves, and asked if she'd read them all.

'Greer, you're a real live bookworm. An endangered species. I'm intimidated.'

'We both read a lot. Mischa prefers non-fiction. He jumps around, always has several volumes on the go. You've probably seen them lying face down in the studio.' She watched Tony as she spoke. He was eyeing her ornate writing desk.

'What an exquisite piece.' He rested his hand on the graceful curvilinear design of a side panel. 'Art Nouveau. Who is it by?'

'It's French. By Guimard.'

'Fantastic, huh? I love that grain and patina.'

She had a vision, banished as soon as it arrived, of the smooth, finely grained young hand sliding down the desk and wrenching open the left-hand drawer. It had a delicate little lock. Feminine. Not much of a deterrent at all. She told herself, Tony is only human, he can't see inside the drawer. Those artless blue eyes don't have X-ray properties.

On the bathroom walls he noticed the criss-crossed tiles of volcanic rock and limestone, grey and whey-coloured, with their unpolished, pitted surfaces. The same design of diamond-shaped tiles, dark and pale, was used in the kitchen behind the sink. And he admired the light terracotta floor that paved the whole house in a jumble of shades, roseate and tawny, full of irregularities.

'Each tile is a miniature landscape,' Greer said to him, 'rutted and full of potholes. That is, if you look closely at it.'

She didn't tell him that, sometimes, she did take the time to look closely. She found the Lilliputian landscapes with all their imperfections beautiful and mysterious, suggestive of pilgrimages or struggling journeys through life. She had said as much to Rollo, who never found such an idea ridiculous, who celebrated objects that were idiosyncratic or skewed. Who shared her compulsion to look closely at things. The defects of flawed objects made them more human and therefore more interesting, they were agreed on that.

Greer believed Rollo's penchant for the offbeat and the imperfect was directly linked to his knack of seeing all sides of a question. Mischa was the expert who dealt in certainties. If you could assign colours to an argument or opinion, Mischa would need only black and white. In Rollo's palette and her own, greys and pastel shades would dominate.

Only the other day she and Rollo had talked about the difference between appearance – the face one showed to the world – and the core reality. The discussion was ostensibly about comedians' lives, but had been prompted, she supposed, by the whole idea of biography; the idea that it should even be considered possible to identify useful truths about any life other than one's own. The unstable brew of influences on character and personality. The necessity to look beyond the surface towards the essence, only to confront a hard truth that the essence was itself made up of a multitude of components, and ultimately unknowable.

'At least for us poor *homo sapiensies*,' Rollo had said, 'with our feeble little brainsies.'

Greer was obscurely reminded of this as she preceded Tony into the main bedroom from the hall. He made the observation that almost every room in the house was on a different level. Two or three steps separated each room or passage from the next.

'That's one of the things I particularly enjoy about this house,' Greer said. 'You have to keep remembering to step up or down. It stops you becoming complacent. Especially in the dark.'

'Well, yeah, I guess these houses were put up aeons before ensuites were even a twinkle in a builder's eye.'

As he spoke he was zeroing in on the red chalk drawing to the left of the bedroom door. 'Mischa, right? Younger, but it's unquestionably him.'

She thought, but refrained from saying, well, that is a moot point. Does Mischa also see it as himself, or as someone he is now disconnected from? She wondered whether Tony's knowledge of his subject would ever go far enough to enable him to pose such questions.

He inspected the initials closely, 'G.G. 5.8.1979.' He straightened up. 'Greer Gordon, her mark, right?'

'Right.'

'It's an accomplished drawing. You nailed him. Not just a good likeness, but a character reference.' He stood and appraised the picture, giving it his complete attention in a way she recognised and respected.

'Verity Corbett said you were a fine portraitist. But she didn't have anything of yours to show me, and I hadn't come across any examples of your work at that stage.'

At that stage. What did he mean by that?

'I think I'd like to use this, if it's OK with you? I mean, in the illustrations.'

He wrote something in his pocketbook. She inclined her head and, as she did so, saw him switch on the little recording device he carried everywhere.

'The drawing is dated August five, 1979. Now, would it be around that time that you left Melbourne? When,' his mouth widened in a smile to leaven the words, 'you and Mischa did your famous disappearing act, to the extreme displeasure of Ms V. Corbett?'

Greer had gone past him to the north window. She rested her arms on the broad sill.

'It would have been about that time, yes.'

Tony bent his head again, minutely examining the picture. 'There's something in his expression –'

Triumph, she thought, he's picked it up. It's unmistakeable.

'It wouldn't –?' He looked at her, taking in her body language. She sensed a subtle change in him, a tensing, a whiff of the chase.

'It wouldn't be the actual day, now, would it?' The pitch of his voice kindled a little with excitement. 'Greer, please tell me that you sat down and you made this portrait on the day you ran away.'

The day you ran away. The five words provoked their

own visions, a sequence of imagined pictures in his mind too. She could tell that by looking at him. But they could only be that – imagined, fanciful, all in the mind. His mind. Could they conceivably bear any relation to the pictures in her own? What was the nature of his imagination, anyway?

Her mental pictures bore the seal, the exclusive imprimatur, of memory. They unwound in her mind's eye like a spool of jumpy images from a silent film. Without access to a projector capable of plugging into her mind and throwing those images against the wall, the biographer's pictures could never aspire to be anything more than approximate at best. The likelihood was that they had nothing much in common with the real thing.

Unless Tony questioned her closely, for instance, he would not know that she had, for reasons she did not intend to go into, taken only one case of clothes and personal effects as she took expeditious leave of her former life. He wouldn't know that this piece of luggage was a black tin trunk painted with her father's name, W. R. Gordon, in white capital letters. It had accompanied him to boarding school in the 1930s and then to Palestine during the war. Years later it had been stored in the garage of the mud-brick house in Melbourne she shared with Charlie, and now it lay in the cellar under this stone house in Italy.

Was Tony even aware that if he was striving for an accurate record he had his back to the wall? He might have the general outlines worked out, but he would never have in his grasp the details, the nuances, which gave those mental pictures visual texture and authenticity.

He must know by now he hadn't a hope of getting much out of Mischa. For certain crucial components in the story, Greer was Tony's primary source. She was the wall that he was backed up against, and her inclination was to refrain from supplying all but the most innocuous of those atmospheric details.

On the day she and Mischa left Melbourne for ever, the lowering skies, for instance, had been on their side. The rain held off as the two of them pushed the back seat forwards and crammed Greer's station wagon with the biggest load it had ever carried. They had stacked it to the roof with paintings and gear, obscuring the back windows, and headed up the Hume Highway in the thin light of a wintry morning. This was the road named after the great explorer, the road that pointed north to the sun. Like a couple of truants in a stolen car they had just let it take them. Mischa had driven non-stop and tirelessly, it seemed, for hours.

They did stop once for beer and coffee and for another pressing chore. There were two phone booths back to back at a highway service station. Mischa called Verity and Greer called her sister.

Josie had reacted with explosive relief and indignation. Where on earth was Greer ringing from, because Charlie had rung in the middle of the night, and turned up forty minutes later completely plastered and dishevelled, looking for her, then driven off again in a dreadful state, and Josie was worried stiff. It's quite OK, Greer had assured her breezily, I gave him the slip. We've gone. Scarpered. We're out in the middle of nowhere, on our way to Sydney. I'll get in touch when we have an address.

She hadn't wanted to listen in to Mischa's call to Verity. It had been short but not sweet, Mischa reported. Short and very sour. Verity had been unamused to hear of their departure, and only marginally mollified by Mischa's declaration that she was still his dealer. He would send pictures down from Sydney for the next show, he reassured her, planned for the following February.

'She must have had a fit of the vapours when she realised I wasn't coming back,' Greer had said airily to Mischa.

The sobering effect of Verity's vapours hadn't lasted, in fact it scarcely survived his hanging up the receiver. As soon as they got back in the car she remembered joining in, although Tony might never hear about this and she'd never thought she could sing, as Mischa plunged into his repertoire of songs from Broadway musicals.

We were intoxicated, she thought now. Blind drunk on the effrontery of what we'd got away with. The sheer gall of it. And in my case there was something else going on below the surface, which must have been perilously close to hysteria. I had run away with Mischa under false pretences. I had not yet got away with it at all, and my gall was of an entirely different order.

She became aware of the need to speak in the lengthening silence. Aware too that without her noticing Tony had finished his examination of the red chalk drawing and joined her at the window. He stood quite close, trespassing on her personal space as if to prompt or dislodge her from this reverie. Or, perhaps, to disconcert.

What was it that he had been asking? She retrieved his question with an effort, moved away from him and said, 'So I did, yes. I sketched the portrait on the day we left Melbourne, you're quite right.' Dreamily, as if she had only just remembered.

'The very day you ran away? Oh, boy. I love it.'

She tossed him a crumb. 'It was done in the evening. Before dinner.'

'Where were you? In a hotel?'

He was not to know that the runaways had come to a grinding halt eventually, brought on by exhaustion and Greer's hallucinatory moment. They had wandered into the scrub to pee, she had looked back at the road and seen the car apparently moving along by itself. After that they'd pulled up at the next roadside motel, simply because it was there and had a room with a double bed and was heaven on earth.

'Somewhere on the way to Sydney. God knows where it was. Goulburn maybe. We went out after I'd done the drawing and found a little Chinese restaurant down the road.'

Tony repeated slowly, 'You'd known each other less than a month, you'd seen him for only a few days of that time, and you'd left your husband for him.' He seemed to be ruminating, eyes fixed on the notebook in his hand and not on his dictaphone. 'So, how did that feel?'

'Feel?'

'Yeah, Greer, *feel.*' There was a distinct undertow of amused irritation. His eyes moved from his notes back to the chalk drawing. 'You know, were you stoked? I see you there, a pair of naughty escapologists in your blue station wagon, right, like in a road movie, setting the compass for Sydney. Well, as a departure it wasn't what you'd describe as strictly orthodox, so it had to be a bit of a blast, didn't it?'

He looked at her then, eyebrows raised and eyes bright with – with what, exactly? She was fairly sure it was with irony. Or guile. Or both.

She said, 'Oh, yes, Tony. It was a bit of a blast all right.'

In order to draw Mischa's head she'd almost had to tie him to the bed, which was another thing Tony would certainly never know. It had been well nigh impossible to get him to stay still long enough for her to sketch his face and to keep his hands off her. And to keep her eyes on his face and on the task at hand, and off the rest of him.

For years afterwards, perhaps for always, no Chinese meal would ever taste as delectable as that one in the obscure, dusty little diner that was only a truckies' pit stop, with its red formica-topped tables and plastic chopsticks.

She decided to throw down a small private challenge, secure in the knowledge that her mental film was locked away unprojected, safe from Tony's prying eyes. 'It was rather good, in fact, the Chinese place. Very good, actually.' She let this hang, then added, 'I remember we had Mongolian shredded beef, Szechuan prawns and mermaids' tresses, Confucius-style. It was nothing if not eclectic.'

They had been ravenous. Greer, in particular, was on the point of collapse. It was their first real meal of the day, and they'd eaten and drunk themselves into a stupor. Following this they had returned to the motel, emerged somehow from the stupor and fornicated into oblivion.

In hindsight this binge and her equal part in it struck Greer as a last burst of excess brought on by a mixture of relief and almost unbearable apprehension. Those two ingredients made for a volatile cocktail. Even at the time it had occurred to her that she was living through a highly personalised version of the calm before the storm.

And it was a short-lived calm, inevitably. A day or two later, after they reached Sydney and found somewhere to live, she had summoned every ounce of courage and dropped the bombshell into Mischa's lap.

Greer sat down heavily on the bed. The intensity of this reel of interior pictures, with their graphic, X-rated content, made her suddenly unsteady. Tony perched on the corner of the bed, quite near her again, and scribbled in his notebook. As she expected, her little challenge had passed safely under his radar. She had an uncomfortable suspicion, though, that he was allowing her time to recover.

'So, do you still make portraits?'

And pigs might fly. Far from allowing me time to recover, he's attacking from the left flank.

'No, I don't.'

'You had a flair for it. I mean, a real talent. What made you stop?'

How was this to be answered?

Tony proceded smoothly, as if to divert the question into a statement. 'Of course, he painted you rather obsessively in the early days. That must have taken time.'

This was easier to pick up on. 'Actually, it didn't take much time. Mine, that is. I didn't often have to model for those pictures. They weren't full-face usually, they were more oblique, like glimpses, or reflections.'

'That's true. If they're front-on, your face is mostly concealed by spots of light. Or in shadow. And that brilliant, disturbing group of pictures, the so-called Shadow period, followed directly on from there, didn't it?'

This was the time when Mischa began painting people, usually but not always variations of herself, with elongated shadows that extended upwards into buildings and trees and threatened to overpower their owners. Then figures with intricate, dismembered shadows, reflected like semi-cubist jigsaws in mirrors or on the surface of choppy water. And finally and most hauntingly, shadows that were detached from their owners and seemingly unrelated to them.

'Yes.'

'Do you think they're in any way commentaries on the past? I've wondered a lot about this, if they could be interpreted as being meditations on his former life?'

His delivery was impersonal and academic. She thought, he has reverted to his art critic mode, which is preferable. But it was an uneasy speculation, and one she had made herself.

'Well, you could try asking him that, couldn't you?'

'I did, but he just tells me it's a mistake to look for meanings in pictures. I've tried, oh how I've tried, you don't believe me – as Agnieszka might say.'

She produced a half smile.

'But the extant pictures from the Australian period were all painted either before, or directly after, the time in Sydney?'

It was a sudden strike, without warning. She gave a cursory nod, expecting something further, and marshalling herself. But he seemed to be content to go off on another tack, ruffling his hair with his hand and drawling almost negligently, 'While you did your own thing. Which didn't include making portraits?'

'No, it did not.'

She had spoken sharply, but he showed no reaction to the tone. Now he behaves as if we're having a completely unthreatening dialogue, she thought, about the weather or the price of fish. Now he looks as if butter wouldn't melt in his mouth.

She glanced across at Rollo and Guy's house. The leaves of the Virginia creeper were coming out. In a few days the flecked stone walls would be invisible, hidden by an impenetrable green cloak.

Two could play at this game. She could see a way out.

She said, 'Stopping portrait painting wasn't a conscious

decision. It just evolved, partly because of practicalities, our madly peripatetic life in those early years. After we had left Australia behind.'

And all that Australia implied. She regretted making even this glancing reference, although Tony seemed oblivious. But she had a foothold now, a stepping stone to safer ground.

'We were always travelling, finding places to rent for a while so Mischa could work. And often living in confined spaces, which, if it didn't mean one room, frequently meant us sleeping in one and him working in the other. Not always, of course. In parts of Asia and Greece, for instance, we often had masses of space.'

'And partly because?' He was acute, she had to give him that. And tenacious, when he wanted to be. Well, she had an answer ready for this too.

'I suppose the reality is that it's hard to have two artists under the same roof. I certainly don't mean that he tried to stop me, he wouldn't have –'

He waited.

'He wouldn't have noticed if I was working or not, really.'

He responded to that with an appreciative laugh. She felt a moment's gleam of satisfaction. Tony might be acute, but he wasn't too difficult to deflect. The reasons she had given him had hardly a grain of truth in them. The simple truth was, she had tried, and failed.

She had tried to work, tried hard, and Mischa urged and encouraged her. At the start she had pushed herself to source materials and embark on sketches. Sometimes she picked out individuals with arresting faces and invited them, often in sign language, to sit for her. When these portraits failed she looked elsewhere for subjects, to land-scapes and urban scenes. But there were endless beginnings, and no endings.

For a long time she would never leave their home base without a sketchbook in her bag. One morning, defeated by the accusing pages of half-made figures and marks that followed the faltering path of her concentration and trailed away aimlessly, she carried a notepad and a novel instead. She had packed the sketchbooks away in the bottom of her father's trunk where they remained to this day, down in the cellar.

At the time Greer had told herself: in some people the artistic impulse is fragile. The reasons for its departure are not always subject to logical analysis. They are shifting and ambiguous, as unpredictable as quicksands. This particular impulse has not died, it is quiescent and one day it will return, she had told herself. My heart is not in it, for now. Meanwhile, I will do other creative things instead and wait for it to return. But it had not returned.

A door in the high perimeter fence that enclosed her safe private landscape had eased open a crack. In her scramble to slam it shut Greer had an out-of-body sensation. It was a fleeting glimpse in which she seemed to observe herself playing for time.

'You've got more than two rooms these days,' Tony was saying, 'you could start up again, and with any kind of an even break he still wouldn't notice.'

'I've got the space now but not the time. Although I suppose one can always make that. If the desire is strong enough.'

'One's capable of anything if the desire is strong enough, and that's for sure.'

She left the room ahead of him. It had been a playful remark, light enough and in the overt spirit of their conversation, but it carried an astringent aftertaste that tainted the air.

The phone rang. The caller was Greer's friend Stella Castles, demanding a fix of gossip, and more of the same. Had the young biographer shown up? How was it going? Would he like to meet a dateless and desperate married woman? Stella was overseeing the restoration of a farmhouse on the Umbrian border, while her surgeon husband, Victor, worked at St Thomas' Hospital in London.

Greer took the call in her study, aware of Tony's presence around the corner in the next room, sifting through the boxes on the living room floor. Yes, the biographer had arrived, she confirmed in a low voice. He was right here actually, so she couldn't talk about him now. She supplied the required ration of amused responses to Stella's inventive litany of complaints about builders, plumbers and Victor. They made an arrangement to meet in a week.

Returning, she saw Tony stretched out on the hearth reading newspaper reviews of Mischa's first show.

'Would you tell me,' he asked when she sat down, his caramel voice warmly involved, 'if you'll excuse me trespassing on such an intimate matter, about the day you first met Mischa? Was it anything at first sight?'

'Strong antipathy, if anything,' she'd replied, matching his delivery. He questioned her closely with the tape running, avid for every detail of the encounter.

'It's the little things,' he said, 'the nuances that I crave. The minutiae of it. Take me there. How was the weather?'

That was easy. If he craved the nuances, he could have a few anodyne ones to go on with.

'How did he look? What was he wearing?'

That was easy too.

'You were there alone in the gallery while he hung the pictures. So what did you say to each other?'

She told him about Mischa's singing. He got a big kick out of that.

'"Jerusalem"? A rock version of the English hymn? You're kidding me!'

'He had an aunt who recited English poetry.'

'Ah, the famous great-aunty Olga. Of course.'

Tony knew all about her. They spoke about Mischa's youthful addictions. Blues, swing and Dixie, American musicals and '50s rock 'n' roll. The hoarded vinyl records, scrounged from anywhere with the help of this maiden aunt who shared his enthusiasms, and played on a wind-up gramophone. Some of these tastes persisted while others had waned.

She relaxed a little. Tony seemed to have turned down another road, to have left the subject of the first meeting behind. Mischa's early life was cushy territory. If he wanted her take on the years before she entered the picture, she was more than happy to oblige. She offered him a glass of wine.

Tony responded with some tableaux of Mischa's existence as a student and embryonic artist in Prague in the '60s. It was obvious that he knew about this period in considerably more detail than she did. He had spent time in the country, checking out the scene. Inspecting for himself the tenements and rooming houses Mischa once inhabited. Following up leads, tracking people down.

He'd managed to unearth from forty years ago, he reported with a sidelong look at her, a residual activist or three who remembered Mischa well. Among them were survivors from a couple of scrimmaging factions in the postwar capital. One had been an entrenched group of older intellectuals, the other a collective of young artists who wanted a Western adolescence for themselves and wanted it now. The tribes intersected at times, when young and old found themselves aligned against a common foe.

'Both sides were politically active. I needn't tell you that Mischa was not a prime mover there. He was born political, not. Is that right?'

'And he was a joiner, not.'

'Exactly. How I see it is, he was always a bit of a lone wolf. Kind of a maverick, with a foot in both camps. He hung out when he felt like it, but he was never one of the boys. That detachment gave him a kind of glamour, but it also caused some rancorous feeling.'

Tony's informants had showered him with grim stories of life after the Soviet invasion of 1968. A somewhat ambivalent view, generally speaking, he told Greer, was taken of Mischa's defection.

'Strong emotions are still harboured there, it must be said. Resentment, jealousy, envy. Especially the last two. He got to shoot through while they were left wading in deep shit. They stuck with it, so now they're holier than him, was the general line. That they could have taken the same escape route as he did tended not to be given much airtime. And nor did his reasons for leaving.'

He broke off and looked at her, eyebrows raised. 'I'm sorry, Greer, am I droning on? Please feel free to tell me to shut up if I start lecturing. I have a bad habit of getting carried away by my subject.'

She thought, this boy has a complete armoury of insinuating, charm-school smiles. That one was ruefully bashful.

'Don't worry about it. This is a house where you can feel free to get carried away any old time. After all, Mischa's your prime suspect, isn't he? Not me.' She flashed a brilliant smile of her own, and saw him momentarily disconcerted.

He bounced back, laughed. 'Right on, then. Well, I guess along with not being political or a joiner he wasn't very into confiding in other people. He kept his reasons close to his chest, so many of them were taken by surprise when he bolted. There was a lot of – speculation.'

She caught the gamey whiff of a bait being thrown into the temporarily placid waters between them. He was fishing for something here. She made a noncommittal sound.

'At any rate, he was the only one of his pals to get out at that time. And my impression was that the stayers were too in love with the cloak and dagger stuff by then. They were outlaws after the Russian tanks arrived. Ferals, with their own incredible underground network. Kind of, you know, a socio-political forerunner of the internet? Talking with them, you could see they had a real nostalgia for that time, in spite of everything. Or maybe,' he caught her eye again, 'it was just the routine nostalgia people have for their misspent youth.'

The lure bobbed below the surface of the water, a sassy red feather.

One of Tony's contacts had put him on to Mischa's formidable elder sister, Grete. Their parents were long dead, but Grete, now in her mid-seventies, lived on in Karlovy Vari.

'Doesn't speak much more than a half-dozen words of English and still managed to scare the hell out of me. She suffers from an odd bunch of ailments – acute intimidatory syndrome coupled with verbal diarrhoea, and on top of that a triple, or should that be a quadruple, humour bypass. Chalk and cheese, Grete and Mischa. You haven't met with her, right?'

Greer shook her head. He must know she had not, or he wouldn't be talking in this curiously tactless way.

'Her browbeaten son translated for me. She was indignant that her celebrated baby brother had never been back to see them. Said the family felt abandoned.'

Was it her imagination, or had there been a faint emphasis there?

Grete had put Tony in touch with a very old retired schoolmaster whose voice, when he could be induced to speak about Mischa, still quivered with aggravation.

'He told me some good stories though,' Tony said. 'Your man was a full-on nightmare student, you'll be amazed to hear. I think the thing was he always did what *he* wanted, which usually was to make pictures, instead of what they wanted. I don't mean he was a really delinquent guy or anything like that. He just –'

'Preferred to please himself?' She had to smile.

'And it drove his parents and teachers completely and utterly bananas, through his entire childhood. And beyond as well, am I right?' He flashed her a grin. 'He had no time for authority figures telling him what to do, basically. Regarded them as muscling in on his turf and making irrelevant demands. But then, on that score, it makes no odds if we're talking sixty years ago, today or tomorrow, does it?'

These were cheeky signals that they were on the same wavelength, sharing mischief.

She opted to play ball. 'It definitely does not.'

'So does he talk to you much,' he went on, 'about the old days? His old life?'

'Not at all.' It struck her, suddenly, where he was heading. He likes to lull me, she thought, before he strikes. She repeated, as if to stonewall him, 'Mischa never dwells on the past. It simply doesn't interest him. Especially nostalgia for misspent youth. I actually believe he finds nostalgia nauseating.'

'Sorry, I wasn't talking about nostalgia here. Anything but, I guess. I mean, you know, past relationships. Significant predecessors.'

She toyed with the idea of feigning ignorance, but his intonation was unmistakeably – as Rollo might say – site-specific.

'You mean Elsa.'

'Elsa Montag, yes.'

'Did you speak to her?'

'Yeah, I met with her. She wasn't too hard to locate. Although I admit, to give the disapproving Grete her due, she wasn't the one who pointed me in her direction.'

Doubtless there would have been plenty of volunteers happy to point him that way. Elsa Montag was the young woman Mischa had left behind in March of 1969, when he skied across the border into Austria.

'I got on to her via her former husband, actually, Pavel. You can always count on a cuckolded politician to hold a grudge.'

'Her husband's a politician now?' She realised her mistake immediately.

'Still is, yeah. He's a survivor. It's Machiavellian how those guys manage to dig themselves in. Old Pavel Montag's quite a big shot in the government these days. Mischa never mentioned his little brush with the underworld of politics Pavel-style?'

She said shortly, to terminate this, 'I wouldn't remember if he had. Mischa loathes politics and we haven't mentioned Elsa or Pavel Montag for years. I told you, he doesn't like to talk about the old days, or about her.'

She could have added, we don't talk about sensitive

subjects too much, I suppose. I'm used to it. Quite comfortable with it, to use one of your phrases. From the start, neither of us wanted to revisit the past. We didn't see the need for mutual psychoanalysis. We communicated very well in other ways.

10

In his bedroom Tony wielded the iron on a pair of brown moleskins. The rust-coloured shirt he planned to team with them, on which he had just done a touch-up job, hung over the back of a chair. As he ironed the crease out of the trousers he spoke into his dictaphone, which was balanced on the end of the ironing board.

'I knew I had to tread on eggshells with her, but I got such a buzz when I found she'd done the drawing the day they made their getaway, that very night, I nearly got ahead of myself and trashed the whole thing. I had to backtrack quick smart.

'She's incredibly nervous and jumpy. Like, she'll be saying virtually nothing, giving one-word answers, then out of nowhere she'll come up with a heap of superfluous detail. All that guff about the dishes they had at the Chinese restaurant their first night on the road. I'm kind of feeling my way with her, approaching things and then backing off a bit, and then having another shot from a different angle.'

He shook the trousers out, examined them and switched off the iron.

'When I introduced the Shadow period she shied right away. She wasn't about to go there, no way. But those pictures have to've been made as a direct reaction to Sydney. And there's the whole question of her portraits too, why she didn't pursue her art. She wasn't going there either. She'd concocted some half-assed story about it being too difficult, what with the travelling and Mischa and life in general.

'She wasn't so averse to talking about his past, although she couldn't tell me anything I didn't already know. She knew about Elsa but had clearly never heard of Pavel Montag. So she's no help on that score. Interesting he didn't tell her the whole story there though.

'It's a helluva grind talking to her. Frustrating. I get stuff, but it's monochrome, it's all dry and pedestrian. I can see all these other things going on in her head and I can't get through to them.'

'You're saturated. Why didn't you take your coat?'

Mischa came stamping in from the terrace outside the kitchen, wet trousers clinging to his legs, hair dripping onto his shoulders and trickling down his neck. He carried a lantern torch with a powerful beam.

'I came to get some food. Then I've got to go back.'

She rubbed his hair with a towel. He submitted to this with his eyes closed.

'If you had a mobile phone you could have called me.' This was a recurrent theme. 'Take off these sodden things first and put on something dry.' She knew this would be ignored, but had a compulsion to say it. His dislocated expression was familiar. He was in another world.

He surprised her by opening his eyes and saying, 'I'm sick of Tony. He's not here, is he?'

'Of course he isn't. Roly and Guy borrowed him for dinner.'

'How much longer is he around?'

'He hasn't been around long. It was you who wanted him to come.' She felt a sharp spurt of anger.

He grunted. 'That was a major mistake, maybe. He talks all the time and prevents me from working.'

'Nothing prevents you from working. It's nearly seven o'clock and you're still going back to work.'

'If I didn't have all his interruptions I would be finished and we could have a proper dinner.' Greer bit off a retort. It was pointless now. He stood brooding over the flames, his clothes steaming. Now and then he looked at her.

Greer took a bowl of thick and garlicky bean soup from the fridge and heated it in the microwave. She put together a quick salad and set it on the table. Mischa's idea of a proper dinner was meaty and substantial, two courses at least. But if he was grappling with something, and it came to a choice between food and work, work would always prevail. She knew that the something might be as modest as the precise placement of two or three brushstrokes.

She selected a bottle of red. He pulled the cork and poured two glasses. They sipped in silence and warmth as the windows rattled against an onslaught of rain.

A high wind had barrelled across the valley soon after Tony had taken his leave. She had stoked the fire, then sat and watched the cold front looming, a bank of nimbus with a glowering, anvil-shaped storm cloud in the vanguard.

'Did Tony tell you he found out where Elsa Montag was living?'

Mischa shrugged. 'That had to happen.'

'He said he found her through her ex-husband. I don't think you ever told me Pavel Montag was a politician.'

'He wasn't. He was on the edge of politics trying to get in. He was a nasty piece of work. I didn't want to speak his name one more time.'

He seemed unmoved, drizzling olive oil and grating mounds of parmesan into his soup, and hoeing into it.

'Tony said you had a skirmish with him. What happened?'

'He threatened to have me eliminated from the planet.'

'*Eliminated*? You mean killed?' It was so unlike Mischa to use a euphemism that she realised he must have read it in a note or a letter. He nodded indifferently and went on eating.

'Could he really have done that? Was that why you left

Elsa?' She found this second question deeply important.

Mischa looked up from his bowl. 'He was capable of that. He was quite a raving madman. But mainly it was a very good excuse to get the hell out of there, and I took it.' She was familiar with the way he could suddenly switch on and give her his entire attention. His eyes, expressive, intensely serious, met and held hers.

The way he blazed into a state of full alert always made her think of an electrical rush, a power surge. She knew that in spite of appearances he was never unaware of what was going on. While he tended to toy with many conversations in a desultory fashion, what she called his spontaneous combustion, a habit of emerging abruptly from apparent detachment and engaging fierily with the subject under discussion, could be dramatic for those who weren't expecting it. When he had got something off his chest he was just as liable to disengage again.

As she was considering what he had just said he added, 'Elsa was temporary, like the others until you. It was a practice relationship that had run its course and was driving me crazy. I told her not to leave him but she did. That was the important thing. You know all that part.'

This was quite true. One of their fervent, cathartic conversations in the car on the way up to Sydney had been about Elsa. It sounded like a clear case of entrapment, and Greer had already known, and known within minutes of meeting him, that Mischa was not one to be trapped.

She asked, 'Does Tony know about the death threat?'

'Probably. He's good at digging.' He looked down again briefly. 'One or two people knew about it. I didn't order them to shut up when I left.' He shrugged his shoulders. 'It doesn't matter, it's a good story, if the lawyers don't muck it up.'

'Did Tony say anything to you about Elsa, how she was?'
He shook his head.

'But didn't you ask if her husband had taken her back?'

'I didn't want to know. I doubt if he did. I can read it in the book if I have to.'

'You don't mind?'

'Mind what?' He had subsided again.

'That it'll all come up.' She felt the well-known exasperation rising, exacerbated by more complex recent feelings. And by irritation that she should still feel exasperated, or even surprised, after all these years. 'She's bound to say angry things, very angry things.'

'So, she slags me off. Maybe I deserve it. It makes the book more interesting.'

'But shouldn't you at least try to find out what she's told him?' She put down her spoon, feeling anxiety building. 'He may be unaware of the emotional blackmail. She could have said anything, exaggerated, made it sound worse. She could have lied and said you promised to marry her. I think you need to put your side.'

Mischa reached across the table for her hand and covered it with his own. 'Whatever she says will be true in her eyes. My side was to get out of there fast. If I didn't get out of there, I didn't meet you. So don't worry about it.'

Worrying won't change anything. It was an ingrained mantra and most of the time she welcomed it, together with his attitude to life: straightforward, uncomplicated, the polar opposite of neurotic. It could also strike her as maddening, illogical and simplistic. That was the flip side. There were times in the past when she had thrown things at him.

She said, 'I didn't ask him either. I don't know why I didn't, I would have liked to hear about her, how she was. He must think we're very odd.'

They continued to eat without talking. Greer thought, Mischa's expression hasn't altered a jot. And yet his mind is not empty, it's sharply focused. It's just that the focus is elsewhere. He has this uncanny ability to carry on a conversation using his peripheral vision, mentally speaking. He husbands his resources. I suspect this is quite unconscious, and a way of conserving his energies. I suppose I should mention that to Tony.

She had one more go at the subject, without much confidence.

'Tony didn't volunteer any details either, then, to you or me. Don't you think that's odd too?'

Mischa had speared a lump of bread and was using it to mop up the remains of the soup. 'What of it? He plays his game, we play ours.'

He went on steering the bread like a racing car around his bowl. Greer conceded, as she had done countless times before: even when he's driving on autopilot using the periphery of his mind, I should never underestimate him.

Mischa went back to the studio, rugged up this time in a hooded rain jacket lined with sheepskin. She had begun to run a bath when the phone rang. The answering machine was not switched on and she was tempted to let the phone ring out, thinking it might be Stella again wanting the low goss she hadn't managed to get last time. The goss on the biographer.

But this time it was Rollo, slightly out of sorts and out of breath, inviting her to dinner post-haste. He had lined up five friends to meet the biographer: Larry and June, a Bostonian academic couple renting a holiday villa up the road for Easter, and three unaccompanied women, Barbara, Dottie and Benedetta. The Yanks had just called – right at the last *minute*, darling, can you believe it? What if we were having *portions* instead of the lamb – to ask if they could drag along their teenage son. Rollo, a stickler for proprieties such as balancing the sexes at table, was put out. Could she bear to make up the numbers?

'Well, I would, Roly, but we've eaten early. Mischa's just gone back to the studio.'

'Just a skerrick on the plate, darling. We can pretend you've got an eating disorder. Anorexia, or bulimia nervosa.' Rollo liked to read the lurid covers of celebrity magazines at the local newsagent.

'Honestly, I couldn't eat another thing. And I'm tired.

I seem to have had Tony coming at me all day.'

'I promise not to put you next to Tony. He'll be up the other end, you won't have to talk to him at all. June and Larry are good value, you'll like them. And you always enjoy seeing Benedetta and Barbara, don't you? And you love Dottie.'

'But I was about to fall into a bath.' It sounded plaintive.

'All right then, we'll compromise. Have a nice quick bath and then pop over.' She heard the hope in his voice.

She said with a spark of mischief, 'But the whole point of the dinner was to talk about Mischa and me in our absence.'

'Did His Majesty leak that? He's so mendacious these days. Well, and wasn't he always? Listen, the clincher is, we're having Maria Paola's chestnut cake for pudding.' He paused for effect, and then added in a meaningful and discernibly crafty tone, 'It might be wise to keep a weather eye on young Tony.'

Drinks were copious at Rollo's dinners. Guy was a dab hand at cocktails, deceptively strong and geared to get the evening off to a flying start. Wine flowed like water. Conversations were likely to become indiscreet.

How might Tony behave? How incautiously might he talk under such persuasive circumstances?

Greer made a quick decision. She would join them in time for the main course.

'Don't worry, I'll make sure we've finished talking about you by the time you get here,' Rollo was saying reassuringly as she hung up.

She remembered the bath. It was still running. She reached it just as the water was about to surge over the rim, and plunged her hand down to let some out. There should have been a chain attached to the old-style plug, but it had come adrift last summer and neither she nor Mischa, who in spite of occasionally still making his own easels was no handyman, had got around to fixing it.

Her hand and arm were scalded painfully red up to the

elbow from the hot water. Mischa always professed to be horrified at the depth and heat of her baths. She made a mental note to get Agnieszka's husband, Angelo, to come and attend to this and a few other chores, as she added some expensive vanilla and mandarin bath cream from a bottle brought by Stella on her last visit. She decided to wash her hair as well.

As she expected, Mischa was still at work in the studio when she emerged. She wrote a note for him. Outside, the rain continued unabated, slamming in gusty squalls against the windows. She hurried to close the bedroom shutters. Smudges of light glimmered from the house across the courtyard: the lights of Rollo and Guy's kitchen and dining room, where the dinner was certainly in full swing.

Tony would be in place at one end of the table, leaning back sociably in an armchair, legs crossed perhaps, his fair skin flushed from the wine and his blond hair boyishly tousled. Greer fancied she could hear the strains of a violin carried by the wind, and then a burst of laughter, fading into the night like a shower of sparks.

She started to dry her hair. She had a powerful urge to monitor Tony's behaviour, to inhibit him with her presence.

Guy was in the process of topping up Tony's glass. Everyone was in agreement: the '99 Brunello was a delectable drop. Only a month ago the *Financial Times*' Jancis Robinson had described it as 'beguiling' and likened a good Brunello to semi-dried plums. But then, as Guy let them know, rhapsodic wine writers had linked Brunellos in recent years with a range of other flavours such as vanilla and morello cherries, licorice, marzipan and dried fruit. The nose of a fine specimen might carry whiffs of pipe tobacco and sandalwood and, yet more resourcefully, nuances of the forest floor.

They were a convivial party, enclosed by curtains and shutters against the elements. Church candles of every shape and size were lined up along the dining table and dresser, throwing a benign, painterly glow over the room and its occupants. The room verged on overheated from Rollo's well-seasoned fire that had roared away all afternoon. On the hearth the pugs lay splayed, impervious to the ravishments of Samuel Barber's violin concerto (selected in deference to the four Americans present).

Rollo had seated Tony between Benedetta, a local potter in her early thirties, and Barbara, a fifty-ish Oxford don with a dancer's posture who knew more, his host informed Tony, than any living soul about the Italian Renaissance. Possibly even more than anyone here at the Castello.

Corbino. Now where did that originate, Barbara had enquired politely. Tony explained that his paternal grandfather had been the archetypal penniless immigrant from Naples who'd made quite good in Brooklyn, before the next generation blew it.

Opposite Tony was the dowager Lady Dorothy Swannage, a well-upholstered and feisty old friend of Rollo's vintage. He introduced her as a collapsed Red and lapsed socialite.

'With, let's face it, dear, an increasing number of prolapsing promontories,' she said jovially, before Tony could respond. 'The descent into dementia is such a bugger, isn't it, Roly?'

'Don't ask me, Dottie, because I know nothing.'

Guy murmured in Tony's ear, 'He wishes.'

Leaning over Tony's shoulder, Guy was contriving to pour wine very slowly into his glass. 'Don't you be taken in by that pathetic, hangdog manner of Dorothy's. It's entirely spurious. She's a professional serial widow with a gimlet eye and unerring judgement, aren't you, Dottie? What's the current body count?'

With the arrival of the minestrone the conversation had turned to Mischa's biography.

'Is there anything you could imagine discovering about a person,' Dottie included in this the Bostonian Larry, an Am. Lit. professor and recent Hemingway biographer, 'that was so horribly bad that even you would hesitate to share it?'

'It's the sly little touches, isn't it?' Guy addressed the table. 'The "even yous". Don't you just love the way she does that?' Dottie flapped her napkin, to laughter.

'In principle I think I'd have to say no.' Larry, as Tony's senior, pre-empted him. 'Given, I'm compelled to say but hate to say it, today's prurient climate. Mind you, all my subjects to date have shrugged off their mortal coils. It might well be a significantly different story, writing about someone who was still very much with us.'

He glanced at Tony for confirmation.

Tony shrugged. 'I can't offhand think of any stuff I wouldn't use. Of course, other living people might be affected, which means there's libel laws to duck. But, hey, isn't truth the best defence? Even the hottest defamation attorneys find it hard to argue with that.'

'But what if, Tony, what if you disinterred a thing –' Rollo looked towards the ceiling, then in the direction of Greer's house, and ground to a halt. He caught Guy's vigilant eye.

Guy was on the ball. 'What if you uncovered a seriously gruesome secret? One that could wreak havoc if revealed. Would you feel it was profoundly incumbent upon you to spread it abroad?'

'He can't answer that.' Larry and June, husband and wife, were in rare agreement on this. It was an impossible question, far too vague. Be more specific, they urged. What kind of a secret? Whose lives?

When there was no response Benedetta spoke up. 'Perhaps you can discover that Mischa has another secret family living in another town?'

The others overrode Rollo's objection that this was too risibly far-fetched to be a realistic moral dilemma. Tony took up Benedetta's suggestion. He spoke rapidly, crossing points off on his fingers.

'Right, let's look at the pros and cons here. Pros are the

obvious value of this juicy info to the biography, the new light it sheds on Mischa's character, all these fresh leads to check out. Cons would be the negative effect on Gigi if she didn't know, ditto the effect on the other family, the strong probability of putting the subject – Mischa – terminally off-side, and that goes for other close friends who'd been left out of the knowledge loop. Like for instance,' he surveyed the table, 'you guys. OK, so,' he paused, 'do I use it?'

He grinned at them. 'You bet. But I'd keep it under wraps until I'd got all the other stuff I needed first.'

'In case of reprisals from us guys?'

'Right on, Rollo. You might retaliate by drying up on me.'

Benedetta said, 'And if he is having a big affair with somebody a long time ago, and the husband of this woman never knows about it?'

'I think you can confidently assume the husband of this woman is in for a surprise.'

'It's never going to happen, Tony. Just think of all the schadenfreude we're going to miss out on,' Rollo lamented, 'just because Mischa's so spotlessly clean. It's enough to make you weep.'

Larry and June's son, Colin, who looked about fourteen and as serious as his father, had been following this. Now he asked, 'What if it was something worse? Like Mischa had murdered someone or something? Or he was a serial killer?'

Tony's laugh was the loudest.

'Good one, Colin. Well, I wouldn't be above using that. Whoopee! Think of the sales.'

'But what if he'd killed a really, really bad guy? And if he was found out now his career would be trashed and he'd be put in prison?'

June and Larry smiled with parental pride.

'Now there *is* a curly one, Colin.' Rollo was keenly engaged. 'Do we turn a blind eye or do we airily trash Mischa's career?'

'Like, say, the guy he killed had been a terrorist.' There

was no stopping Colin now. 'Or he was a Gestapo torturer, an *Ubersturmbahnfuhrer*.'

'Then I think I'd happily reveal the murder, and rely on the expertise of Mischa's crack legal team to get him off,' Tony said.

'Now, hang on.' Rollo's elbows were on the table, chin on his hands. 'Aren't we being too easy on Tony, Colin? The murderee doesn't have to be the full monty of depravity. As long as he's a bit of a stinker, that's all we need.'

He looked at Tony. 'What do you reckon? Is it curtains for Mischa?'

'Sure it is. This is his life story, you can't expect me to sugar-coat it. If he killed someone, whether that guy was a Nazi or the neighbour from hell, the truth will out.'

Dottie smacked him on the arm. 'You pitiless man.'

'I'm afraid so, Dottie. In that scenario, he goes right down the gurgler.'

'And the book soars into the bestseller lists.' June clapped her hands. 'Larry, honey, eat your heart out.'

'Of course, there's no reason why Mischa's artistic reputation should suffer,' Barbara observed dryly. 'One might confidently assume it could only be enhanced by the scandal.'

Rollo digested this. 'So, everybody's interests are served. Mercenary as well as artistic. You've got carte blanche then, haven't you, Tony?' He added, 'Thank you, darling,' as the soup bowls were cleared away by Violetta, a self-possessed sixteen-year-old from the village, one of Maria Paola's daughters.

Tony protested that his interests were at least as artistic as Mischa's and way less mercenary.

Colin's brow was still furrowed. 'But what if he'd got away with killing an ordinary person, a nice guy even, or a woman, and he would be tried for murder in America in a state that has the death penalty?'

This, they had to agree, was something of a different ball game. Tony prevaricated. Larry pointed out long-windedly that in the United States the vast majority of death-row inmates were, regrettably, poor and black. The sad truth was that it wasn't your guilt or innocence that determined your fate, it was the colour of your face and the price of your lawyer.

'Mischa's a rich and famous white dude, Colin,' Tony summed up. 'He'd be laughing.'

'All the way to the bank, and so would you, Tony.' June laughed herself, and stroked her son's crewcut hair. He looked morose, taken aback by his parents' cynical assessment of the unfairness of things.

'What good timing, darling.' Rollo beamed. 'Now we're the full complement. I do like to be symmetrical. It's my only weakness.'

Greer ducked through the door in a cold swirl of umbrella and rain, just as the lamb was being carried to the sideboard to be carved by Guy. After the flurry of greetings, kisses and introductions Rollo seated her between him and Larry, who promptly appropriated her. She was in the wine game, wasn't she? He had just read a provocative article on women winemakers. He sought her views. Did she agree with its argument that they brought a feminine sensibility to bear on the finished product, or was this a sexist premise?

Rollo took advantage of this to signal to Tony. 'Come and help me choose some more music.'

The B. & O. hi-fi, streamlined and top of the line, stood on a sideboard around the corner. The wall above it was stacked with shelves of CDs. Rollo went for a boxed set.

'These nice '30s jazz ladies came last week. Let's have them, shall we? Guy got them off the internet. He's very good at the internet, I can't do it at all.'

He inserted the disc without a pause. 'Now, Tony, what about the little people on the sidelines?' The question was muffled by Ethel Waters singing 'Shake That Thing'.

'Excuse me?'

'I can understand your being keen to tip Mischa in the

poo, but what about the innocent bystanders? You know the ones, they're all over the t-shirts in Covent Garden. "Don't blame me, I'm only an innocent bystander".' Rollo chuckled into Tony's ear.

Tony claimed he still didn't get it.

'The poor unfortunates caught up in Mischa's slipstream. Will you take the same merciless attitude towards them?'

'Are you referring to yourself, Rollo?'

Rollo looked shocked. 'Oh, you can say anything you like about me. Or Guy. Within reason, and as long as it's sycophantic, I don't mind at all. And you don't even have to be sycophantic about Guy. Dear me, no, I'm referring to Mischa's nearest and dearest.'

'That's only Greer, isn't it? As far as we know. Gigi, I mean.' Tony gave an involuntary glance over his shoulder. Greer was not in his line of sight.

'Yes, I know who you mean. Gigi and Greer are two facets of the same complex woman.'

'I'm afraid in a biography, pragmatism's the order of the day. You can't afford to be sentimental. Gigi, well, her story's arguably as important as his.'

'Why? Because Mischa's lean pickings?'

'Because she's a central spoke in his wheel.'

'She's the pivot of his wheel, Tony.'

'Right.' Tony veered away from the older man's gaze, in which there was a discomfiting cast. 'You'd prefer I took a chivalrous attitude to my female talent.'

'Oh, very much so. I'm a sucker for the chivalry, from way back. Call me old-fashioned, but if we're talking cads, Tony, I'll take the gentlemanly bugger every time.'

The tone was flippant but the eyes fixed on Tony were speculative and assessing. Rollo put an effective end to the exchange by leading the way back to the table, where the chat was in full flight. Biography was making a comeback. It had already edged out women winemakers, and threatened to overpower Barbara's rearguard action of Muriel Spark versus Iris Murdoch.

Apart from any more dubious qualities, the biography would be lovely to look at, wouldn't it, Dorothy Swannage said to Tony as he returned to his seat.

Sure, there'd be pages of pics and hardly any words, Tony declared, with a humorous nod in Greer's direction. He wanted every work mentioned in the text to be illustrated.

'Gigi knows,' he said emphatically, 'that I've done nothing else for months on end except hunt down pictures and get the go-aheads from museums and galleries. Not to mention the private owners. They change hands over the years: works you really want go missing, trails go cold. It's been a long investigative haul, I can tell you.'

Larry got the gist of this and turned to Greer. 'I trust he already secured the artist's permission to use the works. That can be a legal and logistical minefield for the unwary.'

'Oh, I think Mischa just consented to anything Tony asked him. Didn't he, Tony?'

She glanced his way. The vigilant blue eyes were already on her, as she had known they would be. There was nothing wrong with Tony's hearing. He seemed well able to follow two conversations at once. Three, if you counted Ella Fitzgerald. His head was swaying along with Dottie's in time with the music.

'Good point, Larry. Yeah, I'm happy to say we cut a deal way back. Mischa gave me the green light to use whatever I could get.' Now he was also contributing to his end of the table's popularity poll of jazz songs and singers.

'He can't renege on the deal if he takes exception to anything you write, Tony?' Larry winked at Greer to signal that this was a joke.

'No way. It's safely signed in visible ink.'

'I'm a bit on the surprised side,' Rollo joined in, 'that London and New York didn't pull rank and insist on a right of veto.' He turned to Greer ostentatiously and raised his voice. 'As an insurance policy against Tony, darling. So they could take exception to anything and everything he writes.'

She shook her head. 'Oh, there's no insurance policy against Tony. Tony is an act of God.'

They appreciated that, and so, she saw, did he. His eyes rested on her for a moment, before he looked to the heavens laughingly. She thought, I'm at the mercy of this young man, and Rollo thinks he is ruthless.

'The d'lovely Marty,' Guy remarked, with a sigh that suggested reminiscence.

Rollo pursed his lips. 'And la Isa-bella figura.'

Greer explained for everyone's benefit, 'Mischa's dealers.'

'Mischa's terribly top-drawer dealers,' Tony amplified. 'Martin d'Avery in London and Isabella Jay in New York. There was some power play along those lines, Rollo. In the end, I'm glad to say, and under pressure from the publisher and from Mischa himself, they caved in. I guess they envisioned they'd get a better book if they gave me a free hand.'

Pressure from Mischa? Greer thought this was highly unlikely. Had Tony meant to say that? She took a covert look at him. As she had imagined, he was leaning back, the epitome of relaxed sociability. She thought, but everything he says is deliberate.

'A better book, as in less constrained,' Larry was agreeing sagely.

'It was Mischa who made Martin, you know that, don't you, Tony?' Rollo waggled his empty glass at Guy. 'Marty wasn't at all top drawer before. He was an underdog, very bottom drawer. Streetwise, though, with sharp instincts and a good eye. He snaffled Mischa, back in the early '80s, and showed him in Pimlico before the Cork Street boys and girls could get their claws on him, and he eventually topped the charts in the chest of drawers stakes. That's when Marty got to be a top dog and changed into a d'Avery. He wasn't a d apostrophe at all before, he was just plain Avery. Not many people know that.'

'Tony knows that, you silly old fart, and you're drinking too much.' Guy slid a bottle down the table towards him with a show of reluctance. 'You can tell when he's had too many, he states the obvious, mixes his metaphors and never gets to the point.'

Everyone looked amused except Dorothy Swannage, who swatted Guy with her napkin. 'Oh, stop it, you dreadful man.'

'Don't worry, Dottie. He's only trying to ruffle my feathers, and it annoys him when he can't. But it's all water off this ducky's back.' Rollo did indeed look supremely unruffled. He sliced into an artichoke heart with obvious relish. 'Yes, Mischa's always had a soft spot for underdogs. Well, you only have to look at Tony. He can confirm that, can't you, Tony?' He gave Greer a stealthy pat as they all laughed.

'Mischa's stayed with the d'lovely Marty ever since,' Rollo went on, 'forsaking all others.' He put on a playful look. 'Mischa's a paragon of brand loyalty, you have to admire him for that.'

'It's laziness. He can't be bothered, unlike you,' said Guy. '*He* changes dealers like other people change their knickers,' he continued airily to the others. 'He's a sucker for the flavour of the month – always thinks they're going to be more elitist and sexy. When he gets stung for even more ridiculous conditions and loony commissions than the previous lot, the old Pavlovian response comes into play and he starts putting out his surreptitious little feelers again.'

Dorothy's protective antennae quivered. To defuse the personal, had Tony had to *do* anything in particular to capture this biography, she wondered. She was interrupted by Rollo. What Mischa had done to deserve it was more to the point.

Tony was self-deprecating in his appointed role as one of Mischa's underdogs. He hoped he was going the way of Martin d'Avery, but he confessed that he had started his working life as a hack in an advertising agency.

'I suppose you can draw on the same skills in a bio,' Rollo mused. 'It's like flogging burgers, isn't it, Larry? Only you have to flaunt the naughty carbs and bad cholesterol instead of the good bits.'

Before Larry could compose a response his wife chimed

in, 'Whatever happened to the idea of a scholarly telling of a life, as opposed to the cynical sensationalism that passes for it these days? No frills, no unsubstantiated revelations, just the plain old facts speaking for themselves?'

She added with a boisterous laugh, 'When Larry goes down that unfashionable route he invariably gets written off as irrelevant, don't you, honey?'

Her husband looked annoyed. Dottie Swannage cut in, 'But we don't know what species of biography Antony is writing yet, do we? It might be ever so scholarly and squeaky clean. Do set our minds at rest.' She gave Greer a motherly smile.

'I'm not sure I know that myself, yet,' Tony said.

This provoked a rumble of disbelief around the table.

'I mean, until I've finished my work here I can't tell exactly where it's heading. Researching a biography's a bit like trawling with a net on the seabed. You sweep up shoals of useless little fish you have to throw back, but once in a while you catch a big guy, and that throws a whole new light on everything.'

He's talking to me, Greer thought, although he directed this with perfect impartiality at everyone. There's an undercurrent of something here. It couldn't be apology, surely.

'Do you mean big as in dolphin or big as in shark?' June asked.

Guy rode over her. 'He means big as in killer whale.' He contrived an expiatory moment with Rollo. 'You have to admit Aggie's lamb leaves your tripe for dead.'

Larry said reprovingly, 'Tony's right. I've always felt the research and the writing discover your pathway for you. Where a biographer places him or herself in relation to the material is critical. I think of myself as a sculptor, chipping away at a block of marble. I chip and whittle away at the surrounding obfuscation until the free-standing subject emerges. It's a gradual process, and only imperceptibly do I realise who it is I'm dealing with. The cut of his or her jib, if you will.'

His wife rolled her eyes. Rollo wasn't having any of it

either. 'I'm sorry, you two,' he nudged Greer again under the cover of the table, 'but all this waffle about trawlers and whittling away just won't do. We're not that easily fobbed off. We need to be reassured that Tony's bio is going to be scandalous and defamatory, and if not, why not?'

'Rollo, if you know something I don't about Mischa, particularly if it's even remotely scandalous, I'm trusting that you'll share it with me and Gigi.' Tony's eyes fluttered at them. 'That's right, isn't it, Greer?'

'You, me and the rest of the world, you mean,' she said.

Violetta carried in strawberries and a cake, Rollo's treat, made in her mother's restaurant from chestnut flour and studded with a pattern of pinenuts and dried fruit.

Rollo took advantage of its reception and ceremonious cutting to confide, 'I don't know, darling. He mightn't have anything incriminating after all. We might have got off unscathed. What do you think?'

'She looked good, long winter skirt and she'd done her hair differently. A bit more around the face. There was a touch more restraint after she arrived. Before she came they were wetting themselves to hear if I'd got anything on Mischa.' Tony had his feet propped on the table he was using as a desk, his face close to the dictaphone.

'And Rollo almost lost sphincter control in his anxiety to find out if I'd got anything on her. They tried to camouflage their seething curiosity under the guise of discussing whether there should be any limits to biographical indiscretion. I was tempted to hand over Elsa Montag, which I guess they haven't heard about because no one said anything, but on balance I thought she was better kept in reserve.

'Also, in spite of their mad rush to let me know they have no loyalties where the biography is concerned, I get a distinct whiff of too much protestation. Rollo and Guy might well consider something like the Elsa thing as like a family secret. OK, maybe, to be written down, but not gossiped about with a bunch of strangers.'

He unscrewed the cap off a litre bottle of mineral water and took a long swig.

'They all drink like there's no tomorrow. Bottles uncorked to breathe, and lined up, and Guy fetching more from the cellar. Great wines, of course, and food. Rollo's treasures everywhere, like being in an Aladdin's cave. And everything bathed in candlelight, an amber glow, like in a Merchant Ivory movie. They partied on till half one having a high old time, and the couple only left then because their kid had been asleep at the table for the last two hours. Dottie Swannage was legless.'

I'll walk you to your house in case you get lost, Guy had said to Tony, but Rollo had overheard and overruled. Not now he wouldn't, he would take Dottie upstairs, where the blue room was freshly made up. He added, sotto voce in Guy's ear, that the dear girl was pickled, she'd only just got over her third hip replacement, remember, and a broken leg on top of it she did not need. Getting Dottie upstairs had been a complicated and time-consuming manoeuvre that kept Guy constructively occupied for quite some time.

Tony emptied the rest of the water into a glass, spilling some. He wiped it off the table carefully with his handkerchief.

'They're incredibly close, in each other's pockets, in this incestuous little commune, you'd think they'd know every last thing about each other. But I'm not at all sure they do.'

11

Greer probed with the tip of her tongue, cautiously exploring the back of her upper jaw. She had her eyes tightly shut. It was as she had feared. She felt only exposed gum where the left rear molar should have been. The bad memory returned, of the tooth coming loose during dinner in the village and finally falling out in her mouth. She'd had to remove it surreptitiously with her napkin so the others would not see.

She let her tongue slide slowly, tentatively, to the side of the empty socket. Nothing there, either. Increasingly full of dread, hardly daring to breathe, she moved her tongue further round, inching along the gum-line towards the front. Sure enough, there were no teeth left. Not one. They had all gone, even the two front teeth, leaving a gaping hole.

Now she recovered in its horror the entire grotesque memory of the night before. As she'd been chewing, every single tooth in her upper jaw had slowly and gradually loosened, one after the other, and crumbled away in her mouth, until finally she had the whole lot scrunched in her napkin on her lap.

She had opened the napkin to steal a look at them and seen, with a shock of revulsion, that they were not her teeth at all. The two rows of gleaming white teeth that were bared in a grinning grimace were Tony's.

She was overcome with nausea and groaned aloud. She was lying on her back and this caused her to wake up with a convulsive jerk, gasping for breath. His face buried in her shoulder, Mischa stirred too.

'Wha's that? What's wrong?' The words came out thick and muffled. His hand caressed her stomach reflexively.

'Oh!' She was still marooned in the terrible landscape of the dream. 'I dreamt all my teeth fell out. One after the other. They were Tony's. It was so awful.'

She pressed herself up against him. He made a soothing noise and wrapped her in his arms. He fell back to sleep instantly.

She'd had versions of this dream before, but not for many years.

In the morning it was light and almost balmy again with just a breath of breeze. April was like that, you could be shivering one day and basking the next. It was never enervating, like the blistering heat of summer, but a more comfortable domestic warmth.

Greer thought the capricious April sun resembled a hibernating animal emerging for a cautious scout around. Or an adolescent person, Agnieszka's daughter, Eva, for example, who, having been stubbornly gloomy for days, surprised you with a burst of transforming effervescence.

Tendrils of sun were beginning to heat the stone on the terrace, bringing the tiny lizards scuttling out in force. But there were still patches of snow on the distant mountain. There remained the possibility of frost, the locals said, until every trace of snow was gone.

She carried her coffee and toast outside. She watched the red tractor chugging in the vineyard directly below, towing a reaper. Mauro, their man of all work, was combing the soil to uproot the grass and spring-clean the roots of the vines. He saw her and waved. Swallows dipped and sailed in front of her, catching the updrafts from the valley. The Virginia creeper on the east wall of Rollo and Guy's house was noticeably greener today, and there were branches of heavy pink blossom on their Judas tree. She thought, mindful of the ironies: all the things around me are starting to come out.

3rd August
Melbourne
We're back in real life. It's evening. It's freezing here, an icy wind was howling as we left the airport. The house was dark and cold, like a portent. Almost feels as if it's going to snow.

I just looked in the mirror. I loathe the way I look. I've changed since we've been away, I think anyone who knew me could see it. C. just thinks I'm exhausted. He fussed round, putting on the heating and getting hot drinks, insisting I had a bath first while he unpacked my things.

It's weird, but my heart feels heavy, like a concrete block in my chest. I'm having panic attacks. The thought of seeing M. doesn't shift this weight, it just gives me palpitations. I'll have to speak to Josie tomorrow before I do anything else. At least then I might have a plan of action, something to put on the table for C.

Before I do anything irrevocable I have to be sure nothing's changed with Mischa. I'll go to him straight after Josie. I feel laden with dread. Heavily laden, and I hate it.

It's all so complicated. Could I be getting cold feet?
Everything might change when he sees me.

She had written in small capitals, after this last sentence:

BUT I DOUBT IT.

'Can I rock up for a mo?' It was Guy, on the path. She closed the diary and covered it with a newspaper.

He leapt up the steps. 'I just spoke to Giulia. Angelo who-is-no-angel-o is coming to start on the pergola when the weather's OK. He wants to know how many mates he should line up. And Jacopo's bringing the forklift on Saturday at eight-thirty prompt.' Jacopo, an errant university student, was one of Giulia's swains.

'Eight-thirty Saturday? Jacopo? In your dreams, dude. Think ten, more likely. Sit down, there's another cup left.' She went inside for the pot.

'All right, dude. You've twisted my arm.'

The small forklift truck would carry their tubs of citrus trees, lemons and limes, grapefruits and mandarins, out into the open from their winter shelter. This was supposed to happen when there was no further chance of frost.

She indicated the distant traces of snow.

'We've had the last frost.' Guy was positive. 'Last night was a shocker, but there still wasn't a trace on the ground this morning.' She was inclined to believe him. He was almost always right about these things.

They talked practicalities. It was a busy time. Olive-pruning and bonfires were in full swing. Vineyard poles and electric fences needed endless repair. The vines were at their most vulnerable now as their tender green shoots, deer magnets, began to bud.

'Giulia's giving Tony a no-holds-barred personalised tour of the winery this morning,' Guy remarked.

'Is she now? Don't worry, I'm sure he's more than capable of defending himself.'

'If he wants to.'

'I thought the feeling of the meeting was he would want to.'

'That's Rollo's take, but he's so hopelessly retro about these things. Young Tonio's not averse to batting for both teams, is my educated guess. You haven't asked me how I thought last night went.'

'How did it go, did you think?'

'I thought it was quite a hoot, didn't you? The food was very good. Aggie's really got the hang of artichokes at long last, after all these years. Weren't you glad you came? In spite of po-faced Barbara. I don't know *what* Roly sees in her.'

He shook his head. 'And what did you make of Larry and June and their pimply son, poor kid? Larry's mutated into the most frightful academic bore. It's blindingly obvious that June can't stand him. I made a bet with His *lèse-Majesté* that she'll have left him by Christmas.'

Guy stretched. 'His blockage has shifted, did he tell you? It must have been the cake. Lo and behold, the royal bowels moved this morning and he's back beavering away in the studio, and may we all be truly thankful, O Lord.'

'Hosanna in the highest. That's *very* good news.'

'Isn't it just? I was getting desperate. You haven't asked me what I thought of Tony's performance last night. Before your inhibiting arrival, of course. Before best behaviour was resorted to.'

'And how did you rate his performance?'

'Well, interesting you should ask. He was rather good value. Although we didn't get very far in our dutiful quest for info about the work in progress. I did notice that he waited until he thought we were all safely plastered before he started asking anything about Mischa. We threw a few innocuous funnies at him to be going on with. Mischa the techno-klutz who can't change a light bulb, who has to be restrained from bawling "Maria" in karaoke bars – you know the routine. Roly told the one about him being the only guest the Savoy has ever had who actually did etchings but never invited anyone up to see them.'

He swilled his coffee in one go. 'I toyed with the idea of putting a few spanners in the works. Mischa the cross-dresser who likes getting into your frocks. The metrosexual who orders moisturiser by mail order. The health freak. That sort of thing.'

'The golf fiend with an analytical mind who cooks the perfect risotto and plays the futures market for recreation.' After she had said this, she was visited by the unsettling thought that it could almost be a description of her first husband, Charlie.

'You got it. It could be the basis of a new game.' They

enjoyed games of all sorts – board, parlour and particularly word.

'So, do you like Tony?'

'Do I fancy him, do you mean? Nice bum, very perky. He's quite a presentable package overall, isn't he? Quite a cutie.'

'I didn't mean do you fancy him. I meant, do you like him?'

Guy looked at her. 'Is there a difference?'

C. is so sweet & kind. It's ironic, I know I could do anything – turn into a raving nympho or an axe murderer, anything at all, not even within reason – and he'd forgive me. He'd never leave me. And he'd always have me back. Whereas with Mischa it's the opposite. I don't think he'd care two hoots if I was a serial killer, but I know instinctively that he would finish things instantly if I was unfaithful. And I'm the same. If I discovered he had killed somebody it wouldn't matter to me one whit. But if he slept with another woman now it would destroy everything.

I think this is the definition of true love, and I'd never realised it before. It's all or nothing, and you must be prepared to make great sacrifices for it. Even to the lengths of giving up the things and the people you previously held dear. I think it can only happen this way, when you can see no alternative except to tear everything apart in order to be with someone. This is what defines a grand passion, what sets it on another planet from the pallid feelings other people mistake for love.

What I feel about Mischa is categorically different from how it is with me and C. It's like the gulf between Anne of Green Gables and Anna Karenina. Or between lazing in a bath and hurtling over Niagara Falls.

The tragedy is that I'll never be able to explain it to C., and he will never understand, although I know he will forgive.

Greer had a clear memory of composing this entry. She had been in bed, propped against pillows, a mug of cocoa on the bedside table, brought by her solicitous husband. After a grimy day's travel lugging their cases on to a ferry and a change of planes, he was relaxing in the bath listening to music.

Beethoven's *Moonlight Sonata* wafted from the bathroom radio down the passage on a current of newly warmed air. The liquid notes of the piano were almost drowned out by the downpour on the iron roof of their mud brick house. She had always loved the sound of rain drumming on a roof, but that night she found it mournful and oppressive.

She remembered feeling complacent about the last three paragraphs. They had taken no time to compose, in a concentrated spurt before Charlie emerged from the bath. Scribbling them down had been, like Stella's telephone call yesterday, only a brief respite from the weight of anxieties.

Now, re-reading those lines which she had once thought self-evidently true and with which she had been so satisfied, she marvelled at their presumption. They were like the proverbial young wine in this respect. And like a cocky young wine, their confidence was to some degree misplaced. There was a vulnerability clinging to the words, and a residue of sadness, so strongly present to her now that she knew it must have been sensed at least subliminally by the writer.

She picked up her pen. In the space at the bottom of the page, she wrote:

17th April 2006
That is not a definition of true love, of course. It's a description of a certain type and stage of love. There can be no single definition, because love takes infinite forms. Perhaps one has to be the age I am now to begin to understand this.
The difference with me and C.

She paused, and crossed this out. She began the sentence again.

The difference was not that Charlie and I didn't love each other while Mischa and I did. The difference was that Charlie loved me deeply, but I was not in love with him.

She laid her pen down and meditated, remembering the piano and the rain, and the clinging sadness. Then she wrote:

And I knew this, but was not brave enough to say it.

'It'll soon be time to put out the ping-pong table.'

Greer and Tony were on the wide lower terrace in wicker chairs, making the most of the fading afternoon sun. They both wore hats, Tony's an old Panama from the rack in his house, one of Rollo's discards. Looked down on from above we must resemble a companionable couple, Greer thought, as if he's an old friend. Or the son of one. It was a sharply destabilising thought, and she shoved it aside.

Tony's little recorder stood on a cane table between them. Its demeanour was reticent and neutral, but she couldn't look at it without wondering what other voices it had heard. What disclosures had it been privy to on the journey that led to this destination?

'Ping-pong? You play down here? That's cool.'

'We play a lot before dinner in summer. Mischa, Guy and I, and anyone else we can rope in. Even Rollo sometimes, although he tends to plant himself in one place and refuse to move. Mischa's surprisingly good. Ferociously competitive.' She gave a laugh. 'We've got photos of him wielding the bat. I'll dig out a good one for you.'

Tony made a note in the pad that sat semi-permanently on his knee. For this alfresco interview he had changed into a white t-shirt and denim shorts, faded and frayed, worn with sneakers and no socks. There were no laces in his sneakers either, she noted. His legs and arms were tanned and toned. He looked like an advertisement for gym membership.

'So, can we talk a bit about your first husband, Charlie McNicoll. He was a management consultant, right?'

'Charlie? Why do you need to know about him?'

Greer was right on the qui vive with this topic, but covertly. She was pleased with the conversational, almost offhand way she put the question. As if it was of no particular import one way or another.

Tony answered in the same throwaway fashion. 'It's just background, but useful, I guess, because you and he were an item when you ran into Mischa. On that red-letter day.' He produced an engaging smile. 'Charlie has a minor supporting role, a bit-part. He's only an adjunct to the main drama.'

'He's a two-bit actor, do you mean? Or a rung up from that?'

A grin. 'At least one rung, but probably not three.'

'What can I tell you?' Is there anything you don't know? Or would you rather hear me incriminate myself in my own words?

'Let's trawl back in time to your first meeting, for starters. When and where was that?'

'We met in London. At a party, the usual thing. He'd been working over there for a few years, at McKinsey's. I was twenty-five, I'd been based in London for three years too, sharing flats, saving money from endless temp jobs and then racing off to do Europe on the cheap.'

'Young and fancy-free. Sounds like fun.'

'It was on the whole, yes.'

'But tough too? A bit of a roller-coaster ride?'

'There were highs and lows, inevitably. But it was a good experience, to be independent and away from home on the other side of the world. We couldn't afford to phone home in those days – long-distance was far too expensive.'

'And no texting or emails either. Things were a whole lot different then, huh? It must have been character-building, overall.' The blue eyes betrayed only polite interest.

'Oh, it was exceptionally character-building.'

It was really quite an art, how inscrutable he contrived

to be. And the picture of languid contentment. He leant back, tilting his hat against the sun.

'Then, after three years of this, you met Charlie McNicoll. Can you give me a verbal portrait of Charlie?'

This was the point at which she could say, why ask that? When I'm almost certain you have already met him yourself and formed your own opinion.

She considered saying this. She hadn't heard Charlie's name spoken out loud by anyone for years. Nor had she said it very often to herself in the privacy of her own mind. Nonetheless, her image of him was as clear, as pristine, as it had ever been.

'He stood out. He was rather classical-looking – tall and dark.' She hesitated. 'Charlie was kempt, as opposed to Mischa, who is definitely unkempt.'

Tony nodded. 'Uh-huh. That's a neat summation. Do you have any photos I could take a look at? From the time you knew him?'

'I may have kept one.' She felt a surge of antagonism. 'But I'm sure you don't need me to tell you what he looks like.' She thought, that's put paid to the matey little thing you thought we had going.

'We're talking thirty years ago, Greer. I'm interested in how he appeared to you, back then. Give me a thumbnail sketch.' His voice was conciliatory but surprisingly firm.

She replied with peremptory speed, ticking the items off her fingers.

'He was sporty, a rower and fast bowler. He came from an old Western District family – that's a rich farming area in the state of Victoria. He was estranged from his family. He'd been to Harvard Business School, he was thirty-one, six years older than me. He was quite worldly, knew his way round menus and wine, had friends with country houses and villas in Provence. Is that enough for you?'

Tony was unfazed. 'He didn't get on with his family?'

'He'd refused to take over the business, the family farm. It caused a rift.'

'What did you think of his parents?'

'I never met them.' She had suspicions about this line of questioning.

'He was earning good money in London, I guess?'

'Yes, he was already very successful.'

'An impressive kind of guy. Not surprising you fell for each other.'

Encrypted here, she could tell, was a glib romantic cameo Tony had drawn up for himself. After leading a fairly rackety existence for three years, the young and susceptible Greer Gordon encounters the well-off, sophisticated Charles McNicoll, a distinct cut above the shabby crew she's been associating with, and eligible to boot. She snaps him up, tout de suite.

She felt an urgent need to correct this Mills & Boon scenario, not only for her own sake but for Charlie's dignity. At least let him be the initial instigator of his fate, rather than a pawn to be duped twice over. She said more gently, 'It was not quite like that, actually.'

There was a distinct beat before Tony turned his head and looked at her. 'It wasn't? How was it, then?'

At least he had the grace to acknowledge the unspoken sequence of images in his mental viewfinder. She turned it over in her mind. It was Charles who had fallen head over heels for her, not the other way round, who had pursued her single-mindedly for the next four years, who had brought up the m word very early on. And who, eventually, had worn her down. Well, that was one way of putting it.

'Charlie was – still is, I expect – an exceptional person,' she said. 'That scarce commodity: a genuinely *good* man, if you know what I mean.'

She made rare eye contact with Tony as she delivered this light but potentially insulting remark. Would he have any idea what a genuinely good man was like? He was nodding. The spruce, photogenic face that Guy found so cute wore an earnest expression.

She felt a compulsion to pursue this, to make sure this

nonchalant boy grasped the essence of what she was saying.

'I knew Charlie very well for nearly five years, and there's nothing bad I would want to say about him. He was a sweet-natured and lovely man.'

'He was mad about you, wasn't he?'

He's been told that, she thought, but does he know what it means? Does he know anything about love?

'Have you ever been in love, Tony?' she asked, on impulse.

His dancing blue eyes conveyed amusement at the topic, and no surprise at all. 'Oh, yeah. In fact a few times. I'm a bit of a love junkie. It doesn't stick, that's my problem.'

As I thought. He knows nothing, like Manuel in *Fawlty Towers*, which he has probably never seen either. She was tempted to tell him that Rollo had all the videos of this famous BBC comedy of the '70s.

'Has it never stuck with anyone? Is the problem usually with you, or with – them?' Why am I being so coy about their genders, she wondered.

'Not for long, and it's usually both, me and them, kind of a simultaneous slide into disenchantment. Which is lucky, I guess. I've seen what happens with the unrequited version, and it's not pretty.'

'Is there anyone in your life right now?'

'Well, yeah, there is somebody I quite like, as it happens. We only just met before I had to fly over here, so we didn't even have the chance,' there was a slight hesitation here and a faraway look, 'to get the show on the road.' He threw her a disarming grin.

Well, two could play at that game. 'So, did you have a nice instructive tour of the winery with Giulia this morning?'

He blinked. 'Sure, yeah, I did. It's an interesting place, the winery. Full of –' He stopped. The blue eyes were slightly out of focus.

'Full of wine?'

He laughed. 'What I meant to say was, you see a totally

different side of this place, it's a whole other world in there. Well, it's your world, I guess, and Guy's —'

She waved this away. 'I'm sorry, that was a digression,' she said. 'My fault. We can do wine another time, can't we? Now, where were we?' The words gave her a pleasant illusion of being in charge of the interview. She knew it would not last.

'Ah, OK. Well, uh, we were talking about you and Charlie, right?'

His eyes went to the tape recorder on the table. But she could see that for a second or two she had thrown him, that in his mind he had been in another country with a person he liked whom he'd recently met, recalling their unfinished business. And then he'd been jerked forwards into a different world, inside the cool winery with Giulia.

They had just got going again when they were interrupted.

'Greer, I hate to be alarmist or anything but there's a whirling dervish on the loose.'

Tony had seen her first out of the corner of his eye, the small figure in a billowing scarlet shirt who was flying at them dangerously fast down the steps from the house. Greer thought she looked less like a dervish than a child's shiny plastic windmill, her arms flailing in concentric circles in front of her.

'I search for you everywhere! Where are you?' Agnieszka pulled up, laughing and panting.

'We're here.' They were amazingly united on this.

'Oh, I know *that*, I see you now. You two are hiding down here from me and having nice little private conversations.' Her petite, eloquent features gave vent to a sequence of expressions, chiding, frisky and finally conspiratorial. 'I like it give you this. I have it all day long waiting to see you in my bag and only now I do it!'

She flourished a shimmering object in Greer's face, and dropped it like a trophy in her lap. Greer saw it was a spiral jotter with a fluorescent lime-green cover.

'I go with Eva after school to newspaper shop with magazine, you know this one, by old ruins wall? We no making decide which colour: she like it one, I like it other one. You don't believe me! There is this green, and also orange one, and nice purple, but Eva think you no like purple. Now you make diary, with lots of detail lists for every day, what thing to do and what buy, and when Mr Tony is coming, and then life is organise, and everything is much better.'

Greer thought, as she submitted to the hug: if only it were that simple.

Agnieszka patted Tony on the head. 'You come last night to the bad boys,' she winked at Greer, 'and eat my dinner?'

'The bad –? Uh, I get you. Yes, your dinner was awesome, Aggie.'

'You like it? It was all finish – you don't believe me – nothing left in fridge from all that big lamb and potato, only bone for doggies, and one little piece cake.' She bent her head to Greer's ear and lowered her voice. 'I like it save for you and I steal from the boys. Mr Rollo he no need any more, he get too –'

She blew into her cheeks to make a fat face and turned to Tony without pausing. 'I learn that way of making artichoke when I go to Perugia. With garlic, rosemary, olives oil. You cut –'

Greer saw an exhaustive post-mortem in the offing. She forestalled it. 'We can't talk now, Aggie. We're working.' Agnieszka had a healthy respect for work. Greer knew this, and was rewarded with a vigorous nod of understanding.

'Sorry, I no interrupt, I leave you all alone again by yourself. But, you must no forget eat your little bit cake. I hide on kitchen table away from that naughty Mr Mischa, he never look under paper because he only man, and man never find anything!' And she was out of there, bounding back up the steps, true to her word.

Greer said, 'Agnieszka is someone, perhaps the only person in my experience, who never walks away. She's either here, and well and truly in your face, or she's vanished in a puff of smoke. It's as if someone's waved a magic wand.'

Tony pulled out a handkerchief and mopped his face. 'Whew. She's a character, isn't she? It's kind of strangely exhausting just being around her.' He indicated the sparkly green notebook. 'What did she bring you, a diary?'

Greer said repressively, 'No, just a notepad. Now then, where were we again?' She had a compulsion to get this nice little private conversation over with.

'Do you mind talking about Charlie?'

Tony pulled on jeans and a long-sleeved sweatshirt as he listened to the sound of his own voice. There were fewer ambient noises on the tape now, less of the twittering birdsong and background mooing of cows. Not long after Agnieszka's visit it had clouded over and they repaired to Greer's kitchen. Even in here a persistent cuckoo punctuated the tape at regular intervals.

'Mind? Not especially. I wasn't hurt by Charlie, it was the other way round, as you must be well aware. To avoid repetition perhaps it would help if you also avoided asking me what you already know.'

They had been seated at the kitchen table with cups of tea and a slice apiece of the leftover chestnut cake they had found, sure enough, smuggled in and tucked under the *Herald Tribune*.

Tony zipped up his fly and replayed the last terse statement. Then he stopped the tape and interposed: 'She was on the edge of her chair all through this interview. Yet she never came right out and asked me *what* I actually know or who I've seen. This was the closest she came, and the most overtly hostile she's allowed herself to get.

'She's in a real bind, because she's assuming I've seen Charlie, but has no way of knowing if he's dumped her in part of the shit or the whole load. Or if he's introduced me to someone she'd far rather I didn't get to meet. And she can't say a word about any of this without giving the shit away.'

He started the tape again. His voice, larded with appeasing balm, said: 'I would like to do that, Greer, but with a biography, in a sense, there's no such thing as knowing. There's just what you think you know. And that is subject to modification and change. You're dependent on what people remember – or think they do – and on what they're prepared to tell you. And everyone has their own take on events, a personalised version, which they've kind of metabolised over the years into their own truth. You have to learn to sort out those who have accurate memories from those whose memories are crap, basically.

'If I've learnt anything on this job it's not to take any one person's version as gospel, however convincing it might sound. It may be just plain bitching, or it could turn out to be total bullshit, right? I think I've learnt – well, I sure hope I have – not to draw any conclusions until I've talked to everyone I can find who's in the mix in some way.

'So, yeah, I'm sorry if I'm a pain in the butt, constantly asking things you think I should know about. It's just I don't feel I necessarily know any stuff properly until I hear it from you. And Mischa of course. Like, you know, from the horses' mouths.'

At the end of this came Greer's voice on the tape: 'Rather than the mouths of asses.'

Tony stopped it there to add something else: 'She gave a little tight smile when she said that. The horses' mouths was risky there, but it kind of paid off. Jokes are cool with her – she gets humour – but you need to pitch it right or it backfires on you. I felt the time was right for the heavy spiel. I expected her eyes would glaze over and she'd be really antsy, but she sat and listened, and I think she heard what I was saying. Although she was tapping a finger on the table. Anyhow, it paid off right away.'

The next words on the tape came from Greer: 'I should never have married Charlie. I knew it right from the start, on our very first date, the evening after we met.'

Tony stopped the tape. 'That came from out of the blue.

I guessed it had to be something important, by the way she leant forwards with her eyes fixed on a point just to the right of me, in that weird way she has.'

Greer had found a sudden desire to relate this story. She told Tony a shortened version, leaving out things he didn't need to know, such as any mention of Charlie's red convertible. None of her other friends in London owned a car. She couldn't even recall what make Charlie's car was, but she suspected that Tony would draw inferences from the fact that he had one.

Charlie had driven her to the theatre, picking her up from the rather grim Arsenal flat – another censored item – she shared with two friends. It was just around the corner from the football ground, where there was a game in progress. Charlie had been impressed to hear that she could lie in bed and guess who was winning by the roar of the crowd.

He had bought tickets (the best, in the front stalls; Greer omitted this) for a new play by one of the formerly trendy, kitchen-sink group of writers. She found that she could not at this distance remember who, or what play it was. Afterwards he had taken her to dinner at a tiny, charming little Italian restaurant in Chelsea (she left this out too), his own stamping ground.

Over dinner they had briefly discussed the play. Greer had remarked that some of the dialogue was Pinteresque. What was that? Charlie had enquired.

'It turned out he had never heard of Pinter,' Greer's voice on the tape had an edge of incredulity. 'I found that almost unbelievable.'

There was a pause. 'Actually, it doesn't seem anywhere near as extraordinary now, when people don't necessarily share so many of the same cultural references. But at the time I did think it was rather amazing. I realised there was an enormous gulf in our interests, I suppose, and in what was important to us. I think I knew then, really, that it could never work.'

'Off the record, did you ever get to ask Mischa if he'd heard of Pinter?'

A laugh. 'I'm sure I never bothered.'

'It wouldn't have made any difference, would it?'

'You're quite right. It would have made no difference at all.'

'So, Greer, why did you marry Charlie?'

It was not the first time she had heard this question. She had asked it of herself, many times.

4th August
Early morning (like 2 am …)
Can't sleep. Tried to watch TV. Can't take anything in. Don't want to go back to bed.

It was a fuckwitted thing to get married. So much that we're going to have to deal with would be infinitely easier if we weren't. It's not as if it's even remotely necessary these days. Even if you were staying together for ever. Why in heaven's name did I agree to go through with it? It must have been hormonal. I'd lived with C. on and off for nearly 5 yrs & never given in. I should have known it was certifiably insane. I should have listened to what my instincts were trying to tell me, right from the start.

All those interminable lists I used to draw up, of the pros & cons. Pros: he was so sweet, so nice, kind, devoted, would always look after me, etc.; cons: he's a businessman, his interests are in commerce not the arts, we've got nothing in common, our minds are poles apart, etc. etc. And all those trips away I took on my own, trying to decide what to do, as if being away from him would decide it one way or the other.

It's so obvious to me now: all that is rampant lunacy. It's obvious to a moron that anyone who can't make up their mind one way or the other should never do it. I should have left him years before, and then this whole catastrophe would never have happened. Why wasn't it clear to me? Why didn't anyone say something?

If only Dad were here, I know he would have warned me. None of my friends were game to say anything, and they must have all realised it was a mad idea. Why didn't someone wise, like a sensible experienced older woman, my mother even (but she was always besotted with C.) take me aside & say, listen, if you have to make a decision — forget it, it's a non-starter, it's doomed, it's wrong. When it's right you'll know. There will be no decision to make, and it doesn't matter how long the list of pros is, they're a total irrelevance, period.

Greer had taken the diary into the kitchen, where the fire lit earlier for herself and Tony needed attention. She read the entry through twice. How ignorant it sounded, how evasive and self-pitying. Were other young people like this, wilfully blind? Or was it just her? She thought of Giulia, beautiful and wayward, seemingly bent on wreaking destruction. Giulia was far too pig-headed to listen to anyone, right now.

But she will probably grow out of it, Greer thought. Most people become less selfish as they grow older. Would Tony think that is what I have done? And Mischa? Or does he think we're both swanning through life without a regret in the world, with never a backward glance? Mischa's work consumes everything, the present moment included. That is both his reason and his excuse. But what is mine?

She had a memory of herself gripped by successive waves of panic that night after their return to Melbourne from the Isle of Pines. Unable to sleep, tossing and turning beside the quiescent body of her husband, who was sleeping the deep sleep of the just. Finally getting up in the early hours, seizing on the diary as if it were a confessional and pouring her heart out. Then lying huddled under a doona on the couch in front of the TV and watching, without comprehending a word, as if it had been some arcane gibberish, a 3 am re-run of *The Sweeney*.

There were two empty lines at the bottom of the page, where the diary entry had ended. Greer felt a need to add something.

She wrote:

17th April 2006
Why did I marry Charlie? I gave in, finally. And at the time, for
obvious reasons, it seemed the right thing to do.

She was coming to the end of the second line, and wrote in
squashed letters between square brackets:

[Cont. at back]

She turned to the back of the exercise book, where there
were a few empty pages, and wrote three more careful paragraphs.

17th April 2006 (cont.)
Until (and perhaps I should add, unless, because I'm not sure
that it is for everyone) you fall in love yourself, it is no more than
an abstract idea. You read about it, people may try to explain it to
you, and you may talk about it yourself and imagine you know
what it is you're talking about.

  But you don't know. It's like trying to speak a foreign
language without any grasp of the key words. Until it happens
you cannot imagine how it will affect you.

  For that reason, even if my mother or some other sensible and
objective older woman had taken me aside, I had not yet had the
experience that might have enabled me to see the wisdom of their
advice.

She considered now how she had answered Tony's question
about her marriage. He would see it as a decisive event. He
would guess there was something of central importance she
wasn't telling him. Since he appeared to be a good detective
it was quite possible, it was more than likely, that he knew
exactly what this was, and was contemptuous of her clumsy
attempts to deflect him.

A mere 50 yards away, Tony had moved over to his favourite
armchair, the winged one with its airy, summery design of

shells, flowers and oak leaves. He listened once more to Greer's explanation of why she had consented to marry Charles McNicoll a mere two months before Mischa Svoboda charged into the Corbett Gallery and derailed her life, as well as Charlie's.

Greer's words came slowly to begin with and the voice sounded tentative, as if she was thinking on her feet. As if she knew, moreover, that this was how she sounded.

'Charlie was always so sure he wanted us to be married, and his certainty made up for my indecision. In a way, it almost cancelled it out. He was so reassuringly free of doubt. You know about his consultancy work, do you? He dealt with firms who were having problems, or wanted to reorganise or streamline their operations.'

The voice gained conviction, picked up a bit here. 'That's what Charlie was very good at: making rapid assessments of companies' strengths and weaknesses. He was accustomed to battles in the boardroom as well as the workplace, and arguing his case for constructive reform. He was used to an interim period of uncertainty, and negotiations and argy-bargy, and eventually getting his own way.'

There was a short interval. Tony sat still, his eyes apparently glued to the empty whirr of the tape, on which the sound of the inevitable lone cuckoo was just discernible. When it resumed the voice sounded different, altogether more spontaneous.

'I'm afraid that's inadequate. But I don't know how I can convey the relentlessness of Charlie's suit, the sheer pressure of his niceness. In the end, they wore me into the ground.'

Tony stopped the tape. He sat staring into space, fingers laced together, then said: 'She was sincere there, you can hear it. Or about as sincere as you can be when you're telling only half the truth.'

12

The conviction came to Greer in the night: I must talk to Charlie. I need to find out exactly what happened when he spoke to Tony. Assuming that has occurred. I think, however, I can safely make this assumption now. I would be extremely foolish to continue to kid myself that there is any conceivable chance Tony has not met and interviewed Charlie McNicoll, the bit-part, but definitely not two-bit, actor in the drama.

So much hangs on the information Charlie has given, or withheld, and not just my place in Mischa's biography or its effect on me. But I must not pursue that line of thought. It leads to uncharted territory. I can't handle it.

She knew that Charlie would have been perfectly within his rights to refuse to speak to the man who was researching a biography of the artist who had run off with his wife. But such a refusal did not square with her knowledge of him. Charlie was never one to sit on the sidelines: he liked his say. Crucially, she felt sure he would have insisted on having his say if he thought he might have any chance of pre-empting the situation.

Meeting Tony would have put Charlie in an exceptionally delicate position. Greer tried to imagine how he might have decided to approach Tony's questioning. He had spent his professional life confronting thorny problems and defending wickets of varying levels of stickiness. This one, however, was in a class of its own.

Charlie was no fool and neither, she believed, was he a vindictive man. In a quandary, his instinct would be to protect the vulnerable. Every actor in this story was vulnerable to a greater or lesser degree, including Charlie himself, but one was arguably at greater risk than the others. There was only one way to find out how Charlie had confronted this dilemma: by speaking with him directly.

There were two obstacles. The first one was almost enough in itself to put paid to the idea. She didn't know any more where Charlie and his family lived. She hadn't had any direct contact with him for twenty-five years. No indirect contact either, come to that. She amended this. There had been one indirect contact, a year or more after she and Mischa left Melbourne. A deafening tattoo on the door at 6.30 am in Port Douglas, Queensland. Mischa had gone to the door spoiling for a fight, only to have Greer summoned from bed and divorce papers thrust into her hands by a surly caricature of a bailiff.

But the last occasion she had heard Charlie's name spoken aloud, until Tony came out with it yesterday, was in Sydney during the five long months she and Mischa had spent alone in that cramped, desolate flat in Darlinghurst.

Those months were a blur in Greer's memory. Immediately they were over she had banished them from her mind. In the same way that Mischa had ceased to think about his time in Prague with Elsa Montag, because it was in the past and done with, she had tried to edit those months out of her life. For a very long time she had managed this quite successfully.

And if it weren't for the biographer's arrival I could have gone on editing them out. Could have, or would have? Just one change of consonant, but a significant, a profound difference. For a quarter of a century, both Mischa and I have conducted ourselves as if those five months and what was going on then had no existential reality. It's almost as if what was happening between us during that time never happened at all.

Looking back, she suspected those months were even harder on Mischa than on her. In all their subsequent years together she couldn't remember him making even one reference to them.

It was at the very end of the five months in Sydney that there had been a conversation in which Charlie was a central but absent player. The conversation was held the day after Christmas, and it had taken place not between Greer and Mischa but between Greer and her elder sister, Josephine.

On Boxing Day Josie made the short flight from Melbourne to Sydney after receiving an urgent summons from Greer. She was intending to come two weeks later, but had changed her plans when the telephone call came and had some trouble getting a flight at such short notice at that time of year. She had not stayed with Greer and Mischa, whose flat was minuscule and crammed with painting materials, but for a few nights – Greer never knew exactly how long – at a small hotel in nearby Paddington.

Greer had a hazy memory of Josie telling her that Charlie had left Melbourne too, soon after Mischa and Greer's precipitate departure, and taken a job in Hong Kong. He'd been headhunted by a US multinational with branches all over South-East Asia. It was a very prestigious post, at least that was a bit of good news, Josie had said at one point, trying to jolly her sister up. Greer thought she remembered her saying that Charlie was initially on a four-year contract, but that there was a strong likelihood of his staying on, if it turned out well, and being posted to other countries in the region.

This information, vague, effectively useless, was twenty-five years out of date. Where on earth was Charlie today? He could be anywhere in the world, working for anyone.

At sixty-two, affluent and well-regarded, he might have retired. Greer found she couldn't even recall the name of the American company he had originally joined. She'd had other things on her mind at the time.

Josie would certainly know where Charlie was living. But Greer had no idea of her sister's whereabouts either. She hadn't seen or spoken to her since Josie's flying visit to Sydney. Since that particular Boxing Day, in fact. Like Charlie's name, but for a different reason, she had not pronounced the name of her sister aloud to anyone for twenty-five years. To protect herself from the pain of loss, Greer had tried never to think about Josie.

After Sydney, when they headed north to Queensland, she had sent her mother, Lorna, their next address in tropical Port Douglas. Lorna had kept in touch, but her letters were reticent. Her mother had found Greer's behaviour incomprehensible and deeply shocking, although she stopped short of cutting the lines of communication. Beyond confirming they were well, she supplied no further news of the immediate family. Neither had Greer asked any questions.

She had stayed in reasonably regular if distant contact with her mother for the first two years, until Lorna's sudden death from a cancer she had first mentioned in a letter that for four critical months had not reached Greer, who was on the move between Bali and Thailand. Since her mother's death there were no Australian entries in her address book. From the day she absconded with Mischa she had cut off all contact with her old friends in Melbourne.

There was, of course, the biographer. Tony would have Charlie's telephone number, no question about that. It would be the easiest thing in the world to ask him for it.

But the second, the insuperable obstacle to contacting Charlie at all was the thought of picking up the telephone and dialling his number without any prior warning. The very thought of having to announce her name to whoever answered the phone was enough to make Greer's blood run cold.

*

4th August

I've done it. I've spoken to Josie, and she's on side. Kind of.

*I bought some brunch things & took them round to her flat —
it seemed safer than going out. Plus some champers (& orange
juice) — I thought it might be needed. It was, altho' J. tried to stop
me on the grounds that it was inappropriate. We made scrambled
eggs & talked for a good 4 hours.*

*Josie twigged practically right away. She's always intuitive.
Well, I hadn't seen her for a few weeks. I wasn't at all sure how
she'd react, I was worried she might burst into tears but she didn't
cry at all, she was good. She would have been pleased if she
hadn't pretty smartly seen that it wasn't welcome.*

*As soon as I got inside the door I dived straight to the point
without putting it off, there was nothing else I could think of to
say. At first she had a complete fit. She thought I must be joking.
Her first reaction was to reject it out of hand. She said it was
impossible, out of the question & I must be out of my mind.*

*I told her about M. The lot. That is, the bits fit to print (not
that that's much). She said I must be crazy, kept repeating that
I'd hardly spent any time with him, how could I seriously
contemplate running away with him, it was absurd. Ludicrous.
Etc. etc. But of course she's never been in love, she's never plunged
off that precipice, and she hasn't a clue. What she had with
Richard was a lot like me and Charlie.*

*Then she got on her high horse. What was I thinking of, it
was so irresponsible & abnormal. When Charlie was so perfect to
me & had done nothing wrong.*

Greer, I can't believe you're saying this, it's unnatural, Josie
had said at first, almost frantically, and then kept repeating it,
her eyes round and appalled. You simply cannot let this
infatuation, your obsession with this man, lead you to do an
irrevocable thing you will certainly regret.

Charlie was popular with her mother and elder sister.
Greer was well aware of their view, held jointly and voiced
often: she had strung him along in a typically irresponsible
and wilful fashion. Her mother and Josie were alike in some

ways. There was an affinity between them, as there had been between Greer and her father.

Think of Charlie, Josie had said, over and over. He's a copybook husband. How could you do this, after keeping him dangling for so many years? How could you do it so soon after you've finally made an honest man of him? When this produced an involuntary splutter from her sister, Josie had blinked and stammered out: it's immoral, Greer, really. If I were at all religious I'd say it was a sin.

Greer had been reminded of her recent encounter with Jean-Claude. The intense tête-à-tête with the young Frenchman on the white beach on the Isle of Pines had led directly to this confrontation with her sister in Josie's characteristically tidy and tasteful sitting room in East Melbourne, overlooking the Flagstaff Gardens. Some of the things Josie was coming out with replicated Greer's own initial responses to Jean-Claude's proposition, practically word for word.

Jean-Claude seemed to know all about passion. He and Greer were convinced they had that elemental knowledge in common. It was what made the idea, this unnatural proposition, imaginable to them. Josie, however, in Greer's opinion, had never taken the plunge off the precipice. To her such a plan was, initially at least, unimaginable.

Why didn't you *do* something, Josie had asked, tight-lipped, before it came to *this*? Why didn't you do something about it *earlier*? Then you wouldn't have . . . She had stopped short, unable or unwilling to finish.

I did do something, Greer pointed out. I got married. Josie's look told her that this had been a truly mad course of action. But she already knew that.

After a while she simmered down a fraction, and I could see that there was a sliver of hope. She was starting to think about it more rationally, rather than as a categorical negative. But she continued to bring C. into it, envisaging endless difficulties. She couldn't conceive of any chance of him accepting the idea.

Tucked away at the back of a drawer in Greer's writing desk was a manila envelope containing a bundle of family photos. They were mainly in black and white because her father, a keen photographer, had preferred it. She retrieved the envelope now and laid the photographs out in chronological order in parallel rows. She had never put them into an album, nor had she taken them out of the envelope for a long time.

Her father and mother, Bill and Lorna, dark and fair, tall and short, playful and serious. Those were the obvious differences that would strike an onlooker. But she knew they were merely surface characteristics that became almost irrelevant once one's knowledge of a person went beyond the superficial. You could have such a deep and intimate knowledge of certain individuals that it verged on the encyclopaedic, and yet to claim you knew everything about them was manifestly absurd. She would never claim that of Mischa, whom she knew inside out and back to front. The source of Mischa's boundless creative life was a private mystery, inaccessible to others and even, she suspected, to himself.

She thought now, for the first time: how well do I really know him? What I know about the thirty-eight years of his life before he met me is negligible. And what of it? I would never have thought much of it, if it hadn't been for Tony. He has brought it home to me lately, rather forcibly.

The photographs were bookended by pictures from two weddings. The first, in black and white, was her parents' wartime wedding in 1944, with the two young people in air force uniforms, holding hands shyly for the camera, carnations in their buttonholes. The last one was the most recent. It was in colour, but still twenty-five years old: Greer's own registry office wedding, no frills by her own request, to Charlie McNicoll.

Her mother, Lorna, was in this snap as well, standing next to the bride. Thirty-five years older than she had been at her own wedding but hardly looking it in her smart turquoise dress and jacket. She also wore a wide smile in which Greer read more than a tinge of relief. Josie stood on Charlie's other side, holding a posy of yellow roses. She too looked delighted that her stubborn younger sister had finally bitten the bullet.

Greer and Charlie wore suits, his a dark lounge and hers a sharp white pants suit teamed with a straw boater. They looked as carefree as the other two, Greer's hat tilted at an angle.

We're both smiling, Greer thought. Charlie has a spray of wattle in his buttonhole and I have an impudent red bottlebrush. Our smiles appear to testify to an identical level of happiness, and no secrets. What can photographs tell you? Less than two months after this was taken, I was gone.

There was a fifth person in the line-up, on Josie's left. A trim woman in her fifties in a maroon coat and skirt, pepper-and-salt hair drawn tightly back in a formal French roll. Verity Corbett. She too looked pleased to be there. Her precise, angular features and sharp retroussé nose were relaxed and directed towards the wedding couple.

Verity was really quite a handsome woman, Greer conceded, in an ascetic way. This comes as a surprise but I can see it now, now I have reached the age she was. I must have invited Verity to be a witness at my wedding, and to the slap-up lunch afterwards at Florentino's, but I had almost forgotten she was there.

Greer looked closely at the photo, recalling Tony's recent remarks, the *aspersions* he claimed to have heard about Verity and Mischa. Tried to picture this immaculately groomed spinster-ish woman with the younger Mischa, rumbustious and unkempt. However much she tried to steer her mind into this groove, it remained stubbornly risible as a theory.

In between the wedding photos was a visual record of a family, not vastly different from most family snapshots. The original wartime couple, and then, around a year later, the joyous arrival of a baby. That was Josie. Josie crawling, then walking. Josie on her first day at kindergarten, clutching her mother's hand. Then another fair, chubby-cheeked baby crawling and walking. That was Greer.

The sisters in the garden with their pet rabbit and later on their Siamese cat and blue heeler puppy. Making funny faces, wearing the gingham summer dresses of their girls' private boarding school. Greer had loved it; Josie had been homesick and eventually switched to a day school. Birthday parties. Teenage parties. The family in swimsuits, on holidays at Aireys Inlet. Josie at her end-of-school formal, long dark hair in waves, slinky dress of blue Thai silk, looking far prettier than she (or Greer, gawky at the time) had any inkling of. The four of them picnicking with friends on another summer holiday at Portsea.

Her father dropped out of the snaps after Greer turned twenty-one. The last photo of him was taken at her twenty-first outside a flower-bedecked marquee in their Camberwell garden. Bill was standing between his daughters, his arms round their shoulders, smiling at Lorna, who held the camera. A week later he was dead of a heart attack.

Her father, mother and Josie were the three people Greer had once known best in the world. Of the three, only Josie was left. People could disappear off the face of the earth without warning. Life was like that, she had seen it happen. People you once loved vanished from your life. People you loved now, and those who were inextricably linked to you, even if you never saw them. People linked by blood.

She herself had vanished from the lives of people she loved. Greer pressed her hands against her face. They were cold to the touch, she could feel the pads of her fingers making white indentations in her cheeks.

Josie was her blood relative, and she was surely still here. Not here, she amended that, but somewhere in the world. Where was that, and more to the point, who was Josie with? Who were the most important people in Josie's life? Greer rocked back in her chair. She thought, I have stifled the anguish of years.

Her sister was her primary point of contact. How had she allowed herself to lose touch completely and absolutely with Josie, of all people?

But that had been part of the plan, hadn't it?

I doused my fears & insisted that C. wouldn't be a problem. It's not as if he doesn't like Josie, or she's a complete stranger. But it does depend totally on him, she's dreadfully right. When I spelt it out to her, voiced the plan aloud for the first time since Jean-Claude & I nutted it out, I saw how much rests on Charlie's co-operation. I will have to convince him it's the best way. I know him so well, I think he will see the logic of it. It does make things a whole lot easier, from every angle.

Josie could see that too, once she could bring herself to get beyond the standard objections. She started to see that for everyone it provides a viable way out of an unfortunate situation. Being a management consultant, C. is bound to appreciate that.

How confident that sounds. Inexplicably so, in retrospect. Did I seriously imagine I was going to convince a man such as Charlie that it was 'the best way'? That he would see 'the logic of it'? The doubts are there, I can feel them, below the surface, between the lines. Would anyone else see I was racked with them?

Not my poor sister. I wasn't going to admit them to her. Or to myself, either. Well, I was intent on getting my way, wasn't I, and Charlie was never going to stop me. I think Josie could see that.

I started thinking we were home and hosed, then she brought up Mother. I said Mum would accept it as the least worst alternative, in fact a vastly preferable outcome to anything else. J. said yes, maybe so, but there was another outcome Mum would like a whole lot better. She had to retreat when I repeated that was not to be mentioned again, it was not on the negotiating table, it was a non-outcome.

Then suddenly she started on Verity. Of all the possible objections that has to be the looniest. She went on about how

Verity depends on me, how she trusts me, how could I not take her into my confidence, etc. etc. I said I was only an employee of bloody Verity, for God's sake, I wasn't married to her. J. shrieked at that, but it more or less threw cold water on the V. offensive.

After that Josie sort of lost heart in the argument for the defence (if that's what it was. Prosecution seems more apt) & I thought I could detect a subtle change in her. A glimmering.

We began to get down to the nuts and bolts of how it could be managed. And what will happen afterwards.

Had she really, really not told anyone, Josie demanded again. No one except Charlie? And he had kept it to himself? No one but Charlie and he'd been sworn to secrecy from the outset, Greer was able to say. I hadn't even got round to telling Mum. And not even bloody Verity either, she added, as a tease. And, oh God, not even Mischa, yet. She'd felt a sickening spasm of anxiety then. Josie had shaken her head. You really are mad, she'd said again. You've no idea how he'll take this.

The secret should continue to be kept, they agreed. Kept watertight between them, primarily for Charlie's sake. That meant there was no time to lose. Literally.

Josie was a librarian. She would organise her summer break so that she could leave home immediately on receiving Greer's urgent summons.

'Or it could be Mischa's,' Josie suggested, but Greer was certain Mischa would not want anything to do with this.

'He may not even want to be with me any more,' she had added, almost blithely.

Where will you go, Josie had asked. They agreed on Sydney. A big city not too far from Melbourne, suitably anonymous, quickly and easily accessible by air. It would be a simple enough matter to disappear in Sydney. They knew virtually no one there.

Josie was adamant about one thing. If she went ahead with this crazy scheme, if this scary proposal ever came to fruition, Greer would have to relinquish all contact with her former life and friends.

'For a judicious interval. Or —?' They tested this, tossed it back and forth. In the end the conclusion was inescapable: the fewer people in the know the safer it was, with the most room for manoeuvre. That meant Greer, Josie, their mother (unavoidable, they agreed, but she could keep secrets) and Charlie.

'And with any luck, Mischa,' Greer said. 'Not that luck's an appropriate word,' she added, before Josie could, 'in the circs.'

But this brought Josie back to the basics, which were nothing at all to be light-hearted about. It seemed inevitable, and most vital of all, that Greer should sever contact with her husband and with Josie herself. And not just for a judicious interval. As far as those two were concerned, for the foreseeable future at least, Greer needed to disappear off the face of the earth.

What happens after Sydney is, hey presto, I do the disappearing act and vanish into thin air. For the duration.

Josie said, through tears: 'It's terrible, but I couldn't go through with it otherwise. Do you see what I mean? Do you see why I'm saying that? Do you understand? Do you promise?'

They were weeping now, both of them, and embracing. Yes, Greer promised, she did understand. She would become ex-directory. Vaporise. It was far better that way. Better for everyone.

Talking about the future, let alone the conversation itself, had an air of unreality about it. In her sister's pale yellow sitting room, gazing out through the bay window at the grey Melbourne sky and spindly trees, it hadn't seemed such a momentous thing to promise to vanish into thin air. Her sister was shifting a weight of responsibility from Greer's shoulders to her own, and handing over the golden key to freedom in return.

Greer thought: and I agreed to disappear, just like that. Perhaps I would have agreed to anything at that moment.

In spite of the tears, it was almost insouciantly that I signed myself out of certain commitments and certain people's lives. For the duration.

How long is that?

She snatched the nearest pen to hand and wrote, at the bottom of the page:

18th April 2006
We thought that this would be in everyone's best interests. Josie certainly believed that it was. But I fear now that it may have been a deeply misguided thing.

She lifted the pen, twisting her hair around it. The happy photos of the close little family of four remained as she had laid them out, in rows in front of her on the desk.

She added seven more words:

I fear it was an insupportable thing.

The diary entry for 4 August 1979 wasn't quite over. There was a brief addendum:

P.S. I'm in a café. I'm wrecked. Stage one is done. Now I have to spill beans to M. and C. (separately, & different species of beans).
What am I doing, making pathetic jokes? It's like in wartime, going through the Blitz, using humour to stave off the fear.

Perched steeply to Greer's left was a hilltop town, and on a spur in the filmy void, a mere smudge on the skyline, another medieval watchtower. The ancient occupants of that tower once warned this little community when peril was imminent. They would have alerted the lookouts in the tower where Mischa was now working to the approach of an enemy. But they were watching for invading armies. Would they have identified a single stealthy infiltrator, with his camera and laptop, his notebooks and recording devices? With his slick, inveigling charm? Would they have identified these disparate items as weapons?

Below her was the sight, reassuring in its ordinariness, of Guy in a well-worn sloppy joe stealing a look through his telescope on the terrace outside the former chapel that was now Rollo's studio. While Greer and Rollo, according to Guy, were away with the fairies a lot of the time, he considered himself a man of the soil, well grounded in reality. He had set up his telescope on a tripod near the little war memorial and the low stone wall, where the land plummeted into the valley. We do a good class of view around here, Guy would tell their wine buyers, but this is the eye-candiest, the bobby-dazzler. This is the g-spot. You can almost drink this view.

Once, after he had observed what a crying shame it was that all the bloody clichés had been used up, they'd launched an ongoing competition to invent some more. It was a tough game – they found it surprisingly difficult to come up with something new, a phrase so pictorial and apt that others cannibalised it and it became a fixture.

Guy claimed this was because the treasure chest of visual clichés was finite. Its emptiness bore witness to the erosion of truth and beauty in their time. They were living through the decline and perilously close to the fall of Western civilisation.

'If we were in the Bronze Age or especially pre-biblical,' he said, 'or even pre the wretched nineteenth century, we could go to town. The cypresses standing like sentinels. The honey-coloured stones. The wine-dark sea.'

There was something about the elegance of their surroundings, he maintained, that invited rhetorical flourish. The reason for this was simple: the land they inhabited was the apogee, the ideal Platonic form of landscape that was a foundation of Western culture.

There was a brief period in which the cliché game had run rampant and made them so self-conscious that it interfered with ordinary speech. It became impossible to say anything about anything at all, since whatever was said sounded crude or platitudinous. The game had reached a natural conclusion soon after this, when Guy came up with what he declared was the ultimate one-word cliché: Tuscany. This perfectly proper noun had been made into something corny by writers, mainly English and mainly recent, who had a lot to answer for. Provence was another.

Greer's kitchen terrace overlooked the valley. On the far side the land sloped away at a steep angle from the thickly wooded floor. Beyond, narrow ridges extended in linear succession to the horizon. She stood out on the terrace and tried to dismiss everything from her mind but this view. She knew it so intimately, so completely, yet it was always surprising.

The countryside surrounded and enveloped her, as it had done since she first laid eyes on it. She always thought of it as her territory, a diorama tilted on its axis, an independent world unfolding in waves. It resembled a landscape painting, complete in itself and self-sufficient, containing a balance of wilderness and cultivation. She and Rollo agreed that it held within its layout everything necessary for beauty, variety and surprise in correct artistic proportion.

Landmarks revealed themselves only gradually. A farmhouse on the near ridge, encircled with bright fields. Slopes of vines in lucid, typewritten rows. A range of barren-looking mountains beyond, and in their foothills the ribbon of another settlement. On an escarpment to the south a classic silhouette of cypresses and umbrella pines.

At this time of year the air was bluish and hazy, blurred on the horizon, a little clearer but still indistinct in the middle distance. Only the foreground was well defined. Our lives have a similar perspective, she thought: the present moment alone is crisp and unambiguous. Yet the present as a concept is riddled with contradictions.

She retrieved as if from nowhere something Charlie had said on their last night together: 'I believe there is no word for "have" in Hebrew. You can't say, I "have" a wife.' This, he said, was because, strictly speaking, there was no way of capturing the present. The moment you tried to speak or write or even think of the moment, it had moved backwards in time and become the past. I feel I have a new affinity with Hebrew, Charlie had added, even if the language won't allow me to express it.

Greer had read about recent research that suggested there was a significant benefit to the mental health of people exposed to trees and nature, even in cities. But as she stared fixedly at the landscape she knew so well it seemed to ripple and change its nature before her eyes. She gripped the railings of the terrace wall. It was almost as if she had momentarily lost her bearings in a world which was not quite as it had been, its landmarks no longer safely familiar.

She thought, what can we do if the present is not here long enough to protect us? When there is a veil that hangs over everything beyond it, even over the day after this one? When all living beings are trapped in the same predicament and no exceptions are made? The truth is, no one can have more than a suspicion of what lies further away. There are no safe bets on the future. It's all guesswork, a bewildering maze of untrodden ways.

She had never imagined the future as a fearful place. Living with someone who inhabited the here and now with such alacrity, such intensity, the future hardly rated as an abstract idea. It was not a presence in her life or Mischa's, not in the way that most of her friends were constantly preoccupied with it.

But a different concept was beginning to assemble itself in her mind. A more concrete way of looking at the future, as an organic entity with visceral links to the past and to the present. It was a disturbing notion fraught with implications she would not, could not, think about. Was this, indeed, how others routinely saw it? Had her inability to do so been a wilful failure of the imagination?

You could influence the present, and through it the future, but you could do nothing about the past. Alone of the three the past was irrecoverable. It could not be changed, and it was potentially merciless.

I know about the past and its tentacles, she thought, but I have been blind. How have I never allowed for the possibility that the future, indecipherable though it surely is, might conceivably exert an influence over the present?

She felt herself caught up in a momentum she was helpless to influence, as if she were on the cusp of a volcanic river, rushing towards the mouth of a distant sea. The forbidden territory that beckoned from the outer reaches of her mind lay in the direct path of the boiling, heaving waters. The amorphous shapes were massed there in the dark, awaiting. She felt as if she were being borne bodily forwards, propelled towards them.

This was the future. It came to her like a blow to the heart.

13

Greer and Guy watched four men unloading huge logs from a lorry in the drive. It was cool today but not cold. A good day for replacing the wormy old pergola that ran half the length of Rollo and Guy's house and along the side garden. It had seen decades of service providing leafy shade, but now it was buckled and in imminent danger of collapse. It would be a tricky operation to save the equally timeworn grapevine it supported.

In charge and the brawniest was Agnieszka's husband, Angelo, a barrel-chested larrikin with a dirty, infectious laugh. The men were lugging chestnut beams 30 feet long. Chestnut was the hardworking wood they called the oak of Italy. It was used when something was built to last. This will see us out, Guy said, *and* our posterity what inherits it from us. Whatsoever that may be.

'Who *am* I going to leave this to?' he remarked to Greer, who was standing next to him. 'The feckless crew of nieces and nephews, I suppose. But don't worry, I'll bequeath you something if I pop off before you. What would you like? The winery?'

'That would be most acceptable.' Greer had had a conversation along these lines some years before with Rollo.

Guy would be his chief beneficiary, of course, but he had promised to leave her something special. From time to time he pointed out items he was setting aside for her: his Californian Bauer pottery, for instance, his Matisse odalisque and the exquisite pair of Gallé vases.

'Who are you going to leave your lot to?' Guy demanded inquisitively. 'Assuming Mischa falls off the perch first, which is a reasonable assumption. Haven't you got a sister?'

'Yes, I have. Somewhere.' A bleak wind seemed to blow around the words.

'I thought so. Tony said you and Mischa both had sisters, and I'd forgotten. You'd lost touch with yours, he said, and so, coincidentally, had M. To lose one is accidental but two looks like carelessness, he said.'

'When did he tell you this?'

'Oh, the other night. Last night, in point of fact. We had a nightcap together. As it were.'

'Did you?' She was galvanised. 'What else did he tell you?'

'Nothing much else, though I was pumping him.' He gave her a sly look. 'It was only a short talk we had. It was rather late.'

'Did he . . .?' She stopped, then made herself continue. 'Did he say whether he'd seen my sister? Did he tell you if he'd seen Josie?'

'No, I don't think he did. Say, I mean. You can ask him yourself, he won't bite *you*.'

He was summoned over to the men, where an animated conversation to do with the preservation of the grapevine ensued in Italian. He smirked at her over his shoulder.

Greer heard a crunch on the gravel and her name called. It was Tony. He wanted to show her something, he said, looking pleased with himself. Something that might interest her. He waved a jaunty hand at Guy.

Tony led her to the upstairs floor of Mischa's studio in the tower, where he had set up three plywood sheets.

Attached with double-sided tape were photographs of Mischa's paintings, all the works Tony planned to refer to and illustrate. The photos were divided into sections under separate chapter headings, with the current location of each picture and the permission of its owner neatly listed on an attached card.

'These are amateurish pics, mostly. I took them as an aide-mémoire. The galleries provide professional transparencies for publication.'

He was still waiting on some of these from various sources. A photographer would be coming in from Florence next week, he told her, if that was OK, to shoot some atmospheric stuff in the studio and surroundings. There were folders of photos still to put up.

Tony took the first sheet of plywood and laid it out flat on one of the trestle tables. 'Chapter One: Karlovy Vari, 1940–1957' had no pictures attached to it, unsurprisingly, but Greer saw four still photographs taken from life. Three of these were blow-ups from original tiny black and white snaps, Tony told her, old and creased but perfectly clear. Greer resisted the temptation to snatch them from the board and pore over them. They were the first images she had ever seen from Mischa's childhood.

She saw a frowning, plump-cheeked baby in a bonnet and long, enveloping gown held vertically aloft for the camera by a grave young woman with a square face and strong jaw, and deep-set dark eyes. Mischa's eyes, but with arched, feminine eyebrows.

'That's Mischa in the embroidered frock with his nice-looking mum,' Tony said. 'He was always known as Mikhal, of course, within the family. Wasn't he a cutie? Don't you just love that grouchy expression? Grete said he was woken up for the photo, and it shows. He was a war baby, so they were probably snatching the moment. And it was probably taken to show him off to his dad, don't you think?'

The next picture had obviously been taken in a photographic studio. It showed Mischa as a small boy seated in front of an older girl standing in a long skirt. Both children were heavily and rather fustily dressed and appeared to be staring intently at something behind the camera. The girl had her hands on Mischa's shoulders.

'That's Grete, forcing him down. He's six years of age here, so it's soon after the war and she's sixteen, but I swear you can already see the word "battleaxe" imprinted on her features.'

Greer scrutinised the image but saw only a stocky girl with a doughy, rather indeterminate face. She looked closely at the well-scrubbed little boy, who was recognisably a prototype of Mischa, only a less emphatic and tidier version. The lower lip jutted out, the eyes were black and bellicose.

The qualities were intensified in the third picture, another formal family group but this time expanded to six members: their father and mother with Mischa and Grete, Grete's Russian husband, who had a look of Prokofiev, and their toddler son. Mischa was a hefty teenager now, with a Bryl-creemed quiff. He looked, as Tony remarked, like one hell of a handful. His parents shared similar pronounced Slavic features. His father was broad-shouldered and burly, with keen eyes under bushy brows like Mischa's and a soft, sensual mouth.

Grete's hair was pulled severely upwards revealing, as Tony didn't hesitate to point out, her high autocratic fore-head and pleasure-averse countenance. This person you are talking so disparagingly about is the de facto sister-in-law I have never met, Greer thought. Has it occurred to you that I might find that offensive? Or was that your intention?

'Mischa's seen these?' she asked.

Mischa was working some distance from them near the south windows, apparently oblivious to the vista with its blandishments as well as to the intruders in his studio. He was humming to himself a tune from *Pal Joey* as he assembled lengths of cedar into a stretcher – what he and Rollo called the cross-and-bracing work. Both artists enjoyed a running dialogue about the practical aspects of their craft, the French papers and Belgian linens, the relative merits of different suppliers and raw materials. Greer never failed to find these discussions, and the obsessive devotion with which they were conducted, riveting.

'I showed him all the photos and he was briefly, well, I won't say enthralled, but he did take a good look.'

She noticed that Tony wasn't bothering to keep his voice down. By now he must know there was no need, since nothing penetrated the force-field of Mischa's concentration.

'I even managed to drag a few quotes about his family out of him.' He made a wry face. 'I've been finding it hard to get anything personal out of the maestro. It's kinda like pulling teeth. Or is it just me?'

She allowed him a tolerant smile. 'It's not just you. He doesn't like talking about himself very much. Especially to strange men.'

Tony looked humorously crestfallen. 'That's too bad. I'm trying not to act overly strange.'

'Perhaps the trouble is with your acting.'

Now he looked really, pleasingly, downcast. 'Well, any tips or crumbs you can offer would be gratefully accepted.'

'Oh, I've got no tips at all,' she said briskly. 'Or crumbs. I warned you before, the maestro doesn't dwell on the past. That includes talking and thinking about it.'

'Thinking as well, huh? Can you really be so sure about that? If you don't mind me asking.'

She glanced across at Mischa. Everything about him was reassuring and solid. She thought, he's wrapped in the protective cocoon of unconsciousness that is his working habit. Neither seeing nor hearing the world around him.

'Yes, I can be so sure. I know him fairly well, remember.' And a great deal better than you do. Except for the time before I met him.

'Right. But —' Tony seemed genuinely perplexed. 'Is he really, you know, that knowable?' He paused. 'That simple?'

'He's not in the least simple. And in his creative life I readily admit that there is a vast area where he is not remotely knowable or predictable.'

'To himself as well, would you say?'

'Perhaps principally to himself.' The mystery of the origins of his work, she had always believed, was the source of his obsession with it. She added: 'His art is a conduit. I think that may be the secret of its hold on him.'

She remembered how she had envied the mystery of his creativity. It had always been an autonomous entity, invulnerable to any outside forces. Unlike her own.

'Art is his way of tapping into his subconscious? Of plumbing the id?'

Greer smiled involuntarily. 'That sounds a touch – glib, if I may say so. I think it's a lot less straightforward than that.' She paused. 'Art is not a means to an end for him. It would be misleading to think of it in those terms. His work is a compulsion, an end in itself.'

'Maybe it's also his way of connecting with the past.' Tony had raised his eyebrows, which seemed to widen his blue eyes.

'Possibly, but if so I doubt if it's in any way conscious.' She thought, here we are, having this very personal discussion about Mischa in his own space as if he wasn't there, and Tony is taping it. It's an incongruous situation entirely of Tony's making. He has engineered it, no doubt for his own purposes.

Tony said slowly, 'It almost sounds like Mischa has some kind of a mental block about the past. His own history. Could this be because he's uncomfortable with it? That's the usual reason, isn't it?'

Is it Mischa you are really talking about?

'It might be the usual reason,' she said tersely, 'but Mischa is not a usual person. As you may have noticed. I think you'll just have to accept that his past doesn't interest him much any more, simply because it's over. When something is over for him it's done with.'

'And that applies to friends and family alike? Artists are notorious for discarding people, I guess, when their usefulness is past.'

This sounded more like a joke than a question, but it did strike her as unduly punitive and she felt obliged to amend it, as if she were touching up a portrait she was making of an image-conscious celebrity. Am I protecting Mischa, airbrushing him as if he were a supermodel, she thought, when he emphatically doesn't want to be protected or airbrushed? Or am I striving to protect myself?

'When he has physically moved on I think he moves on mentally too. But I also think this is largely accidental, it's a by-product of his single-mindedness, his driven concentration on his work. Perhaps it would be different if his sister was living in the next village, I don't know.'

'Did you ever encourage him to contact his parents again?'

He was straightening the photo of Mischa with his family. She wanted to object, to say harshly, why would I, when it was a bond between us? We had both jettisoned our families, can't you grasp even that seminal fact? We were on our own together from that time forward. And on the same imaginative level, too. We saw ourselves in terms that were strictly romantic. We were on the run.

But not, she wanted to add, with the same stakes. The stakes for me were of a different order. I had overturned one of society's most cherished norms. I think I saw myself as a moral outlaw.

She said instead, aware that her voice sounded taut and strained, 'I don't remember speaking about it.' Her voice was always the giveaway.

'I say that because in spite of all the feuding within the family before he left he never fell out totally with them, according to Grete and others. There was residual affection there.' Tony's pitch continued to be light and breezy, but she sensed he was working up to something. He had an agenda. But then it was wise to bear in mind the fact that Tony always had one of those.

'I'd rate it as a fair to average childhood overall,' he went on, 'say six or six point five out of ten, wouldn't you? Not quite as high on the happiness quotient as your own, right? How would you rate yours?'

It was a chatty little question. His teeth flashed in a smile.

'Mine?' She had a sudden mental picture of the family group, the two sisters with their parents at Greer's twenty-first birthday party, the day they had all been photographed together for the last time.

'My childhood was happy, yes.' She looked away, caught off guard by a wave of emotion.

'That was my impression. He never got on with his sister like you got on with yours, did he? Or, for that matter, with his parents.'

Where had that impression come from? Charlie or Josie? Or both? As she attempted to regroup, to grapple with this issue in her mind, he remarked, 'It must be nice, to have had a happy childhood.'

She was aware of his unblinking eyes on her.

'You didn't?'

'Two point five. Three, maybe.' She refused to engage those eyes. 'My mom adopted me out when I was a little kid. She and my dad were never a couple, and she was struggling with another baby from a new guy who definitely didn't want to know me. She just couldn't hack it. Kind of a banal low-rent scenario, I suppose, right?'

What was he doing, here? The eyes were still on her. He laughed.

'My new parents went on to have two of their own biological kids later – that happens a lot, you know? Two more boys. I grew up feeling I was Cinderella, except my brothers weren't that ugly. To look at, anyhow. The only thing I got back from my real dad was his Italian name, Corbino.'

Why are you telling me these things? Why do you imagine I want to know anything about you? No, you don't imagine anything of the kind. You want me to know.

'You managed to do all right, in spite of everything.'

He laughed again, almost gaily this time. 'Yeah, I guess I did OK, didn't I?'

She felt vaguely nauseous, and turned away from him to the fourth photograph. It was larger and in colour, and showed a narrow house, three storeys with a steep gable, Juliet balcony and decorative black-painted fretwork.

Tony had taken this photo only last year. There were different owners now, of course, but they'd let him take a look inside and he'd seen the very room where Mischa came into the world. It was a simple, sweet house, Tony went on, as if this subject flowed naturally from the previous topic, and Mischa lived here until he was seventeen. It must have influenced his aesthetic sense.

Under the heading 'Chapter Two: Prague, 1957–1969' were two postcard-sized reproductions, atmospheric paintings of the city at dusk, with elegant street lamps and lighted windows. One showed a downpour on the Charles Bridge and glistening water on the road. Both were new to Greer, but the artist's youthful virtuosity was evident, even in these small-scale images. Tony touched them in a manner that verged on the reverential.

'These are amazing, aren't they? You don't get much of an idea with prints this size, but he's blended quite dramatic chiaroscuro with elements of grisaille. Gone for and achieved kind of gothic effects with the elongated treatment of the houses. The technique is incredibly confident and daring already.'

Neither had she seen the pair of black-and-white personal snaps pinned here. One was a grainy group shot, which Tony had identified underneath as Mischa's art-school class.

'Isn't this a classic? He's the unwashed hippie here,' he pointed, 'dangling a yard of ash off his fag. How about the long hair and stubble? And the scowl. He's ostentatiously ignoring the camera. *La vie de Bohème*'s the desired effect, wouldn't you say, en route to an absinthe at the Café des Artistes?'

The other was of Mischa looking much as he had when she first met him but a little less wild and dishevelled, standing next to a petite young woman with an hour-glass figure and heart-shaped face. Her face was tilted up towards his and crowned with a halo of dark hair set in neat, shining waves. She was leaning into him, encircling his waist with possessive arms. They were in a rural setting beside water and trees. The caption read: 'With Elsa Montag, summer of 1968.'

Tony said, 'That was taken in the Prague Spring, in the halcyon days just before the Russian tanks rolled in. She's fixated on him but he's looking away from her, it's quite revealing, isn't it, in that half-accidental way you often get in photos? The original was very creased, but it'll touch up OK.'

He took the photo by the corner and laid it on the table. 'They're an incongruous couple. Don't you think so?'

He is monitoring my reaction, Greer thought, conscious of the tape recorder working away on the table in the narrow gap between them. She picked up the photo. She knew Elsa's age to be twenty-four, but in this picture she looked more like an innocent schoolgirl. Her unguarded expression, the devotion and longing on her face struck Greer as almost shocking in their nakedness. Before everything ended in tears, perhaps well before anything had even happened between them, people would have worried about the emotional insecurity of this young woman.

She asked, without needing to feign interest or concern, 'Is this the only one you have of Elsa?'

'Greer, I was lucky to get even this one. She had destroyed everything to do with Mischa. His sister found this. It was in the pocket of an old duffle coat Mischa left behind, and Grete came across it when she passed the coat on to her son, Milos, after it had been hanging in a cupboard for a couple of years. She'd shoved it in the family album and forgotten all about it, until she brought the album out to show me. She was embarrassed to see it there actually. I had a helluva job getting it out of the album so I could photograph it.'

He grimaced. 'Had to resort to the biographer's party trick of pinching it in the end.' He noticed Greer's expression. 'I mean borrowing it. Yeah, she was quite protective of her little brother, in spite of the enthusiastic disapproval regularly dished out.' He glanced at her. 'I guess siblings are like that. Blood's thicker than water, right?'

She thought, what big eyes you have, Mister Wolf. The artfulness of those clear blue eyes was so transparent to her by now that she was surprised no one else had remarked on it. Mischa too was transparent to her much of the time, but never with artifice. He was still humming – now it sounded like 'Stormy Weather' – and wielding a screwdriver. He had his broad back to them, and even at this distance she could pick up his vibrations, his total immersion in the task at hand.

'What happened to Elsa?'

'After he cleared out? It was no picnic, to be honest. Young woman dumped by penniless, oddball artist she'd left her prominent husband for.'

He was being careful to sound neutral, even jocular, she noticed.

'Yes, I am aware of the background.'

'OK. Well, yeah, she disappeared for a while. No one knew exactly where she went.'

There was a thumping full stop here with a questioning intonation. He was seeking a response. Greer shook her head.

'When she turned up again she was in the throes of a pretty full-on breakdown. The first of many. Pavel refused to have her back. She worked sporadically, survived. Life was tough of course for everyone, everything either stagnated or went backwards after the Russians moved in.'

She thought he had finished with this, when he added, 'I think her diagnosis would be severe bipolar, these days. She's pretty screwed up mentally, as I see it. To put it mildly.'

Did he see his own mother as having been similarly screwed up by men?

'Did she ever marry again? Have another relationship?' Greer heard unwelcome notes in her voice, of anxiety and something else more unfamiliar. She collected herself. 'Did she – get over Mischa at all, eventually?'

'Did she put it behind her and move on? I guess not. She doesn't look anything like that picture now, I can tell you. She's a little old grey-haired lady, you wouldn't recognise her. There's a kind of fervent submissiveness about her, but maybe she always had that, you know?'

He was staring at the photograph, running his fingers through his blond-streaked hair, which stood on end like the bristles of a brush, in the currently fashionable manner. He must have put gel in it this morning to get it to behave like that, Greer thought irrelevantly.

'What I think is, it was like she came to the decision way back in 1969 that when she lost Mischa her life would be ruined. And she stuck by that decision, and it duly was. I think that happens with people sometimes, that relinquishing of responsibility for their fate, you know what I mean?'

Greer nodded. She knew exactly what he meant. She felt a tingling in her hands, and realised she had been digging her nails into the palms.

Then he surprised her: 'Your husband, Charlie McNicoll, on the other hand, was not like that. He reacted the opposite way. He made the decision he wasn't going to let his entire life be ruined by losing you, and it wasn't. He got over it just fine. Eventually.'

Now she did meet his eyes. It was as if she had been cast overboard to flounder in a choppy sea and someone, the least likely person, had thrown her a lifeline. She had to make an effort to stop herself from saying to him, from saying humbly: thank you for telling me that.

Mischa came over to them just then, having finished with his stretcher and displaying an example of that sixth sense Greer had always been convinced he possessed. He stood at her side with his arm draped across her shoulder in a reversed reflection of the image, nearly forty years old, that lay on the table in front of them.

Greer said sadly, 'She was very pretty, Mischa.'

'Pretty and sweet. Far too sweet and a hundred miles too trusting for me. I needed a rude and bossy woman. Do you hear that, Tony?' He raised Greer's arm and kissed it from the elbow to the wrist. 'Don't look at those photos, they make me feel old and bad. I don't want them in the book, Tony.'

'Well, I'm always at you for some more modern ones where you're good and old.'

'They would be worse. Paintings can do the work much better. Let them tell the story.'

'That's quite true, isn't it, if you could only decipher them,' Tony said to Greer as Mischa sloped off with a backward grin in her direction. 'The art is the real autobiography of the artist. Did you know he left behind a whole bunch of paintings with Elsa? All his work up to that time. That was all he had to give her, I guess. He had no money.'

'Yes. What happened to them?'

'Well, that's the tragedy of it. If only she'd hung on to even one, but she didn't keep any of them, just gave them away or flogged them at the time for next to nothing. One does pop up very occasionally at auction, like these two here, but mostly they've disappeared off the radar.'

There were few surviving paintings from the third section, 'Between Continents'. This covered Mischa's unproductive years, his haphazard, zigzagging journey to Vienna and eventually to Australia. But 'Chapter Four: The Australian Period, 1976–1981' had two rows of images. Greer recognised every one, even though she hadn't set eyes on the originals for more than twenty years. The majority of them, she saw, had remained in Australian hands.

'This group here,' Tony drew an arc around them in the air with his forefinger, 'are the pictures I'm using from the inaugural Melbourne exhibition, the Corbett Gallery show. I didn't manage to get everything: two I really wanted I haven't been able to track down. Nineteen seventy-nine, when you met, and 1980 were the first bumper crop. You can date the beginning of Mischa's real career as an artist from those years.'

He grinned at her. 'Must have been your ground-breaking influence, right? I flirted with a title for this chapter – 'Mischa Meets his Muse', but he vetoed it on two counts. A, it was tacky, and B, you'd never stand for it.'

'He was accurate on both counts,' Greer said absently. As he spoke Tony had been pulling out some new photographs from the folder. She watched his hands with a feeling of renewed disquiet as he began to put them up. His fingers were tapered, with well-tended nails. The nails looked unusually shiny for a man. She wondered if he could be wearing nail polish.

The first photo was a colour shot taken inside the Corbett Gallery showing a wall of Mischa's pictures. And there was Verity, standing with Mischa at the opening of his exhibition. Verity looked slim and refined in a conservative navy suit with a pleated skirt. She radiated pride, propri-etorial pride. She had been to the hairdresser that morning. Greer recalled her own mental eye-roll at the sight of Verity's hair, newly auburn and newly permed into small immaculate curls.

'What colour's her hair?'

'Sorry?'

'Verity. I just wondered what colour her hair is these days.'

'Hey, that's a good question. Definitely not your standard-issue blue-rinse old lady.' He was taking the question seriously, as she had expected. 'It's like, obviously henna'd, but in an expensive, discreet way that suits her style. Kind of chestnut, or coppery, I'd describe it.'

So Verity had clung to that colour for the rest of her life. She must have regarded it, Greer supposed, as the colour of her greatest success. A success that had turned out to be fleeting, due primarily to the actions of Greer herself. This was an uneasy thought, and yet the overall idea of Verity was not depressing. The woman she remembered was never going to end up as your standard-issue old lady. She had always exhibited far too much attitude.

Next to the photo of Mischa and Verity, Tony had pinned up the typed catalogue of prices. Further along was a colour head shot of a much younger Greer, tanned and smiling, tendrils of blonde hair in her eyes. She remembered Charlie taking it on the Isle of Pines, on their last holiday together.

And there they were, she and Charlie as a couple, wielding chopsticks, looking festive and carefree in their favourite Chinese restaurant. An ice bucket of champagne hung over the side of the table. Charlie had drunk most of that.

Tony's caption to this one read: 'Greer Gordon with her first husband, Charles McNicoll, at The Flower Drum in Melbourne, May 1979'.

She found the choice of photograph and the message conveyed by its selection both poignant and ironic. On this particular night in May she had given Charlie news that had elated him and told him she would marry him, at long last. Was Tony in possession of this highly charged piece of information?

The leaves had scurried in little whirlwinds around their ankles as she and Charlie emerged from the restaurant's bright, soaring interior into the cold snap of Little Bourke Street. It was an autumnal evening, cruelly appropriate, she thought now. Yet neither of them could have had any inkling, as they stepped outside, that the decay and death of their relationship was imminent.

'Was it Charlie,' she asked, 'who gave you this?'

Tony nodded. 'And the one from the Isle of Pines. They're copied off the originals, of course. He picked them out because he said you liked these two.'

Had he really said that? 'He'd kept them?'

She wondered if it was her imagination or whether Tony had shot her an odd look.

'Oh, yeah. He wasn't like Elsa, who burnt all hers. Charlie's a very organised guy. That's how I got to see some of your old artworks.'

Ah, so that was how.

'And he kept every photo from your time together, in two albums. Every picture neatly identified and dated. And a whole bunch of your old family photos as well, in case you want any copies. All in chronological order. You're in there only up to the time you disappeared, of course.'

She could read nothing from his bland expression. He had another photograph in his hand, face downwards. He flipped it over. It was another head shot, and she saw whose head it was. If Tony was planning to shock me, she thought, he has failed, because I was half expecting this.

The photograph was of Josie, looking just as Greer remembered her, but with her glossy dark hair cut in a chin-length bob that was very chic and '20s and suited her far better than the swinging shoulder-length style she'd worn since she was a teenager.

'This is a nice one of her, don't you think? Charlie took it. He's quite a photographer.'

That had to mean Tony had met Josie. Didn't it? But when had Charlie taken it, and where? The background gave no clues, it was nothing but a cloudless blue sky. Josie was wearing a sleeveless orange top and a choker made up of several strands of turquoise beads. Greer didn't recall it and thought she would have, as it was a distinctive necklace.

'It was taken in Hong Kong, that one, circa 1983. About three years after you left.'

That settled that, then.

Tony's voice said: 'You two look very alike in these shots, don't you?'

There was no reply, and he continued: 'Even though you're fair and she's dark, there's a strong family resemblance.'

He hit the stop button on the first tape, and interposed on the second: 'She was seriously rattled by the picture of Josie. Didn't know what it meant. What she thought it most probably had to mean was going to confirm her worst fears. But she still wasn't prepared to come out and ask me.'

He flicked the first tape back on. Greer's voice, sounding distant and cold, said: 'Yes, we were always told we looked alike. It shouldn't surprise you, since we are sisters.'

Tony listened to his own voice saying: 'This chapter's well represented with illustrations from 1979 on. There's all the Melbourne stuff, and examples of works made in Port Douglas and Cooktown, and Darwin the following year. But I've hit a weird blank spot here, Greer. I can't seem to come up with any pictures from the period that came right after Melbourne, before Port. That's the five months' stint in Sydney. Mischa's no help at all, he just switches off, you know how he is.'

There was a long wordless interval in which Mischa's humming could be discerned faintly in the background, before Tony's voice resumed. 'I just wondered if you had any ideas of where I might go rummaging?'

He stopped the tape. 'She clammed right up on me then. Just shook her head blankly.'

He switched his recorded voice on again, sounding as matter-of-fact as if he were discussing the provenance of pictures: 'I guess it was a tricky time in a whole raft of ways, after leaving your former lives behind, having a first shot at living together. Life with an eccentric artist's not easy, huh, even at the best of times?'

He had followed that up with a laugh, quite a hearty one, but Greer had not joined in.

His voice altered. 'I know you used a post office box for your address, but you had a little flat in Darlinghurst in inner Sydney, right?'

Greer's reply was inaudible.

'You didn't see many people. Was it a happy time for you, overall?'

He switched it off again. 'Her expression changes. It's like she's suddenly twigged this guy she's standing next to is a carcinogen. And recoils from me like she might catch something terminal.'

14

6th August
'Tis done. We ran away. 'Twere done in a hurry.

O nly twelve laconic words at the top of the page. Ten, if you allowed the abbreviations. The third sentence was something of an understatement. Greer assumed it was a lazy play on the line in *Macbeth*. 'If it were done when 'tis done, then 'twere well it were done quickly.' She had no memory of putting the words on the page, but she remembered only too well the night with Charlie after she had spilt the beans.

At the time she had thought it the worst night of her life. She was to revise this rating as less extreme on the scale of badness fairly soon afterwards, and on more than one occasion.

She turned the page, but there was nothing more. The date of the next diary entry was early the following year. It was hard to believe that she could have written so perfunctorily, in such a throwaway fashion, about something so momentous. And, more reprehensibly, not only in her own life. The effect on the lives of others, more devastating in the short term, was also more far-reaching.

She thought, actually it would have been sometime the

next day when I took the trouble to scribble those inadequate words. I must have been spaced out. Completely off my trolley, as Tony might say. But the truer explanation, I suspect, is more prosaic and discreditable. I couldn't bring myself to pick up a pen and describe events that reflected on me so badly.

At least, however, she could remember most of what happened. She hadn't repressed those memories, deliberately or otherwise. They were all there, burnt into the hard drive, ripe for retrieval. She picked up the pen, thought better of it and switched to a pencil. It could be rubbed out. This was never going to be easy.

19th April 2006
I left Josie's flat and sat in a café. Then I drove through the city and the afternoon rush hour to Mischa's room in St Kilda. He was painting, still working on what I assumed was the same nude of me sprawled across a bed. I told him without preamble that I was going to leave Charlie . . .

Without preamble was putting it mildly. She had angered another driver by cutting her off and roaring into a parking space round the corner, charged up the rickety stairs three steps at a time and burst into Mischa's room.

A picture lay on a table under the windows to catch whatever grimy light could filter through. He was standing in front of it, his back to the door, swathed in a beanie, scarf and woollen gloves with the fingertips cut out. It was perishingly cold, although she noticed a paraffin heater that hadn't been there last time.

She herself was disguised in a heavy overcoat. She said unsteadily, 'Is that painting me?'

He didn't turn round. His hand froze on the canvas.

'Of course it's you. Have you come back to me?'

'Of course I have. You knew I would.'

'Come here then and don't cry.'

'But I've got a condition to make, first.'

He turned round then and looked her over in her black swagger coat and peaked urchin's cap. 'All right. I agree to it.'

She thought, nobody in my life has ever grinned at me so impishly, with such pure and lascivious delight. If that is not a contradiction in terms. She said, laughing through the renewed film of tears, 'But you don't know what it is yet.'

. . . on condition that we run away as soon as possible. I said I wanted to cut all ties with Melbourne and move to Sydney. It was a big metropolis and we could lose ourselves there. The reasons I gave Mischa for wanting to get away from Melbourne were practical and symbolic, to do with ending my relationship with my husband and minimising the hurt to him. I pointed out that Sydney would be new to me as well. It would be a level playing field for both of us.

I didn't give him any other reason.

Mischa's reaction was . . .

She paused, pencil suspended. How had Mischa reacted? As if she had belatedly come to her senses, that was how. He'd been unsurprised. He was raring to go. She saw now that the way he had regarded it as a bit of a lark, as nothing to make a song and dance about, had made it easier for her. But then, at that juncture, he had only been privy to the half of it.

She told Mischa she would feel much happier if they left Melbourne altogether, because her working life had been there and too many people knew her. She didn't want to run the risk of bumping into mutual friends or, more particularly, her husband every time they went out. It would be less humiliating for Charlie if the runaways, as she was already thinking of the two of them, made a fresh start in a town that was an unknown quantity. That way she and Mischa would be in the same boat, immigrants together.

Besides, Sydney was larger and the art scene was arguably bigger there. She had even said, disingenuously, lying through her teeth, that she was sure Verity would gladly recommend a good Sydney dealer and there was no reason why she shouldn't continue to handle Mischa's Melbourne sales anyway – once Verity bounces back, Greer had added, from the double whammy of losing her star artist and her valued assistant.

She needn't have bothered with all this specious mustering of reasons. It was overkill and quite uncalled for. Mischa had accepted what she proposed without comment or qualification; with zealous enthusiasm and without listening to the detail, most likely, because he was also trying energetically to get her into bed then and there, and was indignant when she refused. Her explanation – that she had not yet told her husband and had to go home to get it over with – did succeed in pulling him up short.

'But that is the only excuse I will accept from now on.'

He thrust her away at arm's length, and they had looked into each other's eyes for a long moment. She'd finally said, with fingers surreptitiously crossed, 'That's just as well then, because this will be its only outing.'

She had put her hand into her capacious coat pocket and encountered a bulging plastic bag.

'I nearly forgot. Close your eyes and open your hands. I've got a present for you.'

She pulled it out and spilt a slender arc of ivory sand and a cloud of fluttering tropical petals, scarlet and gold and purple, into the capacious bowl of his cupped hands.

'The sand was very important to me. It brought back the feeling of being with you, for some reason.' She caught his eye. 'It was so silky and soft, but that's got nothing whatsoever to do with it.'

He looked down at the pyramid of sand and petals and closed his eyes again, 'It is my first and best present.'

She was reminded of the look on his face the day she had first met him. That afternoon he'd been loudly singing and gazing at his own painting of an Aboriginal girl on a piano in a paddock. He had the same expression now. In her diary she had called it beatific, a look of blissful happiness.

'It can't be the best if it's also the first.'

'Yes it can, and don't argue. It is the first *proper* present I have ever been given. Therefore it is also the best.'

On the point of leaving, she had looked over at the painting on the table under the window. 'Do you always take this long to finish something?'

'Are you always so non-observant?'

'*Un*observant, if you don't mind.'

Only then did she see that all along the balcony wall, under the frowzy French windows where he had rubbed a few cursory holes in the dust, the floor was littered with discarded drawings. Limbs, breasts, buttocks, hair, torsos, crossed out, drawn and redrawn, and finally a face she knew. Her face. She circumnavigated them in growing amazement.

'Are all these body parts mine?'

'Don't you know what yours look like yet?'

'Not necessarily. Not from the back I don't. I haven't got eyes in the back of my head.'

'Half of them are necessarily from the front.'

'Why is there only one of my face?'

'Because I can do your face already. I saw it plenty of times in the gallery. The rest always had clothes all over it. Nice white, I mean nice *cream* suits.'

'Not completely always it didn't.' She gazed at his unrepentant face. He was tipping the sand and petals very slowly and carefully into a dusty jam jar. 'All right, it usually did.'

He looked up. 'I prefer that it usually doesn't, do you understand?'

He screwed a lid on the glass jar, and rubbed the dust off against his trousers.

Two finished nudes were stacked against the wall in the corner. One was a charcoal drawing, the other she recognised as the original – the one Mischa had made after their first night together. Their only night together, up to that point.

The work in progress, she saw now she approached it, was radically different. Here the unclothed figure was reclining on her side confronting the onlooker directly, the spine fluidly arched, one leg propped up with the knee bent and the other lying flat and folded inwards from knee to groin. The line of the body and the creamy flesh tones were liquid and voluptuous, but it was the conjunction of body and face that riveted the attention. He had been working on the face. It was soft in repose but alive with a sensuously transported intelligence.

Greer had stood silently in front of it. She thought, he has set himself the riskiest, the most demanding of tasks, to capture the principal components of desire, the physical and the mental, and astonishingly he has pulled it off. She had shivered, but not from the cold, her arms crossed tight around her ribs.

'Well? Do you approve of yourself?'

She had sought for adequate words. 'I think it's the first intellectually erotic nude that I've ever seen.'

'Is that a compliment or an insult?'

'Mischa, it's the most heartfelt tribute to your nerve and technique that I can come up with, right at this moment.'

She had the pleasure of watching his face light up. He had blown her kisses as she drove away on the icy street. All the way home in the car, as she drove to tell her husband their short marriage was over, she held in her mind the beatific smile that she, and no one else, had generated.

I suppose Mischa's reaction was a mirror image of mine: that a future together had been inevitable since we met. Morality did not enter into it. It was how things simply had to be. We both felt gripped at that stage – gripped and energised – by an uplifting kind of fatalism, as if it was predestined for us to be together. I can only think that this somehow cushioned me from the enormity of the blow I was about to bring down on Charlie's head.

I did not return to the gallery that day. I knew I'd cleared my desk and left everything in order before I went away on holiday. Verity had managed without me for three weeks; she would find someone to take my place. It wasn't that I couldn't face her. I hardly gave her a second thought. We did intend to tell her we were going – just not yet.

A kind explanation might be that I was suffering from mental and emotional overload. An unkind and perhaps truer one might be that I had one end in view, and for this all means were justified.

Greer got up abruptly and walked away from her desk into the kitchen. She felt a headache coming and dropped three soluble aspirins in a glass of water. Tony was outside again chatting to, or more likely up, the team of muscular men working on the pergola. They had knocked off and were getting stuck into a tray of beers. She saw Agnieszka emerge from the laundry underneath her house and belt across the parade ground at full tilt. Her body language suggested strongly that she had issues with her husband. Greer watched as she confronted Angelo. Her head did not quite come up to his brawny shoulder.

The little pantomime put her in mind, as it had often done, of a feminist Punch & Judy show in which Judy was the aggressor. The outcome followed the usual pattern. Angelo who-is-no-angel-o did his impersonation of a baboon. He swilled down his beer and capered bow-legged after his wife to the car park, making ribald gestures at her back for the benefit of his workmates.

Greer looked at her watch. It was already 6 pm. She observed Tony stroll across to Rollo's studio, knock on the door and disappear inside.

She returned slowly to her desk. She thought, how inadequate a diary is. It is as difficult to be honest now as it was easy to prevaricate then.

We planned to take away with us all Mischa's works in progress, including another nude of me, which I recognised as a tour de force. Also my current pictures and materials, as I meant to persist with my own portraiture.

Then I drove home. That drive is a blank, but I did stop to pick up some fish and chips.

Even at the time it had seemed wrong that this momentous dinner with her husband should be a takeaway, warmed up in the oven and unloaded on to plates from foil containers. But she hadn't felt up to cooking anything.

She parked alongside Charlie's black BMW in the two-car garage. A side door in the garage opened onto a short path leading to the house, where the extensive ground floor was taken up by an open-plan living area. There was a stone fireplace, and a sunroom and kitchen at opposite ends. Charlie had built a log fire and was relaxing in an armchair, still in his business suit and tie, collar undone, tie loosened, *Time* magazine in one hand and a scotch on the rocks in the other. Brahms' *Violin Concerto*, the first movement, was playing on the stereo.

Two thoughts lodged in Greer's mind as she walked into the house, taking off her coat. First, this is the last time I will ever open the door of my home to see Charlie sitting contentedly there. After I leave this house I will always open the door and see Mischa. And second, I introduced Charlie to this music.

For many years afterwards the atmosphere and the memories surrounding the composition were such that she was unable to listen to even a few bars of it.

I went to Charlie and tried to break the news that I was in love with somebody else. He couldn't take it in at first.

He had risen to kiss her as she came in, as he always did, but she stepped back and blurted, without thinking, the timeworn line of the adulterer.

'Charlie, there's something I have to tell you.' Before he turned his head away she saw his lips whiten with the premonition of shock.

'I've met someone, and I've fallen in love. I'm so terribly, terribly sorry, Charlie.'

Even to her ears the words sounded rehearsed, stiff, banal, reeking of synthetic compassion. Their very ordinariness made her feel suddenly detached from the scene, like a visitor.

'I didn't seek it out, Charlie, truly. I never expected it. I never wanted to hurt you.'

They were standing two metres apart, facing each other. He shook his head, and Greer saw a fleeting expression on his face she had never seen there before. It was a defence-less, frightened look that altered Charlie's entire appearance. He was normally so debonair. Her mask of detachment dissolved in an instant and she began to shake. He took her arm and led her to a chair by the fire.

'Sit down and try to relax. Do you want a cup of tea, or – a drink?'

'No. Yes. Perhaps a drink.'

He'd gone to the fridge and poured her some white wine, topped the glass with soda water, then pulled his chair round and sat opposite, his eyes fixed on her.

'How long ago?'

His first question. It was automatic. She had expected it.

'Less than a month.' She met his eyes. 'I didn't want it to happen, Charlie. It was an accident.'

'An accident.' He gave a half smile. 'A one-off?'

'I really wish that's what it was.'

'But we've just been away for three weeks. You can't mean less than a month.' She saw him computing this, his mouth taut. 'Greer, what exactly are we talking about? Over what period did this – whatever it is – happen?'

'Just – well, just literally before we went on holiday.'

'You mean, really only a few weeks ago?' He looked incredulous. 'Three weeks? Before this wonderful holiday we've just come back from? That was our honeymoon. Did you forget?' He stood up and immediately sat down again. She saw his hands clench and unclench on his thighs.

She looked away. Put like that, it was shaming. 'Only a week before. Otherwise I wouldn't have – gone.'

'A week!' He shook his head in disbelief. 'Why not? Why wouldn't you have gone? I didn't know, did I?' He managed a full smile, without a vestige of amusement in it. 'Why are you telling me now?'

She drew a deep breath.

'Because I – knew straightaway what it was going to mean.'

He got to his feet slowly and refilled his glass, came back and balanced on the arm of her chair. 'Let's not get ahead of ourselves here, dear. There's no point in saying anything both of us might regret.'

He often called her dear. She had never liked it much, associating it with an older generation's endearments. But she had never said anything. On hearing it now she felt two tears squeeze out and run down her cheek, and Charlie's handkerchief wiping them away.

He said gently, 'I'm your husband now, Greer. As of two months, remember? We have an awful lot riding on this, don't we? We can get over this, whatever it is. We can fix it, however bad it might seem at the moment.'

'Fix it' was his typical attitude to problems of any kind, and she had always admired it.

'But this is too bad to fix, and that's the whole trouble, Charlie. When it happened, you see, when it happened I knew, in spite of –' she dropped her eyes, unable to bear his expression, 'in spite of everything, that it was going to change everything.'

'You mean, you were thinking like this before you went away? On your honeymoon?'

The repetition of the word was like a well-placed punch, but she said, 'Not just thinking. I knew, immediately.' She thought of the young Frenchman, Jean-Claude, who had understood. He had said, hadn't he, and it was only last week that he had said it: when it happens, you know.

'And you didn't tell me? You still went away with me, as if there was nothing wrong?'

'I didn't want to disappoint you.'

'Disappoint me?' She thought, he's going to laugh in my face. A lesser man might have spat.

She bit her lip. 'Sorry, that sounds crass.'

'Yes. It sounds crass, darling, because it is crass.' He got up and walked away from her, his posture and shoulders rigid. 'Look, shouldn't we stop beating about the bush? You'd better tell me exactly what we're talking about. Who the third party is would be a good start. Is it someone we both know?'

She shook her head. 'It's Mischa Svoboda.'

I had to tell him who Mischa was.

'Who?'

'The Czech artist we were showing last month.' She hesitated. 'He's very brilliant. I must have mentioned him.'

'I don't remember you saying anything. But I'm relieved to hear he's brilliant.' It was unlike Charlie to be sarcastic, and also unlike him to be topping up his glass before it was finished.

'You've been to bed with him?'

She nodded wordlessly. An engraved silver cigar box that her father had brought back from wartime service in the Middle East lay on a coffee table next to Charlie. They used it for pastel-coloured Sobranies, cocktail cigarillos to offer guests. He selected a green one, saying, 'I won't tempt you,' and lit up. He had not smoked for over a year, and she was shocked.

He drew the smoke deep into his lungs. 'However did you fit it in, dear? I wouldn't have thought there was much time for such a significant dalliance to occur, only days before our little overseas trip.'

He expelled the smoke in a long-drawn-out sigh. Then he stopped short, seized by a sequence of ideas. 'But that was when I was away in New Zealand, wasn't it? I rang and you weren't here. You said you'd stayed with one of your girlfriends. Lambie, wasn't it? Were you with him that night?'

She went to the fridge and poured another drink. 'Charlie —'

'Did you see him today?'

'Yes.'

He winced. 'So. We've established a few things. Including the identity of the lover. What was the name again?' He yanked at the knot of his tie.

'Mischa Svoboda.' My lover's name. Even in the midst of this painful conversation, just speaking his name transported her from that room with its bleak portents to a place of tropical colours and caressing threads of sand.

He questioned me about him.

She rubbed that out.

He didn't want to hear about Mischa.

'I don't think I really want to know anything about this man, Greer, so please don't bother to fill me in. Hearing you confirm he's very brilliant and an artist is more than enough. But,' he got up again restlessly, ostensibly to fetch an ashtray, 'what I do have to know is, when you say everything's changed, what is it you're really saying?'

I told him that I could not stay married to him and we were going to have to separate. He couldn't comprehend this, or believe I meant it.

'Didn't you get this out of your system before we got married? All those years of indecision and messing about, when you kept talking about buggering off and couldn't?'

He had an odd expression on his face, part ironic and part mocking. She thought, I'm not sure that he's taking this seriously.

'I know, but –'

'It's a bit late in the day for this now, isn't it? You should've given me the elbow before, if you were going to. We can't split up now. It would be bloody wrong.' She heard a raw edge of outrage in his voice. 'It's the wrong fucking way round, Greer. It's not the way people do things, not in the famous moral universe you're always banging on about. Surely even you can see that?'

She had gone to his side, tears flowing freely. 'I know it's not. You're right, I should have left before. Oh, Charlie, I know I should. But this hadn't happened before, and now it has and I can't help it. I only wish it hadn't. If I could put back the clock I would.'

The lies were consumed in the flames along with the truths. The long hospitable room, glowing with firelight and jewel-coloured Persian rugs and lamps, did not discriminate. There were no blinds or curtains at the far end, the casual area of pot plants and cane furniture they called the conservatory. Charlie looked down the room through the wide windows into the dark.

'I feel as if I'm staring into the future.' She sensed his tremor. 'Greer, you're not going to –?'

She broke in violently, shaking her head. 'It's too late.'

'What are you going to do about it then?'

'I have to go away.' It was only half an answer to only half his question, but she was gearing herself up.

'Go away? What are you talking about?' He reacted to her expression, looked bewildered first, then disbelieving. 'Do you mean, with *him*?'

'I think so. I do think so. Yes. I'm so desperately sorry to do this to you, Charlie.'

He stiffened but didn't resist as she put her arms tentatively around him. But even as she did this and spoke the required words, the words she knew she owed, she did not feel fully present. Part of her was already out of that glowing room, that comfortable house, that relationship with its myriad complex components, and radiantly on the move.

I'm in transit and I have already left Charlie behind, she thought. I may enfold him in my arms, but it's an empty gesture. My heart has hardened towards him, of its own accord, with no prompting from me.

'Be as mad and contemptuous and furious with me as you like,' she said, the words muffled into his chest. 'Please. Hate me, Charlie – you're entitled to, you're completely blameless, and I deserve it.'

He drew back at once, affronted. 'Of course I don't hate you, Greer,' he had said, wearily. 'Never make that mistake either, along with any others you may be contemplating making. I just simply don't and can't understand you.'

Dinner – the warmed-up fish and chips – had been something routine to do that required no thought. Charlie took a bottle of chardonnay from the fridge and uncorked it. They had laid the table and consumed everything on their plates as if they were subservient children. Greer made a salad, he did the dressing, and they had cheese and crackers afterwards. It was a travesty of intimacy but did serve, briefly, as a respite.

At first they talked desultorily about other things, in a stilted way punctuated by painful pauses. Then they returned to the subject. Charlie was drinking continuously. He had gone through the white and opened a red to go with the cheese. At one stage he said, with a trace of mordant humour, 'Now I know who supplies Pinter with his bloody plots.'

Again she had thought, I introduced you to those plays and now you will probably never want to see another one in your life.

We tried to talk to each other over dinner. He wanted to know how I proposed to manage things.

'What the fuck are you scheming, Greer?'

I told him what Josie was willing to do, subject to his approval.

'Subject to my approval?' Charlie said. His voice darkened at first satirically, and then rose. '*Subject to my approval*, is it now? You sound like one of my bloody company reports, for

God's sake. You've dragooned poor Josie into being your accomplice already, have you?'

He got up from the table in a rush, spinning his chair backwards, and leant over her. 'What the *hell's* got into you, Greer? Are you crazy, or what? Am I supposed to *approve* this? Think of your poor mother, how she's going to feel. Do you really think you can trade in people and their emotions? Parcel up human beings and give them away, and get out of their lives? It's grotesque, isn't it?'

He gripped her by the shoulders and gave her a sharp, barely controlled shake. She sensed his own shock at this as he moved abruptly away from her and rephrased aloud what she had just told him. It was shocking and irresponsible and effing wrong, he reiterated more than once.

'I know it is. But I've got no choice.'

'That's absolute rubbish!' This was shouted close to her ear, and she leapt in her seat. 'Of course you've got a choice, you're not a fucking robot! There's always a choice.'

She thought but didn't say, yes, there may have been a choice once. In the fraction of time before Mischa and I spent the night together, I might have stopped at the cross-roads and taken yours – the road marked 'Charlie'. But once we had made love, to use Mischa's words – those perceptive and true words that our language cannot improve on – freedom of choice ceased to exist for me.

'No. For me there is no choice.'

In their unshakeable certainty the words sounded despairing. Charlie had responded by smashing the flats of his hands down on the table, on either side of her. There was a loud bang. Cutlery clattered on to the floor, and their glasses and the pepper grinder spun and toppled. It was the most immoderate thing Greer had ever seen him do. She was alarmed but not seriously frightened by his behaviour. This was Charlie, after all.

He grabbed his chair and sat down again, hunched over and breathing heavily, staring at the red wine stain as it spread over the white tablecloth. 'Do you really want to know what I think? If you tried to carry this out you'd change your mind at the last minute. When it came to the crunch you wouldn't be able to go through with it.'

Greer said, quite calmly, 'I won't change my mind.'

His head jerked up. 'You may have no conscience now, Greer, but I have a terrible feeling you will regret it, later on when it's too late.'

She said nothing to that. Later on. Regret it. Conscience. They were just arrangements of words. Like freedom of choice, they had no purchase on her mind.

Charlie became angry, and we argued. He had every right to be angry with me. He said it was a choice, and I could choose not to go ahead with this.

But that was the whole point. What he could not see was that I was unable to make that choice. I had already made my decision. I was in a state of certainty.

They watched each other for a moment like wary dogs. Then Charlie straightened up and lit another cigarette. He shook his head several times, as if to steer his mind through a fog and reach a decision.

'This is not the barnyard, dear, where you jump on anyone just because you like his smell.' She had flinched at that. 'Don't kid yourself that I'm going to happily wave you goodbye at your own bidding – not after I've gone through all hell to get us to this place. You can bloody wait for a few months and then see how you feel. How does five months sound? That'll take us to just after Christmas, won't it? To the New Year. You owe me that, Greer, to put it mildly. You owe it to us.'

Greer remembered clearly what had gone through her mind. She'd thought: Charlie's response is that of a primitive, elemental male defending his own property. And then her own reaction, also from the gut: I'm not going to hang around here for five more months. I simply couldn't do it.

She knew how Charlie's mind worked. She knew that however drunk he was, he had taken a position he regarded as right and would not budge from it. And that however fundamentally good-natured he was, he would be a formidable opponent.

At that point Charlie had left the table without another word, poured himself a tumbler of neat whisky and slumped down with his back to her in front of the TV. He switched to an Australian Rules football game and turned up the volume.

Greer grasped the opportunity to retrieve her shoulder bag and run upstairs. She had a small studio that connected with their bedroom, where she drew and painted. She riffled through the filing cabinet for her passport, some family photographs and her diary, and crammed them into a compartment in her bag. It was an instinctive move, and she would have reason soon to be thankful for this foresight.

Behind a curtain in the bedroom was a recess that they used as a dressing area. It had hanging rails and racks of wire baskets full of folded clothes. The cream crepe suit she had worn for the opening of Mischa's show was in its plastic bag, fresh from the dry cleaner. She took it down and was folding it when the sound from the television ceased abruptly. She heard Charlie's feet on the stairs.

'Greer! Are you in there?'

He sounded more subdued than before. He came in, his tread cushioned by the carpet. She thought, maybe he's calmed down a bit.

He said, 'Let's go to bed. We're both whacked.'

He wanted me to wait for five months and then reassess the situation. From his perspective this was entirely fair and reasonable. It was the least I could do.

But I couldn't contemplate it.

They undressed in silence and lay side by side. A full moon gleamed through gaps in the timber blinds.

Charlie had levered himself on an elbow and turned on

his side towards her. She was reminded, and was not blind to the cruel irony, of the painting of herself she had been looking at only hours before.

He said, 'Look, you can go on seeing this bloke occasionally, if you have to. I can accept that. I mean, it can't go on for that long, can it, let's face it? It might get him out of your system.'

She had said, with helpless conviction, 'It wouldn't, Charlie. Nothing will.'

Unexpectedly he had begun to sob, in a jerky, unpractised way that suggested to her a car engine misfiring. She remembered now how she had lain there next to him and observed, with a sadness that was at the same time deeply implacable, the way the chalky light sparkled on Charlie's tears. They looked like trickles of sequins. She had pressed her face to his and felt them, wet and cold against her cheek.

Greer had waited until Charlie's breathing slowed into a heavy and regular pattern. He had drunk such an unaccustomed amount she assumed he must have sunk into a stupor. She went quietly into the dressing alcove and made a pile of winter clothes, scooped them up, slung her bag over her shoulder and ran barefoot down the stairs and out into the garage. It was raining outside and bitingly cold, but in her fervour she was scarcely aware of it. She flicked on the garage light.

Her father's tin trunk from the war was stored at the far end, along with an old fridge, some outdoor furniture and leftover paint tins. The empty trunk was covered with dust and cobwebs. She gave it a cursory brush with her hands, hauled it into the back of her station wagon and dumped the armful of clothes inside.

Then she ran back upstairs. Charlie had turned on his back and was breathing stertorously. She cast around the darkened room for a container and seized on the outlines of the covered linen basket in a corner of the bedroom. She upended it, spilling the dirty clothes on to the floor. With rapid and economical movements she gathered up boots and shoes and threw them into the wicker basket, heaping whatever summer clothes she could cram in on top. She heaved the basket down the stairs and into the car.

She risked a third trip. This time she snatched a dressing gown from the hook and put lambswool boots on her icy feet. Charlie hadn't moved, although his noisy breaths sounded more explosive and spasmodic. Her art materials were in the studio. She closed the connecting door softly and switched on a light, then moved through, snatching up drawing books and works in progress and placing them on the table. The biscuit tin that was her artist's workbox was packed with chalks and crayons. She reached for it, and as she did so she heard a noise from the bedroom.

She inched the door open. Charlie was sitting up in bed. He switched on the reading lamp. 'What are you doing?' The words were groggy with sleep. He blinked in the light.

She said soothingly, 'Nothing. It's all right.'

She hovered in the doorway, her workbox and two sketchbooks tucked under one arm. She saw Charlie taking them in, and her dressing gown and boots. His eye fell on the floor, and the tumbled heap of dirty clothes. She saw it dawn on him.

'You're not *packing*, are you?' With a burst of speed that took her by surprise he dived clumsily out of bed, arms extended. She dodged them and ran for the stairs. Halfway down, the sketchbooks slipped from under her arm. She left them where they fell.

She had reached the bottom with Charlie close behind when he tripped on one of the two spiral sketchbooks and stumbled down several steps. He skidded into her. They both fell. Greer scrambled to her feet, but Charlie had hit the floor heavily and was momentarily winded. She raced for the garage. The keys to both cars hung on hooks just inside the connecting door. She grabbed her bunch and had the presence of mind to take Charlie's too. She hurled those away into the encompassing darkness of the garden.

She slammed the door of the station wagon and gunned the engine. It caught immediately – she had never been more grateful for Charlie's insistence on regular maintenance. In the headlights she saw him burst into the garage and dive between the cars. His fingertips grazed her door handle as she reversed out at high speed. Charlie spun round in his pyjamas.

In his present condition she predicted it would take him several minutes to locate his spare set of keys. Moreover, he had no idea where she was heading. Greer guessed he would lose more precious time ringing Josie. Fortunately, Josie too hadn't a clue where Mischa lived. Verity did, but Charlie would have no after-hours number for her.

Greer put her foot down. In those days she regularly broke the speed limit, but the station wagon had never exceeded it by such a reckless margin as it did on this breakneck journey from Melbourne's outer rim to St Kilda in the inner city. She had driven for a full thirty-five minutes before she remembered she hadn't closed the back doors of the car. In the rear-view mirror she glimpsed the reassuring lid of the trunk. Rather than stop to bang the doors shut, rather than risk capture, she drove on.

When she thought about this turbulent night, which was rarely, and only in the early years, Greer was never entirely sure what she had originally intended to do that evening. Had she really meant to break the news more gently, to discuss everything in detail with Charlie, to give him more time? Did she have Verity's favourite adage, 'Forewarned is forearmed', looming large in the back of her mind as she sorted, coolly and efficiently, through her belongings?

She suspected now that she had acted instinctively, without analysing anything, like Mischa.

Greer had pounded up Mischa's stairs and into his room. There were no coverings on the high windows, nothing but encrusted dirt, and the glow from the street lamps enabled her to pick her way over the debris to the lumpy mattress in the corner. She flung off her dressing gown and boots and slid under the scratchy felt blankets. She was shivering uncontrollably, and the army blankets were appropriate.

She imagined this was what escaping from a war zone must be like. It felt like surviving a perilous skirmish in which she had been in life-threatening danger, and coming home.

Mischa stirred as she pressed her cold hands against him. She always remembered how he had said nothing and evinced no surprise at all, but he was naked and reacted to her instantly.

In the middle of the night I ran out of the house and drove to Mischa in St Kilda. I was still in my nightclothes. It was cruel to leave Charlie in such a way and so abruptly, but I think I was gripped by a superstitious fear that he might otherwise prevent me, physically, from leaving. And I knew that more arguing could not achieve anything other than delay, which I could not countenance.

Very early the next morning Mischa and I loaded up my car and left for Sydney.

In her study Greer read through what she had just written. As a summary it was woefully inadequate, almost to the extent of the one-line dismissal dashed off by her younger self. There was something important she had left out.

Charlie said I would come to regret it later on. And he said I had no conscience. I think it was true that I had none.

She rubbed out the full stop, substituted a comma, and added:

at the time.

15

Tony stood in the chapel, one of Rollo's assertive gin and tonics in hand, before the latest oeuvre. The carved clothes horse with its tossing mane, riding hat and cape was taking sophisticated shape on the canvas.

'I think you're very brave trying to write about painting, Tony,' Rollo had remarked. 'I couldn't do it. I tend to side with Voltaire: we must apologise for daring to speak about art at all. That's how Mischa thinks, of course. He's far worse than me.'

'Greer believes his work is a conduit, but I'm not sure of what. A form of energy, was my best shot.'

'Does she? She's the best judge, you should listen to what she says. Well, all paintings conduct an energy, don't they? Even when their subjects are still and serene, like mine. It's that perfect trinity of light, line and space. Sometimes I think we're nothing but energy conductors, you know, we funny old artists. Nothing but human radios. We channel the energy and the work emits it through colour and light.'

Rollo looked unusually solemn, drink in one hand, paintbrush in the other.

'When I have my blockages, Tony, it's as if all the energy has dried up and I'm not a focus for it any more. That's why the blockages are so deeply depressing. When I'm in one I think, oh no, is this what ordinary people feel like all the time?'

He made a face. 'How awful, I think to myself, to be a normal person and not a human radio. But that's a very conceited idea, isn't it?' He turned on Tony a sharp, searching look.

Tony responded with a vehement shake of the head. 'No way. Artists are privileged people. It must be an enviable thing, to be a radio.'

He watched Rollo poking and prodding at his canvas with a slender brush. 'What do you say to Bonnard's idea that art is all about the primary conception? Trying to grasp that, and make it visible.'

'Oh, I think Bonnard had it right.' Rollo looked down at Tony's little recorder. 'Are you sure the tape thingy hasn't run out? If we're going to heavily name-drop I'd hate it to be wasted.'

'It's on. Trust me.'

'If you insist. Guy always says I'm too gullible. And not only about technology, Tony.' He gave the young man a sportive glance. 'The primary conception, yes, indeed. Picasso said much the same thing, really, didn't he, but in a simpler way? What you're doing is trying to capture the feeling you have when you look at a tree. I've always found that a very useful thing to tell people.'

'Well, that notion goes all the way back to the Greeks, doesn't it? Energy expressed as the form of a thing, its idea. Its essential truth.'

'And takes it a step further. The reaction you have to that truth. The encouraging thing is that everybody's reaction is subtly different. If that weren't the case I suppose art would peter out. Isn't peter a good word? It also means cock, but you don't hear that meaning bandied about very much nowadays, at least not in our provincial little circles.'

Rollo swallowed his nearly neat gin at the same time as making finely calibrated adjustments with his brush to fade the delicate pattern on a china bowl, which was coming into being in the foreground of the canvas.

Tony said, 'Picasso also spoke about aspiring to a truth reached by lying. A higher truth, maybe.'

'I'd forgotten that one. So he did, Tony, so he did. What a cunning little observation that was too. You're right to point it out. If there are higher truths to aspire to,' Rollo waved his paintbrush near Tony's face, 'does this mean we can reach the lower ones along the way? Do we bypass them? Are there gradations?'

'This is the artist's playground, isn't it, Rollo? A vast philosophical theme park.'

'A theme park, that's a good way of putting it.' Rollo became animated. 'I've often wondered about the whole truth question and so has Gigi, your Greer. We wonder together in unison, you know, about all sorts of weird and wonderful things.'

He looked quizzically at Tony. 'Well, it's your biographer's job description too, isn't it? You're just like Goldilocks and the Three Bears. Which porridge are you after, Tony? The higher truth, which might be too hot, the lower truth that might be too cold, or the middle-sized truth that could be just right?'

Tony said tentatively, 'I guess what I'm after is the whole truth and nothing but.'

Rollo took another gulp of his gin. 'Are you really? The whole catastrophe? Well, Gigi and I would say you've set yourself an impossible task because there are too many competing components.'

'The higher truth would be fine by me. Always remembering, Rollo, that it's reached by lying.'

They traded sunny smiles.

Rollo said, 'And we can't have that in a bio, can we? Well then, what about the John Lahr variation? I think it was John Lahr and not Bert. He talks about disenchanting the citizen from the spell of received opinion. He thinks that's the job of the critic, but I think it applies to artists and bio-meisters even more. Good, isn't it? Very succinct and subversive. Someone read it to me from something recently, somewhere. Probably from an old *New Yorker*. It's a *New Yorker* sort of sentence.'

He gazed with renewed zeal at his painting on the easel and picked up a narrower brush with a blunt tip. 'The feeling, the truth and the lying. I'm not sure about your bio, but they're the holy trinity of art, Tony.'

'And the greatest of these?'

'They're inextricably entwined. Feeling, truth, and lying to illuminate, or *exhume* the truth. They're the essential oils, but I'm not sure you can separate them. They would be all you needed if you had to explain art to a Martian, wouldn't they?'

'I guess they would at that. And they'd explain poetry as well, or is that too much of a stretch?'

'I don't think that's stretching it. Not at all. There's a mystical link between painting and poetry, as there is between painting and music – I've always felt that. Well, if it's good enough for the Martians it should do for us as well.'

He wiped his brush and upended it. 'There you are, Tony, we've solved the problem of conveying the essence of art for you. If there was a problem. You've written on Mischa's work before, haven't you?'

'I have a bit. That doesn't mean writing about his work ceases to be an ongoing cerebral wrestling match.'

'Ah well, that must be because his paintings display "an unambiguous ambiguity". Or was it the other way round? That was what one critic famously wrote, wasn't it? Famously or fatuously. An *unambiguous ambiguity*. I'm not surprised it's a challenge, when you have that sort of thing to contend with.' Rollo gave a throaty chuckle and blew out his cheeks.

'I'll try not to emulate that effort. But I can't resent the project as a whole, it's an ongoing addiction for me right now, and has been for a fair while.'

Rollo subsided into the big squashy sofa with his thighs

comfortably spread and patted the seat next to him. Tony sat down, leaving some space between them. It emitted caution. He inserted his recorder there. Rollo regarded it and him benignly.

'You're pretty keen on the art bizzo as a whole, aren't you, Tony? You're not just motivated by a venal desire to see your name in neon lights.'

Tony took a careful taste of his drink. 'Well, any lights would be a welcome bonus. But yes, the art's the thing. I guess it's my grand passion. If you can't hack it, if you can't be one of your pylons, write about it. For better or worse.'

Rollo looked satisfied. 'Oh, always for better. There's no great difference between the practitioner and the scribbler in that regard, I've always thought. Not if they both partake of the passion. It's not such a bed of roses for the lovers though. Have you raised the subject with Gigi yet?'

'I haven't. It's a tricky one.'

'Mischa's passion is his work. The work always comes first, and Gigi knows this. Anyone living with an artist knows they're a step behind in the pecking order. Guy knows it. They have to play second fiddle, and that's not an easy thing.'

Tony began, 'But maybe Mischa –' He stopped, appeared to change his mind and embarked on a different question. 'Do you think Greer – Gigi – resents it?'

'You can keep on calling her Greer if you like, I know exactly who you mean.' Rollo sipped his drink meditatively. He prodded the slice of lemon with his tongue. 'No, she doesn't resent it because she's a sensible woman and knows it would be a waste of time. It's an established fact of life and there's nothing to be done about it.'

'How about Guy?'

A snigger. 'Guy holds it against me, but he keeps his end up. Up, up and away. His Majesty knows how to get his own back.'

He became subdued all of a sudden and subsided into himself. Tony's eyes moved over the stone walls of the studio, festooned with all the decorative flourishes, the sconces and wall-hangings and myriad knick-knacks Rollo called his gewgaws. The windows and the altar, and a couple of pews laden with painterly accoutrements, were the only clues to its earlier function as a chapel.

Greer had told him, however, that an aura of stillness, a contemplative quality, remained at large in the atmosphere, uniquely conducive, as Rollo's work exemplified, to creativity. Rollo had refused to have it deconsecrated lest he lose his divine inspiration.

The silence threatened to become oppressive. Tony broke it. 'You two have had a long partnership, though, Rollo. There has to be a secret there.'

Rollo seemed to buck up. He looked gratified. 'We have, haven't we? What is our secret? We haven't been all that monogamous, not in a big way, so it can't be that. I know what it is. Frequent separations, with my painting and his wine. Lots of trips. They've been a help.'

'Is his wine a passion?'

'I suppose it might be. That means I'm superseded in the pecking order by bottles of Brunello.' His eyes were far away. 'But, do you know, Tony, I think what saved us was Gigi and Mischa. I think we were saved by them coming on the scene. We were at a bit of a fragile juncture, an over-heated stage in the relationship, rather like a pressure cooker steaming away. Their arrival had a stabilising effect. They were the valve that let the steam escape.'

'It was a gamble though, wasn't it? Inviting them to buy into this place. You hadn't known them that long.'

'No, you're quite right. We hadn't known them that long at all. But we didn't need to, you see, we both felt that. We knew they were the right ones. It was just like when you fall in love, Tony. We fell in love with them. We were quite sure and we hardly talked about it. It's all legal and above board, of course. We've got bits of paper that say we each own our turf and bailiwick.'

'And what about the common areas? You all use the

guesthouse, right, and the pool? Do you have a formal agreement for them?'

Rollo baulked visibly. 'Formal agreement? Ugh. What a ghastly idea. No, we just tell each other when we want to book guests in. It works very well. Nobody hogs it.'

'And Mischa and Greer immediately liked the idea of moving here?'

'Well, I think they'd been wandering around for years, living this nomadic life in different exotic places, and perhaps they were ready to stop. Gigi, at any rate. I think she was ready for a home. And Mischa needed a base. Even he was getting tired of packing and unpacking, and things not reaching him because people didn't know where he was. The time just happened to be right. So many important things in life boil down to a matter of timing, don't they?' He shifted his weight.

'Don't they just. Had you been actively looking for a while, then, for people to join you here?'

'Oddly enough I don't think we'd even mentioned the possibility until they came along. Ask His Majesty, his memory's in better nick than mine. No, we were introduced to them in Paris at something or other and we just got on. We hit it off straightaway. And then we found out that they didn't have children, which was an advantage. We didn't ask them if they had any, we were worried it might have been a sensitive subject. We found out in a roundabout way.'

His forehead furrowed. 'I don't know if Gigi would have liked children. I've always left it up to her to raise the subject, but she's never brought it up. Which makes me wonder if it's a painful area. Do you get the impression it's a deep regret, Tony?'

Tony said, 'I haven't asked her about it.'

'But you'll have to, won't you?'

'It's something I'll need to get on to, I guess.' He drank again, somewhat less gingerly.

'Of course, there's no doubt Mischa would have regarded the whole idea of children with complete horror.

He never wanted to be tied down at all. That was why he came to home ownership so late. He was fifty-five by then, you know. He'd been a young man in the swinging '60s – well, I suppose they did the odd bit of swinging behind the Iron Curtain, by osmosis – and he saw the whole domesticity thing as dangerously stultifying.'

Rollo cast a complacent eye over his surroundings. 'Whereas his nibs and I were suckers for the nesting. We didn't hesitate when we saw this place, even though it looked like the aftermath of the bombing of Dresden back then. But, you know, I think Mischa came to see that settling down here brought a surprising freedom in its wake, whereas the old life of endlessly trudging from one place to the next had been quite restrictive, in its own way. That's how life often works, I've found, Tony. Through a series of paradoxes.'

They both jumped at the blast of a peremptory baritone. 'Rollo, are you still breathing in there, or have you died?'

Guy swung through the internal door that connected the chapel with the house, pugs snorting at his heels, and raised an eyebrow at the reclining couple on the sofa. 'Why are you lurking when you could be having a bracing drink on the terrace with a ravishing view? Get a move on, Gigi's already there. We've laid on a good sunset for you, Tony.'

Rollo drained his glass and extended an arm. Guy took the empty glass with one hand and heaved him to his feet with the other.

'What was the name of that exhibition in Paris where we first met Gigi and Mischa?'

Guy ruminated. 'It was a photographic show. Landscapes or nature, by someone with an odd name. An American. What was it? You'd know him, Tony.'

'Landscapes or nature. Not Man Ray then. Stieglitz? Ansel Adams? Minor White?'

Rollo struck his chest. 'Minor White, the very one. I should have known because I bought a postcard emblazoned with a quote by him. I had it stuck up there,' he pointed to a cork noticeboard layered with cuttings and photos, 'for years. "Be still with yourself"', it said, "until the subject affirms its presence". Then we had the great Ice Age of 1985. You've heard of that, I expect? It's when all the hundred-year-old olive trees died. Half the roof fell in here and Mr Minor's *majorly* apposite words got washed away.'

Guy blew a raspberry. 'Having affirmed its presence the subject disintegrated.'

'He may scoff but it spoke to me, that quote, Tony, and it speaks to me yet. I'm going to have to write it down and pin it up again. It's very high on the quotable quote meter. Never underestimate the value of an improving homily, Tony.'

There was another snort from his left. Tony made a note. 'I must remember to ask Mischa about the quotes in his life.'

'Forget it,' Guy said. 'Mischa's not into self-improvement.'

Tony stopped to give Rollo's corkboard the once-over on the way out. He saw photos whose colours were fading to sepia, faces he recognised lunching al fresco under the vines. There were some statuesque lifesavers on Bondi Beach, newspaper cartoons, and postcards of works by Cézanne, Goya and Morandi.

A saucy seaside postcard from England engaged his eye, a woman with a bulbous cleavage standing on a staircase next to an undersized, goggle-eyed man. She was saying, 'I'll just slide down the banister and warm up the supper.'

Directly below this was a postcard from a French series, with a quote from Cocteau. It read, 'Whatever they criticise you for, intensify it.'

Guy saw him looking at this one. 'The story of his life.'

'Tony and I were having an in-depth confab before *he* came barging in and ruined it,' Rollo said to Greer. 'It started off all highbrow and arty and then segued into the realm of intimate relationships. We've enjoyed a deep and meaningful bonding, haven't we, Tony?'

Guy yawned as he levered open a bottle of prosecco

rosé. 'Well, don't inflict it on us, for God's sake. Anything but art and relationships. We think even the bloody bio is preferable to that lot, don't we?'

Eyeing Tony, who was smiling, Greer said, 'I'm not so sure that we do.' Tony returned the look and laughed.

They had ventured on to the western terrace, a small paved extension of Rollo and Guy's garden, to catch the dying rays. There were four or five iron chairs around a marble-topped table. Guy had brought out a tray of glasses and a two bowls of nibbles. He poured four flutes of the sparkling blush-coloured wine, handing Greer hers first.

'Here's to the damn thing anyhow,' Guy said. He clinked glasses with Greer and Rollo. 'Tony's bloody bio.'

'And all who sail in her,' Greer added, telling herself, I will be upbeat.

'Aren't I allowed to drink to that?' inquired Tony.

'Oh no, it's very bad form to drink to your own bio,' Rollo said. He turned to Greer. 'Is Tony going to be in it, darling? Will it be a gonzo type of thing? A bit sluttish and postmodernist, like Hunter S. Thompson?'

'God knows,' Greer said. 'If he's planning a personal appearance he hasn't told me.'

'What do *you* know about postmodernism?' Guy was demanding of Rollo. 'Let alone the tedious Hunter S.T.? He was just a jumped-up T. Capote. It's pathetic, isn't it? By the time he catches on to these terms and gets round to dropping them in a vain attempt to keep up, they've become obsolete. We're into the post-postmodernism now. Verging on the *ultra*-post-post. Everyone knows that.'

Tony had sat himself down on the low stone parapet facing the other three. It was unexpectedly mild and he had rolled up his sleeves to the elbow. His blond hair, with the sun's rays catching it from behind, gave his head a lustrous golden crown. Greer thought, he knows. He's sat there on purpose, to give himself a halo.

'It can't resist a little *carp*, can it?' Rollo was saying amiably. 'Listen to it carping over a perfectly reasonable and well-informed question. Where a biographer plonks himself in relation to the material affects everything else, I should have thought.'

'Quite right, Rollo, and it's funny you should ask that,' Tony said, swinging his legs, 'because I'm considering writing it the way the research has unfolded – is still unfolding,' his quick glance at Greer was like an afterthought, 'in real life. Some of it in the present tense, like interviews and observations. That way the reader will be in on the action.'

Greer looked away. She had a new taste in her mouth, a bilious taste which was nothing to do with the prosecco.

'Do you mean a *Midnight in the Garden of Good and Evil* kind of thing, where the author's one of the luvvies?' Rollo was attending to this closely and leaning forward in his chair, which brought his face close to Tony's crotch.

'Well, very vaguely, yeah.'

'I liked that. Good, cleanish fun, I thought. Nice juicy characters.'

'Of course, mine's a biography rather than a gothic detective yarn.' Tony grinned impartially at the three of them.

'Still, you wouldn't mind those sales, would you?' Rollo looked at Greer. 'I suggested it for your book reading group, didn't I, and they thought it was a very good tip. Did you know Gigi was in one of those, Tony? You could sit in on a meeting, only they won't allow males in. It's full of formidable females with alarming erudition.'

He winked at Greer. 'She's a very intelligent woman, Gigi, you know.'

'Oh yeah, I think I'm allowed to drink to that.' Tony raised his glass and clinked hers before she could take evasive action.

'She's not one of your common or garden artisans,' Rollo jerked an expressive thumb at Guy, 'like some we could name.'

Guy was leaning back in his chair with a practised air of ennui. 'Here we go.'

'In fact she came to the wine bizzo quite late in the

piece. Have you told Tony about your coup de palate, darling?'

She shook her head.

'She's far too modest and self-effacing. I'd better fill you in. Women have an extra layer of skin and can hear higher notes than men, so they probably have more tastebuds as well, don't you think, Tony?' He began to recount at some length the story of Greer's performance in the original blind tea-tasting.

Guy interrupted. 'Americans don't understand tea and they're obdurate in their ignorance, so this means zilch to him. You put hot, not even boiling, water in a cup and when it's lukewarm you add a teabag. Right, Tony?'

'Let him finish,' Tony protested, 'he's trying to educate me out of these brutish habits. So, what's the verdict? Do you put the milk in before or after for peak performance?'

'The jury's still out,' Guy barged in again. 'It was the best kind of experiment because it had a definite result that was totally inconclusive.'

Rollo brandished a bowl of brazil nuts in his face. 'Here, chew on some nice big nuts. You might like some too, Tony. Getting back to the bloody bio, so you're really going to be a major character in it, are you? I'm not sure I'd want that in mine.'

'Well, only in the sense that I'm the guy collecting and synthesising the material,' Tony demurred. 'Comes of being a control freak, I guess. Someone has to do it.'

'Aren't you risking a titanic clash of egos: writer and subject?'

'I'm sure Tony sublimates his swingeing ego in his work,' Guy said. 'Like you don't.' He turned to Tony. 'Remind me to tell you my theory of painters. It's better when *he's* not interminably trying to get his end in. Are you monopolising Tony tonight, G.?'

'I hope not.' She threw Tony a derisory look. 'We haven't booked him.'

Tony said, 'I've got some stuff to do, but after that –'

'You can tell him now, if you like,' Rollo interposed genially. 'I don't need to get my end in any more, unlike you. Mind you, he's not very scientific, Tony. His theories are best kept off the record.'

Tony grinned. 'Allow me to be the judge of that. The record's ready and waiting, Guy.'

'Good, because this is well researched. Fruit of a lifetime's interminable observation.' Guy was topping up Tony's glass. 'All successful ar*tistes*, Tony, have five per cent talent and ninety-five per cent self-belief. You need a messianic ego to succeed. Mischa never wavers. Rollo veers uncontrollably between massive self-doubt and revolting smugness. But the massive self-doubt is simply self-obsession in another guise.'

'Uh-huh. What's your take on this, Rollo? There's no truth in it, is there?'

Rollo looked blasé. 'It's just another way of putting the old inspiration-perspiration, isn't it? A mantra for all shapes and sizes is a suspect mantra, but if it makes him happy.'

'He means, it's true of Mischa but not of him,' Guy said rudely.

Tony said to Greer, 'Is it primarily an ego thing with Mischa? Ninety-five per cent talent apart, I mean.'

She was still processing Tony's laconic disclosure. If he said he was thinking about putting himself into the biography it meant he was doing it.

Tony turned to the others, shaking his head, 'I don't know about you guys, but this man's a huge puzzle to me. Sure, he works of his own volition, but it's like the driving force comes from somewhere outside of himself. I kind of think self-belief is an irrelevance with Mischa. I'm not convinced it's even a part of his equation.'

He looked at Greer again with eyebrows raised. 'Does that make any sense?'

She said, 'Not a conscious part of his equation, anyhow.' She thought, I can't bear this young man. My violent mistrust is so palpable I must be giving it off like an odour; the others must sense it. But even Rollo seems oblivious.

Rollo thrust his empty glass at Guy. 'Do you know what I think? Having your bio written is a bit like being outed. Mischa's in the process of being outed by Tony. Tony can say anything he likes about him in the book. Any way-out theory that takes his fancy. He's – what do they call it in spy thrillers – he's running him. Tony's Mischa's control.'

He gave Greer a stealthy glance she couldn't quite interpret. She thought, Rollo is unusually tipsy tonight. Before Tony could reply, Guy came charging in again. 'The life belongs to the biographer: discuss, with relevance to film noir.'

Rollo's eyes, for the first time, betrayed a flicker of annoyance.

Tony laughed. 'These days the life absolutely belongs to the filmmaker.'

'You're from LA, aren't you, Tony?' Rollo said, with another look askance at Greer. 'Ah, but you'll never sell the rights to this one. Will he, darling? It's far too straitlaced for a Hollywood fillum. They couldn't raise the money. No one would go.'

'Don't be obtuse, Roly. They'll ditch Mischa and give the lubricious yet intrepid young biographer the lead. Anything they need in surplus raunch they can make up, like they always do.' Guy gazed skywards. 'How can I have been shackled to someone for so long and him remain so naïve?'

'You can't make a movie where all the prime movers are still living and litigious,' Rollo objected. 'You see, I'm not as naïve as I look.'

Tony nodded. 'It's true, I found most of the people on my A-list were still around and kicking butt. Far more than I thought there'd be.'

'That's what a young man thinks,' Rollo said. 'Just because his subject is of mature years he expects all the suspects to have kicked the bucket, but we're kicking butt instead.' He sniggered at the others. 'In a bit of an arthritic way. Especially we lucky old A-listers. Although if you don't get cracking with me soon you might lose your chance.'

He threw Tony a roguish look. '*And* there might be a marked shortage of bean spillers to interview. You could be confronting a pitiful paucity, couldn't he, Guy? Dear old Dottie Swannage knows a thing or two about me, but she can't last for ever. My colleague here will fill you in,' he beamed at Guy, who grimaced at Tony, 'but you shouldn't put all your eggs in one basket. It's always a mistake to think one person can be the repository of all the secrets.'

He took a handful of Brazil nuts and crunched them with relish.

Tony said, 'Right. And if it weren't for the new breed of lubricious yet intrepid young biographers I represent, all those secrets might never get out.' He remained deadpan for a few beats, his blue eyes alighting on Guy, then Rollo, and finally Greer, before the onset of the guileless grin she expected.

Greer watched the two older men succumbing to the embrace of his boyish, inclusive charm. As she stood up to leave them she thought, he is deliberately driving me away.

16

'Rollo is different when he's not around Guy,' Tony dictated. 'More serious-minded and thoughtful. Yeah, and perceptive. He's a shrewd cookie all right. Guy's the same whoever he's with. Ditto Mischa. They both have emphatic personalities that are kind of indelible and not susceptible to fine tuning. Not spectacularly responsive to the sensitivities of others. Greer, on the other hand –'

He stopped. As he spoke he rocked backwards and forwards in his chair and flicked through the glossy pages of a book on Sicilian wines he had picked off the shelf in his sitting room. It was inscribed by its English author: 'To Gigi and Guy, *santé santissima*! With lots of love from Kate.'

'When Rollo talked about how artists put their work first, I went, yeah. But then I thought: is that totally accurate here? Maybe Mischa's only been able to do this because his top priority is sorted.'

He replayed these two sentences twice, listening to them with an air of surprise, toying with his hair. Then he added, 'Could be that's the higher truth. All those years before he met her, he didn't get much done. He did zilch. He was all over the place.

'She's something else. Impossibly hard for me to get a

handle on because she's so internalised, suspicious, guarded and uptight. I get little insights of what she's like with other people. She and Rollo are as thick as thieves. I think they get from each other what they don't get from their partners. Interesting he'd say she's the best judge of Mischa's pictures, because she doesn't care to analyse them to me. Has a real resistance to it. She's either got no talent for it or she's frightened by it. She doesn't like me one little bit. What do I think of her? I'm not sure. I provoke her, but I guess I'm kind of neutral about her.'

He pushed the chair back as far as it would go, pressing his heels to the floor.

'We're closing in on the nitty-gritty. Like they say, something's gotta give. All the balls are in my court, and she knows that. I think we need to move things along. It may be a matter of forcing the issue into the open.'

He took his feet off the floor and the chair pitched forwards. It was an old bentwood rocker festooned with fringed suede cushions.

'The timing means it may need to be me who breaks the deadlock, because she knows she's in deep shit but I don't think her pride will allow her to dig herself out of it. Do I have any qualms? Well, hell, I think I may do, actually. Half of one, maybe. I find that kind of surprising. Does it mean I'm more ambivalent than neutral?'

He gave a short laugh and switched off the dictaphone, then flicked it on again and added: 'It means I have mixed feelings rather than no feelings at all. Is that a small step for a man or a giant moral leap?'

The following night he was surprised by a meal cooked by Mischa. The three of them ate casually at one end of the kitchen table, separated by candles and a pot of yellow jonquils. We're having a barbecue tonight, Greer had informed Tony. Mischa is quite a whiz at the barbecue. You can see another side of him.

Tony stayed outside with Mischa on the south terrace

below the house, and observed him setting the outdoor fire-place with balls of newspaper and a tent of twigs. Mischa used a single match to light it, then added branches of aromatic wood from a stack of cut logs. When the flames had settled down and the coals were glowing he laid out three freshwater trout on a rack. The fish had been stuffed with breadcrumbs, garlic and rosemary and brushed with olive oil and lemon. Spring vegetables dipped in oil and garlic and threaded with thyme were heaped up ready to be grilled on the side.

'So, how come you got to be such a dab hand at this?'

The two men stood over the fire, drinks in hand. Smoky aromas of sizzling fish and herbs swirled around their heads.

Mischa said, 'I had expert teaching. It gives Gigi a break and I like it.'

Tony watched him turning the food and prodding the fire. He said, 'I'm trying to understand the kind of person she is, and I'm finding it unexpectedly hard. How would you describe her?'

'I wouldn't,' Mischa said promptly.

'But you of all people must know her really well.'

'I don't know her really well at all.'

An asparagus spear rolled over and threatened to fall in the fire. Mischa retrieved it smartly with tongs. Tony was about to ask a follow-up question when Mischa added, 'I know what she shows me. She is a mystery in other areas. That is a good quality in a person, Tony. You should look for it.'

'You and she do seem to be very different people.'

This produced a broad grin. 'Ah, you've noticed. She is a woman. Luckily for me.'

'And from the way you got together, a woman of strong feelings, I guess.'

This emboldened statement produced a full-on laugh. 'A piece of luck for me again, Tony.' He moved the fish to a quieter corner. 'And she makes very good vino, which is third time lucky.'

When they brought up the trays of food and seated

themselves at the table Greer told their guest, 'Barbecues are almost the only time he ever cooks, and I love it.' She passed him a plate.

'It's a bit of a male thing, I guess, being outside and grilling food on an open fire,' Tony said cautiously.

'Oh yes, very he-manly. So it's OK to say he does it very well.' She laughed across at Mischa.

'And he tells me he was shown the ropes by an expert?' Tony helped himself to the grilled baby artichokes and asparagus, and the salad of broad beans, tomatoes and wild radicchio. He had waited to raise this question with her, she noticed. He was a fast learner, although he needn't have bothered to wait in this case.

Mischa's eyes were on his plate, but Greer knew that this was one moment in his past he would neither dismiss nor fail to acknowledge. It was part of a set of incidents, a seminal group of memories whose afterglow helped to define their relationship, even to this day. She had always felt it was a key determinant of their survival, their continuing narrative as a couple.

Tony should have some small inkling of this. She said, 'Yes, it was on the drive between Brisbane and Port Douglas. We met some people who invited us to their place for a barbecue. Beer, barbecues and blokes, it's a religious ritual in country Australia, so Mischa was press-ganged into doing his bit. They found he was rather good at fires, in fact, I seem to remember they put him in charge.'

All the same, she was surprised when Mischa expanded on this. 'We made friends with them at a New Year's Eve party in a pub.'

And both of them stopped eating when Tony said, 'Well, guess what. I met with some of those people and they send their regards. They remember you very fondly.'

Almost immediately after Josie's arrival in Sydney, as soon as the next day, Mischa had flung his painting materials and Greer's trunk into the car and the pair of them had embarked on the first leg of the long drive up the east coast to the tropics of Far North Queensland. They had an unspoken need to put as much physical distance as possible between themselves and the site of recent past events.

Unlike the mad dash from Melbourne to Sydney five months previously, on this occasion they had kept inside the speed limit. And, unlike that previous drive, this was a sober journey with no singing, and precious little talking either. Which was scarcely surprising. Both of them were in a state of something not far removed from post-traumatic shock.

On 30 December they had motored down the main drag of a Queensland country town in the sluggish afternoon and passed a run-down pub that looked like a picture on a postcard. In its heyday it had been a handsome three-storey hotel built in the gold rush of the last century, with wide wraparound verandahs on two levels. It seemed quite natural for Mischa, without saying anything, to stop, reverse fast down the empty street and park under a tree. They had climbed, silent and tired, out of the dusty station wagon and booked a room. It was an airy bedroom on the top floor, basic but clean, with double doors opening on to the humid verandah.

Their own silence was challenged at once. They found they had stepped into a hive of activity. The hotel had been bought by ambitious new owners and preparations for tomorrow, New Year's Eve, the biggest night of the year, were in full swing. They opted to stay on for it, more through inertia than any anticipation of fun. It turned out to be a wise decision.

The old year yielded to the new in the hotel's lush, overgrown beer garden, crowded with local merrymakers. It was a night of stifling heat that became, somehow, anything but enervating. There were streamers and fireworks, a jazz band in pork-pie hats with a groovy black sax player, a seafood buffet, beer, champagne, the works. The night was intoxicating, in every sense of the word.

In later years, just a languorous whiff of frangipani was enough to transport Greer back to that garden and that particular New Year's Eve. The flowering shrubs seemed to float in the air in the gathering dusk; the creamy yellows of the frangipani and the purple bougainvillea, and the saffron and shocking-pink hibiscus. And the heavy foliage of the trees, draped with tendrils of tiny star-shaped lights.

They had found themselves drawn, or rather coerced – no refusal brooked – on to a family table of nine spanning three extrovert generations. As the evening wore on they had exchanged names, taken puffs of the odd joint that was being openly passed around and told stories that verged on the indiscreet.

They ventured on to the dance floor when the band slowed down, with Greer leaning against Mischa for support and her face glued to his chest. To sensuous renderings of 'When I Fall in Love' and 'The Way You Look Tonight', they had clasped each other tightly for the first time in months.

A TV was wheeled out and they watched the festivities in the state capital cities. They had counted down the seconds until the new year, and whooped and whistled along with everyone else. Then they'd kissed each other hard, embraced their new mates and countless uproarious others, and sung 'Auld Lang Syne' holding the hands of strangers in a circle that swayed and lurched.

Greer hadn't drunk alcohol or smoked anything at all for ages. The unaccustomed effects combined to mask her exhaustion and remnant aches and pains. She had even for a time found herself co-opted with Mischa into the conga line, snaking through the pub and out into the road under the lid of the velvet night, weaving between the worn verandah posts of the town. The rhythmic chants and the rise and fall of their footsteps were almost drowned out by the hypnotic buzz of cicadas.

These protracted revels supplied the blast of normality needed to melt the ice that had come between them. Sometime in the early hours of the new year, after stumbling upstairs to their room that looked out on to the drowsy street they had recently conga'd along, in spite of being pickled and physically and emotionally drained, they had managed to make love.

Mischa had approached this milestone slowly, and with a tenderness that unlocked Greer's constricted heart. After they hauled themselves out of bed late the following afternoon, with him safely down the hall in the shower, she wrote in her diary. It was the first entry she had made for quite some time and, in fact, the last one she would make for a quarter of a century.

New Year's Day 1980
We're back together. Permanently and irrevocably. It has to be symbolic that this, the first day of the new year, is for Mischa and me the day of our reconciliation.

I feel flooded with relief and profound thankfulness, quite unlike anything before in my life. This feeling is like a spiritual experience, although I know it's horrendously sacrilegious to say so. Under the circumstances.

We were both on an unbelievable high last night, in spite of being (or maybe because of being) knackered and sloshed (totally, times two). The high lasted the whole night & we haven't come down from it yet. We had the best time. We met some surprisingly nice people too, or they seemed nice. In the state we were in we probably would've liked Stalin or Charles Manson. We're going to see some of them again tonight.

After the party we came to bed. In the aforementioned blotto state we hardly knew what we were doing, but that was a good thing – it made us forge ahead oblivious. We just . . . I was going to say, threw caution out of the window, but that's not how it was at all. It was, though, utterly different from before.

M. was so sweet & gentle with me, so tentative at first and controlled. He whispered at one stage he felt as if I was a virgin, and it was true, that was how it did feel. He let me guide him. In a way it was as if this was the first time for him too, although his restraint and self-control could only have come about from experience. It was not explosive like before, but gradual and infinitely more delicate.

I will never forget how tender he was. Never.

It didn't hurt but afterwards I cried, I couldn't help it. That made him cry too. It hit me then what all this has been like for him. Not that I haven't been aware of Mischa and his feelings for every moment of every day of the past five terrible months. But I saw it with a new clarity.

We didn't even fall asleep straight afterwards but lay in bed, watching the sunrise through the wide-open verandah doors and talking. We spoke a bit about sex & jealousy. We know we've each had plenty of previous experiences, we just don't want to hear anything more about them. Charlie, Elsa & the rest, they're simply meaningless names to us now.

And I want to hereby put the past, and I mean the immediate past, out of my mind. I intend to banish it.

If you don't make a point of remembering a thing, it doesn't lodge in your psyche. It does not become a memory. Eventually, it fades away. That is what this will do.

After the barbecue Tony was keen to make a start on collating Mischa's library of musicals. Greer left them with brandy and the soundtrack of *Crazy for You*. From her study she could hear Tony singing a few bars of 'Nice Work if You Can Get It'. He had a light tenor not dissimilar to Fred Astaire's.

She sat with her arms clasped across her chest, the steady light of two candles glowing on the desk. There was no draught. The flames burnt without a flicker. She remembered very well the complicated tears she had shed. They were uncontrollable. It had been like a pent-up dam bursting and flooding over.

Had that confident method of erasing a memory worked out according to plan?

She thought, I am sitting here in candlelight as my predecessors must have sat, in a room in a stone house that is part of an isolated hamlet. What would you see if you were to put this little group of buildings, where four people live in close proximity, under a microscope? You would see an organism, a complete ecosystem detached from the outside world.

Detached, yes, but also dependent on it in countless ways.

If you extended the breadth of the magnification, the surrounding countryside would enter the picture, and you would see how the wider world connects with this hamlet. Extend it further, much further still, and you might fit first the country and eventually the whole planet under an over-arching lens.

Did I deliberately set out to put the world at a distance? That is what everyone does, in a small way, when they construct walls around rooms inside their own houses. But I have gone beyond that, haven't I? I have tried to barricade myself against my own past.

You could see craters on the moon through Guy's tele-scope, or on a good day the stones of the distant watchtower astride the ridge on the horizon. Through high-powered telescopes astronomers could leave the boundaries of their small world and venture out into the universe. They could write stories of the birth of galaxies and witness the fallout from events that had happened billions of human years ago.

And you didn't even have to be an astronomer. Every-one on the planet could do this, in a more limited fashion. Every inhabitant in the world had a telescope, their own built-in, individual version, and it was more versatile than a conventional model. Through it they might try to visualise the future, but with no guarantee of success. They could also revisit the past.

The mind was a miniature observatory, with the added capacity to look backwards in time. Greer saw this clearly. Each mind was autonomous, able to construct and decon-struct, write and rewrite the narratives of individual lives.

Your personal observatory, though, was restricted. It was subjective. It could only operate on a limited scale, your own private frequency, constrained by your existence as a human being. To believe you could barricade yourself in perpetuity against the fallout you had generated – well, that had to be a delusion.

If she were to steal a fearful glance through her own

telescope Greer knew already and only too well what she would see out there. A mass of prowling, indistinct shapes. But there was something she had not realised until this night, sitting in candlelight in her study. It felt like a momentous scientific discovery, a moment of pure illumination.

Whether she looked backwards in time or whether she tried to look forwards, it made no difference. From either end of the telescope, the view was the same.

If you don't make a point of remembering a thing it doesn't lodge in your psyche. It does not become a memory. Eventually, it fades away. That is what this will do.

If she focused the lens of her mind's eye it could bring those shapes into sharp, into hardcore relief. Even though she had not done it, and could not bear the thought of doing it, she knew that this was true. It proved that the writer of those words was mistaken.

No matter how well you succeeded in banishing them from your mind, certain memories did not fade away. They might retreat. They might lie in wait. It was as if they had minds of their own.

It has been a long dark night of the soul. Thanks, you up there, whoever you are, for letting Mischa and me make it through against the odds. Thank you Lord, thank you God, Jesus, Allah, Buddha, Mohammed, Krishna, Confucius, and all the spirits of the Dreamtime, the Wandjina, and especially you, Venus, the goddess of love.

And my fairy godmother, the tooth fairy, and anyone else I've forgotten to thank.

At this moment in time, in this wondrous new year, let it be recorded: I am truly happy.

Oh yes, Greer could see that in the writing. The words fairly danced off the page, with their euphoric loops and whorls.

She deciphered them with a sense of wonder. The entry

read like an overheated acceptance speech at the Oscars. Effusive thanks for making it through, dished out to every deity that sprang to mind, but no mention of those at whose expense she had made it.

Had there been any residual scruples? There was no evidence of them here, no acknowledgement of what had taken place less than a week earlier. No vestige of a qualm. Just an oblique reference to 'the immediate past'. The writer had stuck to her guns, maintained her stance of selectivity to the last.

The writing was oversized in its exuberance and the entry ran over a double page. It could easily be torn out. Greer held the two sheets of writing between her fingers. How light and fragile the pages were, and how combustible. She sat at her desk, staring at the pages as if to erase or nullify the words by force of will.

She looked at the walls of her study, shadowy and mysterious in the candlelight. She imagined those who had come before, tried to locate their phantom imprints in the air, to pin them down. What had been the nature of their transgressions? This room had not always been a study. What had it been?

It was a small space. It had probably been a child's bedroom.

Ripping out those pages would be a cowardly act. Such vandalism would not destroy the past. And it was an insult even to think of trying to explain, or excuse. Why was she trying to explain it anyway?

At this moment in time, in this wondrous new year, let it be recorded: I am truly happy.

What could you say to that? She laid down her pen and locked the notebook back in the drawer.

17

G reer and Mischa had stayed on in the country town hotel for two more days. They were recovering, and not just from the aftermath of New Year's Eve. Both evenings they ate with people they had met that night, first in a big group in a local pizzeria and then at a smaller backyard barbecue. It was an intense pleasure to sit at a table and eat and drink, talk and laugh with ordinary people. It had all the freshness and charm of a new experience.

'They remembered you very well,' Tony had repeated at dinner. 'I got the feeling they'd reminisced about meeting the two of you a lot over the years. They were taken up with the romance of it all, how you were on the run from past lives and lovers.' He turned to Mischa. 'They followed your later career with great interest.'

Part of the enjoyment had been the knowledge that the two of them were passing through and would never see these nice people with whom, to be honest, they hadn't much in common, again in their lives.

'How on earth did you find them?' Greer had asked in amazement. Mischa seemed to have moved on. He was intent on making a wavy line of cracked pepper on his plate with the blade of his knife.

'Ah. They found me. One of their kids, who wasn't even born back then, was a student at a Sydney art school. He saw my website and then his dad emailed me.'

Greer was not worried. Neither she nor Mischa would have let slip anything incriminating about the immediate past in Sydney. Neither of them could face thinking about that, let alone speaking of it.

Tony went on, 'They said you'd had some pretty riotous times together.'

Greer said, 'Oh, we did. It was quite wild and woolly. So much so that I can't remember too much about it.'

Mischa looked up from his plate and engaged her in the eye. 'I remember all about it. It involved mainly drinking. They said when the revolution comes and all painters are banned, at least I can make survival food on a fire.'

For the five months preceding that barbecue Mischa and Greer had lived like a couple of hermits in the city. They were closeted together: Mischa working at a manic pace that seemed to Greer increasingly violent and disturbed, and Greer growing more distraught. They had occupied the same tiny flat, but they hardly, it seemed in retrospect, exchanged more than a few words each day.

For the last four months they hadn't even shared a bed. Mischa had dossed down on the lumpy couch in the same room he painted in. He had stopped smoking soon after their arrival, of his own accord. Just given it up one day without a word.

There were hookers, drug dealers and plenty of other artists outside on the pockmarked pavements of Darling-hurst. It was a countercultural quarter of inner Sydney they had gravitated to, full of Art Deco flats and cramped Victorian terraces, the front doors opening directly on to hilly, narrow lanes lined with plane trees.

Winter had yielded to spring and then the searing heat of December, the first month of summer. But in all that time Greer hadn't seen another person set foot in their little flat, with the sole exception of Marlene, the craggy-faced drag queen who lived in a studio across the landing and befriended Greer.

If it hadn't been for Marlene, a woman imprisoned in a tall man's body, and their afternoon breakfasts in pavement cafés or heart-to-hearts perched on the bed in Marlene's overpowering bed-sitter, Greer thought she might quite likely have gone mad. Marlene's gaudy room, strewn with peacock feathers, stilettos and g-stringed jockstraps, with glitzy Viennese mirrors and '30s Berlin cabaret posters on the walls, had been her only refuge.

They had one other visitor, but as fate would have it Greer had been shut away with Marlene when she arrived. Verity turned up out of the blue, only a couple of days before Christmas. Mischa's reaction was such that she cut her visit very short. She was out of there in next to no time. Greer wouldn't have known a thing about it if she hadn't opened Marlene's door just as Verity was emerging from the flat. She had dived behind Marlene's broad back, and Verity had continued on her way down the stairs.

Verity did have time, however, to see the paintings. They were hard to avoid, being all over the sitting room floor and in deep piles around Mischa's sofa. She would have drawn her own conclusions from those.

Even Josie, when she eventually flew in with her suit-cases, had no occasion to step inside the flat. There had been nothing for her to pick up there, because Greer had bought nothing. Of the two sisters, Josie was the practical one, the forward planner. Greer had been in no doubt that Josie would arrive well prepared.

'They were happy to talk about New Year's Eve in Queensland, about Port Douglas, her divorce papers, you name it. I say "they" but it's mainly her, of course. Safely out of the danger zone she becomes almost garrulous. Well, anyhow, compared to how she gets when you approach the no-go area.'

Tony was doing his housekeeping, stripped down to a pair of boxer shorts, stretched out on the bed with his hands behind his head. On the front of the shorts was a red apple with a large bite out of it. He was staring at the ceiling and speaking into his dictaphone. The second recorder was at his side.

'He enjoyed playing with the fire, didn't overcook like people usually do. At dinner I said the fish tasted incredible, which it did – juicy and fresh with a wonderful smoky, herby flavour. I was rewarded with a child-like beaming smile of pure pride. It was quite sweet how he took the whole cooking stuff so seriously. It's probably because it gives him something constructive to do with his hands. Simple yet macho, no fiddling around with measurements and recipes. That would definitely not be the go.

'We stood out there together side by side like a pair of old drinking buddies. I was nearly stupid enough to quip that we were like one of those men's groups where they make campfires in the woods and reconnect with their masculine side. Howl at the moon, and all that stuff.

'I did say nearly. The fire must've made me reckless. Or maybe it was the beer, or even the moon. It was a clear night and a big moon up there. Serendipitous. After I'd broached the subject of Greer's strong feelings I figured it was as good a time as any to raise the Elsa ship from the seabed. I figured it was best to be direct.'

He threw a switch on the other recorder, and listened to himself say, 'So getting out of Prague was a smart move, relationships-wise.'

There was a grunt on the tape. 'It was a smart move everything-wise.'

'Mind if I ask a delicate question?'

Another laugh. 'Try it. I am just capable of being delicate.'

'You left the country pretty smartly after the death threat you assumed – very reasonably, I'd say – was from Elsa's husband, Pavel Montag.' Another grunt. 'There was that, and the political situation, and the whole damn thing with Elsa. Her instability and possessiveness. But in the absence of such a serious threat, would you ever have got around to leaving?'

There was a pause. Tony interposed, 'He shunted some things around the grill, then made direct eye contact.'

Mischa's voice said, 'Yes. I had to leave anyhow.'

'I guess in that situation there was a whole bunch of reasons to choose from, right?'

Tony hit the off button. 'That was a dumb thing to say. I could tell he wasn't about to hand over any free points. So I made a daring executive decision. Nearly made me break out in a rash.'

He flicked it back on. 'Did you know she – Elsa – was supposed to have gone away and had a child after you left?'

A pause. 'Supposed?'

'It was rumoured. Strongly.'

'Later I heard about that rumour.'

'Do you mind if I ask if it could have been yours?'

'You can ask that.'

'OK then, Mischa, could it have been your child?'

'How do I know? The mother would know better than me.'

'She denied everything. Screamed at me. Broke down in tears, wouldn't listen or say anything on the subject. But enough people told me about it that I had to ask you. They said she'd been pressuring you to marry and have a child. It hadn't happened with Pavel. She suspected he was sterile. That seems to have been pretty much confirmed later on, in his other marriages.'

Tony had paused at that point. There was nothing on the tape but the sound of cooking food sizzling and spitting.

'You've always been very open, right, about not wanting to be tied down with kids. I guess Greer accepted that.' Another silence followed.

'People who knew you said what Elsa was doing was blatant moral blackmail. I should tell you they said it was a daughter. They all said the word was she had a baby girl.'

Mischa had not responded. Tony looked at the second hand of his watch. It had moved more than three-quarters of the way round the face before he heard his own voice again. 'I guess I have to ask this, though. Did you know she was pregnant before you left?'

'That was not a conversation I wanted to have.'

'You mean, you refused to talk about it?'

'I mean, she knew my feelings on the subject.'

'So she knew better than to bring it up?'

'What does she say?'

'She doesn't, you see. She gets hysterical, claims it didn't happen. The thing is, Mischa, I don't think I believe her.'

'Just write what you like then.'

'I want to get things right.'

Tony stopped the tape again there. 'He shrugged and downed his beer. He's of the old school. He wasn't about to tell me she was neurotic and devious and chronically smothering. You have to admire him for that. Most guys his age would've just said she was a bitch.'

He picked up the master tape and strolled around the room speaking into it. 'Did she or didn't she? It could be like, say, she's already told him, he gets the death threat, and he takes the heaven-sent opportunity to get the hell out of there. Maybe she's told Pavel, or Pavel finds out somehow.

'*Or*, and what I'm leaning towards is this, she doesn't get around to telling him. She's been putting it off, she knows only too well what his reaction would be. Then, after hearing from Pavel, he exits from her life in a hurry, and she's lost her chance.

'Whatever, she goes to another city, has the kid and gives it up for adoption. Or finds an orphanage. And that's when she loses it, in both senses of the word. She has her first breakdown.'

He put the dictaphone down, then picked it up again.

'He was quite cool and impassive throughout this, but with one exception. When I said it was rumoured to be a baby girl I sneaked a look at his face in the firelight, and I think I saw a tiny reaction there, a little twitch of the mouth, like that ghosting on his new pictures. Maybe, and I think just *maybe*, he was struck, like for the first time, by the completely revolutionary idea that he might have a grown-up daughter. Momentarily struck dumb with it.'

He passed a hand over his face. 'And just maybe not entirely displeased in spite of himself? In spite of it flying in the face of everything he's always said? Secretly, that is. He was never going to let on to me. He didn't say or do anything at all for quite a stretch. Just stood there staring into the fire and poking at it, and moving the veggies around. But there was a kind of relaxing, like a softening of his features – I wasn't imagining it.

'With any other guy, and I mean *any* other guy, I'd never in a million years dream of broaching such a sensitive subject just before we were about to sit down for a cosy meal together. But Mischa, well, it's like she says, he's not an ordinary guy in any respects. A few minutes after that little exchange, in which he gets confirmation that he's most likely got a daughter running around somewhere, here we are, a homey little trio, sitting round the kitchen table making carefully oblique references to the cathartic little interlude in the tropics when they began to have sex again.'

He paused before adding, 'It's not exactly admirable, his attitude, he's not going to win the Nobel Prize for ethics – well, neither is she, for that matter, no fucking way – but you have to admit it's pragmatic. There's nothing he can do about it now, is how he sees it. It's water under the bridge.'

Tony switched everything off and went into the bathroom to clean his teeth. He unscrewed the tube, squeezed some brilliant blue gel on to an electric tooth-brush and set to work on the outside top row. Halfway along he stopped and wiped some splashes off his chin, returned to the other room and retrieved the recorder.

'What's really, really interesting will be if he decides to try and track her down. He's got more of a chance than me.

But it wouldn't be easy, it mightn't work out, and the very idea could be anathema to him. I wouldn't want to predict which way he'll turn on this. Well, that makes two of them, doesn't it?'

Greer and Mischa had pulled themselves together after what Tony identified as their cathartic little interlude in the tropics. They pushed on further north, beyond Capricorn, and dug in for an extended period in languid, luminous Port Douglas, just below the sixteenth parallel.

There in the tranquil aftermath of Sydney Mischa threw himself back into productive work while Greer made a few futile attempts of her own. She wasn't unduly worried at that stage. At that stage an extended holiday was all she felt capable of. She thought of that time as the honeymoon she'd never had.

Their landlord bought Mischa's second painting, which set the ball rolling. There was a lot of disposable income floating around in that corner of Far North Queensland. Many pictures were sold on the spot, as they were painted. Private commissions came in. There was never enough surplus to send down to Melbourne. Verity never did get her follow-up exhibition.

'We were irresponsible,' Greer had admitted to Tony, aware of Mischa's glad eye on her. And full of the joys of spring, she did not say, and the bliss of being young and in love and highly sexed. New-found freedom was a big part of that, she did decide to add. Verity, through no fault of her own, had become a symbol of apron strings and the unlamented past.

But it was a notably bad move, Greer conceded aloud, to put an already smouldering Verity so drastically offside, to let her down again with such cavalier disregard. Tony verified this. It was adding insult to injury. He said Verity had felt herself shoved offside with a capital O.

'And I'm afraid it was categorically due to your evil influence, Greer. Not only did you spirit Mischa away, you also made him sever his links with the gallery. You had nothing to do with any of it, in her eyes, Mischa. She was still besotted with you. She'd have given her right arm, she told me, to have those Queensland pictures.'

He gave Greer a teasing look. 'But she was remarkably balanced and even-handed where the works were concerned. I truly believe she wouldn't have minded one itsy little bit if the whole lot had happened to be of you.'

To begin with Greer had found it disquieting, the disconnect between their laid-back life in the sun and the sometimes confronting subjects of Mischa's paintings. In Sydney there had been a stark correspondence between what was going on and the nature of his work. She had assumed this would always be the case, and was disconcerted when their comparatively idyllic days in Far North Queensland threw up uneasy images.

At first Mischa had painted Greer, but nearly always obliquely, in backward or sidelong glimpses and partial reflections, often in veiled or washed-out light. And following on from that came the period, not an extended one but intense, of dishevelled figures with shadows, long and looming or distorted, and then, unnervingly, detached and unrelated.

Over the years Greer had come to think of each picture as having two distinct, separate provenances: its coming into being and its subsequent history. She saw the products of Mischa's creativity as mysterious, independent entities with lives of their own, just as she knew Rollo did with his own works. Rollo blamed his pictures for his episodes of painter's block, accusing them of sabotaging him. He boasted that at other times they were capable of being charmingly amenable and co-operative.

In Greer's opinion Mischa's images did not reflect his state of mind in any direct external way, although you could (and critics did) analyse them and make plausible cases for psychological expressionism. But not always, or even that often. Some subjects she was at a loss to relate to anything.

Mischa's artistic preoccupations appeared, apparently from nowhere, and vanished or went into abeyance with the same quixotic spontaneity.

He himself did not change according to the mood of the work in progress, Greer informed Tony. She could see he was resoundingly unconvinced. And nor, she told him, did Mischa's own mood impinge on what he produced.

Always excepting, of course, and this she did not tell Tony, the time in Sydney. The Sydney period of Mischa's career was an exception to every rule. Not that it was ever identified as such, since it had to all intents and purposes ceased to exist. This was because there was no evidence for it. In the canon of Mischa's work, there were no extant paintings to bear witness to any Sydney period.

18

21st April 2006
Last night I dreamt of two men. I was with Mischa, it was now,
in the present time, and nothing was changed. But unbeknown
to him I was having a wild, tumultuous affair with a much
younger man.

The mood of the dream was frenetic. High anxiety alter-
nating with electric excitement. I was mired in terrible guilt, yet
felt powerless to end this affair. I rushed to see my lover in
secret, when our intense erotic encounters were punctuated by
urgent talk. He was pressuring me to leave Mischa and run
away with him, and part of me desperately wanted to do this.
I felt pulled and torn between the two, unable to imagine
leaving Mischa, and yet intoxicated with the rediscovery of
passion.

Then it came to me suddenly in the dream with a
shocking, revelatory force: I am in love with the two of them.
And with that, just as I was half aware of emerging from the
dream, I was hit by a second, almost simultaneous realisation:
they are not two different men at all. They are the same man.
They are Mischa now, and Mischa as he was.

Greer lay in bed alongside Mischa in the immediate
aftermath of this dream, unable to move, at once

drained and exhilarated by the feverish emotion of it. She closed her eyes and tried to draw back the mental curtain, to re-enter the roller-coaster journey with its searing, conflicting feelings. She tried to envisage again the face and hands of her younger lover, who was also Mischa, but they were not be retrieved.

She felt she must tell it, write it down, before it faded away or vanished entirely in the way that most dreams did. She ran in nightdress and bare feet from the bedroom to her study, unlocked the desk drawer and wrote rapidly at the end of the diary on one of the empty pages that followed her last entry. Quite why she felt compelled to make a record of it she did not know. Neither did she feel the need to analyse anything – the dream or her intentions. It was enough to put what she could of the story of the dream on paper while she still marvelled at it.

It sounds odd to say this, perhaps, but in the drama of this dream there was something poetic. It was like a duel, a choreography involving the mind and body, with a wholly unexpected denouement that tied up all the ends. It had been such a frantic, high-octane ride, and its final mood contained an enormous component of relief – the realisation that I did not need to leave at all. When the dream ended and I came down from it, I was not in the least depressed, but instead strangely uplifted.

Mischa slumbered on unaware of any of this, but it was already dawn and Greer found herself disinclined to return to bed. The scent of wisteria surged through the open windows and she felt energised, better than she had felt for the past few weeks, since well before the biographer's arrival. It was a novelty, this giddy sensation of wellbeing. It had become unfamiliar. She thought, why am I feeling like this? There's no reason for it. He is still here. Nothing has changed. It can't possibly last.

She threw on jeans and an old t-shirt and sweater, aware that for the first time in weeks she had not thought about dressing for Tony's benefit. It was too early to fetch the paper and mail from the village but the temperature was mild. She made coffee and drank it outside on the steps, listening to the birdsong and watching the tepid light creep over the grass.

Some instinct – not a noise – made her look across to the neighbouring cottage, Casanova, Tony's house. She was in time to see Guy emerge from the front door and run down the steps with his loose, loping stride. He saw her, inevitably, and executed a little pantomime, an exaggerated start with finger to the lips. He came over.

'G. What on earth are you doing abroad at this ungodly hour?' He dropped down beside her on the step, yawning.

'I could ask you the selfsame thing.'

'It's only just after five. Obscenely early. Shouldn't you be tucked up in bed sleeping the sleep of the just?'

'Indeed it is. Shouldn't you?'

'I have been. I've finished.'

'Well, so have I. Do you want some coffee?'

When they repaired to the kitchen terrace with a fresh pot she told him, on impulse, about the dream. He rated it highly.

'It's rather profound, in its way. And quite sexy. I'm impressed. And envious: I don't think I've ever had a profound dream. Or at least not a profoundly sexy one.'

'Nor had I. It could be a first.'

'What prompted it? Tony raking up your libidinous past with his probing archeological excavations?' He yawned again.

She let him think she considered. 'Maybe that was it.'

'Or is it guilt? You're not having it off with the versatile Antonio, are you?' He favoured her with a droll look from under drooping eyelids.

'Not on your life. It's too crowded in there already. Who knows what you might trip over.'

After Guy had gone she wandered, on impulse again, over to Mischa's studio. She passed the big cypress close to the sitting room window, where her nesting doves were cooing.

It had several little recalcitrant branches jutting out at right angles and disturbing the symmetry. This happened to some cypresses, but not all. It was caused by snow, Guy claimed. Sometimes they were self-correcting, and the branches would fold back up into the sinuous body of the tree all by themselves.

She put her shoulder to the main door. She hadn't bothered to bring the key. It had a businesslike iron padlock which Mischa had left unlocked, as he usually did unless they were going away or there had been a recent visit from the insurance company. She crossed the floor and went up the stairs to the main studio. She had a good idea by now what she was heading for.

Tony's masonite sheets were laid out on a trestle table under the soaring windows of the south wall. The studio was still dimly lit, but without switching on the lights she could see at once that he had completed his chapter headings and posted new illustrations. Most of these were paintings, but there was a significant quota of new photos attached to some sections. She wasn't interested in those. She only had eyes for the chapter Tony had already brought to her attention. 'Chapter Four: The Australian Period'.

She skimmed along the row of images. Mischa at his first Melbourne exhibition; Mischa with Verity at the opening; Greer herself on the Isle of Pines; she and Charlie at the Flower Drum restaurant. Her eyes came to rest on the head shot of Josie, in the orange top and turquoise beads, with her stylishly bobbed hair. Tony had appended a new, single-line caption to this photo. It read: 'Josephine (Josie) McNicoll, *née* Gordon, Hong Kong, 1983'.

Greer took in the brief words. For a second or two it was almost as if she had written them herself, there was such an inevitability in the message they carried. She thought, so this was what they did. This was their solution. Why am I not surprised? My reaction is quite unambiguous. First and foremost, above anything else, it is pleasure. I think it is true to say that I feel unalloyed pleasure, for my sister and for

Charlie. And yes, there is also unalloyed relief. It's what I would have wanted, what I'd hardly have dared hope for, let alone put into words.

And yet, if I'm to be honest, I think the germ of the idea was always there, in the far recesses, and not only from the moment I unleashed the plan on Josie.

Josie must surely have made a better wife for Charlie. In Greer's mind Josie was always the one he should have fallen for. He had just happened to meet the less suitable one first.

Josie was the practical sister, always immaculately turned out, whatever the occasion or time of day. The one who had a weekly appointment at the hairdresser. The social one who loved entertaining and devising grand celebrations. It was Josie who did all the organising for Greer's twenty-first birthday party, right down to matching corsages for the sisters and their mother. Later, Greer had thrown away her wilted flowers while Josie had pressed hers into an album.

A sequence of pictures arrived unbidden in Greer's mind. Engraved invitations on a mantelpiece for 'At Homes' and cocktail parties. Josie and Charlie hosting a formal dinner at a long table with lashings of silver cutlery and sparkling crystal. The two of them dolled up to the nines in a late-model convertible with the top down, en route to some smart business engagement or other, or perhaps to a ball.

Their wedding. Greer's mother, Lorna, had been circumspect in her letters, but she would not have withheld such information as this. The marriage must have been arranged soon after Lorna's death. Where had it taken place? In Hong Kong? She saw Charlie in a dinner suit and Josie in an off-the-shoulder gown with a veil and train.

Charlie's preference was always for a full-blown, traditional church affair. He agreed to the registry office to appease me. Well, he would have agreed to anything. This time around, though, the bride and groom would have been of one mind. The groom was divorced, of course. Perhaps the ceremony had been held out of doors on someone's sweeping lawns with a view of the sea.

There was another aspect to Josie's personality. From childhood Greer had always been aware of it, because she had so often been on the receiving end. Josie liked to look after people. She was a nurturer. If there was such a thing as a defining characteristic, this was hers. She was the kind of traditional young woman everyone tended to describe as slightly old-fashioned. As maternal. Which was a painful irony, because Josie had known since her teenage years that she could never bear a child.

I grew up knowing she was a deeply maternal person, Greer thought, and with the knowledge that her biology had dealt her a killer blow. I was able to make use of both halves of that information for my own ends.

Before leaving the studio she looked over Mischa's works in progress. There were two large examples of what were already being called his Displacement pictures. One showed a crowd of people massed in the foreground and disappearing into the distance. All were staring in different directions, wildly. Since early last year Mischa had been drawing more than usual on paper, in crayon, charcoal or pen and ink. Here he was employing marks, impressionistic but emphatic, to blur the boundaries between static and moving images. Lines and ghosting in pale wash around the bodies suggested movement of limbs, fluidity and flux.

He had sketched a rough, idealised cityscape around and among the figures. It appeared to be partly in ruins and partly a futuristic metropolis. Just off-centre was a blank area, almost like a gaping hole in the canvas.

In the second picture on the west wall two characters, not identifiably male or female, were looking from right to left and appearing to age before the viewer's eyes. The facial contours were in segments, Cubist-style, fragmented yet not spacially detached from each other. Behind them in the background strange shapes and shadowy figures were looming. In front of them, again near the middle of this picture, was an empty area of nothingness.

As with others in the series a seething sense of transience

and loss pervaded the scene. Standing in the studio, as the sun's rays intensified by the minute and spilled through the east windows, Greer tried to pin down exactly why this was. Was it the restless interplay of line and medium that created this feeling, or an urgent, tensile quality that was intrinsic to both compositions? They seemed to be in suspension between points of essential information, rather like the stop-start narrative of a dream. The gaps in the pictures were suggestive of dreamscapes, too.

Greer looked at the shadowy shapes massed in the background of the second picture. She had not seen that one before. He must have started on it yesterday.

The whole studio was bathed in rosy morning light as she descended the stairs and pulled the heavy door closed behind her. Dew was all around, glittering on the leaves and grass and sparkling off the planes of gravel on the path. She and Guy had visited the local gravel pit late last winter, after torrential rains turned the path to Mischa's studio and sections of their access lanes into rutted quagmires.

She had been struck by the industrial activity of the pit and the heavy machinery that ground stones and rock into different grades of gravel, spewing it out to form sleek geometric heaps in the shapes of pyramids and rhomboids. The following day she took Rollo down to show him. Rollo was fascinated by the hermetic hive of activity, so much at odds with its bucolic surroundings. Who would have thought it?

Greer walked across the parade ground on the springy grass dotted with daisies, poppies and buttercups. Her feet in their rubber-soled sneakers were sodden with dew. It was still too early for anyone else to be about – only the birds, which were in full harmonic voice. The energy that had possessed her since she awoke from the dream of the two men who were the same man was still there, but it was tempered since the visit to the studio with impulses that were less clear-cut. She glanced behind at Tony's cottage. His bedroom window was open, but the front door that Guy had eased back on the latch remained tightly closed.

She skirted the side of the chapel and took the track that clung to the ridge, heading north alongside rows of twenty-year-old olive trees, then down a little pathway to the swimming pool tucked into the side of the hill. It boasted a grotto, which showed off a bronze sculpture of an athletic youth, made early on in their tenure by Rollo at a studio in Rome.

A single magisterial olive tree presided over the pool in the lee of the hill, one of only a handful to survive the freak winter of 1985. It was four hundred years old, and known to them all as the grey eminence. Greer leant against it, running her hands over its extraordinary trunk, a work of art in itself, furrowed and twisted into fantastical shapes and protuberances.

The four full-time human residents of the Castello would describe themselves as irreligious, perhaps profoundly so, yet she suspected even Mischa if put on the spot might not deny a spiritual connection with this tree. To Greer and Rollo it had the status of a tribal elder, a fellow owner-occupier with its own legitimate claim to the land. It was a living being with the wisdom of age and a personality – quirky, dispassionate – clearly defined. She sometimes climbed it, just as she had swarmed up trees incessantly in her childhood, with Josie craning to get a glimpse at her through the foliage. But this morning she had something else in mind.

The pool was still covered with a tarpaulin. This would be removed as soon as the unpredictable spring weather settled a little more. Then the deckchairs and loungers would be carried out from the pool house (which was more accurately a shed) and placed around the green water. It was green because of the colour of the tiles Rollo had chosen to line the original excavation. He thought green was cooler and more allusive than the usual blue. He told Greer that he realised much later he'd had a subliminal vision of Marvell's 'green thought in a green shade' when he set about creating a garden pool.

Guy had planted a clump of umbrella pines after the concrete was poured and the tiles laid. The trees had grown up now at the far end of the pool and the water reflected their slender outlines and elliptical crowns. It was a generously sized pool, long enough to swim laps. To Greer and to many visitors, especially in the height of summer, the place had the indolent aura of a sacred site.

She left it and followed the path as it wound upwards again, skirting the olive orchards and then joining a narrow road that descended into a hollow. She arrived at a high-walled enclosure guarded by a pair of lofty, rusted iron gates. This was the cemetery, and Greer never came here without thinking of *The Secret Garden*, a book she and Josie had read aloud incessantly on one country holiday.

She pushed open the gates, which were never locked. Marking each corner of the cemetery and presiding over it were four majestic and very old cypresses. When they first arrived at the Castello Mischa had painted them in a series of pictures known as 'The Guardians'.

With its high stone walls the cemetery was a suntrap. Even now, on a mid-April morning, the sun was starting to heat the headstones scattered over the ground. Some of the graves were plain stones, modest and nameless. Others were iron crosses. Many had inscriptions that Greer could recite with her eyes closed. 'Here lies the dear soul of Amadio Nardi, *la famiglia inconsolabile*'. Emilia Brogi was described as 'honest and hard-working'. Her family was also inconsolable. Assunta, 1922, was 'an exemplary mother and spouse'. Another woman was described as 'a generous Italian mother loved by her children and friends'.

Some of the letters were flattened, the inscriptions obliterated by time and weather. Marianna had died young, her family desperately hoped to meet again their darling daughter. Ernesto Belloni was an affectionate husband and adoring father who had died unexpectedly – *moro improvisamente*.

One Franco Cebrun had a big, rough-hewn chunk of granite for his headstone. Greer always pictured him as a hearty fellow on the obtuse side, rather like Agnieszka's spouse, Angelo. All the same, Franco had a long inscription: 'My love, *amore per te, ti amo, tua per sempre*. Death will neither separate us nor diminish my great love for you'. Signed only P. Next to it on a small simple stone, 'To my father with love, Lucrezia'.

A husband and wife had their sepia photograph attached to their tombstone. On the large oblong tomb at one corner a family mourned the irreparable loss of their husband and father. His photo was still mounted there, a grave, pudgy-faced man, *dui sio ricordo prosero*.

Greer sat down on a flat, warm stone empty of writing. She peeled off her sweater. Already the air hummed with bees, a hint of the somnolent summer to come. If she were to die suddenly, what would they write on her headstone?

When she had a spare hour or so and the weather was warm she sometimes brought a book down to the cemetery. She found it a tranquil spot for reading, and its simple record of loss and devotion touching. There was no room for equivocation here, just emotion expressed in a few words. Or feelings revealed by omission, or not at all. These people came from families who had spent their days in close proximity. Living cheek by jowl in a hamlet far smaller in area than a village, they must have known one another intimately.

Too well, perhaps? Was there room for secrets? Personal ones, certainly. The stone walls were thick and soundproof, and forgiving. She had cause to be grateful for that. But the consequences of certain bigger secrets would soon have been visible to all and impossible to hide. Feuds, sickness, broken bones. Love, reciprocated or unrequited. A fact of life, such as a death. Or a conception.

In this confined place milestones such as these could not be concealed successfully for long. Most of those who now lay beneath these stones had passed their whole lives here. Sloughing off a former life and leaving the family behind was not an option for them, in the main. They were obliged to keep their emotional baggage with them because there was nowhere else to leave it, and only when they died was it allowed to slip away.

These former residents had more blood relatives living close by, but probably no more close friends than their successors in this hamlet. There would have been far fewer names listed in their address books, if they had such things. But most of the people whose names they did know, and not necessarily friends or relatives, they must have known through and through.

In fact, Greer thought, they probably knew more people intimately, in the sense of seeing them constantly and following their life stories, than any of us do now. These days, instead, people pore over the synthetic lives of celebrities they will never meet.

She looked from one grave to another. The little inscriptions bravely defied the years and tried to confer a measure of immortality. The death of one member of this tiny community must have affected them all. For better or worse, for richer or poorer, it would have had some impact on everyone.

How many important people had she lost in her life? How many were there of whom she could truthfully say, I loved you, and I am inconsolable for your loss? It was not a difficult question; the answer came instantly. Her parents, an aunt, and the one grandmother she had known well. Four people only.

And in the future, for whom might she grieve? Whose were the names, announced in the night after a knock on the door, or in a quiet phone call from a hospital? Whose were the names with the power to take her breath away? This was not hard to answer either. Two names with that power came up immediately. Mischa and Rollo. Guy too, most probably.

And a fourth name stepped forward from the past to claim her sure and certain place on the list. Although she had not seen or spoken to her sister for more than twenty-five years, Greer had no doubt that Josie's name would have that power.

But there was another name. There was someone else, someone to whom she was intimately related, yet whose given name she did not even know. Someone to whom she was more closely related than anyone in the world, more closely even than to Josie.

Sitting on the stone that had become hard and cold, Greer knew she had scaled the perimeter fence. She had left the safe house far behind and was out there, exposed and open, in the area of dark formless shapes and shadows without identities. She had set foot in the forbidden territory of her mind.

She was aware of a single piercing thought. It was unguarded and she knew at once, and with absolute clarity, that it contained the nucleus of her fears.

All the surrounding horrors were real enough — they were profound problems and she had instigated them — but they were essentially red herrings. They might appear to be intractable, but like all human outcomes they were not set in stone. Things were not immutable — that was their nature. There were influences that might be brought to bear. One of these, she thought, surely the greatest of these, whatever its testimony, was the truth of the matter.

Greer saw now that her dread had been of something else altogether. Something so specific and shocking that to have been unaware of it, to have thrust it away for so long, seemed nearly beyond comprehension. She told herself: I will now confront this fear. Because there is now no alternative, I know that. I must do it because there is nothing else to do.

No, those are not the reasons. Because I am, at long last, ready. Because I cannot resist it any more. Because it is irresistible. And because I want to do it more than anything. These, and only these, are the reasons.

Put your head down between your knees and take deep slow breaths.

This instruction from a school first-aid manual, repeated several times, had an effect. The single anxiety was more fundamental than the vague apprehensions she had refused to identify or confront and now thought almost trivial. It had a definition, because she had finally brought herself to name it, and it was crueller because, unlike the other problems, it was beyond her influence. Its source was the fragile thread of another's life.

If you refused to acknowledge something, did it exist? If you didn't express it in words, was it less likely to come to pass? She thrust these questions away like some specious residues of a former faith. Into her mind the words arrived, already arranged in sentences, seemingly of their own volition.

What if he were to have died without my acknowledging his existence?

What if he were to have died without my knowing him?

19

Greer's reflection looked back at her, steely and unblinking, from the octagonal mirror in the bedroom. She asked herself, is the alteration visible? There should be something new in the expression of the eyes because I am different. I have undergone a change, perhaps even an epiphany, and that must have left its mark. If I were painting a portrait of this woman, it would be necessary to locate a subtle shift in the emotional territory of her face.

I believed I had an epiphany once before, as a result of a momentous conversation with a young stranger, sitting on a beach on the Isle of Pines, New Caledonia. How strange that I should have believed that. But perhaps it's not so strange at all, because the two are linked. In a funny way they are part and parcel of the same epiphany. And yet they are poles apart. They are the opposite of each other.

She went to her desk and took out a pencil and a sheet of writing paper. With fast, unhesitating strokes she sketched from memory the nuance of expression she had just studied. The face in the drawing regarded her evenly. It was the face of a woman who had lived with some intensity. The expression conveyed an impression of something discovered. Greer had the sense of retrieving another thing, long mislaid. She thought, I have not lost my touch.

Tony was not in his cottage. When she reached the studio and pushed open the door of the upper level she heard the low buzz of male voices. Mischa and Tony stood under the south windows. Mischa's head was bent. Approaching, she saw he was looking at one of Tony's small photographs.

Greer said to Mischa, whose face was angled away, 'Show me.'

She was quite unprepared for what she saw, but she recognised it instantly. It was a photograph of a twenty-five-year-old picture, Mischa's painting of her reclining on her side, a sensual and serious nude figure, one leg raised and bent at the knee, the other folded into the body. He had begun that painting while she was holidaying on the Isle of Pines with Charlie, consumed with longing for Mischa.

Greer and Mischa had carried it, unfinished, to Sydney, where she had last seen it leaning against the wall of their sitting room. Instead of continuing to work on it, Mischa had rolled it up soon after they arrived and put it aside. She had expected never to see it again.

Tony said, 'I'm feeling kinda sheepish about this, Greer. When I told you I hadn't found any works from the Sydney period, that wasn't a hundred per cent accurate. There was one. This one. This stunner came up for auction last year, coincidentally just before I got to Australia. The State Gallery of New South Wales acquired it. The curator nearly creamed his chinos when he saw it, he told me. Well, and who wouldn't? It's an iconic work.'

Greer's eyes were riveted on the picture. Although it was more than two decades since she had last set eyes on it and the reproduced image was small, she could detect important changes. The lines of the torso, which had been sketchy, were complete and emphatic; the background had been filled in with dense pigment. Against it, the archetypal female form glowed with a translucent pearly sheen.

The work had the self-belief of a painting triumphantly

accomplished. She searched Mischa's face. He must have heard about this sale. He hadn't told her. There was something in his expression she couldn't read.

He put his hand on her shoulder and said, 'I gave it to Marlene.'

Immediately she knew what it was about Mischa's expression. His face looked exactly the same as it did when she uncovered one of his hidden stores of chocolate. He looked like someone who had been found out.

Tony was going on, in a conversational fashion, 'It was the first time this particular work had surfaced, so I was able to trace that sale back to the guy that offloaded it. Well, I'm not sure she'd like me calling her a guy. The sassy old gal who owned it.'

Greer said, more to herself than to Mischa or Tony, 'Dear, funny Marlene.' It was painful to pronounce that name again. It brought back a past she had repudiated.

It brought back crossing the landing to unburden herself in the perfumed boudoir of Marlene, the uber-female who revelled in girl talk. Invariably finding her in a state, obsessing about waxing her legs or wailing over ladders in her stockings or the bunions from her tight, teetering shoes. It brought back finding Dietrich on the turntable, most likely, because this self-annointed namesake of hers was always falling in love, while insisting she never wanted to and couldn't help it.

Within minutes of Greer's arrival the two of them would be shrieking with laughter over some silly thing. The laughter was cathartic, verging on hysteria. In those days both of them, for their different reasons, were teetering on the brink.

'Marlene, right. Now there is a name to conjure with.' Tony's uninhibited gaze swerved between the two of them.

'She'd hung on to that painting all these years, since Mischa left it out for her. Said she'd always regarded it as her superannuation, her sole family jewel. She could only bring herself to part with it when she was on her uppers. The job market's not that crash hot for drag artistes who are way past their prime.' He grinned at them. 'She referred to it as her garage sale.'

Selling the picture had put Marlene squarely back in the black.

'She told me with great relish that she'd joined the fat pussies and paid off her apartment – not the same shitty old dive she had back then, she said to tell you. I checked out her place, it's a riot. She said to be sure to say that as a result of her garage sale she fronts up to shareholders' meetings now and creates quite a stir, which I can believe, *and* she has a harbour glimpse to die for in divine Elizabeth Bay.'

His eyes went with an air of invitation to the dictaphone. Greer was still looking at Mischa.

'I've got the address for you. In Evans Road.' When they didn't respond, Tony added, 'She was good interview talent, Marlene. One of the best. And I'd rate that as one of your best too, Mischa, huh? That Sydney picture?'

Mischa said, 'That was not a Sydney picture. It was done in Melbourne.'

'Before you left. Mostly. Yeah, Marlene told me that. She knew its history. I guess you must have told her about it one day, Greer.'

'I guess I must.' I guess I told her about just about everything in those days. I had to. There was no one else to tell.

'She still has the postcards you sent from Port Douglas and Cooktown. She said to send you her fondest love, and you'll always have a special sequinned place in her heart.'

Greer saw on Tony's face the iridescent memory of Marlene. He added, 'Oh, and she said these days she pulls suits in the corporate world like you wouldn't believe.'

Mischa's hand still rested on Greer's shoulder. The sunlight lay in oblongs on the studio floor. It was dusty, Greer noticed. She must get Agnieszka in here. Mischa always hated it when she did that.

Tony asked, 'Were there any other survivors?' They looked at him and away again.

'Surviving pictures, I mean. From the great Boxing Day bonfire of 1979.'

Greer heard her own soft intake of breath. At the same time she was reminded incongruously of the Bristow comic strip set in an office, with its references to the Great Tea Trolley Disaster of 1963. Tony's voice was light and innocuous, as if he was fully expecting to hear an amusing anecdote. So that was how he was going to play it. Well, playing it down was probably preferable to up.

Mischa said, 'I burnt the others.'

'Out the back of the block of flats. On a total-fire-ban day. And the cops slapped you on the wrist with a fine. Why did you do it, Mischa?' The voice, buoyant, might have been asking why he disliked team sports.

'I got rid of them because none of them were any good.'

'Did you agree with that, Greer?'

'Agree with what? That they were no good, or they should be burnt? Or that he was fined for lighting a fire on a day of total fire ban?'

'I understand you weren't there at the time he did this,' Tony said in a softer tone, 'but what did you think about the quality of the work he put on the bonfire?'

'Oh, I —' She hesitated. She felt dizzy all of a sudden and short of breath. 'I don't —'

'She didn't like them because they were full of shit, Tony,' Mischa roughly interrupted. 'That's all there is to say on the subject. Go away and get over it.'

He propelled Greer across to a trestle table with bench seats. Table and benches were covered with books, magazines and newspapers, sketchpads, empty mugs, stray CD boxes and an old cassette radio.

Mischa brushed a space for both of them on a bench. He put his arm round her. Greer leant against him with her back to the table. She looked at the dust on the floor. *Put your head down between your knees and take deep breaths.* She had thought she might be about to faint.

Tony, unruffled, squatted on the end of the table and placed his little tape recorder in front of him. 'Verity showed up one time while you were in Sydney, not long before you left, right? Said she saw Mischa but not you, Greer. Neither of you had been in touch for months and she was stressed out, not knowing how the works for the next show were coming along.'

His eyes flicked to Greer and away again. 'She remembers the paintings very well. No way did she think they were shit. No way in the world. She particularly remembered the self-portraits, because she'd never seen Mischa make any before.'

And he would never make any again. Greer closed her eyes against the images, but they were burnt on to her retinas. The heads, all of them Mischa's, splattered with marks that were slashed into the paper like wounds. The bodies, his and hers, grossly distorted and asymmetrical. Shadows, ominous and malevolent, looming over hospital beds. Writhing contortions. Changelings.

Mischa had always employed different styles in the same picture, held in bold, finely judged equilibrium. It was his trademark. This was the first and only time Greer had ever seen him produce work that she feared was out of control.

Mischa said, 'Verity was talking through her hat. She was always biased in favour of me.'

'True, but she said those pictures were pretty remark-able, Mischa. She was taken aback by them. Said they were confronting and bleak, but really strong. She likened them to Goya's "The Disasters of War". When she heard what happened to them she was so shocked and appalled she said she nearly threw up on the spot. Not her *exact* phraseology, but –'

Tony jumped visibly as Mischa sprang to his feet without warning and yelled, 'Don't tell me her opinion! I don't want to hear what she thinks! I didn't want her to see the pictures, I didn't want her to show them and I didn't want them shown in the future! Not to anyone, do you understand?'

Mischa dropped his shoulders and exhaled hard, looking

down at Greer, whose head was bent again. He said in a more normal voice, 'We don't want to see them again, Tony, so my decision is, there's no point to cart them around. Better they go up in smoke.'

His eyes settled on Tony's dictaphone. He seized it, vaulted on to the table and thrust the small gadget in his face, like a singer with a microphone. 'Don't worry, people, I did the right thing by my crazy pictures! I got a green plastic bucket and went and scattered the ashes in the cemetery so they could have a view of the sea!'

Greer got up. She said quietly to Mischa, 'It's all right, I'm OK,' and to Tony, 'I'll be in the house.'

She crossed the floor fast, concentrating on planting her footsteps one in front of the other. As she went she detected a note of excitement, carefully supervised, in Tony's modulated voice.

'Is that right? No kidding. You went out on Boxing Day, that same night, with the ashes from the fire?' And then conversationally, as if it were of no great moment, 'In a green plastic bucket, huh? And which cemetery would that be?'

Outside the studio Greer made a beeline for the house. She was feeling nauseous, the way she used to feel before exams. There was no one about, for which she was glad. She didn't want to see anyone just now, not even Rollo. It was Saturday, she remembered. Jacopo and Giulia were reputed to be coming this morning with the forklift. She glanced at her watch. They were due any minute but they were bound to be late. Probably an hour at least before they showed up.

In the kitchen she sat quietly and drank a glass of fizzy water, which was supposed to be settling. The early morning energy, with its concomitant gust of wellbeing, had gone. She felt detached, and at the same time resolute. She didn't want to think about or work out what kind of resolution this might presage. It was just there, surrounding her, the way the force-field of Mischa's creative concentration surrounded him.

She went into her study and took out the diary. Before opening it she sat with her elbows on the desk, chin in her hands, looking at the sketch she had made earlier of herself. Finally, she opened the diary at the back and wrote without preamble, as she had told Mischa without preamble that she was leaving Charlie.

21st April 2006 (later)
The waters broke at 3 am on Boxing Day morning. That it happened to be Boxing Day was immaterial – we had not celebrated Christmas. Mischa and I had been painfully silent all day.

Marlene, my friend who lived across the passage, had gone to an Xmas lunch party. She came back in the evening with bags of leftovers, turkey and pudding. She banged on our door, very drunk, mascara running, with two cold bottles of Veuve Clicquot, & made Mischa open one of them then and there. We went down to the concrete yard where we put the food on Marlene's card table and she sat me on a chair bolstered with her Thai silk cushions.

We were a forlorn trio, in the tiny boiling hot courtyard in the twilight, among the overflowing rubbish bins. I drank two glasses of champagne. They drank the rest.

It was the champers, Marlene insisted, that oiled Greer's carburettor two weeks before her due date. This was an uncharacteristically masculine analogy for something that was a deliberate ploy on her part, as Marlene informed Greer in the car in the early hours of the next morning. It had had the same galvanising effect on her sister-in-law. She more than anyone knew that by this stage in the piece Greer was fighting a losing battle against discomfort, distress and desperation in roughly equal parts.

By this stage in the piece, moreover, Marlene was having trouble keeping her hostility towards Mischa under wraps. And vice versa. Looking back, Greer thought Mischa had been in a catatonic state for weeks, scarcely responsible for his actions. But even as that had made him incapable of looking after her, it hadn't stopped him working away in a kind of rampage of productivity.

On the afternoon of Christmas Eve, before her show, Marlene had insisted on taking Greer to a Croatian clairvoyant in the Cross she'd heard amazing things about. The woman, who was younger than Greer, had scrutinised her client's palm and at once pronounced her to be a passionate woman. Moreover, Greer was besottedly in love and she was soon to have a momentous experience.

These things had a reasonable chance of being true, given Greer's burgeoning appearance, but the fortune teller had taken note of her client's set face and gone on to say, gravely, that she could see big, very big difficulties. There was a major impediment preventing these problems from working out. Greer knew what this was, didn't she?

'But will they work out?' Greer had wretchedly asked her. The girl, who seemed pleasant, was looking increasingly uneasy.

'There seems to be a solution, but it's –' She was obviously reluctant to go on. Seeing this, an agitated Marlene had hustled Greer up and out of there, voluble with apologies for her own feeble-mindedness in suggesting this stupid outing.

Marlene had tried to persuade Greer to come to Christmas lunch with her. 'They're darling people, darl, you'll adore them. You've seen nothing till you've seen the seven stripping Santas, they're a scream. It'll do you good to party, you can't be moping on your own.'

To Greer's half-hearted protest that she wasn't alone, Mischa was there, Marlene had retorted that he might as well be in Timbuktu. But the idea of paper hats and mincing Santas made Greer feel sick.

The waters had broken while she was on her way back from the bathroom, in the narrow passage between it and the bedroom, where she had been sleeping alone. They had flooded across the floor, which was on a slight tilt, and trickled through the doorway into the sitting room where Mischa slept on the sofa.

Greer had stood there, rooted to the spot, stunned by the amount of liquid that gushed out of her. Her first thought was that Mischa would be horrified. Her second thought was to call Marlene. Marlene had made Greer promise to come and get her the moment it happened, whatever time of day or night it happened to be. Even if Marlene was high-kicking in the chorus line, Greer was to haul herself up on stage and drag her, pun intended, darl, into the delivery room.

Marlene brought a bucket and mopped up the water while I rang Josie. This was not the problem it might have been, as Josie, mindful of premature surprises, had been organised for ages. But she now had to find an early seat on a plane. I didn't have to pack a bag for myself either. Marlene had had it ready for a month at least.

I didn't wake Mischa. Marlene and I went to the hospital. Marlene insisted on driving, although she wasn't feeling well.

She put a line through the full stop and added the words '*at all*'. In truth, Marlene had been feeling exceedingly ill in the aftermath of Christmas Day and had vomited out of the driver's window on the way to hospital. The blasé nurses at the Royal Women's, Paddington, were used to everything. No eyelids were batted at the tall, disastrously hungover person of indeterminate gender and ravaged make-up who presented herself as Greer's dedicated birthing coach.

In spite of that she insisted on staying the distance and was a tower of strength for me.

They were whisked straight to the delivery suite. Marlene had wielded wet flannels and held Greer's hand, encouraging and urging her on in between mad dashes to the bathroom. She had the presence of mind to deliver a crash course in breathing techniques, and they breathed through the contractions together as the cycle intensified.

Marlene had accompanied Greer to two antenatal classes. Greer suspected Marlene had continued to attend the course after she herself dropped out. Her own absence from the classes was symptomatic of the way she had blundered through the past five months. Apart from rubbing her stomach with cocoa butter several times a day because of her horror of stretch marks she had done the bare minimum, medically. In spite of the ballooning evidence to the contrary, she hadn't wanted to admit that this was happening.

Josie got there just in time.

By midday, amazingly, and with almost an hour to spare. If she was bemused by the presence of Marlene, Josie hadn't shown it. Marlene, however, had not been inclined to yield her position as primary support person, although she was looking increasingly green as the last hour wore on. She and Josie had jointly soothed, breathed and mopped Greer's brow to the finishing line.

Before the fact and encouraged by Marlene, Greer had been adamant she would have an epidural and everything else on offer. In the event, the breathing and muscle relaxant, together with a certain stoicism she hadn't known she possessed, got her through. When eventually she demanded pain relief it was too late, the finale was imminent. She and Marlene had screamed in unison.

In the days that followed, driving north with Mischa, dancing on New Year's Eve, she thought the fact that she hadn't had any analgesics to speak of must have speeded her recovery.

Most of it is a blank but I do remember the moment of giving birth. Being told to give a short, very strong push followed immediately by a push at half strength. And then the sensation of something sliding out of me, quite slowly, over what seemed like several seconds.

And then, dimly, someone saying it was a boy. A perfect boy.

She didn't see him. Had she signed papers, forms? She had no memory of it, but that didn't mean a thing. Beyond being wheeled into a ward where there were several other new mothers, she had no memory whatsoever of the hours immediately following the birth. But she knew she couldn't have stayed the night. Had she signed herself out of there? Had it been necessary, or could you just discharge yourself if you felt like it?

She did remember walking out slowly with Josie beside her. It was definitely not completely dark outside, but the light was fading fast. Josie must have been carrying him. She didn't remember.

Much more vivid was the recovered sensation of glorious lightness. And the overwhelming feeling of liberation. She had felt — there was no way round it, in spite of the bulky pad she was wearing and the soreness — as if a key had been turned in the lock, a bolt drawn back and she'd been unleashed on the world anew. As if the judgement was not guilty by reason of unsound mind, and she had been released from a life sentence.

Of saying goodbye to Josie, which she must have done, she had no memory at all.

Her pen hovered over the page. There were some things, weren't there, that should not be written?

I don't remember anything else until I was back in the flat. The aftermath is nothing more than a blur in my mind.

There was something else, however, that did have to be said.

I think I deliberately did not look at the baby, so that he would not have any existential reality for me.
So that I would not have to make myself forget him.

Mischa was not in the flat when Greer got in, she did remember that, and Marlene was out as well, tripping the boards at Les Girls. Greer scribbled a two-word note, 'I'm back', and stuck it on the floor inside their front door, then showered and manoeuvred herself into bed. She had been fast asleep when she heard Mischa's heavy tread. She came to with a start.

Mischa had opened the bedroom door and stood silhouetted against the light from the passage. In her befuddled state he seemed to be carrying, of all things, a green plastic bucket. Had Marlene forgotten to tip out the waters?

Whatever it was, he'd put it down without saying a word and crossed the threshold, stripped off his clothes and got into the bed where she had slept alone for months. He avoided touching her, just left a space between them and fell deeply asleep instantly, as if he too was monumentally exhausted. He seemed to smell of smoke, but she'd thought she must be imagining it.

By the time she awoke the next day it was mid-afternoon and Mischa had already packed the car. Her clothes were in the tin trunk, and he had put it on top so it was accessible. He'd even thought to give the Port Douglas post office as a forwarding address for any outstanding bills.

There was no sign of Marlene, which was not unusual. She was often waylaid on her way home from work, describing it as 'Taking a little detour'. But this meant that Greer could not say goodbye. She wasn't inclined to argue the point with Mischa. To say each was as desperate as the other to get the hell out of there was an understatement if ever there was one.

Greer had always had a key to Marlene's flat. Before leaving the building she had made time to compose a farewell note. The note was short but emotional and deeply heartfelt. It was Mischa, Greer now recalled, who had wrapped the key in it and been the one to deposit it inside Marlene's room, while she herself negotiated the steep and narrow stairs for the last time.

Greer slept most of the way to their first stop, and it was a few more days, after New Year's Eve in fact, before it occurred to her that not one of the pictures Mischa had painted in Sydney had travelled with them in the car.

20

There was activity on the parade ground. The plants and citrus trees that had been bedded for the winter, the lemons, limes, mandarins and grapefruit and all the flowering shrubs that were susceptible to frost, were in the process of being lifted from the sheltered stone outhouse they called the limonerie by the forklift truck operated by Jacopo. Greer stood on the lawn, summoned with Guy to supervise.

'Give me half an hour,' she said to Tony when he came for her, but he had spotted Giulia and she didn't have to worry about him.

She thought, I am operating on autopilot, as Mischa often does. I appear to be here among the daisies chit-chatting with Guy, but I am in another, harder, place. I am preoccupied with something other than this, something that Guy knows nothing of, with my unquiet mind thrashing around in the undergrowth. Being ambidextrous, just like Tony.

Tony and Giulia were playing sheepdogs, confronting the excitedly barking pugs and giggling like children. Jacopo, designer sunglasses shading coal-black, heavy-lidded eyes that didn't miss much, had hoisted one of the heaviest tubs with the crane arm and swung it out and around.

'See the youth cavorting,' Guy said. 'Doesn't it make you pea-green with jealousy? What wouldn't you give, and so on.'

'Every dog has its day.'

'That's no help and no consolation. I want my day back. I'd be prepared to enter into a Faustian contract for it. Wouldn't you? Go on, I bet you'd love a second go at youth.'

'I quite like my present age. And I'd probably make all the same mistakes. It's hard enough identifying exactly what the mistakes were.'

She could bandy words with Guy with scarcely a conscious thought, but the careless mendacity of the last sentence brought the anxiety sweeping back in a wave that threatened to knock her off her feet and suck her under, like one of the dumpers that caught you unawares on Bondi Beach.

Guy, though, was always susceptible to appearances. 'Who cares what the mistakes were? What one craves is the delectable chance to make them all over again.'

'We'll put the lemons where they were last year, shall we? At intervals along the drive.'

He nodded absently, shading his eyes. There was a burst of hilarity. Now Giulia was perched on the forklift, giving orders.

'Tony quite likes the hetero ideal, you know. The yin and yang of it. It's the pleasing artistic symmetry of straight-ness that appeals to him. He's got a point, I suppose. You can't quarrel with the building blocks of nature.'

'I thought it was the pleasing artistic symmetry of it that had you worried.'

He made a face. 'There's more 'n a slip 'twixt theory and practice.'

'Proverbs for our time, by G. Crewe. A losing battle, you think, in this particular instance?'

'I think. It hardly ever works, not in my experience. Not in the long term. Not when there's a strong pull the other way. Mind you, if it could work, our Giulia's the girl to make it happen.'

'Don't give that scenario another thought. There'd be pistols at dawn. Three ways. What about the big blue hydrangeas? Door of Rollo's studio?'

'One on each side.' Guy had a distant look.

'There's symmetry for you.'

He was leading up to something.

He said, 'How are you rubbing along with Tony? He's doing a thorough forensic job, I imagine. You must be finding out all manner of boring things about Mischa's past. Yours too, no doubt, though perhaps less boring, who knows? He's an inscrutable cove, young Tonio. Annoyingly discreet for a biographer.'

'He's doing a thorough job. Annoyingly thorough. We're rubbing along. And you?'

'Kind of you to inquire. I was thinking of asking him back, as it happens.'

'Back?' She was on high alert, in an instant.

'Back here for a stretch in the summer. I thought he might like to write some of it at Casanova.'

She was caught unawares again, and this was one walloping dumper she hadn't seen coming. Guy saw the flinch.

'Do I detect a dose of the disapprovals?'

She drew a slow breath. 'Perhaps a smidgin.'

'You're not keen?'

'Well, I – no. Not terribly keen, as it happens. What does Roly think?'

'Oh good God, I haven't floated it with His Lordship. It's a completely unilateral impulse.' Guy looked amused. 'He's got no say in the matter, any road.'

'It wasn't always thus.' She felt another wave hit her, this time of sadness.

'It wasn't, but it is now. Don't look so funereal. Tempus fugit, and all that. He's eighty-one next month. Officially.'

'Yes, I know.' Desolation swept over her.

'Eighty-one going on eighty-three. Or ninety.'

Rollo's birth certificate had been stored in a part of Somerset House that was bombed in World War II. Guy always swore he had jumped at the chance to put his age back, and Rollo always swore this was a vile slur. Greer kept her stance carefully neutral.

'When you want Casanova for anyone he can work in a room chez nous. And doss down chez nous, what is more.' Guy eyed her. 'You needn't see him very much. I'd keep him busy.'

She knew the innocent look in his eye too well.

'You've already invited him, haven't you?'

'I have, actually. Sorry.'

He rubbed his hands together, as if to brush off a fly or some imaginary dirt. 'Listen, it's not all beer and skittles, you know, back at the ranch. There's been a bit of fraying at the edges. Don't put your trust in those false prophets intimating immortality. In love or in life, for that matter.'

'I'll bear it in mind.'

What if he?

What if he were to have?

'We could do with an injection of youth here, don't you think? A shot of adrenalin. Do us all good.'

She could not answer.

'I might need a few ancillary services on the home stretch. Tony'd make a fair to middling aide de camp, don't you think?'

She had never been miserable in Guy's company. Now she felt anguish.

'Guy. You're not thinking –' She could not pronounce it. The prospect was too appalling.

He knew perfectly well what she would not say.

'Let's not count the chickens or tilt at windmills before they're hatched. Sufficient unto the day, and so forth.'

'You didn't finish.'

'Sufficient unto the day is the necessary, thereof. Will that suffice for you right now?' He was not about to take this seriously, she could see that.

Tony had said goodbye to the others, and was prancing towards them with a spring in his step.

*

She filled the kettle for tea while Tony squatted on the floor with the boxes, the cardboard cartons he was still calling 'the archive'. Greer had dredged up an unnatural calm from an unknown source, like some sedative borne on the breeze. But there was a snap, only slightly muted, of anticipation in the air. She thought, Tony is on tenterhooks.

She brought the tea and a plate of biscuits on a wooden Florentine tray that Rollo had given her. It was a bit souvenir-ish, Rollo had said with a bashful smile, handing it over very early on in their relationship. A bit on the touristy side, with all those gilded twirls and swirls. But some touristy things were allowable, weren't they? Greer had discovered later that Rollo had touched up the gilt himself and it was an old tray, not one of the souvenir shop repro-ductions at all.

Before Tony could leap up for it she handed him a mug. She wanted to dash, even if only for a brief interval, his complacent expectations. She decided to kick off this session with a little interrogation of her own.

'How did Verity know where we were living in Sydney?'

At the time Greer had been too upset and distracted to worry much about the implications of Verity's surprise visit. But it must have been a godsend for Tony. Mischa insisted he had only ever given her the post-box address.

Tony took the staccato question with equanimity. 'Ah, that. It was all because of the flowers.'

'Flowers?'

'Mischa sent flowers for her birthday. A week before Christmas.' Tony coughed. 'I'd say the motivation was guilt, wouldn't you? Not having contacted her or sent her any new pictures. Et cetera.'

She thought, he can't resist the et cetera.

'The Sydney contact was the florist just down from your apartment. Verity did a spot of sleuthing.'

A cautious smile. 'I guess they let their usual defences down, with a genteel lady like her. No way was she going to be a terrorist. Or a mugger.'

Greer said tartly, 'They probably thought she was his mother.'

'She did say it was her Miss Marple moment. Mischa couldn't hide the pictures from her when she suddenly blew in like that. There was no way he could stop her from seeing them. She said the works were everywhere, drawings and paintings all over the floor. She had to take her shoes off and tiptoe around them all to get to the bathroom.'

Past the couch strewn with Mischa's bedclothes.

'So yeah, Verity guessed —' a trace of discomfort, 'how you were. How both of you were. But she didn't know any more of the story than that. And she kept your secret loyally, you know, Greer. Never told another soul. That's what she said, and I believe her.'

So I misjudged Verity.

Tony drank some water from the bottle. 'I have to say that she didn't divulge a word to me about the content of the pictures until she'd first determined what I already knew. She was very scrupulous, Greer. Like Marlene. Marlene said her bee-stung lips were sealed. She wasn't about to blow your cover either.'

She was baffled. 'Then —?'

'Here's the amazing, serendipitous thing.' Tony's voice had risen and accelerated. He resumed more soberly. 'From my viewpoint serendipitous, maybe not so much from yours.'

He glanced from under his lashes.

'A woman got in touch with me, right, about a Frenchman she used to have a bit of a thing with years ago. The French guy's name,' he enunciated carefully, 'was Jean-Claude Clement.'

This she had not expected. '*Jean-Claude*?' Greer felt a tremor run down her spine.

'Jean-Claude, yeah. I never got to track him down himself, well, not so far, but there was this former medico colleague of his from Canberra. She's a professor now at one of the teaching schools and she contacted me. She'd read something about my book, or she'd seen the website, and she remembered her French boyfriend relating a weird tale about meeting you on a beach on holidays. It was years ago she heard it, she said, but it always stuck in her mind.'

Tony paused. 'After the holiday Jean-Claude had come across a review of Mischa's Melbourne exhibition in some weekly paper and he showed her. He remembered the artist's name because it was unusual.'

Why did I disclose his name? What a foolish question. Because I couldn't resist. Two words, two arrangements of letters. It transported me, just to say those words out loud to a stranger on a beach. She saw blinding sun and an expanse of ivory sand.

Tony was musing. 'This happens to biographers, I guess. Especially the way technology is these days. Sometimes you only need one contact to point you in the direction of the –'

He hovered, looking uncertain.

'Of the truth?' That gave him a frisson, too. She saw it in his voyeuristic eyes.

'Of the whole truth, yeah.'

She said, 'You're never going to get to the whole truth, Tony. Only a partial version. You'll have to accept that.'

He didn't believe her. She could see it in his confident eyes and the assertive tilt of his head.

Greer stood up and said curtly, 'I've decided there's no point in prevaricating any furthur. You had better come out of the biographer's tactical closet and tell me who you have seen and spoken to.'

Their eyes met. Tony's were wide and bright. She sensed relief, also barely suppressed excitement. He said, 'Right on, Greer.'

She was looking down on his upturned face, eager and boyish. She moved away and opened the window, and balanced on the wide sill with her mug of tea. Sounds drifted into the room. Her doves and a cuckoo, cows from the farms across the valley and the traverse of a distant jet plane high in the stratosphere. Tony was fiddling with the flap of his satchel. The inevitable dictaphone sat on the floor.

Greer said, 'I think I'd prefer not to have that thing on any more, if it's all the same to you. Which it's not, of course, but I'm sure your excellent memory will fill in the gaps. Not to mention your vivid imagination.'

He touched it and responded with a reassuring smile. 'It's safely off, Greer.'

'Then you can put it away, out of sight.'

He tucked it into the back pocket of his jeans promptly. She had a desire to pick him up by the scruff of the neck and shake him.

Instead she said, 'I gather you've seen Charlie and my sister, and spoken to them. Where are they living?'

'OK now. Let's see.' He frowned and screwed up his eyes. 'They keep a house in Sydney, in an upmarket neighbourhood called Hunters Hill, but Charlie's on a three-year contract in Shanghai right now. I was able to catch them on one of their Sydney visits. It's a grand old house, turn-of-the-century sandstone, with lawns sweeping down to the water and a jetty for their boat.'

Greer braced herself. 'They have a child.' In the rising inflexion of the last syllable she heard the ghost of a question. It was easy to fall back into the old habit. To clutch at straws, while knowing they had blown away. To clutch at straws you did not need any more.

Tony got up, pirouetting off the floor with one hand. She thought, Guy would like it, but that little display of athletic prowess is wasted on me. He sat back in a chair, the denim satchel resting on his knee.

'Yeah, well, they had three kids, but they've all flown the coop now. Two are away at school. One's at the national uni in Canberra and the other's doing postgrad in the UK. Sussex, I think it is.'

'Three?' She was confused.

'They adopted two, because – well, you know how your sister couldn't have kids of her own? She had that very rare thing when she was young –'

'A form of Asherman's Syndrome.'

'Right. So they adopted two Chinese race babies. Girls. Pretty cute kids – there were photos everywhere. They're grown now, of course.'

'So they were sisters for the . . . for the first one?' She heard herself speaking the words distinctly and slowly, as if she were addressing a child. And felt herself rocking in the open window, backwards and forwards. This had been a childhood habit, when awaiting a reprimand for some transgression. She straightened up, her hand on the ledge.

'Younger sisters for Will, yeah.'

Will. She saw him throwing a frisbee on a beach to his younger sisters. She pronounced his name experimentally, tentatively, in her mind.

'They called him William Charles Gordon McNicoll. William for your dad, and Charles for his. Gordon for, well, for you. And for Josie too, of course. But he's always known as Will.'

She looked at Tony. Here was the messenger with the tidings, the repository of the knowledge. His round head with its halo of bright blond hair like stalks of spiky corn was bent now, his hands riffling through the folders in his case. She felt she was seeing him with new eyes. He was not the person she would have chosen, but he was all she had.

'He's all right, Will, is he? Is he in good health?'

The strident questions had emerged, bludgeoned themselves out into the open before she thought to frame them in any different way.

She stood up again, feeling Tony's gaze on her, and turned to stare out of the window at her cypress, and the valley beyond. The familiar sloping landscape looked like an incomprehensible map, some unknown country spread out before her. The land trembled behind currents of warm air. It seemed to have no connection to her.

Does Tony know why I sound so stilted and strange? Why there is a lump in my throat? Does he have the remotest idea that this is the first conversation on the subject I have ever had with anyone in my life?

'He was doing very fine, Greer, when I last heard.'

She had her back to him and he couldn't see her face. There were small cotton-wool clouds scudding high in the sky. To her horror, she felt tears welling. She squeezed her eyes shut and brushed at them with her clenched fists.

'When you last heard? But how long ago was that?' Now her voice sounded muffled and gravelly to her ears, and foreign, like the voice of another person.

'Not so long. Just before I came here.'

He's speaking to me encouragingly now, comforting me as if I were the child.

'And you – did you actually see him?'

'Sure I did.'

Tony must have got up, she felt his hand resting lightly on her forearm. 'And I have a photo to prove it.'

Instead of throwing him off she allowed herself to be guided to the armchair next to his. He was taking something from his case, one of his manila envelopes.

He hesitated. 'Do you want to see it?'

The question was so absurd she had to stop herself from seizing the envelope and tearing the paper to extract the colour photograph, a ten by eight print. Instead she saw her middle-aged hand extend itself as if in slow motion and slide it from his smooth young fingers with their shiny manicured nails.

She lowered her eyes to the photograph in her hand, but at first saw nothing. Her vision was still blurred. Acutely conscious of the presence of the young man next to her, she laid the image on her knee and pressed the cold palms of her hands against her eyelids.

She unfolded her hands slowly, like two doors opening outwards, keeping her thumbs pressed to the corners of her eyes and her head lowered. That way Tony could not see her face when she looked on the likeness of her son for the first time in her life.

What she saw at first was what anyone might see. A lanky youth, dark-haired, wearing jeans. He was standing outside a house with a lacy iron balcony, a house in the style of the inner-city Victorian terraces she remembered.

It was an oddly formal photograph. The young man was not lounging but standing stiffly, as if to attention. His arms, blue shirtsleeves rolled to the elbow, were folded in front of him, his feet planted wide apart. He presented the camera with a challenging stare, chin jutting, unsmiling.

She thought, he is like a soldier presenting arms. He is good-looking, there is strength and vigour there. A look of Charlie. A dependable face. That is what anyone might see. This could be any testosterone-fuelled young male. But what is it that I see? Because I am the single person with the closest possible relationship to him.

I am his mother.

'He asked me to take it.'

She hadn't heard. Her head close to the sheet of paper, she was momentarily unaware of anything else. Just this image, with its uncompromising body language. Her son was signalling to her.

Tony waited before saying again, 'Will asked me to take the picture.'

She removed her hands from her face and put them in her lap. She thought, I have no defences against what is coming.

'He asked you?'

'For you. He wanted me to bring it here for you.'

Because there was something else, something Tony was not saying. She knew it, from his flickering, evasive eyes and the hawkish stance of the young man in the photograph. She wanted, for a few more precious moments, to be ignorant of it.

'Tell me – about him.'

'He looks a bit like you, Greer, don't you think? The same high-bridged nose. He's a very cool guy. You'd be proud. He's an architect, working on low-cost housing, for Asia mainly. Very socially responsible and politically aware; plans to set up his own outfit in a couple of years.'

There was warmth in his voice, liking. She had a startled memory. A conversation on the lower terrace, when she'd asked Tony if he had ever been in love.

'Is he – I mean, does he have a partner?'

Tony lifted his eyes and turned them on her. A distinct glint of amusement. 'He's engaged to be married, Greer. Lovely girl, too. Rebecca. Long dark hair with red high-lights. Great figure. She's just done her Finals, in architecture like him. They're living together. She was with him.'

He raised his eyebrows and flashed a reminiscent smile. 'Yeah. It was very obvious they were crazy about each other.'

'Really, engaged? Already? Do you have a photograph of Rebecca? When are they getting married?'

She felt dazzled, overwhelmed by the quantity and import of Tony's information. She was unsure how to broach the most pressing subject. From being drained of all response, now she had a thousand nervous, buzzing ques-tions.

'You've got me there. Some time this year, that's for sure.'

'What did he –' She sought to rephrase this. 'Tell me the truth about this, Tony. What was Will's attitude –'

She stopped, confronted head-on with her renewed vulnerability.

Tony gave her a sidelong glance but didn't address the unformed question immediately. He swallowed. She saw his Adam's apple bobbing.

'When I met with him his parents were in Shanghai. I hadn't, you know, got around to contacting them yet. So they didn't actually know anything about the biography. I'm talking about Charlie and –'

She tried to put a brake on her impatience. 'Charlie and Josie, yes. His parents. Yes, I know.'

Her voice was husky. What was he getting at? He was rummaging in his denim briefcase again. He pulled out another of his dictaphones. It was labelled. How many did he have? He forestalled her objection with a gesture and shook his head.

'There's something I think you need to hear. I feel very bad about this, Greer.' He licked a little bead of sweat from his upper lip.

The foreboding choked in her throat like swirling smog. He switched the recorder on. At first she heard only the piping of birds. The liquid warble of an Australian magpie. And then Tony's noncommittal introduction.

'Interview with William McNicoll, March twenty-one 2006. We're sitting in William's back garden in Rozelle, Sydney —'

A second, energetic young male voice interrupted. 'Hang on, what's the point of this? I can't tell you anything about my father's life before I was born. I wasn't there, right?'

'It's not about your father. Sorry if I didn't make that quite clear on the phone. I'm researching a biography of your mother's partner, Mischa Svoboda. The artist.'

'Then you've obviously stuffed up, mate. You've got the wrong person. My father's name is Charles McNicoll and he's certainly not an artist.'

'He can't even draw recognisable stick figures, Will, can he?' A young woman's light-hearted voice chimed in.

Tony again. 'It's your mother's partner I'm writing about. Your birth mother, Will. Greer Gordon.'

There was a short pause.

'You've got the name right, yes. My actual mother was Greer, Mum's younger sister. But you're on the wrong track, mate: she's dead. I never knew my real mum. She died when I was born.'

Greer said, 'Turn it off.'

Tony touched the switch. He avoided looking at her, sucking in his breath.

'I'm more than sorry, Greer. That's what they brought him up on and I swear it never occurred to me.'

'How did he react?' She found herself on her feet and

pacing the floor, the photograph tightly under her arm. She felt ill. 'No, *give me that*. I want to listen to it by myself.'

She snatched the recorder from Tony's hand.

In her study, she put it on the desk and shut the door. She knew how to operate it, she had watched Tony often enough. There were a few minutes left to run on the tape.

Tony's response. Taken aback. 'They might have told you that, but Greer is very much alive. She lives in Italy with the well-known Czech artist Mischa Svoboda. You've probably heard of him? She's a winemaker, herself.'

A short pause and an altered tone. 'Oh, jeez. Look, I'm really sorry if this comes as a shock to you, Will. Greer and Mischa have been an item since, well, since before you were born. Since about five months before, right? I just assumed you knew all that. I didn't mean to break it to you like this. I honestly had no idea they'd given you a different story. I guess they figured it was the least hurtful way out of a tricky situation. Least hurtful to you, when you were growing up.'

'What the hell are you talking about?' Slowly, more puzzled than hostile.

'Greer split up with your dad, you see. She'd fallen heavily for this new guy.'

'Are you saying he's my father?'

'No, no, she was already pregnant with you when she met Mischa. She was working in an art gallery, right? He was a pretty wild character, Mischa, back then, but obviously a huge talent, and I guess she didn't feel he'd be accepting of –'

An emphatic interruption: 'Another guy's inconvenient brat?'

'Uh. Possibly. Yeah.' An exhaled breath. 'Anyhow, I'm sure she had her reasons. She handed you over to her older sister to look after from day one. I guess they flew you straight from Sydney to Hong Kong, where your dad was by then.'

'A kid would've cramped their style so she donated it to her sister who couldn't have one? Is that what you're saying?

And everyone swapped partners? Jesus. Had Dad switched over to Mum before I came along?'

'Well, I haven't met with your mum and dad yet so I can't be specific, but I guess they must've told you pretty much what happened after you were born?'

'They told me a story. Here's how it went. There was a period of grieving. Mum came over to help look after me. Then a year or so later they fell in love.'

'Yeah. Well, I'm sure that's probably pretty accurate: that they lived in the same house but apart for a while, and hooked up later. There's no doubt your dad had been mad about Greer and was pretty devastated when she ran out on him.'

Another pause. Then a long-drawn-out, almost amused groan. 'For Christ's sake. She ditched Dad when she was already pregnant, farmed me out to her sister and wrote me out of her life. Where'd you say she lives?'

'Italy.'

'Whereabouts?'

'In Tuscany.'

An incredulous laugh. 'Tuscany, yeah, that'd be right.'

The light, musical voice: 'Excuse me, can you turn that off?'

'Shit, is it still on? Yeah, turn the fucking thing off. In fact give me the tape —' There was a scuffling noise. 'No, on second thoughts, don't. Just leave it. Put it all in your book, OK? Verbatim.'

A click, then silence. Greer sat motionless at her desk. The blood had drained from her face.

Tony's voice came back on the tape.

'The poor guy was pretty shattered, finding out cold like that. I tried to tell him more about her, the artists' colony where she lives and so on, but he didn't want to know. He did get me to repeat at what point Greer had met the Czech lover. Too late to get it aborted, was it, he asked me. Pretty much, yeah, she would've been over three months gone, I had to tell him. I suggested he should maybe think about going over there and meeting with her, but he just snorted and said he'd rather go surf with the sharks.

'But he did add, almost throwaway, when I was leaving, that I could take a picture of him outside the house and hand it over so she could see what she'd spawned. In case she had any residue of interest. Not that she'd give a fuck, in all probability, he added. Not a flying fuck.'

21

G reer went to the back of the house and took the uneven path that sloped down to Mischa's studio. The pugs had emerged from the bushes and they trotted after her, snuffling and panting. Greer knelt to pick one up. She held its tight little body like a warm, pulsating barrel against her face. Only minutes had passed since she first heard her son's recorded voice. She still held his photo in her other hand.

She looked up at the crown of the ruined tower, where it leant into the sky. The high, fretted clouds that had been around earlier in the day were all blown away, but there was a flat heaviness in the air. She put the dog down and pressed her face against the stone. Faint, disembodied sounds of string music came from within, where Mischa was working, and floated down. She listened to a few bars: it was Schoenberg's *Transfigured Night*.

She remembered Mischa's most recent compositions. The two unfinished pictures, each with running figures and strange, empty holes in the canvas. The impression they conveyed, that some crucial piece of information had been left out. The impression of loss.

Greer thought, they are like jigsaws with missing pieces.

And then: how could I ever have imagined anything was accidental in Mischa's pictures?

I can't talk to him. Not yet. I am not ready. She turned away and retraced her steps.

She sat with Rollo, side by side on the couch in his studio.

'Well, you must meet each other right away, darling. You need to see him and he needs to see you.'

She had ignored the dictum that he was never to be disturbed when working, save in an emergency. Rollo had seen at once, without being told, that this was one. He had said nothing, but had put down his brush, switched off Wagner and gone to her.

'I can't do that. You've heard the tape.'

'Forget about the tape,' Rollo said briskly. 'That's his initial response. He's just had a great big shock. His world has been turned upside down. He's responding by being aggressive, like a cornered bull. That's a normal, healthy young male response. Now he's had time to get used to the idea, natural curiosity will have asserted itself.'

'This only happened a few weeks ago.'

'Weeks are years when you're young.' She saw Rollo dissecting the photograph, every detail of it, as she had.

'He didn't exist, and now suddenly it's as if someone has waved a magic wand and, abracadabra, he's materialised and he's part of our world. He's very dishy, darling. I can't stop looking at him.'

'But he's not part of our world. I chose Mischa over him. He will never forget that and never forgive it. How could he?'

'In our youth we've all done unspeakable things for love.'

'But this is an unforgiveable thing, isn't it?'

'You didn't know him then. He was a newborn. They have no personality, do they? Babies are just unformed clay. They're like a blank canvas.'

He doesn't get it, she thought. Even Rollo doesn't understand. But I'm not surprised that it's incomprehensible to him. It would be beyond the comprehension of any normal person.

What must it be like for my son?

'I didn't take the trouble to get to know him.' She thought, this is what despair is like.

'Life changes every one of us. If we're lucky enough, we can take advantage of that. Look at you, for example.' Rollo took her hand. 'You're not the same personage now as you were twenty-five years ago. Not the same at all.'

She looked at him. *Is that true? Am I not?*

'I think I'm the last personage in the world he would want to know anything about, Roly.'

He gave her a small, intimate smile. 'I knew there was something, you know. I just didn't know what it was. It must have been a big, oppressive secret to carry round.' He stroked her hand. 'I'm glad you've unloaded it. That has to be a good thing, doesn't it?'

'I avoided it by ignoring it. By making it into something that never happened. You see, Roly, I haven't been account-able for it.'

'It's important to be accountable, you're quite right.' She had known she wouldn't have to explain this point.

He was still studying the photograph. 'It's not too late to take it on, you know.'

'But I think it is. I think it is too late. How can I take it on now, when it's something I should have lived with all my life? I should have acknowledged it instead of burying it like some . . . like some shameful thing I wasn't responsible for. No amount of sackcloth and ashes is going to undo that.'

'I don't mean a hand-wringing kind of penitence, darling. That would be of no use to anybody. There's really only one person you need to be accountable to, other than yourself, of course, and that is —'

She interrupted, 'Will. To my son.' She shook her head. 'But I've no right to describe him like that.'

'Whatever has happened, you're still the biological parent. You have the inalienable natural right.'

'No. When I gave him away I surrendered my natural right.'

'But rights are nothing but human constructs, aren't they? Riddled with faults and holes like their poor, unfortunate creators. They're there to be superseded, rewritten and improved on. Surrendered,' he glanced sideways, 'and then miraculously resurrected.'

'Oh, that's the sort of thing I used to think, Roly. That they were just words. And if you repeated words often enough they would lose their meaning. They would cease to exist.'

'Now, let's not get ourselves sidetracked by silly old semantics. Think on this thing. Your son is alive.' Rollo gave her one of his probing, almost intrusive looks.

She took a deep, shuddering breath. *Yes, my son is alive.*

'And you are both living in the world. You are both inhabiting our funny, imperfect world – don't forget those qualifying words, they're very important – and I think, dear heart, to invent any excuse not to meet him and take the first steps, however *imperfect* and faltering, to acknowledge your accountability would simply compound the transgressions of a former self.'

Greer thought, he looks exhausted by this speech. I think he managed to deliver it all in one breath.

He gave her a follow-up smile and a little squeeze and added, 'Discovering that his mother is a fallible human being won't necessarily destroy him, you know.'

She kissed him on the cheek. His skin was thin and papery. She felt a renewed chill.

'Guy's invited Tony back in the summer.'

He evinced no surprise. 'There you are, I knew His Majesty had a penchant. Well, we both have a bit of a one, let's be honest about it. I'm using the royal "we" here. He and I liked each other, didn't we, so I suppose we have a similar taste in men. But that's naughty, he should have cleared it with you and Mischa first. Do you disapprove, darling?'

She said, 'I don't know what to think.'

'If you decide you do, you can supersede Guy. Rewrite the rule book and boot the young Turk out.' He gave a rumbling chuckle.

She went back to Tony. He was in the sitting room, working on his laptop. Writing about her, she had no doubt. He had a bottle of mineral water on the desk, with a decorated tile placed under it.

She was unworried now about what he thought of her. She had no interest in trying to influence that. There were other concerns of greater moment, matters of fact rather than chance or opinion, and these she did have some residual power to influence.

At the sight of her Tony switched off his computer. There was an unfamiliar expression on his face. It was apprehension, she realised. He expected her to be angry as well as upset.

Very quickly, before she could change her mind, she said, 'There are some important things I didn't tell you. And incidental details you couldn't have known about. So that you have a more accurate idea of how things were. That is, if you'd like.'

Tony leant forward, his face alight. 'Oh yes, Greer, I would most certainly like.'

She allowed him to turn on the recorder. If he did not have basic, accurate information he would undoubtedly get things skewed. That would be worse.

It was incumbent on her now, wasn't it, to take responsibility? The beans were spilt, the secrets were out. Most of them. Others remained in her keeping. She could decide which of these she wished to give away.

'She's changed towards me. Or maybe it's not towards me, but her attitude's different. To questions about the past, to a whole bunch of stuff she'd glossed over before. What it means is we're coming at the whole thing again, from the top.'

Tony replayed a section of the recording he had just made.

'She's showing a different side to me now. Why's that? Because she knows I know, so there's no point pretending any more. But it's not only that. There's something else going on here. It's almost like she's become a collaborator or confidant.'

There was a television in the corner of the room. He switched it on, and watched a few minutes of an Italian drama series involving groups of students in shared apartments. Then he spoke slowly to the recorder again, eyes still on the screen. A couple had gone into a bedroom and were having a strenuous argument while stripping off their clothes.

He said slowly, 'I think what she's decided is, she wants to let me in on the last big secret. She wants me to get what falling in love was like for her. For them. Maybe she even wants Will to get that. Why? Because she knows it's the key thing in their story. Well, I guess it's a key thing in life, period.'

His hand lingered over the switch. 'Is love the important thing in itself, or is it what it can do to you? And what it can make you do?' He gave a little laugh and added, 'Hey, I can't believe I just said that. Was it really me?'

His mobile phone rang. He fished it out of his jeans pocket.

'Hi.' A pause. 'Oh, OK, good. What's that, you are? Oh yeah, sure I can —'

Some time later there was a knock on the front door. He ran down the steps, calling out that it was unlocked. He heard it creak and groan as it was pushed open.

'Hey, so you made it! Let me welcome you to the Castello.'

Mischa answered the telephone. This was a comparatively rare occurrence, as he disliked talking on the phone. Greer had been considering getting one of the new devices, where you could see the person you were talking to on the computer screen. Being so visual, Mischa might quite enjoy that.

He came into the bathroom, where she lay under a cloud of bubbles. He stood over her, brandishing the phone like a weapon.

She hissed, 'I told you I didn't want to talk to anyone. Say I'm asleep.'

'He said wake her up. It's the husband you had a long time ago before me.' He held out a towel. 'Dry your hand.'

'It's Charlie?' She was electrified. She took the phone.

Charlie's voice sounded as if he was in the next room. It had not altered a whit.

'Greer? I'm sorry to ring you unannounced like a blast from the past, and probably an unwelcome one at that, but there's something –'

'Quick, tell me, what is it?'

He said calmly, 'It's important but not life-threatening. Everyone's all right. I probably should have called you before, but I've been flat-out. It was a triumph of detection to get your number.' She could hear him deliberating.

'Is it him, Charlie? Is it to do with Will?'

'Well, it is, actually, yes. He's on his way. I strongly suspect he's going to turn up on your doorstep at any moment. Both of them, in fact. Will and his fiancée, Rebecca Levy.'

Her mind had shut down. After a pause he continued, 'We only just found out that they'd gone. They left a day or so ago without telling us, of course. As they do. You've spoken to that biographer by now, I suppose? Devious bastard, isn't he?'

'Yes, he is.'

'You do know what happened to Will?'

She said, 'Yes. I thought he didn't want anything to do with me. I could understand that, completely.'

'Well, no, he didn't. It was all very unfortunate, the way he found out. Cold, like that. He was very angry about being lied to. Angry with us, with you, with the whole box of tricks.'

She interrupted, 'Charlie – is he in love?'

'Josie can tell you about all that stuff better than me. Here, I'll put her on.'

As if they had been chatting every week of the last twenty-five years.

'*Josie?*'

They were weeping again, as they had wept before, a long time ago, in Josie's flat overlooking the Flagstaff Gardens. That afternoon Greer had been about to disappear off the face of the earth, for the duration. Hearing Josie's voice again at the end of the telephone from the other side of the world, high and breathless and familiar, the duration seemed very long. In another way, seconds later, it didn't seem that long at all.

Greer and Mischa lay in bed. It was late, but for once Mischa was still wide awake. Greer could tell his mind was working away at full pelt. She fancied she could pick up the disturbances in the air. The atmosphere between them was vibrant with unspoken thoughts.

She thought, this is how we are, Mischa and I. We operate on tangents for much of the time. Our thoughts intersect and veer away. We touch and then we separate and then we touch again. That is how it is.

Eventually she said, 'I'm glad about it. The picture, it's a wonderful work. I'm happy that it was saved.'

'It had a good subject,' Mischa said.

'You did work on it again, after all. You finished it. It must have been – it was on that Boxing Day, wasn't it?'

'Yes. On that Boxing Day I worked on it after all. I finished it off.' He turned on his side to look at her, although it was too dark to make out her features. 'It kept me busy while you were out.'

While you were out. She marvelled at that. Out. Such an innocent little word, to carry such a weight of meaning.

'Why did you give it to Marlene? You never liked her.'

His response was unhesitating. 'Because she helped you

when I couldn't. It was the best thing to do with it.'

'Yes, it was. And I'll make contact with her again.'

She turned this over in her mind.

'If there had been no biography, none of this would be happening, would it? It would still be buried. All of it.' And my son would still be living his life oblivious to my existence.

Would I still be oblivious of him, too? This new question struck her as so confronting it verged on the unthinkable.

Mischa made a noncommittal noise. He remained in the same position, immobile. She thought, he is unusually tense tonight.

'Is it a good thing, though, Mischa? Overall?'

Because this was you, wasn't it?

It was you, Mischa, who set this in motion. You said yes to the biography. You didn't clear it first with your dealers. More to the point, you didn't say anything to me. It was your doing alone. Was that because you knew that if I heard about it I would put the kibosh on the idea?

Did you set it in motion knowingly, and on my account?

He said, 'I'd rather hear what you think, Mrs Smith. Overall.'

Greer searched for the invisible shadows imprinted on the walls of the bedroom. The previous occupants of this house must have had secrets, must have had their big secrets too, for which they had been accountable. She was convinced of that. But then, they had little or no choice in the matter.

She thought, there is an opening. A glimmer in darkness, a crack in a wall. I have been handed a choice.

'I think – no, that's not right, Mischa –'

'Yes?'

The single syllable was laconic, but she knew he was one hundred per cent on the case. He lay beside her, still motionless, waiting.

She tried to gather her thoughts. They were undisciplined, swarming all over the place. She thought, there are changes afoot in my life. In our lives. He knows that.

'I know it's a good thing.'

'How are you feeling?'

The surprising question rebounded. He had hardly ever asked a question like that. This time she answered without pause for reflection.

'I feel relief.'

He moved against her. She felt the tension go out of him, his breath on her face. She rested her head against his chest. He traced her cheekbones with his finger. They were wet.

She said, 'Other things too, Mischa. Lots of other things. I don't think I know how to describe them yet.'

'I don't have to kill him, then?'

'Him?'

'The biographer.'

She waited until afterwards, until he fell deeply asleep – it was not a long wait – before she got up and went into her study. From a pigeonhole in her desk she took out a sheet of writing paper.

21st April 2006

I've heard the tape of your meeting with Tony Corbino. I've seen your photograph, Will. And now I hear the news from Charlie and Josie – the first time I've heard their voices in twenty-five years – that you and Rebecca may be on your way here.

What can I say to you, Will? And to you, Rebecca? Because it's your business now too. I know you are engaged to be married.

Your attitude to me is understandable. It is entirely justified. The question is, why? Why did I do what I did?

I trust that this diary, which I am going to give you in the hope that you may bring yourselves to read it, will go some way towards answering that question. I think I knew all along, from the day of the biographer's arrival, and perhaps subconsciously very much earlier, that one day I was going to give it to you.

You may not wish to read it, and I should warn you that it will not be an easy read. Nor do I emerge from it with any credit.

What is written here does not in any way excuse, but I hope that it may, however baldly and inadequately, explain what must otherwise seem inexplicable. Perhaps the one virtue it does have is honesty, although there are limits to that which will not be lost on you.

If you reach the end you will have some insight into the young woman I was (not much older than you are now). To what extent I am still that person is not for me to say.

Whether it hit you like a thunderbolt, as it did me, or whether it grew on you more slowly and flowered, the experience of being in love must have changed the two of you profoundly.

I can only hope that this may help you both, not to forgive the unforgiveable, but in some way to understand.

She lingered over the last sentence, as if to imbue it with some miraculous power, before folding the page in half and placing it inside the front cover of the diary.

22

Greer came into the kitchen dressed in jeans again and a loose cotton shirt. It was going to be another balmy day. She could already hear bees. The beams of light that lay across Mischa's breakfast debris on the table had more warmth in them. He had slept well, so deeply he had hardly moved all night. He had got up early, whistling. She had slept too, but fitfully.

She threw open the north windows. The creeper on the south wall of Rollo and Guy's house opposite was greener today, the stones nearly hidden. The light breeze was drenched with wisteria. She gulped the perfume like a narcotic, drawing it deep into her lungs.

Then she heard a murmur of distant voices and saw them. There were three young people standing at the east end of the lawn, by the low wall at the precipice of the valley, grouped around Guy's telescope.

Two of the three had their backs to her. She did not know them, but she knew who they were instantly, without a moment's doubt. The third person was no surprise. It was Tony, positioning the telescope so the girl could see across the valley to the lookout tower on the far ridge.

Greer stood at the window and watched them, hypnotised

by the three figures. Tony was leading the other two away now. He was opening the gate to the right of Rollo's chapel. He must be going to take them along the winding path across the slope of the hill, the path that led down to the swimming pool and on to the little walled cemetery.

She would have known Will from his walk, more of a saunter, which was Charlie's loose-limbed walk, even if his photograph had not imprinted itself on her mind. He was swinging the young woman's hand. Rebecca was tall too, taller than Tony, with her wavy hair caught in a band and tumbling down her back.

The three figures disappeared from sight down the path. Greer stared at the small patch of ground behind the gate, where they had briefly been and then vanished. She stood at the window, transfixed.

They had been here, on this land, only a short distance from where she stood. It was as if a magician had waved his wand and magically they had come into her world, just as Rollo said yesterday. Then he had waved it again and they were gone.

Were they really here? Had she seen them at all, or was it a hallucination, a dream glimpsed and then irretrievably lost? She had set eyes on Jean-Claude that day, only to find herself unable to recall any detail of his face. But Jean-Claude was no figment of her imagination. He was real, he was a character in her story, and he had passed on the secret. Tony was around to verify that.

What if they never come back?

She felt herself disabled by the thought. Suppose they had been spirited away by a pied piper, young and charismatic like them, but blond-haired and full of guile? She fought a blind urge to chase after them, foolishly calling out her son's name. She fought against the rising panic of bereavement.

Tony has no reason to spirit them away. On the contrary, he has every reason to see this to its conclusion, since he engineered it. Of that I have no doubt.

She turned away from the window with its vista of emptiness, crossed the room, then ran down the steps and into her study. She breathed in the deep, calming breaths, the method Marlene had once taught her, in a time of *extremis*, and she had never forgotten.

She pulled out the diary and unfolded the sheet of paper she had written last night. She read it through once, folded it and replaced it inside the front cover.

Then she opened the diary at the last page. There was one more piece of information she had to impart, an urgent postscript. Although it was of fundamental importance she had been unaware of it until just then when, standing at the window and feeling bereft of something she had never had, she discovered it for the first time.

22nd April 2006
I should not presume to say what I am about to tell you, Will,
but I find that I can't help it. I am unable to leave this, my first
communication with you (could first imply second?) without
telling you this, one single thing that rises up and overpowers all
my other inglorious feelings.

There is no evidence I can give you for what I am about to
say, I know that. And there is no point in denying that in the
years since you were born I have been fortunate and often very
happy.

But there are certain things so deeply buried that one is
unaware of them until a trigger, a person, or an experience,
unlocks them. I already knew this, of course, because the events in
this diary are themselves the consequence of one of those
cataclysmic discoveries.

And now I have found another, and it is almost beyond
belief to me that I did not know this before.

There was a love requited, and a love given away. I cannot
deny that, Will. But please try to believe this. It is also true to say
that I have missed you for every day of your life.

Acknowledgements

I am indebted principally to the Sesti family of Montalcino. My gratitude goes to Sarah, Giuseppe, Elisa, Cosimo and Petroc, not only for their time and patience but also their generous hospitality and joie de vivre.

Other friends contributed a great deal, and in many ways. Warmest thanks to Kathy van Praag, Caroline Moorehead, Anne Chisholm, Jeremy Steele, Helen and Ross Edwards, Pamela Traynor and Christopher Bowen, Kristin and David Williamson, Jane, Andrew and Tara McLennan, Robin de Crespigny, Sophia Turkiewicz, David Marr and Eva Buczak.

At the all-important business end, Sophie Hamley, my agent at Cameron Creswell, and at Random House Meredith Curnow, Roberta Ivers, Catherine Hill, Jessica Dettmann and Judy Jamieson-Green were all a delight to work with.

Also by Virginia Duigan

Days Like These

There are certain friends with whom you don't have to pretend

Lou, a freelance journalist, leaves New York after the breakup of a long relationship. Taking refuge in Mim's North London house, the nerve-centre for a group of old university friends, she becomes drawn into an escalating series of personal dramas.

Days Like These is about women behaving badly. It is about love and loyalty, deceit and disaster, and the onset of moral choices. In a world where you can touch most things, what – and who – is untouchable?

Told with wit, humour and sophistication, *Days Like These* tests the bonds between friends.

'A tremendous first novel possessing real charm, a kind of freshness and guilelessness that is very potent – and a toughness and reality that I genuinely applaud.'

William Boyd

Virginia Duigan's first novel was *Days Like These* (2001, 2008). She also wrote the screenplay for the 1996 movie *The Leading Man*. *The Biographer* is her second novel.

She has worked as a freelance journalist in Australia, Britain and the United States, as a broadcaster and scriptwriter for the ABC, a literary editor, theatre and film critic, and book and restaurant reviewer.

She lives in Sydney and London.